GIVING IN TO YOU

THE GIVING TRILOGY: BOOK ONE

L.M. CARR

Cover Design and Interior Formatting:
Juliana Cabrera at Jersey Girl Designs

Second Edition: April 2018

ACKNOWLEDGMENTS

Anyone who knows me knows how much I loathe roller coasters. I hate anything that makes my stomach flip and turn. This book, however, has been the ultimate roller coaster ride, and I've loved every minute of it. When I started writing, I never expected to enjoy the thrill of the ride so much. From the first day when I wrote my character's names down on a piece of paper, it has been an incredible journey filled with highs and lows, twists and turns, laughter and tears.

None of this would have been possible if I didn't have the endless and unconditional love and support of my husband, Damian. I can't thank the love of my life enough for listening when an idea popped into my head or when he helped me figure out the little details. You are my everything.

To my kids, Michael, Julia and Emily. Thank you for listening about these fictional characters and putting up with me when I talked about Adam and Mia like they were part of our family. I can't count the number of times they waited for me while I lost myself in the story, assuring them that I only needed a "few more minutes." I love you guys more than you'll ever know.

To my sidekick and partner in crime, Mary, you encouraged me from the very first time I told you what I wanted to do. You've been my confidante, beta reader, researcher and "unofficial" editor. Thank you so much!

To the girls who read my story, encouraged me and always offered "brutal honesty." You have my love and thanks!

Prologue

VIOLENT SCREAMS ERUPTED DEEP FROM WITHIN ME, tears flowed down and stained my face as I blinked trying desperately to see the snow-covered road that twisted and turned ahead of me. I barely noticed the passenger who was pleading for me to slow down, spewing lies and insincere words of apologies that they never meant for this to happen, they never meant to hurt me. This couldn't be happening to me. Meaningless words infiltrated my ears as my head pounded through the sobs until I heard nothing at all except the sound of my own ragged breathing. Days later when my eyes slowly fluttered open, he was gone. I was left alone and empty.

Chapter One

AFTER SUPPRESSING A SMALL CASE OF ROAD RAGE WHILE following behind a vehicle in which the driver is either Miss Daisy or is having a heart attack at one of our town's few traffic lights, the black SUV finally starts to pull away, creeping slowly through the intersection towards the center of town.

"Ugh! Green light means go! C'mon, you moron!" I yell, banging my palm against the steering wheel. Brady looks at me, tilting his large head in confusion. I offer a smile and pat his head, letting him know my annoyance is not his fault.

I turn left and park haphazardly in my driveway, racing to get out and stretch my body to release the tension and stiffness after the long drive. The 1,900 mile trek home from Texas kicked my ass.

Even through the delirium and exhaustion that threaten to overtake me, I open the back door and take a deep breath as my eyes roam the dark kitchen. I smile at the thought of being home.

Toeing off my black Converse, I collapse onto my bed, fully clothed. My pillow is balled up beneath my cheek. Brady jumps up, curling beside me. Within mere minutes, I'm pulled into a dreamless state of slumber. I am home. Finally.

"MIA!" ARMED WITH A BEAUTIFUL WIDE SMILE AND A warm hug, Shelby's lean, tanned arms wrap around my back and squeeze tightly. A huge grin spreads across my face as I tighten my arms around her petite body and we wobble from side to side.

"Hi, Shelby. Miss me much?" I tease, tugging on her long blonde ponytail. It's only been about a month and a half since we've seen each other, but God knows I've missed this girl! Brady clumsily comes barreling past the butcher block island into my small, cozy kitchen, almost knocking us over with his large, black body. His loud yelping, long tail wagging, and jumping around like a lunatic makes me think he's missed Shelby, too.

"Holy shit, girl! Did you lose weight or what? You're a skinny bitch!" Rolling my eyes and shaking my head, I snort my response telling her that she's just as crazy as ever and quickly remind her that she's the one who's still the same size as when she was sixteen.

When she finally releases me, Shelby squints her pretty green eyes, steps back to eyeball me from head to toe, and asks with watery eyes, "How are you? You good?" *Am I good?* That's a great question. After what happened last spring, I think I am good, not great, but good enough so I simply nod and offer a tight smile.

Pushing the screen door open in the kitchen, we walk out to the backyard. I've already got the fire pit going and have a large pitcher of margaritas sitting on the worn side table. I'm looking forward to spending the last few days of summer with Shelby before we begin our new school year. It feels so good, like old times before the pressure and drama of last spring. I won't make the same mistake twice. Fool me once, shame on you. Fool me twice, shame on me.

As we sit back and relax in old, repainted Adirondack chairs, sipping margaritas from salt rimmed glasses, our conversation flows as if we hadn't spent the summer apart. Even though we've sent · texts a few times over the summer, I give her a detailed account of my summer adventures while visiting my brother in Texas.

Josh, my older brother by three years, is in the United States Air Force. A few years earlier, when he was stationed in Germany, he met a fellow Airman named Araceli, a beautiful Mexican-American woman with dark skin and flowing black hair. They fell in love and married six months later, eventually moving stateside to San Antonio. They now live in a cozy Spanish-styled home in a quiet suburb outside of the base like many other military families. I can't imagine being in the military, having to moving around every few years.

Thankfully, my family has lived right here in this sleepy little town where "everyone knows everyone." Where even the butcher at the market knows your favorite cut of meat and the locals know that attending football games on Friday night is almost as important as filling the pews at church on Sunday. But growing up in a small town can have its disadvantages, too. Like I said, everyone knows everyone.

DRIVING HALF WAY ACROSS THE U.S. IN MY JEEP Wrangler with only a dog as my companion was nothing compared to the scorching heat of San Antonio in July. I found every opportunity to be outside, running or hiking, enjoying the beauty of Texas as much as possible. Although some days I really wanted to lay in the hammock under a palm tree, relaxing with my Kindle and a glass of lemonade or, in my case, a big-ass margarita, but I couldn't sit around for too long doing nothing. Too much time on my hands made my mind drift, thinking about things that I shouldn't. Thoughts about things that I once had, but now don't, always tried to creep up. Thoughts about things I want, but won't allow myself to have, surfaced to the forefront dragging me down to a place I never wanted to be again. Ever.

"You're awfully quiet over there," Shelby says with raised brows, placing her phone down on the side table. "You thinking about that summer hottie?" she asks, waggling her perfectly arched eyebrows.

I close my eyes and scrunch up my sunburned nose. "Oh, yeah.

That's it. You totally caught me!" I scan the tall trees and the little path that leads down to the water as I debate whether or not I want to tell my best friend that I actually did meet someone...and had sex with him. Instead I raise my glass to toast, "To the end of some things and the beginning of others."

I should tell her about Max, my brother's Air Force buddy, because she'd be pissed if she knew I was holding back. Since it was my last night in Texas and Max was going back to Germany, we decided that shot after shot of Patron Silver sounded like a really good idea. Letting my inhibitions go, I accepted his challenge and lost, finding myself in the back seat of his white Land Rover with nothing but my cowboy boots on. It's a good thing I'm never going to see him again; I don't think my brother would like the idea of his little sister screwing his best friend. *What was I thinking?*

Guilt consumes me for keeping Max a secret so I throw her a bone about another guy.

"You know Luis, Araceli's brother?"

"Yeah, he's a priest or something, right?"

"He's pastor with a little church in Mexico."

Shelby looks at me with one eyebrow arched up, questioning me. "Okay..." she drags the word out. "Why are you telling me this?"

"He asked me out. I guess he's liked me for years and finally had to nerve to say something," I say, trying to sound nonchalant.

Shelby's eyes widen with curiosity. "Did you go out with him?"

"Uh...no! He's like 5'1 and he's a holy roller. He doesn't drink or swear. I don't think he's ever even had sex." I laugh. "We'd never get along."

"True story. You do have a potty mouth."

"Fuck you, I do not!" We break into a fit of drunken giggles.

After making another pitcher of margaritas, Shelby, a newlywed as of May, shares details of her honeymoon on the Caribbean islands of Turks and Caicos with its sandy beaches, turquoise water and endless sun. Shelby, the little slut, doesn't hold anything back. I admit to getting a little embarrassed, a red flush spreading over my cheeks when she reveals almost every erotic detail, even telling me about all the places sand found its way into and how flexible her husband is.

"Wanna see some pictures?" She jiggles her eyebrows as she grabs her phone from the side table and unlocks it.

"You have pictures? Oh my God! Mike would kill you!" I screech, leaning over to have a look at these pictures.

I always wonder why it's considered rude when guys kiss and tell—women are the worst!

With the tequila flowing freely through my veins, I look up at the moonless sky with its infinite stars and try to find the constellations. Shelby has sex on the brain because she swears that she sees a penis one.

"Look!" She points to the dark sky. "There's a shooting star. Hurry, make a wish, Mia."

I grin and indulge her playfulness. My eyes close, and I silently wish for one small thing. I wish for the one day, the absolute moment in time that I know I am exactly where I am supposed to be. My life will be what it should be.

"Whatever you wished for, it'll come true. I just know it." I love this girl; she's a hopelessly romantic drunk. "You'll find him."

My eyes roll dramatically. "Why do you think my wish involves a 'him'?"

"Because it does!" Her eyes widen and her mouth opens as she gives me a "duh" look.

Him. I need to change the subject of me and a "him." Not such a good combination for me. Let's just say I've not been so lucky in love and was a little more than turned off when, last spring, I walked into the restroom of a local bar to find *him*, the guy I was sort of dating, balls deep in someone else. I should've grabbed her hair and smashed her face against the sink that she held onto or punched him in the face, but I didn't; I simply ended things right then and there. There was no need for explanations or further humiliation as I felt my heart seal shut. I wish I could say that I've never been more mortified in my life, but that would be a lie.

That night in the bar was when I decided that I wouldn't date anymore. I don't need a man. After all, tucked away on the top shelf of my closet is a shoe box full of BOBs and plenty of batteries. That works just fine for me. Whoever said dating should be a time of fun, drama-free sex before you settle down, clearly hasn't "dated."

Unable to keep her eyes completely open, Shelby tries to wiggle her eyebrows. Her words slur, "C'mon, Mia. You know he's out there. You just gotta get back out there." She tips back the rest of her drink and sets it down. "Play the game. Get back in the saddle." Her arm whips over her head, circling awkwardly like she's trying to lasso a young calf. "Woo hoo! Take another chance."

"You're drunk." I chuckle at her "philosophy" even though I don't really find it funny or even necessarily agree with it. There was a time in my life when I believed in love. I was that young, naïve girl who thought that just because a boy said he loved you that he meant it. I thought when a boy told you that he wanted to marry you, he meant it. I thought giving him everything was enough.

Shelby and Mike are the exception because at sixteen years old, Mike meant every word he said about loving her. Not everybody is so lucky. Reality slapped me in the face so damn hard, it made my head spin like Reagan's in *The Exorcist*. My eyes fill with tears and I blink furiously before they fall heavily down my suntanned cheek.

Reaching over to place my glass down on the table, I look over at my drunk best friend who's looking into her empty glass asking where her drink is and wonder to myself how at twenty seven years old, I'm alone. Maybe somewhere deep down I do want the happily ever after. Maybe I really do want the white picket fence, 2.5 kids, and a sexy husband who is insanely in love with me and adores everything about me. Maybe I do want love. Or maybe I just need to shut the fuck up and refill my drink.

With that thought, I struggle to sit up, lean over and smile a drunken grin. Reaching over to grab Shelby's hand I say, "You know what, Shel? I...I...fucking love you. You, Shelby Warren, oops...I mean...Matthews," I giggle and continue, "...are my best fucking friend." Her heavy eyelids look up at me, an even bigger drunken grin on her face. "I...I...fl-flove you, too."

Chapter Two

THE FAMILIAR AND USUALLY WELCOMING SOUND OF Brady's deep bark wakes me up. I open one eye, moan, and immediately close it, groaning when the pounding in my head gets louder. "Shhh, give me a minute, boy, will ya." I pull the hood of my sweatshirt down low over my aching head.

My mouth is dry. It feels like I've swallowed a bag of cotton balls and all I taste is dirt. Not that I've ever tasted dirt, but I imagine this is what dirt would taste like. As I lie there promising myself to never, ever drink that much again, I think about last night.

I vaguely remember Mike standing over me while I slept uncomfortably in the Adirondack chair long after the fire went out. I think he tried to wake me and help me inside, but I couldn't walk so he carried me to the couch. I remember running my hand through his closely shaved head, giggling at the feel of fuzz at the nape of his neck before lacing my fingers behind his thick neck and telling him that I loved him. I think I even may have kissed his smooth cheek. Good God! I can only imagine the look on his ruggedly handsome face and the sense of relief when I told him that I loved him for loving my best friend. Mike driving over here in his police cruiser to get Shelby after she didn't answer his calls or texts proves that he's one of the good guys.

Slowly raising my head off the couch, reluctantly opening my eyes, I find Brady pacing frantically near the kitchen door. I sit up slowly, hoping and praying that the contents of last night don't make an unpleasant appearance. With dirty, bare feet, I shuffle through the kitchen to let him outside. I palm my head, trying to smooth away the pain. *Damn, I feel horrible.* I pop a dark roast K-cup into the Keurig to get my blood flowing and I lean forward against the island, waiting with my head bowed. Thoughts of last night come rushing into my mind. Oh, God. What drunken confession did I make this time?

I grab my ball cap from the hook by the door, pulling the brim low to shield my eyes from the sun as I push the squeaky screen door to sit outside with my coffee in hand. It's a gorgeous, bright and sunny late August morning. Brady bounds towards me with a tennis ball wanting to play fetch. Sure, it's a little early and I think I'm going to vomit and the trees are spinning around me, but I indulge him. I still feel a bit guilty that he was cooped up for so long as we traveled home from Texas two days ago.

The realization hits hard that I'm only going to have a few more mornings like this before I head back to work, so I lounge in the Adirondack that Shelby sat in last night, sip my coffee and look through the trees at the quiet lake. My body slouches into the chair and I pull the cap lower onto my face, hoping the strong coffee settles my stomach. *I am never drinking that much again. Ever.*

I close my eyes, breathing in the morning air, enjoying the warm sun on my head when I feel it. I feel the black cloud hovering over me, taunting me with fear, doubt, and sadness. My pulse starts to quicken as it begins to consume me, encasing me in a bubble of despair. I won't let this happen, not this year, not ever again. I've just had an amazing summer visiting my brother. Spending time with my niece, Ashley, and nephew, JJ, was good for me, but it always leaves me wanting more. And more isn't something that I'll allow myself to have. It's not in the cards for me. Breathing deeply through my anxiety, I'm relieved when the black cloud starts to dissipate.

Knowing that the remedy for my sudden bout of depression is a good run, I drag my sorry ass inside along with Brady, guzzle down a large glass of water, swallow three Excedrin, and shower quickly before changing into my running gear. After brushing my teeth, pulling my honey-blonde streaked hair into a high ponytail, I stare at my face in the mirror. Big, brown, sad eyes stare back at me. *Get a grip, girl. Get a fucking grip.* Brady's ears perk up, the circling around and yelping begins because he knows what it means when I open the door to the broom closet in the mudroom. "Atta, boy. Let's go!" I bend down and kiss his wet nose after securing his retractable leash to his collar.

My elderly neighbor, Mrs. Longo, waves hello to me and shouts, "Hey, Mia. Welcome home, darling!"

"Thanks." I jog in place, releasing one ear bud as I call back to her with a wave and a promise that I'll stop by later with Brady for a visit. I swear the woman, wearing her favorite rice picker hat, will someday collapse and die in her garden, after spending hours each morning in the blazing sun, pulling weeds until there isn't a single weed left.

Starting to jog away slowly, I chuckle quietly to myself, remembering the time I asked her why she weeds so often. With a devious smile and a wink, she told me that it keeps her hands agile to "take care" of Mr. Longo. Good Lord! I could never again look at the old man the same way, with his plaid shorts and golf Polo tucked in, belted above the waist.

With my ear buds stuck securely in my ears listening to Maroon 5, I pull back on the leash, unable to let Brady set our running pace until the Excedrin kicks in and I no longer want to vomit. I look around my quaint neighborhood, taking in the summer sights around me. Full green maple and oak trees line the quiet street on each side, providing shade as children run and play in their yards. A bouquet of pink balloons tied to the mailbox declare a baby girl has been added to the Cummings family. Further down, a white "DeGennaro Realty" sign stands at the edge of the well-manicured lawn of the McDonnell's huge brick house. I guess Grace McDonnell, the former town librarian for over fifty years, was finally moved into an assisted living community.

A smile spreads across my face as childhood memories flood my mind. My childhood was like a Norman Rockwell painting; I can't remember one bad thing except maybe for high school. Long, summer days riding my yellow bike and playing hopscotch on the sidewalks with my best friend, lemonade stands, hide and go seek, building snowmen, sledding down the Miller's backyard slope with Josh and his friends were just the normal things we did. We played outside until dark, only coming in when our mothers called for us. Almost every childhood memory I have included my best friend.

With a quick shake of my head, I try to erase the memory of her showing up at prom wearing the same dress as me. She tried to convince everyone that I copied her, but I knew the truth. She could have picked out any designer dress and her father would've gotten it for her. Me? I had to shop at the mall, but I was okay with that.

My God, all of that seems like a lifetime ago. Back when I was just a girl and things were simple, before the harsh reality of life set in.

"Easy, boy, easy." I pull back on Brady's leash as we round the corner into Peterson State Park; the place I consider my refuge. Its beauty is unparalleled with its open fields, a rolling river and steep waterfalls which lead to smaller streams that Brady loves to splash in. Any of its endless hiking trails all lead to the magnificent summit that overlooks the sleepy suburban town below. On a clear day, you can even see the calm waters of Long Island Sound in the far distance. It truly is nature at its finest.

Unhooking Brady's leash, I follow him over to the stream and gulp down the rest of my bottled water. He barks and jumps around trying to catch the tiny minnows until he's soaking wet.

"Stay here, boy." I point my finger at him like I mean business before I walk over to refill my bottle from the free standing water fountain. I keep a close eye on him because he's got the attention span of a fly and will run after anything that moves. I chuckle as I watch him until my attention is drawn to the sound of little voices behind me.

"Shit!" I mumble, scrambling to grab my disobedient dog before he runs over to the excited, young voices approaching us. "C'mere, boy." I squat down and wrap my arms around his big body, thinking that I should demand a refund for all those stupid training classes. After securing his leash, I stand and turn around to greet the voices that are now calling out, "Brady! Oh, hi, Miss Delaney." *Nice, I'm an afterthought next to my dog.*

I immediately recognize the faces of former students who've grown a few inches since they were rambunctious second graders in my class. "Hi, Jake. Hey, Ben. How are you boys?" Telling me all about their summer vacations seems like a feat within itself because Brady is all over them, yelping his pleasure, showering their faces with sloppy, wet kisses. Try as hard as I might to control him, the boys love every second, rubbing his belly and head.

Noticing their green jerseys and footballs, I ask, "Football practice?"

"Yep," Jake answers.

I spot a small group of parents sipping their Dunkin' Donuts coffee while their younger children run and play nearby. This is a big football town especially during the fall months when everyone dresses in green and white to cheer for the undefeated State Champions. This is the way life is in a small town.

All three of us turn around when we hear someone whistling and calling the boys' names.

Squinting in the morning sun, my heart beats a little faster when I see who's walking in our direction. *Crap!* It's their coach and I know him...very well. Unfortunately.

The boys start complaining but quickly comply. "Awww...I guess we gotta go," Jake says giving Brady one last belly rub before running off. "Bye, Miss Delaney. See ya at school next week." I hear Ben say, but I'm no longer looking at him. My attention is drawn upwards to the beast of a figure approaching me.

"I'll be there in a sec, boys. Start with a few laps for a warm up," his deep voice commands.

I take a long drink of water to quench my thirst, relieving my cotton mouth and look anywhere but at him. No one seems to notice us—everyone is just going about doing their own thing. So why do I suddenly feel like I'm on stage and I've forgotten my lines? My heart begins to race as a flush quickly spreads across my face. *Oh, shit! Why does he have to be here? Why does he have to look so damn sexy with his khaki shorts and olive green Army t-shirt that fits perfectly around his sculpted torso? Oh, Lord, kill me now!*

Looking in every possible direction around me just to avoid his gaze, I look up as he saunters over to me with an air of confidence. His dirty blonde hair is a little longer than I remember causing it to peek out from under his Red Sox ball cap. His skin is perfectly tanned, showing the definition in his biceps accentuating his black tribal band tattoo. He's staring at me with piercing blue eyes, blue like the ocean. *Damn, he looks good!* His body stops within a foot of mine. His eyes lower, traveling up and down my body, his lips smirk with a devilish grin.

"Hello there," he purrs, leaning in to hug me as he places a lingering kiss on my cheek. "Welcome home, Mia. I've missed you," he whispers in my ear. *Breathe, Mia. Breathe.*

"Hi, Shane. How are you?" I barely smile, trying desperately to sound nonchalant as I quickly pull out of his embrace.

"Well, I had a good summer, but it just got a whole lot better." *Oh boy, here we go!*

"Really? And why's that?" I blurt, not buying his bullshit in the form of flattery again. I'm not typically rude, but just seeing him, catapults me back to that day last spring.

"I told you I missed you." He reaches out, tucking a shorter piece of layered hair that's fallen out of my ponytail. I swallow hard. *No, do not fall for his touch. Do not fall for his words. Not again. Remember it's all bullshit.* "I like your hair. You changed the color, didn't you?" he asks as he twists it in his hand, letting it slide through his fingertips. I want to snatch my ponytail away and slap his hand down.

"Yeah, I did. It was time for a change. I got tired of the same old boring brown. I thought I'd spice it up a bit with some blonde highlights." I stare at him defiantly, wondering if he understands the full implication of my words. "What's that saying?" I tap on my chin for effect and look up at him. "Oh yeah, you know the one, 'Blondes have more fun.'" I narrow my eyes and smirk, my words drip with sarcasm, hoping he remembers the specific event to which my words allude.

"Mia, come on...Don't be like that. I said I was sorry. You wouldn't even let me explain." He holds my arms and sways me from side to side, trying to ease the animosity that's seeping out of my pores.

Hearing a quiet, but definite grumble, I turn to Brady and realize that he's been waiting this whole time. *Why can't guys be like dogs? Fun, loving and LOYAL?* We both just stand there looking at each other, brown eyes to blue.

I wonder if he's thinking about the look on my face when I walked in and found him with his pants around his ankles. Or is he thinking about how he hounded me for weeks afterwards and I wouldn't give him the time of day? Or maybe he's thinking that if I'm desperate enough that he'll get one more fuck?

Whatever he's thinking about, he doesn't say. It doesn't really matter. It's over. And it never should have started in the first place.

"Hey, Coach! You ready?" a faraway voice calls to him. "It's hot as hell out here. Let's get these kids outta here early." I glance past Shane to see Tanner, another guy from town. "Oh, hey, Mia. How's it going?"

"Hey, Tanner. I'm good. You?" He mutters something about

how he'd be better if it weren't already almost ninety freaking degrees out.

"You need to go," I remind him and turn to leave when he reaches out for my hand, rubbing his thumb across my knuckles. Turning slowly, I see that boyish smile that I've known forever. I used to think it was endearing, now I think it's just bullshit.

"C'mon. You said you forgave me..." His voice trails off, his cheeks flush with embarrassment. "At least call me? I'd like to see you. We can go for a hike or a run. We could have dinner and talk. We can start over."

My eyebrows shoot up to my hairline in disbelief.

"C'mon, I'm serious. You've been gone all summer. I've missed you, Mia."

Lies. All lies. "Yeah, whatever. We'll see...It's hot. I have to go." I finally turn in the direction of the hiking trails without as much as a quick, backward glance. How did things between us get so serious and awkward? I really should've listened to my instincts and kept that one in the friend zone. But once again, I listened to my heart not my head.

Running. Running is good for me. It fuels my body and frees my mind. My legs carry me faster and faster up the trail while beads of sweat pour down my forehead. My hot pink Lycra running shirt is drenched; the sweat oozing through my skin probably reeks of stale booze.

Flashbacks fill my mind of running this trail with Shane. His big hands roaming all over my sweat covered body when we reached the summit. I can feel his warm lips crashing into mine, his mouth kissing me all over, his hands digging into my hips. *Fuck!*

I don't want to think about him because it makes me think of her, and I most definitely don't want to think about her. Although we never claimed to be exclusive, it was sort of implied while we enjoyed each other's company, whether we were working out at the gym, taking graduate courses in administration together and having some pretty fucking fantastic sex. I remember waking up next to him and then storming off when he almost uttered the dreaded "L" word. I was angry because he was trying to make it something more than what it was. It was just sex, at least that's the story I kept telling myself.

"Let love in." Those were Shelby's words last winter. Her futile attempt to get me enrolled for an online dating site was a bust, even when she promised to manage the account for me. The online dating scene was not lacking in hot guys, but I always wondered, "If they're so hot, why are they on a dating site?" It's not that I couldn't *get* a date, I wasn't interested in dating because, in reality, I was just becoming interested in life again.

Shane was the first guy I let my guard down for and look how that turned out! Growing up in the same small town, our paths always crossed. After freshman year, Shane left college and joined the Army, serving his country, traveling to distant lands. He had some great stories and adventures about his time abroad. He eventually went back to college, got his degree and is now a physical education teacher and football coach at the local high school.

Although my brother was my hero and I did everything that he did, joining the military wasn't something I'd ever thought about. I dreamed of going to college to become a teacher, marrying my high school boyfriend and starting a family. I had my life planned out. My life's plan was pretty damn perfect. At least that's the way it seemed. It was perfect until that dream abruptly became a nightmare. In one night, my dream was shattered beyond imaginable repair. So many lives irrevocably changed forever. All in one night.

The burn I feel through my legs has me pushing myself to run harder and faster as if I'm running from those memories. Brady slows his approach as we reach the summit. I pull the cinch bag off my back and grab another bottle of water. The water, although no longer cool, is still refreshing to my parched mouth. Muffled laughter consumes me as Brady laps crazily at the steady stream of water flowing from the bottle, trying desperately to quench his own thirst. I lower myself down on the flat rock that juts out, letting my tired legs dangle over the edge, massaging the muscles in my thighs and calves.

The view from here is absolutely, breathtakingly incredible. For miles and miles, all I can see is the place I've always called home. Small houses in between thick oak and tall pine trees spread across the town. The little white congregational church has been rebuilt after the fire burned it to the ground, the elementary school has its new playground and a new strip mall is thriving in its early stages. It all appears to be back to normal...except for the abandoned lot with a dilapidated fence still around it and warning signs to keep out. Unshed tears pool in the corners of my eyes as I stare at the lot and remember.

Some nights when my dad had to work late, my mom and I would take a ride down in our green mini-van to visit him and bring dinner. My dad was the foreman at DeGennaro Manufacturing, the industrial plant was our town's largest employer. I always felt like the cool kid walking around with my dad because he was kind of the boss. That was until Gina walked around with *her* dad, Mr. DeGennaro. He was the owner so he was the *real* boss as she would often remind me. She was my best friend and although we were as different as we could be, we were inseparable.

Mia and Gina. Gina and Mia. We were two peas in a pod. Even when we dressed alike, it didn't matter that she had fair skin, blonde hair and blue eyes or that I had olive skin with brown eyes as dark as my hair; we were perfectly paired. We used to think it'd be cool if we married each other's brothers so we could really be sisters.

As kids, we spent so much time together that she even called my mom "Mima," short for Mia's mama. Gina's parents divorced when she was only a few years old; her mom would pop in every couple months to "visit." It was heartbreaking to watch Gina get her hopes up that her mom might love her enough to actually stick around, but she never did. For years, I watched my best friend cry for days after her mom left again, abandoning her children for a life on her own.

Unfortunately, the bevy of women who slipped in and out of Carl DeGennaro's bed weren't exactly stellar role models for a young, impressionable girl. I think Gina loved spending time with my mom almost as much as she loved spending time with me.

I glance at the church where my parents renewed their vows and remember their whispered words.

"Daniel Delaney, I love you madly. I'll love you with every breath I take."

"I love you more, my sweet girl. And I'll love you until the last breath I take."

My parents were passionately in love with each other. Although their displays of affection often garnered snickers and groans of disgust from Josh and me, we knew, without a doubt, that our parents loved each other and that they loved us. We didn't have a lot of money growing up, but my parents did the best they could on one income and, somehow, it all worked out.

Our family and the DeGennaros got along really well, even spending holidays together at their house because it was bigger and could accommodate their large, extended Italian family which included Gina's older brother, Christopher, and lots and lots of uncles. I never knew they weren't really "uncles" until I finally figured it out. I'll never forget one Christmas my Uncle Carl lifted a glass filled with homemade wine and made a toast to my parents. "To Dan and Ellen, you both have brought much love to us. May we always have our family." Some of the uncles cheered, "La Famiglia" or "Buon Natale." Gina and I clinked our glasses of grape juice and pretended it was wine.

But that was a long time ago. A lifetime ago. Our families don't speak anymore. For some, it's because they can't, for others, it's by choice. Gina and I aren't friends anymore. My best friend broke my heart in the worst way possible. Not once, but twice.

BRADY CIRCLES AROUND UNTIL HE FINDS A SPOT UNDER a tall pine tree to begin his break. Leaning back to rest on my palms, I whisper, "Hi, Daddy." A small smile creeps across my face as I picture his dark hair covering his dark eyes and handsome rugged face. In my mind, he always has on his grey New England Patriots sweatshirt. It was what he was wearing the last time I ever saw him. "I've missed you."

Quiet words flow from my mouth as I tell my dad all that has transpired over the last six weeks—well, most of it anyway. I don't think my dad wants to hear about his daughter getting it on in the back of an SUV. Talking to my dad was as natural for me as breathing. He was always there with me, even if it's just in spirit. I was his little girl and he was my beloved daddy.

The midmorning sun is getting hotter, the humidity in the air rising. My ponytail will soon look more like a squirrel's tail. Knowing that I have a long list of things to do, I pull my knees in one at a time to retie my laces for our run back down. It's the sound of breaking twigs behind me that distracts my closing thoughts, causing me to pause in my one-sided conversation.

Expecting to see someone familiar from town, I glance over my shoulder, turning my head to the unwelcomed guest who interrupted my private time with my father. Standing there, wordlessly, a man comes to an abrupt halt a few feet behind me. I freeze immediately. I don't recognize this person and my instincts tell me to run. Run far away from him because staring at me is this incredibly and impossibly beautiful, tall, tanned man with the most gorgeous dark chocolate eyes I've ever seen. My eyes roam over his body and I notice he's only wearing pair of running shorts and his t-shirt is draped around his neck. On my way back up his body, I notice there's a bottle of water in one hand. A flawless face boasts features that are perfectly proportionate except for his nose which appears to have been broken at some point and is slightly crooked. Covering his chiseled jaw is probably a few days' worth of sexy scruff. This nearly naked man tilts his head to the side, looks at me darkly and then smirks.

"Whew! What a view." I hear him pant; his voice is deep and sexy. Maybe he's waiting for a response, but I don't give him one. I seem to have lost the ability to speak. "Um...is there someone here? Were you just talking to someone?" He looks around probably wondering who I am talking to because clearly I'm alone. Had I really been talking out loud? Could he have heard the conversation I was having with my father? He places his hands on his knees and leans over, breathing deeply, trying to catch his breath. His head hangs low, but his dark eyes drag lazily up and meet mine. There's intensity in his stare. He looks like a predator about to eat his prey.

I swallow nervously when I realize that I'm staring so I turn back and lower my gaze to secure the lace on my other sneaker. I can hear him taking ragged breaths and I blush instantly, wondering if that's what he sounds like after he comes. Adrenaline causes my heart to beat a little faster and louder; the sound of it rings in my ears.

When I look back at him, his breathing is almost under control and his eyes watch me carefully. Brady's eyes open and his ears perk up when it finally registers that the voice he heard wasn't mine. I inhale sharply as I stand up and prepare to leave. He's just a man. So what if he's the most gorgeous man I've ever seen. So what if he has a perfect smile with a killer body, he's probably dangerous or an asshole or maybe he's both. A dangerous asshole. This time I will follow my instincts.

I use my hands to wipe off the back of my shorts and then walk over to give Brady a few rubs on his sleepy head, telling him that it's time to go. My eyes involuntarily look at the man close to me. His muscular legs support his body as he bends over. Finally, he stands upright to his full height, which has to be over six feet, and he wipes sweat from his dark brow with his t-shirt, exhaling a loud sigh.

I feel like a voyeur as I watch those dark eyes of his close before his head tips back and he pours a full bottle of water directly over it covering his wavy, dark hair. He rakes his hand through his hair, the water flowing south. I wonder what it would be like to run my fingers through that hair. He opens his eyes slowly. Almost as if to torture me, he pours water into his cupped hand and brings it to his face, scrubbing his eyebrows and jaw, and then spreads water across his chest which is sprinkled lightly with dark, curly hair. Holy shit! That's freaking hot. I think my sweat drenched t-shirt isn't the only wet thing that is in need of a changing.

My eyes close briefly as I silently bid my father farewell. Again, the voyeur in me is back. I honestly can't help but watch as his eyes close again before he pours the last of the water over his head. It flows, mixing with his sweat as it travels down over his chiseled, hard chest onto his washboard abs, following the V trail into his black running shorts. I think "V' has just become my favorite letter of the alphabet. Talk about sex on legs! Embarrassment floods me when I realize that my traitorous tongue slipped out, and I've just licked my lips.

"Ahhh...that feels much better." He opens his eyes, runs his hand through his hair and smirks. Brady, now fully awake and up from his power nap, is ready to play again. He bounds over and rubs himself up against the man's long legs. I want to step forward and scold him for being a bad dog, but my feet are planted in cement, keeping me still.

"Hey, boy. Come here, buddy." He squats down to rub Brady's head and ears. Oh no! Brady has made an instant friend for life. "You're a good boy, aren't you?" he laughs, talking to my crazy sidekick of a dog. "Are you a good boy? Or are you a naughty boy who likes to get into all sorts of trouble?" His dark eyes look up and pierce mine as he grins roguishly.

Oh, so this is how this is going to go down. Got it! I dramatically roll my eyes, purse my lips, and let out a disbelieving chuckle with little humor, knowing full well we aren't talking about my dog anymore. Are you freaking kidding me? What a jerk! Who does he think he is? Who cares if he is absolutely perfect and has an amazing body and is looking at me like he wants to eat me alive? Who does he think he is invading my quiet time, making comments like that? I don't think so. And that, my friend, is my cue. Time to go.

"C'mere, boy. Time to go, Brady," I command.

"Hey. I'm Adam."

I watch him cautiously as he stands up and reaches forward, extending his long, damp hand, humor displayed on his face. Does he really think that I'm going to shake his hand? God only knows where that hand has been! I'm not a rude person by nature, but something about this guy rubs me the wrong way. Hah! Who am I kidding? I'd love for him to rub the buzzing flesh between my legs.

I just stand there and stare at it like it repulses me. After what seems like minutes, hours or days, his eyebrows rise and he asks expectantly with a charming smile, "And you are?"

I swallow hard, but my words refuse to come. I won't answer him. He's probably just another good looking, okay gorgeous guy, looking for a piece of ass. NOT interested. Thanks, but no thanks.

Looking straight into those dark eyes, I finally find the right words to answer him. "I..." I say shyly at first and then with a stern look and an edge to my voice continue, "am leaving." The utter look of disbelief on his face is priceless. *Take that, jerk!*

"Let's go. Come on, boy." With Brady's leash in my hand, I walk confidently around his gorgeous body and his stunned face and race down the trail away from the man. Finally, I listen to my instincts which tell me to run. Run far away.

Chapter Three

STILL REELING FROM THE EVENTS OF THE MORNING, from seeing Shane and then meeting that sexy man, Adam, who had my heart beating faster and the lower half of my body clenching tightly, I decide that I need a shower and to get on with my day. A sense of pride overcomes me for not giving in to the temptation to relieve myself of the pent up pressure while in the shower. Oh, hell! I'm such a liar! I totally got it on with my showerhead.

Honeydew melon scent fills the room as I lather my neck, my arms, my shoulders, my long legs and everywhere in between with lotion. My eyes instinctively close as I imagine Max's hands, then Shane's hands, then Adam's hands touching me, caressing me, holding me. Brady's bark jolts me out of my erotic daydream. *What the hell?* Damn, even in my mind, I'm a slut! I shake off the dirty scenarios and walk over to the old, duct-taped suitcases that have been abandoned in the corner of my room since my return and I pull out a bra, a thong, a pair of cutoff denim shorts and a white tank top. Not really wanting to do much with my long, wavy hair, I throw on my old tattered New England Patriots ball cap again and head out to my Jeep.

It's a beautiful day so I decide to take advantage of it and leave the soft cover top off exposing the dark leather seats covered with discarded cups of coffee and bottled water. The music on the radio blasts with me singing along about it being the best day of my life even though it really isn't. I decide then that I really need to pick up the garbage before it flies out as I drive. The stupid latch on the seat is stuck again so I have to climb up the runner to reach into the back leaving my ass up in the air to fend for itself. Muttering profanities at myself for the condition of my vehicle, I suddenly have the sense that I'm not alone.

I look around over the hood of the truck thinking it's either Brady or maybe Mrs. Longo, who often comes over unannounced or uninvited. There's no one in front of me, so I turn back. But a movement at the end of the long, asphalt driveway catches my attention. A blurry figure runs past and is gone. I shrug my shoulders at my paranoia as I continue to pick up empty coffee cups, water bottles and candy wrappers. Suddenly, I have that feeling of being watched again. I raise the curled brim of my hat which has fallen over my eyes and look back to the end of the driveway.

Adam, the beautiful, arrogant man, stands there looking me. Our eyes lock instantaneously, but he isn't smiling that perfect, cocky smile, instead, an intense look, possibly one of annoyance or anger, is etched across his face. He isn't just looking at me or watching me; it feels primal and possessive like he's staring, trying to reach down into my depths of my soul. It's kind of scary, yet hot at the same time. *Oh, crap! What the hell is he doing here?* In all of my life, I have never felt that magnetic pull that I've always read about—but I feel it now. His chest, now covered with his damp, grey t-shirt, rises and falls as if he's trying to control his breathing. Adrenaline courses through my body, my core tightens instantly. I'm sure I'm going to have to change my underwear again.

I want to look away, but I can't—he's mesmerizing, bewitching me with his eyes. I force myself to break our connection and look away from him, blinking rapidly as if I've been awakened from a dream. I quickly step down from the Jeep and look back, but he's no longer standing there. My driveway is completely empty. My eyes scan the long driveway and around the backyard with no sign of Adam anywhere. A part of me wants to sprint to the end of the driveway to see if he's still there to confront him, but the sensible side tells me to keep still. I'm left standing there beside my burgundy Jeep, holding a bag of garbage, with nothing but a million questions. Where the hell did he come from? Why was he standing there? What was with that look? Who is this Adam guy?

The look on his face was so intense; it felt like he was trying to convey some secret message that was only meant for me. Listen to me! Secret message? Magnetic pulls? *Oh, please!* Guys that look like that aren't interested in girls like me. He's probably pissed off because I brushed him off at the park. What did he expect me to do? Fall at his feet and worship the ground he walks on? Yeah, that's probably it. I doubt a man who looks like an Armani underwear model gets the brush off often especially by a lowly, small town, school teacher such as myself. I can only imagine the bruising his ego took. I wonder briefly if he could be like Ted Bundy; a handsome, charming serial killer who moves from town to town evading capture. Maybe I should be afraid because he knows where I live. Maybe I should call Shane and have him come over for a while. No, I'm not ready to see him yet. Maybe I should call Pete, but he wouldn't be any help; he'd just lick the man to death. Or maybe I should stop by Smith's Firearm Supply and load up on a few extra rounds of ammo.

By the time I finally head out to run my errands, it's late in the afternoon and the August heat packs a punch. I have my list and I'm determined to get back home so I can open a bottle of wine, grab my Kindle and relax. Bank. Post office. Grocery store. Liquor store. Pet store. Having been gone almost six weeks, I have to pick up my mail that was on hold at the post office.

I drive through town, smiling at all the familiar places and faces, beeping my horn at people I know. The Killers keep me company during my afternoon drive through town. Waiting at one of the few traffic lights, I bop my head, tap the steering wheel and sing off key about Mr. Brightside, when to my left, I see blonde hair blowing in my peripheral vision and I feel the weight of a stare. No, not a stare. An "I fucking hate you. I wish you were dead" glare. *Seriously? I haven't been home for three days and this shit starts again. Ignore it. Ignore her. You're better than this, I remind myself.* I wish I could just ignore it, but I can't. So I do what my mom taught me to do, "If you can't beat 'em, join 'em." With the most indifferent look I can muster, zero expression on my face, I turn my head to face Gina and stare at her. I want her to know I'm bored with her and her games. It's time to grow the fuck up and behave like an adult not a spoiled brat. I have no doubt that if she were able to shoot beams, she'd zap me into oblivion. The hateful rays from her blue eyes could just quite possibly melt the lens on her fancy Prada sunglasses as she glares at me.

She says nothing to me. She doesn't have to. I know perfectly well how she feels about me. Funny thing is I feel the same exact way about her.

"Mia, you said you liked the dress. You didn't say you were definitely getting it." Gina looked at me in the mirror as she applied more lip gloss.

"Oh my God! You knew I had it on hold because I had to wait for my dad to get paid." I shook my head and crossed my arms. *"Why would you do that?"*

"Give it a rest, Mia. It's not the end of the world." Gina pulled the door open and brushed past my boyfriend who was standing there wearing a black tux, waiting for me.

"Looking good, Dylan." She patted his cheek as she passed by.

Dylan's eyebrows rose in confusion. "What's up with her?"

"I don't know. She's been a real bitch lately." I grabbed his hand and headed off to the dance floor.

A quick beep of a car's horn snaps me out of the reverie.

"Mom, the arrow is green," a small voice pipes up. "Go, Mom, go!"

My eyes move to the back of her shiny, silver Mercedes convertible and notice sitting there are two little girls. One I recognize immediately as her blonde haired, green eyed daughter who looks exactly like her father, but the other, a dark-haired girl, I don't recognize at all. Without a word of acknowledgement to her daughter, Gina's sleek car lurches forward, taking a sharp left towards the outskirts of town. *Well, that was fun! Always a pleasure to see you, too.* NOT!

I can't change the past. It is what it is. I've decided not to dwell on it any longer; I'm going to have a fresh start. I was beyond thrilled when our small town got the board's approval to build a new elementary school, combining all Kindergarten through fifth grades. The only drawback is that now I'm going to run into Gina more than I'd like to since her daughter, Sophie, is in second grade.

Running errands seems to take longer than usual because I run into everyone and their mother in town. I promise Miss Jones that I will visit after church. She was my nana's oldest and dearest friend who loved me like a granddaughter. It's kind of sad that she never married or had children of her own. She was so good with kids. *I wonder if that's what people will say about me when I'm old. Poor Mia Delaney, never married, never had any children. She lived and died a spinster. What the hell do they know anyway?* Truthfully though, the thought does make me a little sad.

As I checkout, placing my items on the conveyer belt, the sound of deep laughter draws my attention to the front of the store. Curiously, I set the pint of chocolate ice cream down and look up from my carriage full of food and freeze when I see that sexy man from the park. Adam looks freshly showered, wearing khaki board shorts, a white t-shirt and a Yankees cap. He pushes a carriage with a young boy, wearing a similar blue cap holding on to the front of the carriage. *Again? He must have moved here over the summer because I'm pretty sure I know everyone in this small town and I definitely do not know these two.*

Wanting to hide myself, I pull my cap down low over my head, needing a reason to look down and avoid eye contact at any and all costs, I pull my phone out of my back pocket and send a text to

Shelby.

Me: Hey, lush. Still drunk?

An immediate response pings.

Shelby: No way! Sex is an amazing way to sober up!

Me: Lucky bitch!

Shelby: I know, right!

Me: Come over tonight? Can you bring me a hot guy? I'm dying here! LOL

I knew her answer would be no. She's married now and can't come hang out with me whenever she wants to.

Shelby: Can't tonight, babe. Mike sends his love. ● But I hear there's fresh meat in town.

Fresh meat? What is she talking about now? I swear she's such a drama queen.

"Damn, he's fine. Mmmmm...mmmm." My head snaps up. I look at Angie, the sixty-something year old part-time cashier, who has suddenly stopped bagging my food and is looking out into the store towards the produce section. My eyes follow the direction of hers, and I realize then that she's referring to Adam, whose hand is wrapped around a massive cantaloupe, squeezing it gently, sniffing it to check for ripeness. Oh Lord! Those hands! I can only imagine how that would feel to have his hands on me or that nose skimming over me, down my neck, over my...

"Girl, look at that ass! I bet the rest of him looks that good, too." Angie's southern drawl in full effect. I shake my head and laugh under my breath, embarrassed by my dirty thoughts. I turn to face her, hand over some cash, and whisper, "Angie Jackson! What's the matter with you? Aren't you happily married? Don't tell me there's trouble in paradise at the Jackson home, is there?" I mimic her southern drawl perfectly. The dark brown skin around her eyes crinkles as she purses her lips and smirks because we both know that she and her husband, Clayton, who owns an auto repair shop in town, are head over heels in love with each other. "Mia, girl." She snaps her teeth. "You know better than that! Honey, just cuz' I can't touch, don't mean I can't look! But, you...you *can* touch, girl."

I feel the flush of my face come quickly. "You're crazy, Ang. That's why we all love you." Dropping the change into my pocket, I load my grocery bags back into the carriage, and head outside into the hazy, hot, and humid August air.

When I get back home, I am thoroughly exhausted and grateful that there were no more sightings of Adam. After putting my groceries away and eating a bowl of cereal, I plop myself down on a bar stool at the island and begin rifling through the tall stack of mail, sorting it into two piles. Junk. Junk. Junk. Really? I won a sweepstakes? I thought Ed McMahon was dead. Junk. Junk. My eyes widen in surprise when I spot the return address of the large, manila envelope from San Antonio Public School District. Save. My brother's suggestion to always keep my options open couldn't have come at a better time.

Chapter Four

My therapist once said that most people usually follow their instincts. When danger presents itself, people of sound mind will typically run away from it. It's that fight or flight instinct, I guess. I like to consider myself a pretty good judge of character and am usually right to follow my instincts. Usually. Not always.

After tossing and turning all night, my mind kept wandering back to the man from the park who then glared at me in my driveway. He's dangerous, I can tell. Not dangerous in he'd lure me and kill me kind of dangerous. Dangerous in the kind of man who will take a woman's heart and shred it into a million pieces and not care about the consequences. A man like that isn't looking for a lifetime of love—he's looking for a night of lust.

A million questions race through my mind as Brady and I round the gate to the park's entrance. Brady picks up the pace, knowing what he wants to do and I'm happy to let him lead me straight to the stream that flows beneath the old, wood covered bridge. I sit down on a picnic table, take a drink, and look around.

College kids set up a volley ball net, stretching out the lazy days of summer. A young couple strolls hand in hand, the swell of her belly protruding out from under her pink cotton sundress. Shrills of laughter and delight draw my attention to the newly installed playground area where children swing and play without a care in the world.

I sigh heavily, releasing all the pent up "what ifs" from long ago that some days slither to the forefront of my mind. I rebuke myself for wallowing in a moment of self-pity. "Let's go, boy!" I call to Brady, as I climb the long "expert" trail marked with a black diamond.

Looking out over the town, I'm surprised that I didn't notice earlier all the new construction that's been taking place recently. The new school was a big focus of our town for the past few years and before that, well, I guess I didn't really pay attention to much going on around me.

Two hours later, as the sun begins its evening descent, I pull back on Brady's leash as we make our way back into my neighborhood, slowing our pace to cool down. I'm lost in thought, making mental notes of all the things that I still need to do this week to get my classroom ready, when my attention is drawn in the direction of a huge, shiny, black SUV driving slowly, approaching in my direction.

The driver's tinted window is lowered a quarter of the way, but the rest remain closed. With the sun glare impeding my sight, I raise my hand to my brow, hoping to catch a glimpse of the driver. I smile and admire the beauty of the luxury vehicle; I inherited my father's appreciation for fine cars.

There are several houses that have been put on the market recently. I wonder if the driver is moving slowly to look at one of them. It would be great to have a young family around. I'm more than happy to offer some insight into our neighborhood and the families who live here. Don't get me wrong, the Longos are great if you like to play Dominoes or setback on the back deck all afternoon. Mrs. Longo told me once that she and her husband were quite adventurous in their younger days. Strip poker was their card game of choice back then. I can't help the cheesy grin and laughter that erupts from my mouth as I picture Mr. Longo in his tighty whities. I realize that I'm still staring at this approaching vehicle as I laugh to myself. I must look like a crazy person!

Suddenly, the vehicle picks up speed, the window closing before

I can see the face of the driver. I just stand there, dumbfounded, wondering who that was. I mumble to myself about not wanting the car's occupants to move into my neighborhood because they drive way too fast for a residential area. When I look down to turn off my iPod, I notice goose bumps cover my skin, up and down both arms.

What's up with that?

Chapter Five

THE LAST WEEK OF SUMMER VACATION IS SPENT WORKING in my classroom. I love this time of year. Stapling up new bulletin boards, attaching name tags to desks, and arranging my classroom perfectly for the new group of kids are some of my favorite things to do before the first day of school.

Noticing my travel mug of coffee is once again empty, I make a quick run to Dunkin' Donuts to satisfy my caffeine fix. I am a self-proclaimed coffee junkie. I pull into the drive thru as I usually do, but I quickly cut across the parking lot and nearly collide with an Audi when I see Pete standing behind the counter.

Pete is one of my oldest and closest friends. We've been friends since Kindergarten and he was my first crush in second grade. He was my first kiss in eighth grade. I loved him like crazy until he told me that he'd never love me like *that*. Pete, the boy I wanted to marry, the boy whose name I scribbled all over my notebooks, loved boys. That was the beginning of his insistence that everyone call him *Peter*, not Pete. Lucky for me, I've been grandfathered in. Stepping out of my Jeep, I wave sheepishly, utter an apology to the scowling driver of the Audi, and step inside.

A huge burly man stands in front of me, shielding me. When Pete finally notices me, he nearly drops the frozen Coolata he's making and runs around the counter. "Oh. My. God!" Wrapping his arms around my back, he pulls me close to his tall, lean body and swings me around through the air like a rag doll.

"Dude! Put me down!" I laugh, swatting his hands away. His beautiful hazel eyes sparkle with genuine love and happiness to see me. "I heard you were back...days ago." He narrows his eyes. "Do you have any idea how fucked up it was that I heard from Angie Jackson that you were back? *Very* fucked up!" His eyes roll dramatically as he steps back behind the counter to make us each a cup of coffee and yells something about going on his lunch break. Lunch break? It's 10:30 in the morning. I guess 10:30 sounds like a good time for lunch when your work day begins at 4:00 a.m.

I love hanging out with Pete. He's so happy and carefree. I get an earful about his hot new boyfriend, but I'm quick to cover his lips when he starts to tell me about his sex life.

"Fine. Tell me about yours then," he demands.

Every summer he begs for details about the juicy hookups that he swears I have. My exaggerated tales of dark erotica and dabbling in BDSM with some unbelievably, handsome billionaire are just that...tales. Pete spends way too much time reading romance novels. I chuckle at his words that I'll find the one when the time is right, but it only serves to reopen the tiny wound in my heart that hasn't quite mended since last spring.

"Hey, Peter. We need you," an older woman calls, pointing to the long line of people waiting to be served.

"Ugh! I gotta get back to work. Promise you'll call me later?" He leans down to kiss my cheek as I promise to have him over for dinner or drinks by the fire pit soon.

"SHIT!" I CHOKE ON THE LAST BIT OF COFFEE WHEN I pull into my usual spot on the far side of the school parking lot. I reach back to grab my bag and notice the black SUV, a shiny Escalade, from Sunday is pulling into the lot, parking in a spot designated for visitors. The mustard yellow New York license plate confirms that it is the same vehicle. A feeling of trepidation courses through my body and puts me on alert. Curiosity begs me to spy on the driver who opens the door to exit, but I'm a total chicken shit. Instead, I scoot down, lowering myself while searching blindly for the cup holder with one hand and pulling the lever with the other to recline my seat, and I quickly manage to conceal myself. *OK, Mia?! Seriously? What is wrong with you? Chill out!*

I wait and wait. And then wait some more. Finally after twenty minutes or so I peek over and see Shelby's white Honda Civic pull into the lot. Sitting upright, I glance around and adjust my seat to its upright position. I wipe the sweat from my brow, pull my hair into a messy bun, and go over to help Shelby with her boxes and bags for her classroom.

Why does just seeing this car have me on edge? It was odd how the driver slowed down and then sped up as I approached. I'll have to ask Mrs. Longo if she's ever seen it before. I'm thinking we might need to start a neighborhood watch or something.

"Hey, you. What's going on? You...um...you look a little flushed," she says, reaching into the trunk to retrieve her boxes. "Can you grab those for me?" She nods toward the oversized bag and the small, white rectangular box topped with a perfectly knotted gold bow.

"You okay?" she asks curiously as she closes the trunk.

"I'm fine. It's just hot as hell and you're *late*." I lie, glancing over my shoulder towards the double doors leading into the building.

"Sorry. Mike wouldn't let me leave 'til he gave..." I hold up my hand to silence her.

"Ugh...I get it...I get it," I say in mock disgust. "God, you two are like...freakin' rabbits." Yes, my best friend is a sex fiend.

Setting up Shelby's room doesn't take nearly as much time as mine did. But then again, I did mine alone last night. Only the custodian was there and he offered little help except to tell me to close the windows before I left.

Being the perfectionist that she is, Shelby insists that she needs to change the color of the bulletin board paper because it doesn't match the new border. She grabs her phone and leaves in search of perfect bulletin board paper in the storage closet on the second floor.

I see the slim box that I carried in and open it, revealing a brass name plate with fancy black letters engraved boasting "Mrs. Matthews," her new name. Hoping to surprise her, I carefully take the name plate into the hall and secure it in place outside her door. I breathe a quick puff of air onto the name plate, using the bottom of my t-shirt to wipe it until it shines. "Perfect!" I grin and whisper. "Absolutely, perfect!"

The sound of footsteps rounding the corner diverts my attention and I casually turn to see who's there. I'm looking forward to meeting some of my new colleagues now that our schools have merged.

"Well, thank you for coming in. It was a pleasure meeting you," Mrs. Chapman's high-pitched voice croons. I start to greet my principal but freeze immediately when I see Adam standing beside her.

"Likewise," his voice answers as he transfers a manila folder from one hand to the other to return her handshake. They both look over at me. *Why, dear Lord? Tell me why this gorgeous, mysterious man is everywhere I turn lately. Maybe he is a stalker like in a bad Lifetime movie. Either way, hopefully he won't remember me.*

Saved by the bell is seriously the understatement of the century when my cell phone rings, begging to be answered. I smile feebly at my boss and the mysterious man and walk back into Shelby's room.

Seeing Mom's name makes me smile. I feel badly that we haven't talked much lately. I swipe my phone and answer with enthusiasm, "Hi, Mom." Walking over to the windows overlooking the parking lot, I listen absentmindedly as she rambles on about her friends and how she feels abandoned by her children because Josh and I don't see or call her often enough. She's a little dramatic. I look out around the parking through the classroom window and notice the Escalade is still parked there.

"I know. I know..." I interrupt, not able to get a word in edgewise. "Ma, I hear you! You don't have to yell. Will you please just calm down?" I can't take it when she gets herself all worked up; I need to call the doctor and have him adjust her meds again. "Okay, Ma...I gotta go. Okay...yes. I know, Ma...I will, Ma. Yep...love you, too."

I close my eyes and press my forehead against the window, taking deep breaths, reminding myself that she isn't well and even though I am twenty seven years old, I'll always be her baby. Life hasn't always been fair to her. I guess I truly am my mother's daughter.

"Fucking shit!" I curse, tossing my phone onto the desk, watching it slide towards the edge nearly falling to the floor. I quickly and quite ungracefully scramble, reaching out and save my phone before it succumbs to iPhone suicide.

An "ahem" startles me. My eyes snap up immediately. Wearing black dress pants and a light blue dress shirt, Adam leans against the frame of the doorway, his arms crossed against his chest. His face is sexier than before with a thicker scruff in place.

"I hope that vocabulary isn't part of the curriculum at this school," he smirks. "I've heard great things about this school and its staff," he continues. *What? Oh, my God! Shit, I hope he's not a new teacher here. Oh no! I bet he's the new assistant principal. Last I heard, the vacancy had not been filled yet and the search continued on. Crap! That would be awkward!*

"Oh...um...no," I stutter as my face begins to flush. "I'm sorry you heard that. That was a personal matter." I mentally curse my mother and her craziness.

Wondering where Shelby is, I straighten myself out and look beyond Adam into the empty, quiet hall. His eyes follow mine, a slow grin appears, as he turns and looks behind him toward the door and then back at me. Does he think I'm looking for an escape route? I feel like a small, helpless animal trapped beneath the spell of a predator. I swallow hard, waiting for him to speak or for Shelby to arrive and help a sister out.

His eyes are on me like he's studying me, then his eyes flash around the room. "So, you're the teacher?" he asks thoughtfully, looking around, presumptuously stepping further into the room.

"Yes, I'm a teacher." My voice is small. I fidget with my phone to calm my nerves.

"This is a nice room. It's very...clean, creative, and...purposeful." A wicked grin appears. "I like rooms like that." I swallow hard again because I can only imagine the kind of room Mr. Sexy here is talking about. Who does he think he is? Christian Grey or something? *Okay, Mister. Time to go!*

"Yes, it is a nice *classroom*." Grabbing my bag, I tell him quickly that I was just on the way out, hoping that he'll get the hint and leave. But no, he stands there ogling me from head to toe. I watch with fascination as he inhales and exhales resolutely. Finally, his cheek pulls back in a side smile and then he simply nods and turns to leave. I can't help but stare at how nicely his ass fills out his expensive dress pants. His strong and confident gait exudes pure sex. Oh dear God, a shiver tingles through me. If he's the new vice principal, I just might have to transfer. There is no way I can *work* under him when I want to *be* under him.

Just as he crosses the threshold of the doorway, Adam stops, peering considerately at the brass name plate on the wall. "What did you say your name was?" he asks. He looks disappointed.

My eyes flash to meet his. "I didn't," I answer indignantly.

His lips pucker to contain his amusement. Adam's eyes quickly close and reopen as if he were shaking off a negative thought. "Well." He looks at the name plate, his brow furrows. "It was a pleasure seeing you...again. I look forward to seeing you around."

He walks toward the front entrance of the building but stops abruptly just as he reaches the double doors. He pauses and glances back at me dejectedly while his mouth opens to speak before closing quickly. The forlorn expression on his face makes me feel guilty for being a bitch so I offer a conciliatory smile as an apology for my rudeness.

As if debating his next move, he briefly shakes his head and sighs. Is this really the same man who eye-fucked me at the park? Why couldn't he just introduce himself like a normal person? This Adam may be a gorgeous, sexy man, but I can tell he's trouble. It's written all over his face. Huge red flags wave feverishly in my face. I definitely need to heed the warning and steer clear of him.

Half an hour later Shelby finds her way back to the classroom with colorful rolls of bulletin board paper and we finish setting up her room. My cheeks feel about as red as the paper she chose.

"Well, it's about time! Where the hell did you go? China?" I snort, grabbing a roll of paper from her before she drops it, wondering how she even managed to carry all this stuff.

"I stopped to say hi to a few people. I wasn't gone that long. God, you're moody today. What's your problem?" she asks as she measures and cuts the perfect length from the roll of paper. Am I really that transparent? I know she knows me well and all, but really? "What's got you all hot and bothered?" If Shelby only knew how *hot and bothered* I am!

"Nothing! It's hot. Let's get this crap done and over with, Miss Perfectionist. I'm starving and I want to head to the lake." These are both good excuses because I always want food and I love the lake.

"Did you see Shane here?" she smirks, nodding for me to take the corner of the paper so we can hang it up.

"Shane? Why would he be here?" I grab the paper that slips through my fingers.

"Rumor has it that he applied and interviewed for the assistant principal position."

"No way!" My eyes bulge, my pulse quickens because there is no way in hell that I can work side by side with Shane. We used to coach together, but this is different. Things are different now. I swear I'll transfer to another school in another state. If Shane and Adam both work here, I don't know what I'd do. Hell, I'll have to quit my job! That application sitting on my kitchen island just might become a reality instead of just an option.

We pick up salads for a late lunch and spend a few hours down by the lake sun tanning, enjoying the last days of freedom. I don't mention anything about Adam because there's really nothing to tell. I stretch out on the blanket, soaking up some vitamin D.

I walk along the beach alone, tossing rocks into the lake when I feel his eyes on me. I look up to see Adam standing chest deep in the clear water, his eyes beckon me to follow him. I look around for Shelby, but she's gone. The beach is deserted; Adam and I are the two solitary occupants. Behind him, the sun smiles and sets beneath the horizon of the lake, promising to return tomorrow. Adam steps back further into the water, concealing his luscious mouth and hard body, yet his dark, mesmerizing eyes still summon me to come closer. I want to run to him and wrap my arms around his neck and squeeze him tightly between my legs. I want to feel that body against mine.

"Mia, c'mon. It's time," his sultry voice calls to me.

I smile seductively and whisper, "Yes, Adam. I'm coming."

Just as my toes sink into the cool sand, taking small steps towards him, my body freezes and tenses; ice flows in my veins.

"Mia...it's time to go, babe." His voice is softer this time, sweeter even. My tired eyes flutter, adjusting to the yellow and orange glow of the sun and I see Shelby standing above me. "Seriously, wake up! We have to go."

My body thrusts upward into a sitting position, panting heavily as I search the calm water for a pair of chocolate brown eyes. This man invades my thoughts and now my dreams. Shelby folds her beach towel and starts to pack up her bag. The look on her face is doubtful as she asks if I'm alright; her last question confounds me.

"Mia?"

"What?" I ask, packing my bag.

"Who's Adam?"

Chapter Six

THE FIRST DAY OF SCHOOL IS NERVE WRACKING FOR teachers and students alike. Even teachers get butterflies the night before. It usually goes pretty well; thankfully there aren't too many tears in the second grade. Day one is all about getting to know each other so my goals are simple: get to know the kids' names, feed them lunch, and get them home safely to their parents.

This year I have nineteen students in my class. I've known most of the kids since they were babies or even in their mama's bellies. One of the six new students to our school is Madison Lawson, a quiet, little, dark-haired beauty. I quickly learn that she likes to be called Maddie and that she moved here over the summer with her dad and her twin brother, Luke. Tears well up in her eyes when Becca, one of the other girls in the class, asks about where her mom is. Very stoically, she responds, "She's in Heaven." How sad! My heart splinters into pieces for this little girl. I offer a smile and diffuse the awkward situation, reassuring Madison that I'm excited to have her in my class and promise that she's going to have a great year.

Dismissal time rolls around before I know it. I separate my class by dismissal procedure: students who are picked up by their parents stay with me, bus kids go with Shelby. I'm not looking forward to the long line of parents waiting to claim their children at the end of the day. I volunteer for this afterschool position because lots of teachers need to rush home to their families and take their kids to dance lessons or soccer practice. I don't have to rush off to be anywhere. No one is waiting on me.

Part of my job is to monitor and call children who wait anxiously to be picked up. This is the worst part of the day because parents love to gossip as they wait in line. Being the professional that I am, I ignore the chatter and snickering that I hear and just smile, welcoming all the beautiful, fit, stay-at-home moms picking up their children. But when Mrs. Cummings comes in with her newest little one, I drop everything and cradle the sweet baby girl, named Hannah, in my arms. I nuzzle her neck because babies smell so good; it's the smell of goodness and innocence rolled into one. Goofy baby talk and exaggerated smiles pour out of my mouth until the baby starts to fuss so I hand her back immediately, thanking her mom for the opportunity to hold her.

I glance at my watch. I hate when parents are late to pick up their kids. With a huff of annoyance, I'm relieved that the line is dwindling down slowly, only a few children remain. Why don't they just take advantage of the public school transportation that's offered? The rolling of the custodian's cart draws my attention and as I turn back to the line of parents, I'm stunned when I come face to face with Adam who steps up the table with a look of delight on his breathtaking face.

I swallow hard. "May I help you?" A look of confusion mars my face, wondering why he's waiting in the line with parents who are there to pick up their children. Dressed in an expensive charcoal grey business suit, crisp white shirt with a loosened light blue and silver tie, he leans forward to sign his name on the line twice. He's a lefty.

A kid? He has *kids*? He's married? But I didn't see a ring? Oh. My. God. How embarrassing! What a major douche bag! I want to slap him or kick him in the balls for being so forward with me at the park. I wonder if his wife knows what an asshole he is.

"Good afternoon, Mrs. Matthews." He grins, his eyes flashing up beneath long lashes. I momentarily lose the ability to think rationally or speak when he looks at me. "Um...good afternoon," is all I can manage to squeak out. Before I call out the names of the children he's been given permission to take, I ask for some form of identification because I don't recognize him as a parent.

"Sure," he responds, reaching into his back pocket for his wallet.

"Here you go." He starts to hand me his license but doesn't let go right away. I look at him as he waits for me to take it since both our fingers have an edge of the license. He wants to play a game; I can be patient. After a few seconds, I release my hold and turn my hand so my palm is facing upward. I look like a parent demanding something from her child. He smirks and places the rectangular card in my hand. When I look at his license, I notice just two things. The first is that it's from the state of New York and the second thing is that even in the generic DMV photo, he's insanely gorgeous. Figures!

"Thank you." I smile as I hand back his ID. "Just so you know, it's standard protocol for new students. School safety and security measures are strictly enforced since..." I realize I'm starting to ramble. I tend to ramble when I get nervous. The sound of throats clearing tell me that the two parents behind Adam are growing impatient.

I look down at my list and call out the names of the children he's picking up. "Madison? Luke? Your..." I hesitate because I'm not sure what to call him. Dad? Uncle? Brother?

"Father," he answers my unspoken thought. "I'm their father." His eyes look directly at me. Holy DILF! His daughter is the new student in my class! Oh, crap! How will I ever stand to see him all the time?

My cheeks flame when the children jump up to greet him. The smile on his face is genuine and loving as he scoops them up, one in each arm, kissing them. "How was your first day of school?" He listens intently as they each answer him with "Good" or "It was fun.

I made a new friend..." Their words fade as they walk toward the door, but just before Adam is out of view, he looks back over his shoulder and catches me staring. What does he do? He smiles like he's got a giant freaking secret.

Every afternoon that week, I find myself eager to get to my dismissal post so I can shamelessly gawk at him. I mean, it is part of my job to look at parents and to talk to them, right? I try to be inconspicuous as I watch what we like to call the "Pretty Committee" moms dote on Adam, offering to set up play dates. Hmmm...I wonder if they mean for the kids or for themselves. I wonder what their husbands would think of their generous offers. One mom hands him a business card for her gym, telling him that she'd love to train him. Train him or fuck him? Really, people? Have a little self-respect! I can't help but laugh at their desperate attempts to get his attention.

Unfortunately, Gina, dressed to the nines, is always there to pick up her daughter, too. Jealousy hits me like a ton of bricks when she and Adam walk in together, talking intimately. How can they be so friendly? I watch as her fingers reach up and brush off his shoulder. I've seen that move a million times; I doubt he has anything on his shoulder anyway. His smile is warm and genuine, playful even. It's a smile one would give to a lover. That's it! It has to be! She's probably sleeping with him—it's what she does best.

From what Madison has told me, they just moved to town over the summer. Of course, Gina would be the head cheerleader of the welcoming committee. I'm sure she's giving him a lot more than just a tour of our charming little town.

"You know, if you want, I could just start picking up the kids every Thursday. What do you think?" I overhear Gina ask Adam, who is intentionally staring at me, his brow is slightly furrowed. He doesn't respond. She must notice his inattentiveness because she follows his line of sight and meets my eyes. Her blue eyes narrow, shooting her notorious death glare at me. I simply look back at him, no smile, no kind gesture. Nada.

"So what do you think?" she asks as he signs his name twice. "Sure," he responds, never taking his eyes off me.

"Hello." Adam smiles at me, his face softening. What a douche nozzle! He's seriously got to be the biggest asshole to stare at me while his lover looks on. Like Gina needs another reason to hate me.

"Hello," I answer back with a small smile of my own, before he moves along to gather his children.

All week, Gina's glares get longer and stronger every single day. The hardest thing to understand is why *she* hates *me* so much. I never did anything to her. I'm not the one who took something that I had no right to, shattering her heart into a million pieces. It's not possible; you'd have to have a heart to shatter and she is a heartless bitch.

"I can't believe you just did that?" I shriek and wipe off the chocolate frosting she smeared on my face. I want to cry as I look down at my ruined halter dress that's covered in icing.

"Oh God! Can't you take a joke? I was just kidding." She glances around nervously at our families who've gathered for our high school graduation party.

"Gina!" Uncle Carl yells, snatching her up by the arm as my mother rushes over with a damp cloth.

"What? God, all you guys think she's so fucking perfect."

"Watch your language," my father warns sternly.

"Whatever," Gina's blonde hair whips around as she pushes her way through the crowd, bumping shoulders with Josh.

BY FRIDAY AFTERNOON OF THE FOLLOWING WEEK, I'M eager to pack up my things for the long Labor Day weekend and am looking forward to the annual cookout at Shelby and Mike's place. I sit on the edge of my desk and tap out a list on my phone of what I need to get for the BBQ when a quiet knock at the door interrupts my thoughts, causing me to look up.

Standing there in the doorway is Adam, dressed casually in jeans and a white button down shirt, now sporting a sexy beard with a puzzled look on his face. This guy must be really indecisive with things. One week his face is almost completely clean shaven with just a hint of a five o'clock shadow. The next week, he seems to let his beard grow in shielding his strong jaw. Beard. No beard. Make up your mind already. But the reality is that he looks gorgeous either way. I shake my head and smile when I realize that he's not alone; he's holding the hands of Madison and Luke, the little boy that I recognize as one of Shelby's students.

"Hi, Mrs. Matthews," Adam saunters in slowly, a wary look on his handsome face. "I'm sorry to interrupt, but my boy, Luke, forgot something in his desk." *Mrs. Matthews? Why would he think I'm Mrs. Matthews?* I rack my brain for a clue and then I remember. *Ah, yes!* The name plate. He must've seen it on Shelby's door. I remember now that he called me Mrs. Matthews the first day of school.

The confused look written across my face is mistaken for annoyance because with a tentative look on his face, he asks, "Would you mind if he grabbed it? The kids are going to their grandparents' house for the long weekend." His eyes bore into mine like he's trying to tell me something, like he's trying to send a message. My telepathic receiver must be broken because I don't get it.

A giggle erupts from Madison as she looks up at her father. "What are you giggling about, silly girl?" he asks sincerely, smiling down at his daughter.

"Daddy, this is my class!"

I can't contain the smug smile on my face as Adam realizes his mistake. It's an honest mistake since there's only a foot between our classroom doors and I was standing in Shelby's room when he walked in.

"Wait, what?" he asks, his eyes darting back and forth between his daughter and me. "Seriously?" Adam turns quickly to the doorway, steps out and looks at Shelby's door before turning his eyes back to me. Slowly, he walks back, contemplating his words.

I step forward, extending my hand to greet him. "Hello, Mr. Lawson. I'm Miss Delaney, Madison's teacher." His mouth presses into a hard line trying desperately to hold his laugh in, but it doesn't work. His laugh is just about as sexy as the rest of him.

"Wait, let me get this straight. You're not Mrs. Matthews? You're not Luke's teacher?" He waits for a response.

I simply shake my head. "No, I'm not."

His voice drops to a whisper, "You're not married?" *What an odd question to ask!*

"Dad, seriously?" asks Luke, already heading to the door.

Adam grins uncomfortably and just stares at me. "Okay, then. Now that *that's* cleared up." He claps his hands together and ushers his children out. Just as he starts to walk out, he looks back over his shoulder and grins at me, shaking his head in disbelief or perhaps relief. Of which, I'm not so sure.

I smile back at him. My cheeks flush with amusement. Blood flows quickly through my veins causing things that should not throb at work to throb.

I finish my list and text my brother before tossing my cell phone into my work bag, and proceed to follow them out, watching them enter Shelby's classroom. I hear the conversation as Adam briefly explains to the custodian why he's there. I should probably stand in the doorway since Shelby left early for an appointment, but I convince myself that it's fine and start to walk away. What's he going to steal? Expo markers?

As I get ready to turn the corner of the hallway leading out to the door, I hear Adam's voice. "Go ahead, bud. I'll be right back." His deep voice comes closer as he walks with heavy steps in my direction.

"Excuse me, Miss Delaney." I turn around to face him and am met with angry, dark eyes. "Why didn't you tell me who you were?"

His voice is stern. He steps closer, walking right into my personal space like he owns the place or has a right to be so close. A little presumptuous, aren't we? "So let me get this straight. You're not married and you led me to believe that you were?"

Is he insane? I never said anything like that! I breathe deeply, slowly preparing my answer and smirk. "Mr. Lawson, I did no such thing. It's not my fault you made an assumption. You know what they say about people who assume, don't you?" I'm not really sure why I suddenly feel contentious toward this man. He seems to press my buttons and, oh Lord, I'd be lying if I said I wouldn't mind him pressing some other buttons.

The last thing I hear before pushing my way through the double doors and climbing into my Jeep is his sexy chuckle and him murmuring, "Nice. Real nice."

Wanting to feel every ounce of sunshine, I decide to roll back and secure the convertible top. The parking lot is already empty; everyone trying to get a jump start on the long weekend. My phone alerts me of an incoming text from Shane telling me to have a great weekend and asking if we can get together soon.

Just as I finish my text to him thanking him for the thought but declining his offer, I see Adam, with a juvenile backpack slung over each shoulder, walk out of the building, hand in hand with his two adorable kids. He looks absolutely ridiculous, yet so sexy, so completely happy, all at the same time. Luke is helped into the back seat first. Then Madison's high pitched squeals of delight make me jump. It's at that moment that my appreciation for him as a father grows when he scoops up his daughter, tosses her into the air, ending it all with a kiss on her forehead before securing her in the back seat. It's quite a disparity between this good, loving father and the arrogant man I met a few weeks ago at the park.

Chapter Seven

MY SIMPLE PLAN FOR THE NIGHT, WHICH INCLUDED A hot date with my Kindle, is thrown out the window when my college roommate, Kate, calls and invites me out to some new dance club in the city. Even though I am tired and really should just stay in and rest, I catch a two hour nap before rummaging through my cramped closet, looking for something to wear. Ahhhh, yes! Perfect! The short, black dress hugs my body like a glove. Poor Brady whines, knowing he's on his own tonight.

Sometimes, it's hard being a teacher in the same small town in which you live. I don't want my personal life to get mixed up with my professional life. I am always aware of my behavior outside of the classroom. But I am more than Miss Delaney, second grade teacher and girls' basketball coach—I am Mia Delaney, a twenty-seven year old, sexy, and single female on the prowl. I know what's expected of me in my role of responsible teacher, educating America's future and all that, but I'm going to allow myself this one night to indulge, let go, and have some fun. It's my one night to be a little reckless and carefree like Kate. There's a reason she's earned the nickname Krazy Kate. After all it's not like I would know anyone there. The whole dance club scene isn't really my thing, but I'm looking forward to a night out with Kate.

I'm a little out of my comfort zone. Needing to control the agitation running rampant throughout my body, I open up a bottle of white wine and sing along to Pink while I raise my glass to Brady, who looks away from me. I think if he could roll his eyes at me, he would. It's just about 9:00...I run down my list: sexy, black dress? Check. Killer heels? Check. Flawless makeup with a smoky eye? Check. Tousled dark hair falling in waves? Check.

I take a quick selfie and text it to Shelby letting her know that I'm going out with Kate and telling her that she's to send out the search party if she doesn't hear from me by tomorrow. It wouldn't be the first time she's had to come find me. Kate has been known to go MIA. Shelby responds, "Damn girl. You're dressed to impress! Or maybe to kill! Have fun. Be safe. Love you."

Kate, already inebriated, barges in through the kitchen door. I place the empty wine glass down and lean in for a quick hug. It's not a Shelby hug, but a hug none the less. Kate looks great, like she usually does. Her thick blonde hair is pulled into a sleek, high ponytail, showing off her newest tattoo, an infinity sign, which is prominently displayed on the nape of her neck. Her body, long and lean with curves in the all the right places, is to die for. She's one of those lucky bitches who can eat whatever she wants and never step foot in a gym or maybe her daddy knows a good plastic surgeon. Pulling the phone out of her silver clutch, she snaps a few photos of us and includes them in a group text to people I've never met and probably never will. Our friends don't really run in the same circles.

After giving Brady a quick kiss on the top of his head which Kate thinks is disgusting, I grab my small clutch, turn off all the lights, except for the small lamp on the hall table, and lock the doors.

A tall driver dressed in a dark suit waits by the black town car. "Kate! You got us car service? Seriously!" I snort.

"Come on! It'll be fun. We can drink and dance and if you find someone you like, you can bring him back here and fu—" Kate's words are cut short when her eyes snap up to the driver who is staring with raised brows. "Sorry, Phil. I'll behave. I promise. I mean it this time." The words slur seductively from her pouty mouth.

The back seat is soft leather and comfortable. Kate sings along with Jason Derulo and adds her own gestures about doing more than just talking dirty to her. The upbeat music pipes in as the air conditioning offers needed relief from the humidity. Driving through town, I wonder who can see us in here behind the tinted windows. It's not often you see a luxurious town car here. Well, that's not entirely true. The DeGennaros, they all have nice, fancy, expensive cars.

My thoughts drift back to Gina's 13th birthday party when her father rented a black, super stretched limo to take thirteen wild teenagers to the movies and then to dinner at a fancy Italian restaurant which was owned by one of the many uncles. We were all so impressed and honored to have gotten an invitation!

When we finally arrive at the posh, upscale club, aptly named Pulse, it's already jam packed, wall to wall, with beautifully dressed women and gorgeous, sexy men. Maybe there's a prerequisite to be allow in, I laugh to myself. Good thing I'm here with Kate in that case; I doubt I'd even be allowed to stand in the line. The doorman, a "friend" of Kate's, ushers us in quickly, bypassing the long line, garnering us stares of jealousy and looks of disdain.

A tall, leggy blonde hands us each a glass of bubbly pink champagne as we wind our way through the throng of people. The new wave, techno music is loud and the lights are dim except for the flashing of a strobe light in the far corner of the club. Perfume and cologne waft through the air. Walking closely behind Kate, I take in the scene as we pass the dance floor where hands are roaming all over bodies, gyrating, practically having sex on the dance floor.

This club boasts several massive, mahogany U shaped bars and plush seating areas. Thick, dark red leather couches are arranged in small clusters on the far end with a scattering of high top tables nearby. From anywhere in the bar, you have a good view of the multitudes of partiers.

Our bodies are thrust forward as we laugh and dance to the beat of the fast, techno music. I wave my arms up in the air, swaying my body carelessly, dancing with no one in particular. The bottle and half of champagne that we drank in the car on our way over to the club has loosened my inhibitions. Watching some of these people bump and grind for the world to see is not something I'm used to witnessing up close and personal. My eyes follow their bodies as they move together, almost becoming one. Even though I want to look away, I can't. It's erotic and sensual; I'm mesmerized and turned on. Sexy, well-dressed men stalk around looking at the beautiful, half-naked women like predators circling their prey, lust filled eyes roaming up and down their bodies, wanting to devour them.

Suddenly I feel hands on my hips as someone dances closely behind me, pressing something very hard into my ass. My body tenses immediately and I step forward into the crowd, freeing myself. A raspy, deep voice close to my ear interrupts, "Hey, beautiful." Ignoring the voice that can't surely be for me, I look at Kate who's staring at me with raised eyebrows and a sly grin on her drunken face.

"What?" I shout over the music, leaning in closer to hear her.

"Someone wants you." She nods her head indicating that I should look behind me. *Seriously? Me?* That huge bulge pressing into my ass was for me? This guy must really be in need of glasses or is blind because there's no way he is calling me beautiful, not with Kate right here next to me. I mean, I'm pretty enough and all, but Kate, she's gorgeous and everybody knows it.

My head turns back to meet the voice who's waiting for a response. My eyes rake upwards from his white, button-down shirt over his throat, finally settling on his full lips. Deep, green eyes embedded in olive skin smile back at me. *Wow! Gorgeous man alert!*

"Hello," is all I can manage to say. I'm suddenly aware of the throbbing and pulsating of the music around me. Or is the throbbing coming from within me?

"Hi. I'm..." He looks up above me, thoughtfully, and says,

"Devin." He extends his hand to me and I place my hand in his. "Hi. I'm Mia." I smile at him. My hand is gently pulled and raised to his lips. His eyes are focused on mine as he places a lingering kiss on my knuckles before pulling me flush against him.

"Hello, Mia." His eyes search my face. "You haven't been here before, have you?" He smiles. "Welcome to Pulse." He swivels his hips, pressing his hardness into my belly.

"Thanks. It's a pretty cool place, but it's kind of like a... meat market." I laugh nervously at my joke. Devin looks at me considerately, his face illuminated by the strobe light. "Let's get you a drink. You might need it."

"Oh, okay," I answer, but Kate's voice interrupts me when she leans and tells me that she'll be right back because she sees some people she recognizes. "Kate! Wait, I'll go with you." But she doesn't turn around and I'm left staring at her ass as she makes her way over to a group of friends who've just arrived.

"C'mon. Let's get you that drink," Devin commands as he places his hand on the small of my back and leads me over to one of the last vacant couches, placing our drink order with yet another leggy blonde. While we wait for our drinks, Devin and I make awkward small talk. He tells me I look beautiful, sexy, and edible.

"So you've never been here before. Tell me why?" he asks, his eyes keep roaming over my body like he's buying a car.

"This isn't really my kind of bar, actually. I'm not into this scene," I answer honestly.

"That's too bad. Believe me, after tonight, you'll be coming here over and over again." His lips pull back in a devious grin. Something tells me he's not talking about my attendance to the club.

Devin runs his hand up and down the cocktail waitress' legs, lingering close to her ass when she bends over to deliver our drinks. Her eyes dance with delight at his affection; I'm thinking that her job description doesn't just include serving drinks. Our conversation continues as if he hadn't just groped this woman in front of me. He mentions that he's one of the club owners. He seems to be early to mid-thirties and I'm impressed that he's an entrepreneur, finding success in the entertainment industry. The loud music makes it difficult to hear so he leans in closer, practically on top of me, grinning at me roguishly. I should feel flattered when he says that he noticed me the minute I walked in, but I don't.

Feeling uncomfortable, I shift my body away from him, looking around the club, pretending to see someone I know just to gain some space. It's hot enough in here without the added heat radiating from his body; my pulse is starting to race. Maybe that's where they got the name from. My wild friend is nowhere to be seen at the moment. A sense of unease creeps into me when I realize that aside from Kate, I'm surrounded by absolute strangers who are probably all pretty drunk or well on their way. I'm all for going out and having a good time, but you need to be smart about it. And something about Devin makes me uneasy, triggering my anxiety to kick up a notch.

Devin slides closer to me, placing his muscular arm around my shoulder, pulling me to him. "Mmmm...enough talking. I can't wait to slide my cock into you. Baby, I'm going to make you scream so fucking loud when you come," he growls after biting down hard on my earlobe. His tongue slides down and he licks my neck. You know that moment in a movie where time stands still and the camera circles the main character and she's like, "What the fuck is going on?" Yeah, that just happened!

Without wanting to send myself into a full blown panic attack or causing a scene by punching him in the face, I hastily excuse myself to the ladies' room. *He wants to fuck me? He doesn't even know me! What the hell kind of club is this?* Now that I look around, I see the signs that this is no ordinary dance club. The mass of tangled bodies grinding and gyrating should've been a clue. I curse Kate to the pits of hell; I'm so going to kill her for bringing me here!

When I decline his offer to walk me, Devin reaches forward,

grabs my hand, pushing it against his bulge, and assures me that he'll be waiting right here. My eyes spit fire at this crass, rude, asshole of a man before I turn to leave. A sense of desperation floods me as I look around searching for my friend. I just need to find Kate and get the hell out of here. This isn't the place for me.

After waiting in the long line that snakes down the dimly lit hall, I squeeze my way through moving bodies, exiting the bathroom hoping to find Kate so we can leave. There's another door at the end of the hall which is illuminated by a black light, but there's no line. Maybe it's the VIP bathrooms or something. I send Kate a text asking where she is. I lie and tell her that I'm not feeling well and that I need to leave sooner rather than later.

My eyes roam back and forth across the dance floor, the crowded bar and finally up to the second level. I didn't notice all the smaller balconies perched above me, each one like a hotel balcony, overlooking the club. My body follows my eyes, rotating in a full circle as I count at least twenty balconies full of people, kissing, touching or watching. I can only imagine what I must look like if someone were watching me. They'd see a foreign tourist, gazing upward in awe at the massive skyscrapers on the streets of Manhattan.

Continuing to search the faces on the balconies, I still don't see my soon to be ex-friend, Kate. An intense chill, like a charge of electricity, shoots straight through me from my head to my toes because instead of locating my fiery friend, I meet a pair of dark, familiar eyes, watching me. Standing tall with long, outstretched arms, his black sleeves rolled up, strong hands grip the railing; an angry faced man who looks very much like Adam Lawson stares directly down at me. *What the fuck?* It can't possibly be him, can it? I mean really, what are the chances that this mysterious man is here at *this* particular club, on *this* particular night, in *this* city. His dark eyes are intense; the lower half of his handsome face is covered with a thick, dark beard. There is no doubt in my mind that it's him; even my body knows it's him, as moisture pools below. *This can't possibly be happening to me! Why the hell is he here? He doesn't look like the clubbing type and he's a father for God's sake. A hot father but a father nonetheless.*

I want to look away. I try to look away, but I just can't seem to tear my eyes away from his gaze. A sultry, redheaded woman wearing a shimmery, tight green dress with a deep plunging neckline exposing her full breasts, wraps her arm around his and whispers in his ear. I watch enraptured as he slowly, almost deliberately shakes his head from side to side indicating an answer of "no." For a moment, I feel like he's not answering her, but somehow talking to me, telling me "no."

Our staring contest ends when a drunken woman, dancing wildly, knocks into me causing me to stumble forward and lose my footing. Devin's arms engulf me immediately. "Hey there, beautiful. You okay?" Embarrassed, I smile and reassure him that I'm fine, readjusting the hem of my little black dress, pulling it down to cover my ass. I love this dress, but it leaves very little to the imagination.

Devin's eyes are glazed over; he looks like the devil himself. A nervous chuckle escapes, wondering where he keeps his red suit and pitch fork. I glance back up to where Adam was just standing only seconds before; disappointment floods me because he is no longer there. He's gone. Blinking furiously, I recall all that I had to drink—I must be drunker than I thought because I'm hallucinating. *Seriously, Mia. Chill the fuck out! Adam Lawson, here? Really?* Maybe he has a twin brother or a doppelganger.

Grabbing my phone that I feel vibrating in my clutch, I receive a text from Kate letting me know that something came up and she left, but that Phil, our driver, will take me home when I'm ready. *She left? What the hell?*

I tap out my response, "Not funny. Where r u?"

She responds immediately, "Sorry. ILY" She loves me?

You stupid bitch, at the moment I hate you! Faster than my fingers can move, I respond, "Meet me out front. We are leaving. NOW."

What was I thinking coming out tonight? This is Kate. Wild, carefree, irresponsible Krazy Kate. It's not like I can call Shelby or Pete for a ride; it'll take them almost an hour to get here and I'll never hear the end of it about going out with her. They're not really fans of the notorious KK. And tonight I can't say that I disagree.

Devin, still standing in front of me, leans down into my ear, a smile on his lips. "Hey, you ready to get out of here?" *Uh...YES, just not with you!* "I have a VIP suite upstairs. A couple of friends might join us." Devin's eyes light up and he smiles lustfully at me. What? Maybe it's the effect of too much alcohol too fast, but I feel like I'm in the Twilight Zone. I'm waiting for Ashton Kutcher to come out and tell me I'm being punked.

"Actually, Devin, something's come up. I'm sorry. I've got to go." I lie. His eyebrows rise up in disbelief, his smile now twists into a snarl. "What do you mean, 'You're leaving'? You can't just leave? It doesn't work that way. I CHOSE you." Devin's words sneer in my face as he grabs my arm so hard that I know I'll have a bruise in the morning.

I swallow hard as I look at him, anger filling me. My words are confident, but my body feels anything but. "You need to get your hands off me." I search the crowded club for someone to come to my rescue, but no one seems to notice what's going on between us. I would imagine that we look like everyone else with hands roaming and groping.

Devin drops the hold of my arm and backs away, seeming to realize what he's done. "I'm...I'm sorry, but you can't just leave," he stammers, before reaching out to grab my hand, pressing it along his pants where his erection is firm. "Devin, let me go!" I push against him. He bends down into my ear and whispers, "This is for you. You'll be begging me for it. I can promise you that."

That's it! I see red and lose my shit. "Who the fuck do you think you are?" I yell. In an instant, the image of my brother, teaching me how to throw a proper punch, races across my mind. Never in my life have I been so angry. Never in my life did I want to literally put my fist through someone's face. Scratch that—that's not entirely true, but you get my point. I'm pretty pissed.

Before I realize what's happening, I step back and throw my weight forward as my fist flies and connects with Devin's face. Blood immediately flows onto his lips and chin, staining his white shirt. "You fucking bitch! You hit me!" Devin's eyes widen as he clutches at his bloody nose. I stumble back into the crowd instantaneously, needing to get away from him and far away from here. The last thing I need is to get arrested for assault.

Immediately, I spot an illuminated sign and push my way in that direction. I send up a silent prayer and plea that Phil is there waiting for me and that Devin, the asshole, isn't following me. The music seems to be louder and more people are packed into the club. I can't imagine they're not violating some occupancy law right about now. Fighting my way through the crowds of people strolling into the club, I realize that it's an entrance not an exit. People are being ushered in as I'm trying to get out. It's not until I turn to look for the exit sign do I realize it's located in the back corner of the club; it's in the direction that Devin went and I don't want to take my chances of running into him again.

The humidity in the air is stagnant, thick and heavy as I stomp out of the club, swearing to myself that I'm going to kill Kate. The line to get in seems to have gotten even longer, wrapping around the corner. Lust is smeared all over their faces. It's almost ironic that I can't wait to get out and these people can't wait to get in. It's just a stupid club. A fucking weird club with men who think they can take what's not being offered.

Damn it! Where is he? Annoyed at myself for even coming out with Kate, I scan up and down the street looking for Phil, walking quickly even though I've got a blister forming on my toe. That's what I get for wearing four inch stilettos. The humid air is thick, causing my beautifully coiffed hair to frizz and stick to the back of my neck. Mumbling to myself for my own stupidity for wearing these shoes, but more importantly, for coming out with Kate, I head towards the parking lot thinking maybe Phil has parked the car there and is waiting for me. I wish I had gotten Phil's number. I should text Kate, but I'm sure whatever took her away in the first place, is now preoccupying her time.

On each side of the lot are cars, waiting patiently, silently abandoned temporarily while their owners party at Pulse. Porsche. Range Rover. Camaro. Mercedes. BMW. Lexus. Audi. Maserati. Corvette. It's like a luxury car show; it's the who's who of fancy, expensive cars. But, no town car and no Phil wait for me. *I'm so going to kill her!*

A chill shoots up my spine, goose bumps spread across my arm when I realize that besides the sounds of muffled laughter and distant techno music, it's eerily quiet and dark. Shit! I didn't think to bring my pepper spray or more importantly, my gun. *Yeah, it didn't exactly go with my LBD and it definitely wouldn't have fit in my clutch. And I can't exactly cross state lines with a .22 cal.*

The sound of an engine starting claims my attention. It purrs in the distance, slowly coming towards me before stopping completely; its headlights blinding my eyes. The driver's door opens, heavy footsteps and a dark figure slowly approach me still a few yards away, but this ominous presence scares me to the point of immobility. I quickly open my clutch and unlock my phone, getting ready to call 911 if need be. *Yeah, a little dramatic, I know, but hey, I'd rather be safe than sorry and end up a statistic.* I look around for the fastest and shortest way back to the club, back to the sound of drunken laughter and pulsating music. Like a slap in the face, it occurs to me that I'm about to come face to face with Devin. His gait, deliberate and determined, indicates that anger still flows in his veins, tension radiating from his pores.

As he stops, only a few feet now separating us, his face is darkened by the light behind him. I take a small step back and begin to utter an apology.

"Look, I'm really sorry I hit you, but I don't..." The terror is clear in my voice. I strain my eyes to see the expression on his face, but it's too dark.

"Why? Why are you here? Why would you come to a place like this?" A hostile yet quiet voice cuts off my words. Confusion mars my face at his questions. *Just because I didn't want to have sex with him means I can't come to dance club? What the hell is his problem?*

"Why? Why would you come *here?*" The words are strained, as if spoken through gritted teeth, trying to comprehend the unfathomable. At that moment, I feel so terrible for punching him in the face. Well, now that's not true. The bastard deserved it! My silent words scream, "I don't know why I'm here. My dumbass friend brought me and abandoned me. You said you wanted to fuck me and you put your hands on me, you asshole," but words fail me. I am mute.

"Answer me," he demands, tension radiating from his body, his fists tightening. Almost instantly, I'm snapped out of my reverie. His voice. It's a familiar voice. The shadowed figure and voice come closer. I am still mute not because I *can't* speak; his voice has rendered me speechless. I'm not sure if it's the tone in which he speaks or the questions and commands he hurls at me.

Cars pass by on the street behind me. I pray and plead that at any moment Phil will come around the corner, looking for me and offer to save me. *A man to save me? Am I a fucking damsel in distress? Hell, motherfucking, no! I don't need a man to save me!* I mentally kick my own ass and buck up. I am Mia Delaney. I am Dan Delaney's KAD. My father's words about me being his kick-ass daughter who shouldn't put up with a man's shit are what I need at the moment. The silent pep talk provides all the courage I need.

"Excuse me?" I retort, my voice laced with disdain, fueled by my anger. I need to be smart about this. I need to stand up for myself and not back down, but I don't want to exacerbate the situation because this asshole is already volatile.

"Listen, I think you've got the wrong idea," I continue speaking, trying to placate him while I back up slowly, not wanting to turn my back to him. The smell of his cologne wafts into my nose, causing me to momentarily and involuntarily close my eyes and inhale, as he steps forward, closing the space between us. I open my eyes. The courage I felt just seconds before vanishes and the instinct to run and hide kicks into high gear. My body tenses with fear that he's going to reach out, grab me, pull me into his car, rape me and kill me. I know it. My heart pounds frantically in my chest with fear that this might be my last few moments of life. The feeling of being hurt by this man is overwhelming.

"This...this isn't a place for someone like *you*. You don't belong here. Just go home." The compassion in his voice is oddly comforting. Maybe he's remorseful for having mistreated me earlier.

"Okay," I say calmly, trying to pacify him. "You're right. I'll go."

The passenger's window slightly rolls down a woman's voice calls out, "C'mon, baby. Let's go. Unless she's going to join us..." I catch a glimpse of her and see that it's the redhead who stood on the balcony hanging possessively onto the arm of the man I could have sworn was Adam. I'm pretty sure the man in front of me just flinched at her words.

Why would Devin warn me off if he's leaving with someone? Confusion and annoyance furrow my eyebrows. I realize immediately that this man standing before me, is taller and leaner than Devin. His body reveals a quiet strength.

"Why are you still here? I told you to leave." He's completely serious and apparently completely delusional.

Oh, no he didn't! My emotions are on a proverbial seesaw, teetering back and forth from anger to fear and then back to anger. I'm not a violent person, but this person in front of me produces such strong emotions and I'm about to explode. Again. Fuck appeasing. Fuck relenting. *Fuck him!*

Angry Mia and Fearful Mia are like a bad science experiment when mixed together, they explode and erupt. Everything I learned about keeping calm, assessing the situation to diffuse it, goes out the window because I'm...well, I'm just pissed off. Like really pissed off and scared shitless at the same time. I don't take orders very well from anyone, especially strange men in a club parking lot.

"What the fuck? Who the hell are you to tell me what to do? And you, my friend, need to back the fuck up before I pepper spray your ass!" I shout defensively, opening my clutch. I've been manhandled one too many times tonight. He doesn't move, but neither do I. There's a tension, a magnetic force keeping me there drawn to him.

"Go. Home. Now. And. Don't. Come. Back. EVER.'" Through gritted teeth, he enunciates each word calmly sending shivers down my spine and triggering a deep throbbing between my legs. *What is wrong with me? This man is threatening me and I'm thinking about sex?* I stand there trying to digest his words, my eyes narrow in contemplation. I don't want to push my luck; I'd like to come out of this confrontation unscathed. Intelligence wins out over emotion.

My eyes narrow again. "Fine! I'll leave...but not because *you* told me to." I point my finger at him. The woman calls him again, even more impatiently than before. "Looks like someone is pulling on your leash, my friend," I say defiantly while kicking myself mentally for being obnoxious and provoking him.

I back up slowly, turning in the direction of the club's entrance and walk with quick steps away from the man with the familiar voice. The familiar voice follows me out onto the sidewalk and steps out from the darkness of shadow. I look over my shoulder to see if the domineering prick is still there. This man stands there watching me walk away. I gasp loudly when a passing car illuminates his bearded face briefly—it belongs to Adam Lawson.

Chapter Eight

TUESDAY MORNING FINDS ME WITH A NASTY HEADACHE and a sour stomach. I drank way too much this weekend. Moaning loudly, I stretch my hand out to reach over to give Brady his morning belly rub. I groan even louder, mentally slapping myself because I should have known better than to go out with Kate. It wasn't the first time she'd ditched me. One time in college, I went to use the bathroom and Kate, drunk as a skunk, literally left me alone at the bar while she ran thirteen blocks all the way to our dorm room. I didn't talk to her for weeks. Needless to say, I was beyond angry at having to find a ride home in a taxi cab. *Again*.

Trying hard to keep my eyes closed, praying for the nausea to pass so I don't vomit...again...a muffled laugh escapes my lips, remembering my silly antics at Shelby and Mike's Labor Day cookout. *Oh, I'm sure we'll be talking about this one for a while.* Cheeseburgers, beer, hot dogs, beer, BBQ, beer, brownies, beer, potato salad, beer...I'll have to run a little harder this week to work off all the crap that managed to find its way into my mouth. All weekend, I sent all of Kate's calls to voicemail and left her apologetic texts unreturned. Damn her and her disappearing act! She really fucked up this time. I'm going to need a few days, maybe weeks, before I can talk to her.

This is going to be the longest day ever. I mean EVER! Brady's soft snores assure me that it's still early enough that I can get at least another hour of sleep. When I finally wake up, I realize I've overslept and now have to rush to get myself to work on time. Not exactly the right way to start off. I feel like shit. Plain and simple. After showering and dressing quickly, I pull into Dunkin' Donuts drive thru to get an extra-large cup of coffee with a double shot of espresso. The drive thru window opens to Pete's laughter and calls for "high-fives."

"Shhhhh...you're so loud!" I close my eyes and rest my head on the steering wheel as I wait for my coffee.

His laughter does little for my headache, but does jog some memories of me giving a fair share of "high- fives" to anyone and everyone at the party. I think at some point I even high-fived myself. I must've been fun to watch. I can only imagine the videos that are sure to circulate! They better not show up on YouTube.

Regretting my poor decisions for overindulging and oversleeping, I mentally rebuke myself and mutter words promising to never, ever drink that much again. Ever. *Shit!* I feel like I keep making that same promise over and over.

My biggest problem when I arrive at work is to decide how I'm going to open the heavy double doors at the front entrance of the school with a very sore hand wrapped in an ace bandage. So much for knowing how to throw a punch! Not to mention all the hand slapping and high-fives.

Since my hands are full, I wedge the door handle in between two fingers, wincing at the pain that shoots through my hand. A string of muttered curses fly from my lip-glossed lips when I realize that I've just spilled coffee down the front of my red and white sundress.

"Goddammit! Shit! What the fu—" I mumble.

Snickered laughter startles me, drawing my eyes straight to the beautiful, amused, freshly shaven face of Adam Lawson.

"Good morning, Miss Delaney. Let me get that for you," he offers kindly, opening the door for me and then reaches for my cup of coffee.

"No, thank you. I've got it," I answer, my resolve strong, although I wince and inhale as the pain again shoots through my hand.

He gives me an incredulous look with his eyebrows raised up. "Let me. I insist." His voice drops to a deep tone, similar to the one he used at the club, while his eyes bore into mine and he steps forward to close the gap between us.

I reluctantly give in and smile, passing my coffee to him. When our fingers graze one another, I'm flooded with a current of heated energy that surges through my body, turning my cheeks pink.

"What's wrong with your hand?"

"Nothing. It's fine." I lie.

Somehow I don't think he believes me when he peers at me, his lips part and then close, saying nothing in response.

"Thank you," I concede, sighing heavily as I enter the building.

Adam walks back into the building alongside me. We silently pass the office and walk into my classroom, finally stopping at my desk where I set my bags down and reach for my coffee, taking care not to touch him, and mumble sheepishly, "Thanks again."

Either he doesn't hear me or he has something else to say because he just stands there with one hand in his pocket, looking at me blankly. There's a flurry of activity out in the hallway as parents come in to drop off their children for school. I wonder why he's still here. Shouldn't he be at work already?

I walk over to the sink and grab a paper towel to blot the coffee from staining my dress. His eyes follow me and he watches me carefully. I can't believe I've spilled coffee on my new dress.

Adam saunters slowly over to me. "You missed a spot." His eyes travel from my face to my chest and then back up. My hand is engulfed in his as he guides me to the mark, wiping the stain near my cleavage. "It's right here."

I should slap his hand away. I should step back out of his reach, but I can't. I don't want to. I am incredibly drawn to this man in front of me. He has me hypnotized just by his presence. "There you go. You've got it." He grins, knowing how much he's affecting me. Bastard! I need to get the upper hand here.

"Um...is there something I can do for you, Mr. Lawson?" I ask in my professional teacher voice before walking around him and taking a small sip of coffee.

"Well..." He turns and grins wickedly. "I was actually hoping there was something I could do for *you*." He lets that last word float out there, waiting for my response. Oh, dear Lord. There are so many things that he could do for me. The list is endless. The possibilities are endless. *Hello, Mia. He's the father of a student in your class!*

"Excuse me?" I choke on my coffee.

"I'm not sure if Madison has told you, but I own my company. Being the boss has its benefits." He smiles, his eyes gleaming with humor before continuing, "One of the nice things about being in charge is...I can do whatever I want, whenever I want. I don't answer to anyone. Ever." *That's great for you!* I have a boss to answer to and she's not going to be happy if I'm late to pick up my class.

"Okay..." I drag my response, wondering where this conversation is heading.

"My work schedule is..." he hesitates, "very accommodating. I'm available to help out whenever you need it." *Oh, Mr. Lawson, you have no idea what I need!* I can almost feel that hard body pressed against me, making me moan in pleasure. I shake my head to clear my erotic thoughts.

He continues, "Field trips...class projects. I'm very good with my hands and I'd like to spend some time in you..."

My eyes widen and then narrow. "Excuse me?? What did you just say?" The last sip of coffee catches in my throat, causing me cough and sputter.

The look on his face has me confused. "I said, 'I'd like to spend some time in your classroom.' You know, I'm available pretty much whenever and am willing to do whatever you need, Miss Delaney." His voice drops to a sexy growl. I'm pretty sure we're not talking about making popsicle-stick picture frames or weaved construction paper placemats.

Holy shit! Did I just imagine that whole thing? I could've sworn he said he wanted to spend time *in me.* Maybe Shelby's right—I need to have sex. Fast.

My eyes open wide, a slight flush on my face. "Wow! That's a really generous offer, but unfortunately, I don't get to choose who helps out for things like that. The office handles all of that stuff. Sorry." I offer an apologetic smile.

"Hmmm...that's really too bad," he hums. "So, that's it?"

"Yep, it would seem so," I reply.

"You really won't accept my offer?" he asks with humor in his voice. His eyes glare at me. "Any possibility of me coercing you?" He grins, toying with me.

"Nope. Sorry." I glance at the clock, thinking of all the things I need to do before my students come in.

"C'mon. Everyone takes a bribe once in a while. I think we can work something out, don't you?"

"A bribe?" I laugh. "I don't think so. I play fair and I play by the rules." I take another sip of coffee, my eyes flicking up to meet his gaze.

"What if I were to say...blackmail you?" He drops his voice to a playful tone.

"Blackmail? What are you talking about?" I eye him skeptically.

He steps in, closing the space between us as he whispers, "Choose me and I won't tell anyone about that vulgar little mouth of yours." His tongue slides through as he licks his lips.

Vulgar mouth? What is he talking about? How would he know that I have a potty mouth?

"I have no idea what you're talking about." Play dumb. That's a good way to go.

"I think you know *exactly* what I'm talking about." He smirks.

We're at a Mexican standoff—neither one of us willing to relent.

"That's too bad. But maybe I've found your soft spot..." His eyes drop to my lips, watching me sip again. My throat burns as I swallow and stand silently. I want to scream, "Nobody has ever found my 'soft spot.' I don't think it really exists, but I'm happy to let you try!"

"Here's what I propose," he says insistently. "If you make sure they choose me, I'll bring you coffee every time I come." He waits for my response to his offer. A giggle nearly erupts when I imagine a cup of coffee arriving via a little parachute at all hours of the night whenever he "comes."

"We'll both get what we want. It's a win-win, don't you think?" His eyes dance with humor. The thought of this glorious man *coming* is definitely not something I need in my head as I start my day with a roomful of six and seven year olds.

I need to appear unaffected so I remove the lid and blow slowly. "Whew. That's hot." My eyes look straight at him, clearly amused by his offer. "Again, that's a really generous offer. I'll keep it in mind. There aren't too many dads offering to help me out." I need a diversion or I just need him to leave. "Well, I hate to cut this conversation short, but I really need to get ready for the day." I smile professionally. "By the way, your daughter is doing a great job. I'm available for a conference if you have any concerns."

The ringing bell signals the start of my work day so he extends his hand, blocking my path. "Thank you, Miss Delaney. Thank you for considering my offer and for being *Madison's* teacher."

I place my hand in his, praying that he doesn't notice how sweaty my palm is. Adam's eyes, full of lust, look at me as his hand closes gently around mine. My hand is raised gently to meet his full lips; he places a lingering kiss on my knuckles. "It's always a pleasure to see you, Miss Delaney."

Maybe I'm still drunk or just a little, tiny bit buzzed because the room starts to spin around me, and I feel my body sway slightly. I miss the contact immediately when he releases his grip, walking out without another word.

Unfortunately that feeling dissipates, near orgasm forgotten, the moment I turn the corner and see Gina standing there talking to him. His tall body leans down and whispers something in her ear, before he throws his arm casually around her, leading her out of the building. The sound of her hyena cackle grates on my nerves and screeches in my ears like chalk on a fucking blackboard. *What the fuck? Did I just imagine that whole thing? Maybe I really am still drunk. Or maybe he's just a gorgeous man-whore.* Asshole!

THE NEXT FEW DAYS ARE UNEVENTFUL AND FLY BY quickly. Thursday afternoon Shelby and I find ourselves at The Pour House for a few, well-deserved cocktails. People flock in and fill every space in the tiny bar—friends and strangers drink and laugh together, welcoming the near end of another week. A couple vacates a high top table so Shelby and I grab it and sit comfortably, drinking our wine, chatting about our students, the parents and about how the first few weeks have gone. I don't mention to Shelby about Adam's generous offer. I wonder briefly if he's offered the same to her. She is Luke's teacher after all. Something deep down tells me not to.

Even after ordering a second glass of wine, I still feel wound up. I keep thinking about the look on Adam's face—it was priceless. I didn't mean to be a bitch to him. Well, maybe I did...a little. Each afternoon, his flirtation was met with my defiance and opposition. I hate guys like Adam Lawson and all they stand for.

The moment Adam stepped up to the dismissal table the smile that graced my face disappeared.

"Hello, Miss Delaney. And how was your day?" He smiled, scribbling his name.

"Fine," I spat out. No smile or amusement showing as I quickly moved him along so I could attend to the next parent in line.

Clearly he didn't get the hint because he didn't move. "Are you sure? You seem upset...with me." His eyes tightened like he's trying to concentrate on my face.

"Why would I be upset with you? I don't even know you." Brain to mouth filter must be broken again.

"Well, if there's anything I can do to put that beautiful smile back on your face...please let me know." A devilish grin appeared on his handsome face as he turned to get his kids.

When the next parent arrived, I had a smile back in place and I greeted them with kindness and professionalism.

"Hello? Earth to Mia..." Shelby's voice snaps me out of my daydream.

"What?" I snap back before uttering an apology along with "please forgive me" eyes while I run my hand through my long hair then smooth my eyebrows with my thumb and index finger.

"Damn, girl. Didn't you hear me? I've been calling your name for like five minutes. What's up with you? You've been off," she hesitates, "all week."

I try and laugh it off as nothing, my betraying shoulders shrug. "I don't know...I guess I'm a little stressed. It's not a big deal. I'll be fine."

"You lying little bitch!" Her eyes full of amusement. "Seriously, what's wrong? Tell me!"

I don't really know what to say. I can't even pinpoint what's bothering me.

"Oh. My. God. I know you! This is about a guy, isn't it? Shane? Did you sleep with him? Are you guys getting back together? I swear to God, I'll kick his ass if he hurts you again."

Her questions fly at me one after the next and I manage to dodge each one of them. I tip back the rest of my wine and place it down on the worn, oak table. "Well," I reply, "I'm not sleeping with Shane and we're definitely not getting back together so there'll be no need for ass kicking."

"But..." she prompts, "it is about a guy."

"Yeah, I guess it is sort of about a guy, but not really..." I confirm, reaching for her glass since mine is empty.

"Mia, seriously! What the hell? Spit that shit out already!" She reaches to take the glass back. "And don't drink my wine, you lush!"

My laughter only serves to prolong the inevitable, causing her eyes to narrow at me. So I divulge all about Adam and his constant, unyielding flirting. Shelby's eyes become animated as she delights the predicament I find myself in. She's convinced that I should give in and enjoy what he's offering, until she hears about the one name that could change it all: Gina. *That* is an absolute game changer.

"Excuse me, ladies," the cocktail waitress interrupts our conversation when she sets down two more glasses of wine. "These were sent over by the gentleman. Enjoy." She nods to someone across the room.

Looking around the crowded bar, Shelby and I try to figure out who is the mystery man who sent over our drinks so we could thank him. I recognize most of the patrons from town; no one stands out or is paying any particular attention to us.

"It's nice to know we've still got it, girl!" Shelby raises her glass and clinks it with mine. "I'll be right back." A sinful grin washes across Shelby's face, after she hears her phone signal an incoming text.

"Wait! Where are you going?" I laugh, demanding that she give me her phone as I reach across the table, trying to grab it out of her hand.

"My husband misses me. Do you mind?" she chides, pulling away from me.

"Yeah, right. You're such a little slut. You're going to send a selfie again, aren't you? Good thing you're married now!"

She struts off in the direction of the ladies' room, but I'm quick to yell, reminding her that "friends don't let friends drink and send selfies to wrong numbers." Let's just say I've mistakenly been on the receiving end of one of Shelby's texts and I've seen a whole lot more than just her pretty face.

I glance around the noisy bar, noticing how much louder and busier it is now than when we first arrived. There are people everywhere. The manager sets up a microphone in the far corner for open mic night.

I check my phone for any new messages. I tug at the silver, circle pendant that hangs from necklace and run it back and forth between my fingers, a telltale sign of my agitation. Then I tap my red fingernails against the engraved name on the wooden table top waiting for Shelby to return. As I slowly sip the wine, a feeling of paranoia overcomes me. It's not creepy, I just feel like someone's watching me. I feel it deep within me with parts that have been dormant for a long time.

A few minutes later when a table of four gets up to leave, I have a clear view of a man staring at me. Our gazes meet, but I feign indifference when Adam smiles and raises the glass of amber liquid to his mouth, taking a slow sip before saluting me with a slight nod. Without meaning to, I roll my eyes at him. This man is everywhere and he's got some nerve. This must be some fun game to him. One I'm not interested in playing.

I'm not a rude person. I'm just rude to jerks who like to flirt mercilessly and then walk away with their arm draped around another woman. I look over again just in time to see his blonde female companion, who was busy on her phone earlier, walk away from the table. She's tall, curvy and beautiful. She's not the same woman from the club. A man like Adam probably has got so many women that he numbers them like cattle.

Shelby returns to our table, giddy and buzzed. She notices my gaze and follows it. "Whoa! Who is that fine fucker?"

"No one."

"Hah! No one, my ass," she snorts. "Who is he?"

I scoff and lean over casually to whisper in her ear, "That fine fucker is none other than Mr. Adam Lawson aka Luke and Madison's dad." My eyebrows rise in a "see what I mean" look. I reach into my bag when I hear an incoming text alert.

"No, way! Seriously? He's hot!" She peeks over her shoulder. I have a perfect view of him. He sits with his back against the chair, his eyes, now stern, are cast down to his phone. I watch as his chest rises and falls with each inhale and exhale. His fingers work swiftly tapping out a message and then he waits. He taps again.

"Yes, he definitely is hot," I answer, keeping my eyes down as I tap out my own text. "But he seems like a pig, if you ask me."

"Uh, Mia...you might want to get ready because that pig is walking this way."

My eyes snap up in attention. I drop my phone into my bag, quickly grabbing my glass. I plaster the biggest, fakest smile on my face as if Shelby has told me that I've won our nation's largest lottery jackpot.

I know he's approaching before I actually see him. I can feel his presence. I can smell his scent. My nipples harden; my body starts to tingle below.

"Miss Delaney! What a surprise! It's wonderful to see you with a smile on your face." His deep voice comes very close to my ear. My eyes close involuntarily and I inhale his clean, masculine scent. Yep, I've definitely had one too many glasses of wine.

My nervous hand begins to twist the stem of the wine glass between my fingers. He sets his glass down beside mine. His finger brushes against mine as his gaze drops from my eyes to my lips, searching my face. Hello? Inappropriate! Does this man not know boundaries? What's with the touching?

"Hi! I'm Shelby Matthews. I don't think we've met," Shelby interjects, thrusting her hand out, reminding us of her presence.

"Ahhh...Mrs. Matthews. Forgive me. I'm Adam Lawson." He draws her name out slowly and intentionally, his head turning in my direction and then back to Shelby. "My son, Luke, is in *your* class," he states that fact as he shakes her hand. I watch with anticipation for the kiss that never comes.

"Yes, Luke's a great kid. Very bright. Very polite."

His expression is one of pride. "Thank you. That's very kind of you to say." He pauses, "But you should see him at home. He's quite the wild child." His attention is now fixed on me. "And Madison? How's my Maddie girl doing, Miss Delaney?"

He raises his glass to his lips, ice clinking when he tips back the last of his drink, those dark, sexy eyes never leaving mine.

I swallow hard. "She's fine. I mean, she's doing well. She's a sweetheart." I don't know what prompts me to ask the next question. I chalk it up to liquid courage. "Is she like her brother?" His eyes display his confusion. So I clarify, "Is she a wild child at home? You know, like her brother?" Holy shit! It sounds like my voice, but this attitude isn't me. It's him. He makes me a little edgy and belligerent.

When his cheeks pull back into a wide grin, a small crinkle appears around his eyes. His words are playful when he answers, "Hmmm...good question. We're still trying to figure that out. She's definitely way more reserved so I'm working on getting her to open up. She doesn't always do as she's told, but don't cross her; she can be quite feisty at times." I know that he knows that we are not talking about his daughter.

"Hah! I love her already!" I laugh as I lean in close to his ear, my warm breath whispers, "It's the quiet ones you have to watch out for." Adam's body stiffens momentarily and then he inhales leisurely. I smile and pull back to sip the last of my wine before raising it in the air. "Cheers." Yep, I'm officially drunk.

Dark eyes stare at me, trying to figure out his next move. Our staring contest is over when his attention is diverted to the woman who is now heading back to their cozy little table for two. A slight frown mars his face. He exhales, "Well, ladies. I don't want to keep you." Turning to Shelby, he extends his hand. "Mrs. Matthews, it truly was a pleasure meeting you. You keep that boy of mine in line.

Crack the whip if you need to." Shelby blushes and smiles. "Will do, sir. And please call me Shelby." That little wench! She's melting into a puddle of teenage hormones right before my eyes and she's married!

Trying to avoid any more strained moments, I thrust my hand out and plaster on the cheesiest grin I can manage. "Goodbye, Mr. Lawson. Enjoy your evening."

"Yes, you as well..." he hesitates. Maybe he's waiting for me to say "call me by my first name," but I don't. "Miss Delaney. It's Miss Delaney."

His large hand closes around mine, leaning in close enough to hug me or kiss me. I smell his cologne or body wash, and Dear Lord, he smells divine!

"You...Miss Delaney, have an absolutely beautiful smile..." he murmurs, his breath tickling my ear. "I can put that smile on your face a million different ways." He pulls back and slowly releases my hand, his eyes never straying from mine. "Ladies." He nods and walks back to the table where Ms. Curvy Blonde awaits with a puss on her face. Shelby stares after him and sighs. That earns her my squinty evil eye.

Chapter Nine

FRIDAY. WHO DOESN'T LOVE FRIDAY? IT'S DRESS DOWN day, payday, and the start to the weekend. It's also the day we have our "share" time in our class. To say that I'm very interested to see what a certain dark-haired little girl has brought in to share today would be a serious understatement. Is it wrong that I think I might gain some insight into her father? Yes. Is it wrong that I don't care? Probably.

I sit back with anticipation as Madison waits patiently, watching her classmates share what they've brought in. Apprehension spreads across her adorable face when she reaches into her pink backpack, unwraps a purple cashmere scarf, revealing a pair of old, well-worn ballet slippers, dirty, tattered tape covering the toes. A proud, beaming smile appears, but quickly diminishes, a quivering lip replaces it after Lizzie, another student, comments that the slippers aren't even hers, basically calling Madison a liar.

"They are mine! Well..." she hesitates, tears forming in her eyes, "they were my mother's, but they're mine now." She quietly stuffs the slippers back into the bag, burying her reddened face, no doubt to hide the tears that have spilled over onto her cheeks.

My heart splinters into tiny pieces right there. I inhale deeply, reaching over to grab a tissue off my desk when the bell rings signaling time for afternoon recess. Madison takes the tissue but keeps her head down. I lower myself and whisper in her ear, asking her if she wouldn't mind staying inside with me during recess so we can talk. She doesn't respond at first. I assure her that she's not in any sort of trouble. "I'd just like to talk to you. Would that be okay?"

I usher the rest of the class to the door and tell them to follow Mrs. Matthew's class outside to the playground area while Madison moves to sit at her desk.

I slide a chair over from the reading table to sit by her and smooth her hair away from her face like my mom used to do to me and ask what's got her so upset. She shrugs her shoulders, hiccupping through a few remaining tears.

"I miss my mom." To know the pain of loss as an adult is hard enough, but for a child to know that pain absolutely shreds me.

"Aw, sweetie. I know it's hard when you miss someone. Want to tell me about her?" No response just another hiccup. The small chair scraps loudly when I move it closer to her so I can gently rub her back.

"You know, it's okay to miss people. It means they were important to you. I miss people every day. My mom lives all the way in Florida and my brother lives all the way in Texas. Both places are pretty far away." I continue rubbing circles on her back. "I get to see them sometimes, but my dad...he's in Heaven like your mom." The confidence in my voice surprises me since I usually get choked up talking about my dad.

Finally, she lifts her red-rimmed eyes, her face stained with tears and looks at me. "Your dad's in Heaven?"

I nod, offering a small smile. I share some of my favorite memories of my father: teaching me how to swim, how to play softball and even how to hook a worm. Her nose scrunches up in disgust at that last bit and then she smiles. "You know," I continue, "it really is okay to miss your mom. I bet you have some great memories."

Her face beams. "She was a ballerina. A real one, but then she got sick. Now she's in Heaven."

"Wow. A ballerina? She must've been beautiful and graceful. Do you dance, Madison?"

A silent nod is her response. "Daddy just signed me up. I go with my best friend, Sophie. She's in my brother's class." Sophie? Gina's daughter? They can't possibly have known each other that long since they just moved here over the summer. That's interesting, but I wouldn't be surprised if Gina hasn't made her move already. After all that's what she does. She's like a King Cobra who slithers her way into people's lives and then devours them.

"That's awesome. I bet you're going to be great!" I smile.

"Yeah, it's fun. But I'm not as good as Sophie. She's been dancing for a long time. After dance, me and Sophie and her mom always get frozen yogurt at Peachwave."

I know I shouldn't try to garner information from a little girl, but curiosity wins out. "And where's your dad? Doesn't he take you to dance class?" I know I'm prying, but honestly, I just can't help myself.

"No." She shakes her head sadly. "He works a lot and Thursday is his late night. Sometimes I sleep at Sophie's house." Seriously? What responsible parent would willingly let their kid sleep out on a school night? I wonder if Adam sleeps there, too. Another piece to the Adam Lawson puzzle.

When the bell rings, signaling the end of recess, I pull Madison in for a sideways hug, thanking her for talking with me and remind her that she can always talk to me. She wraps both arms around my waist and holds me close. Her cheek presses against my stomach. I feel something shift deep in my soul. *Breathe, Mia, breathe.*

"You're the best teacher ever, Miss Delaney." I've heard those words before over the years, but for some reason, this feels different.

As dismissal draws near, my pulse starts to quicken and I find myself reapplying lip gloss for the umpteenth time. I just need to be professional. This isn't even about me or how he's driving me crazy with his flirting. No, this is about a student in my class. This is a teacher talking to a parent, sharing a concern about a student. *Yeah, right!* I can't even convince myself.

Repeating it in my head like a mantra, "Good afternoon, Mr. Lawson." I imagine myself looking directly at him, asking to speak to him privately. I practice the words over and over while parents sign their children out for the weekend. I can do this. God, this would be so much easier if I had a few drinks in me! I smile inwardly, shaking my head at my own craziness, when SMACK, I come face to face with the bitch of all bitches. She saunters over, looks me up and down, signing her name not once, not twice, but three times indicating that she's picking up Adam's children as well. *Well, fuck me! They are together! He is a pig!* I want to scream, "*Run Adam, run far. Get away from the viper.*"

A small chuckle escapes my lips at the mental image. Gina snarls, venom spewing from her mouth, her eyes narrowing into slits. "What the hell are you laughing at?"

"Nothing. Nothing at all. And please watch your language. You are in a school with children around." Condescension drenches my words.

"Whatever!" The bitch rolls her eyes at me and walks away. I watch as she rounds the corner out of the building, her high heels tapping against the linoleum tile.

After the last two kids have been picked up, as I gather the sign out sheets for the day, I hear a little voice calling my name. Madison's arms are around me in an instant, causing me to step back into the table.

"Hey there, sunshine. What's the matter? Did you forget something?" I smile down at her, wondering if she needs to get something from her desk.

"No. I just wanted to give you a hug because I won't see you until Monday and that's a long time." Big brown eyes surrounded by full lashes look up at me.

"Aw, sweetie. That's so nice. But you know—" I start to say.

"Madison!" Gina's angry voice hollers and echoes throughout

the hallway when she sees Madison's arms embracing me. "What are you doing?" Her voice patronizing. "Let's. Go. Now." *What the hell? Why is she yelling at her?* I feel Madison's small body stiffen for an instant.

My eyes drill holes into her. "She's. Coming." I say pointedly at Gina.

"Well, I gotta go." She smiles sadly. "I'll see ya Monday."

Just before they're out of view, I can't resist, even though in that split second I know I should.

"Hey, Madison, tell your daddy I said hi." Mia. One. Gina. Who the fuck cares!

Chapter Ten

MONDAYS SUCK! PERIOD. FIVE DAYS IS NOT ENOUGH time to recover from the weekend, from the laughing, to the crying, to the almost peeing myself ten times over. It's been so long since I've felt that carefree.

Friday night, Pete and I lounged by the fire pit, sharing two bottles of wine after enjoying Chinese takeout. He had me either choking or spitting out my drink too many times to count. The best was when he gave me a detailed account about how *Fifty Shades of Grey* has improved his sex life. And he's gay! Ah, Peter, with his gorgeous face and killer body, complete with washboard abs, will no doubt someday make someone very happy—at least in the bedroom he will.

Saturday and Sunday were lazy days spent running, baking, and playing with Brady down by the lake. The end of summer was drawing near and it was a relatively quiet end to the weekend except for the sound of an obnoxiously loud car driving around the neighborhood late Saturday night.

It actually felt a little too quiet, a little lonely. I called my brother and spent time talking to my niece and nephew, promising them that I would visit again soon. His complaints of running nonstop with his kids annoyed me a little bit because some people would give anything to trade places with him.

Shane finally succeeded in setting up a "non" date, just as friends, because he knew that's the only way I'd even consider going. Too much has happened. Too much hurt to forgive. Too much pressure on my fragile heart. Friends. That's what we were before we decided to become more. We've agreed to meet up for pizza Wednesday night. I quickly declined his offer to pick me up, opting to drive myself. *A girl needs her car for a quick escape if needed, right?*

My non-date with Shane is still on my mind when I walk into the building Monday morning, juggling my coffee, purse, workbag, and my lunch bag. A familiar voice stops me. "Excuse me, Miss Delaney?" Why does the sound of my name coming from that mouth make things tingle below my waist?

"Yes," I answer, turning in his direction. "Can I help you?"

"Please, please, please. Can you do me a huge one?" Huge one? Why does everything Adam says make me think of sex?

I'm floored. "Excuse me?"

Adam stands there in a perfectly fitted, navy blue suit, holding two lunch bags, a blue one with Ironman on it and a pink one with Madison's name embroidered on it. He looks absolutely ridiculous but devastatingly sexy at the same time.

"I'm running late to a meeting and my kids forgot their lunches." He tips his head to the side, giving a pleading look. "Please?"

I look at him dubiously, wondering why he just doesn't bring them in himself. "You do realize that the office is right there." I look behind me, stating the obvious. "I'm sure you can manage walking through the door." I smirk.

"I would, but then Mrs. Chapman starts talking to me and you know...Please. I'm begging," he says giving me the "'how can you say no to me" look.

"Fine. Whatever." He strategically places the lunch bags on my two extended fingers and catches me staring at his face.

"Thank you so much. I owe you." A genuine smile plasters across his face.

"You know, Mr. Lawson, for being the boss and having a job,

you sure do come here a lot." I joke.

His eyes widen and then narrow. "Believe me, Miss Delaney, I would love nothing more than to come here." His eyes drop lower over my body. "All. The. Time." His grin is devious. *Bastard! He got me again.* He reaches around behind me to open the door since my hands are completely full, ushering me in as if he were a true southern gentleman. I know better. He's no gentleman—he's a wolf in sheep's clothing.

"I'll see you later, Miss Delaney."

You bet your sweet ass you will, you fine fucker! Oh. My. God. *What has gotten into me?* I smile politely back at him and step through the door.

"Thanks," I say as I step through the open door, whipping around to catch him before he leaves.

"Oh, Mr. Lawson, don't be late for dismissal...I might be gone before you have a chance to come...to pick up your kids, that is." *Take that, bastard!*

The door closes behind me and I don't even give a thought about glancing back. Please, who am I kidding? I want desperately to see the look on his face, saying, "Game on!"

EACH AFTERNOON THAT WEEK, THE ROUTINE IS THE same.

"Hello, Miss Delaney." He blesses me with an All-American, "I've got a secret" grin.

"Hello, Mr. Lawson." I smile back.

Each day I find out more and more pieces of the Adam Lawson family. Since it's raining today, our students will have indoor recess. Shelby and I decide that our classes can combine and play together in our rooms. Luke, Madison's brother, comes over to join some of the boys in my class. I hear him tell his friends that he's going to play football this year, but he's going to miss some practices because he's going to sleep over his grandparent's house. He is a carbon copy of his father. He's a real boy's boy. Tall with scraped knees, a missing front tooth and head of wavy dark hair that flops onto his forehead just like his dad's. He either hasn't discovered hair gel or doesn't care to use it since he's only six years old.

A light knock at the classroom door draws my attention and I see Sophie, Gina's daughter, standing there with an anxious look on her face. Damn! I didn't think about this when I agreed with Shelby to combine our classes for recess. It's not that I don't want her to play in here; she's just a painful reminder of the past.

"Hi, Sophie." I smile genuinely at her. Her green eyes dart every which way but at me. "Do you want to come in and play?"

She shakes her head from side to side but doesn't reply with an answer.

"Are you sure? Are you looking for Madison? I think she's over there," I say, pointing to the area by the green rug where Madison is playing a board game with some friends. "C'mon, I'm sure she'll be so happy to see you. You can even surprise her," I whisper as I encourage her to enter.

"No. I...I can't," she squeaks.

"You can't?" I laugh, surprised. "Sure you can, honey. I don't mind."

"No, I can't. My mom would get really mad. I'm...I'm not supposed to talk to you," she mumbles.

What? Her daughter can't talk to me? I'm not the enemy here. Has she forgotten that she's the one who broke my heart and wrecked my life? Not the other way around! What a bitch!

"Well, sweetie." I struggle to smile, my lips pull into a tight line. "I don't want you to get in trouble or anything."

"Um...can Maddie come play in my room?" She looks at me with those beautiful emerald green eyes that are too familiar.

"Sure. Let me get her."

I'm still in shock when Madison jumps up and heads in to

Shelby's room to play. *She told her kid not to talk to me? Did she forget the same DNA was once shared by both of us? How could she forget?* She has a beautiful, healthy, living physical reminder every single damn day.

THAT AFTERNOON, I MAKE A QUICK RUN INTO THE grocery store to get a few things for home and work.

"Here you go, darling. Just the way you like it." I reach over the glass counter to take my package of trimmed chicken breast.

"Thanks, Lee. You're so good to me." His thickly parted hair and Coke-bottle glasses hide the wrinkles near his eyes. He hasn't aged very well, but he's as sweet as ever.

"It's no problem. You just drop off some of that delicious stuffed chicken and we'll call it even."

"You got it!" I smile at the butcher who's known me since I was a kid.

Just as I start to push my squeaky carriage towards the dairy section, a little voice calls my name and I turn to find Madison running in my direction. She wraps her arms around my waist, squeezing me hard.

"Hi, Miss Delaney!" She tips her head back to look up at me.

"Hi, Maddie! What are you doing here?" I smile at her and glance around looking for Adam or maybe even Gina.

"I'm shopping with my dad. He's over there." She releases me and points behind her. I see him round the corner with his phone to his ear. He's looking down at the floor, seemingly deep in thought. He disconnects the call and looks directly at me; he stares at me standing there with his daughter. I watch as he walks over to us. I can't make out the look on his face. Annoyance, maybe?

"Hi." He smiles at me.

"Hey. How's it going?" I can't help but ask after I just saw the look on his face. Before Adam can answer, Lee comes from behind the counter without his butcher's apron. "Now don't forget about that stuffed chicken, darling."

"I won't. I promise." I smile back.

Adam's eyes follow Lee as he walks towards the front of the store, leaving for the day.

"A friend of yours?" he ridicules.

"Yeah, something like that. He's totally my type," I whisper and let out a chuckle.

"How do you stuff a chicken?" Maddie asks. "It doesn't sound very good."

"Madison!" Adam scolds her while stifling a laugh under his breath. "Sorry about that."

"It's fine." I assure him with smile because kids sometimes say the funniest things.

"So what do you think?" I hold up a jar of cinnamon applesauce and a natural flavored one.

"I like that one!" She points to the cinnamon jar. "My gramma always buys the one without sugar." Her nose scrunches up in disgust.

She tells her father that we're going to be celebrating Johnny Appleseed's birthday and eating applesauce for snack. I quickly count the jars in my cart and realize that I don't have enough for the class.

"Will you need some help with that project?" Adam asks, smirking.

"Project?" I grin, my eyes widening with humor. "I don't think scooping out applesauce qualifies as a project." I laugh. "I think I can handle it, but thanks for the offer."

"I told you I'm available to help out anytime."

"I'll keep that in mind." I feel confident as I answer.

"Please do."

"Dad, we can get some applesauce?"

"Sure."

The three of us walk together, back a few aisles to get more applesauce. There's a current of tension between us. It's almost tangible. After a few moments of awkwardness and we've gotten our items, I turn to face Madison and her dad.

"Well, I've got to get going." I address them both. "I'll see you tomorrow, Maddie."

I look at her father who's standing next to her, carefully watching our interaction.

"Goodbye, Mr. Lawson. Have a good night."

"See you later, Miss Delaney."

If only he knew that I would see him later...in my dreams.

By WEDNESDAY, I'M MORE THAN READY FOR MY NON-date with Shane that evening. The few texts that I received from him were light-hearted and funny. I'm thankful he has kept his flirtations to a minimum.

Walking into Mario's Pizzeria, I find him sitting there in a white Boston t-shirt and navy board shorts, waiting for me while he scrolls through his phone. A huge smile crosses his face when he finally notices me standing there.

"Wow! You look great!" He stands up and leans in slowly to kiss my cheek, waiting for approval.

I don't know what's so great about what I'm wearing. My cargo pants rolled to the ankle paired with a cardigan over tank top and red Converse isn't really all that, especially because it's a "non"-date after all. No need to dress to impress.

"Thanks." I accept the compliment as I slide into the booth and pour myself a glass of water. We decide to share a meat lover's pizza and a pitcher of beer. After a few minutes of awkwardness, we fall into a comfortable conversation about my summer trip to see my brother. Tears stream down my face when he shares his adventurous mishap of changing the diaper of his newest niece. I'm so thankful when he tells me that my principal, Mrs. Chapman, and the Board haven't made a decision on the assistant principal position yet. I can tell that Shane is hopeful that we'll be working together and, as much as I don't want to admit it, I find myself enjoying the time with Shane. We used to be really good friends.

Pushing myself away from the table, I rub circles over my full stomach. "Oh my God, I'm stuffed!"

Shane's eyebrows shoot up in amusement. "Well, you *did* just down half of a loaded pizza and drank more than half the pitcher of beer!"

"Shane Davis!" I chide in mock horror. "Where are your manners? I always thought you were a good guy? Nope, I was wrong. You are a dirty dog!"

He looks sheepish.

"You're going to make me self-conscious about my weight now."

I cross my arms, feigning hurt, pushing my ample boobs up. I don't miss the way his eyes drop to my chest. *Yes, idiot, this is what you gave up for a quick fuck in the bathroom.* Feeling slightly self-conscious, I tighten the cardigan around my chest, hiding my cleavage.

"Aw, c'mon, Mia. Don't be like that." I'm not sure if he's referring to the fact that I've shut down the peepshow or because I know he's a dirty dog.

"Fine. Whatever," I tease, rolling my eyes.

Then with a look of hope, he continues, "If you want, we could start running together again." And there it is—the elephant in the room. An awkward lull comes between us as all conversation comes to a halt.

God, I hate this. I really do. Shane was always the guy that every girl wanted. I'm pretty sure he had the same girlfriend all throughout high school. He always seemed so loyal. Well, he did until last March.

Shane's rough hands reach across the table, curling his fingers around mine, his face remorseful. "Mia, I'm sorry. I really am. I shouldn't tease you about how much you eat. And while I'm handing out apologies, I'm sorry again for last spring. I know I fucked things up with you. I know I hurt you. You have no idea how truly sorry I am." His thumb rubs back and forth across my knuckles, his eyes pleading for mercy. "I know it's a piss poor excuse for being such a douche bag, but I was really, *really, really* drunk that night. I don't even really remember much of what happened. I remember being at the bar with you and then Gina..." His words abruptly cease when he mentions her name. The truth in his remorseful words rings loud and clear. "I'm just really sorry." I know he didn't mean to hurt me, but he did. Nothing can change that fact.

"Shane," I sigh his name, pulling my hands out from under his. "Look, we were friends before we decided to be anything else. We were just having a bit of fun, right?" *Wrong! He knows as well I do that that's not true.* He was the first guy in a really long time to find his way into my heart whether I wanted him there or not. Who would've thought that I'd be here comforting him? He's the one who got caught with his pants down. Literally! I pour myself another glass of water and keep my palms wrapped around the glass.

"But that's just it, Mia. I don't want to be just friends with you." His blue eyes bore into mine.

"Shane..." I beg for him to understand.

"Please give me another chance." His voice is pleading, his eyes searching my face for a sign, any sign that his words are not in vain.

I shiver when I run my hand along my arms and feel goose bumps lining my skin. The bell on the entrance door diverts my attention, causing me to look in that direction.

In walks Adam, casually dressed in weathered jeans and black v-neck t-shirt, talking on his cell phone. Soon after he ends his call, he slips the phone into his pocket and looks around the restaurant, his eyes landing directly on me. A stern look quickly appears and then disappears as he shifts his attention to Shane and then back to me. I watch silently as he walks up to the counter, pays, and then proceeds to carry out two large boxes, pushing the door open with his back.

I feel like I've been caught with my hand in the cookie jar, a slow blush creeps up on my face. I continue to watch him as he holds the door for a woman to enter, smiling at her as though he'd like to eat her for dessert. The only acknowledgement I get from him is a sideways glance and smirk before he leaves.

What the hell? No, "Hello, Miss Delaney." No sexy "I've got a secret" smile. Nada! It's really not that big of a deal so why do I feel so annoyed and disappointed at the same time.

Chapter Eleven

LATER THAT WEEK I FIND MYSELF ANTSY, NEEDING TO expend some extra energy. Knowing that I've been slacking off running every afternoon, choosing to let Brady play catch down by the lake instead of at the park, I set out early Saturday morning for a long hard run with Brady in tow. Sweat drenches my head, drips down my back, the burn in my legs screaming for reprieve. My steps slow down as I reach the summit, my quiet place, but the pounding of my heart thunders rapidly when I notice a lone occupant sitting there, quietly looking out over the town. *Really? This can't be happening to me.* This man has occupied my thoughts and dreams for some time now yet an escape from him is nowhere to be seen.

Sweat glistens off his broad shoulders, the well-defined muscles of his bare back beg to be touched. Brady, my traitorous dog, races over to him.

"Hi there." He smiles and turns his lean body to face me. "Well, aren't you a sight for sore eyes." His hand runs over the dark hair that has fallen over his sweat covered forehead, exposing his unshaven face with its heavy stubble.

I look at him dubiously as I gulp down the rest of my water. My eyes roll, my lips purse letting him know I think he's a liar. "Mr. Lawson, you seem to be all over the place these days."

"Well," he states and looks directly at me. "I am new to the area so I'm just trying to meet the locals. I want to take advantage of all this little town has to offer." His eyes blatantly sweep down the length of my body.

"That's nice," I blurt out sarcastically. "Where are your kids?" He ignores me and asks a question of his own.

"So, you're a local girl?" His lips pull back into a knowing smile.

"I am. Born and bred here."

He uses his hand, brushes away small pebbles and dirt on the ledge beside him and pats the spot. "Sit."

I smirk and take a seat next to him. "I will only because my legs are tired not because you told me to."

He narrows his eyes and laughs at me, shoving his hands through his hair again after wiping them off on his running shorts. His arm brushes against mine, a jolt flashes through my body. *Get a grip, Mia!* He wipes the sweat from his brow with a blue t-shirt.

"So, Miss Delaney, give me tour." His gaze is now over the town outstretched ahead and below us. "What keeps a beautiful woman like you in this small town?"

"Hey, what's wrong with my small town?" I nudge him lightly with my elbow.

"Nothing really. It's just that there are a lot more opportunities in bigger cities."

"Bigger is not always better, you know," I retort.

"Oh, I disagree. Bigger is *most definitely* always better." He leans close to me, his face only inches away as he gives me a cheeky grin and a sideways glance. An embarrassing chuckle escapes me when I realize that I walked right into that one. I bite down on my bottom lip trying desperately not to laugh, shaking my head at my foolishness.

We sit there for what seems to be an endless amount of time. I point out all the places of interest and the history behind each one. Memories of my childhood rush to the forefront of my mind. I try to think of a single bad memory from my childhood, but the truth is that it really was perfect. At least it seemed that way to me. The only painful memory, if you can even call it *painful,* was when Josh decided to make a ramp in the street and broke my yellow Starburst bicycle in half. Literally. His body ended up stretched and sprawled out beneath the broken frame. I'm not sure if I cried more for my brother or my broken bike.

"Oh my God. That's a funny story," Adam says, laughing at my play by play of the incident. "Did he at least buy you another bike?"

"Of course! My father made him pick up an extra paper route to pay for a new bike. There were no freebies in our home. You had to work for everything and if you broke something, you had to either fix it or replace it."

"Do you still talk to your brother?"

What an odd question? A goofy grin spreads across my face as I answer, "Yes, we're very close. I talk to him all the time. In fact, I was just visiting him over the summer."

"Sounds like you have good memories."

"Absolutely! I had a wonderful childhood. This was a great place to grow up," I smile answering truthfully. It wasn't until I was older that things changed.

He listens intently, as I continue the tour, nodding in approval of the town. "It's a nice place to raise kids."

"It is."

"What happened to that place?" I know he's looking at the plant because there's a hint of sadness in his voice. Maybe he thinks a small town can't afford to rebuild, but that's not the case at all.

I clear my throat to swallow the lump that has now formed when I point to the vacant lot. So many lives were altered forever in one night. "That was a manufacturing plant. There was an explosion and it burned down several years ago." My voice sounds foreign to me, devoid of any emotion.

"An explosion? Did anyone get hurt?" His face transforms to genuine interest as he squints his eyes to inspect the lot.

I don't want to answer this question. The hurt and devastation of that night will be evident on my face and I don't want his pity or anyone else's for that matter.

"Yes, one person," I answer solemnly, gathering my hair to readjust my ponytail.

"Really? How bad?" he asks, still looking straight ahead.

"How bad, what?"

"How badly did someone get hurt?" He seems oddly concerned.

"He died," I whisper.

He finally turns to face me. "Did you know him?"

I swallow down a lump the size of a half dollar that threatens to choke me. My eyes close, willing the tears to stay at bay.

"I did. He was my father."

"Your father? My God, I'm so sorry." Dark eyes look at me with what exactly I don't want to see. Pity. I can only imagine what the look on his face would be if he knew the other events of that fateful night.

"That's why I come here. I want to feel close to him, to talk to him. He was my everything." I smile to myself.

Adam turns to face me, and raises his hand to brush my layered bangs away from my face. "I am so sorry."

After sitting in silence for some time, each of us lost in our own thoughts, a pontoon boat on Lake Whitney captures his attention. Adam listens intently as I tell him about my years on the lake, and then he smiles when I point out the path that runs through my heavily wooded backyard and leads right down to the shore. The lake was my second home.

"So that's your house right there?" He leans in close to me, pointing to my home which is barely visible amongst the thick trees.

"Sure is," I say proudly. I love my house; it's the only place I've ever called home.

"That's a big house for one person." He says it like it's a question, not a statement.

"Not really. Besides I don't live alone," I toss out. His eyes study me.

"You live with your mom?" he asks.

"No."

"Roommate?" Oh, he is so fishing for information. I think like this game.

"Nope."

"Boyfriend?" he hesitates, skepticism oozing from his question.

"Definitely not!" I shake my head, snorting a bit.

A look of relief washes over his handsome face.

"So...who's the lucky person to share the place you call home?"

I can't take it anymore as laughter erupts from my belly. "It's just me and that guy." I nod at Brady resting beneath the shade of the trees. "He's great, but he's such a bed hog."

"You think you're funny, don't you, Miss Delaney," he says with a cheeky grin.

Okay, enough talk about me. It's time to find out about a certain, sexy father. Let's see what his story is.

"So what about you? What brings a city slicker like you here?"

"*A city slicker?*" He feigns being offended, but his deep laugh makes me smile. "I was right. You *are* a comedian."

The buzzing of his phone interrupts us. I wait with a look of expectancy, my eyes wide and round as he looks at his phone and responds, "Hey, Chris. What's up?" I can only hear one side of the conversation and it sounds like he's setting up a meeting. "Okay, yeah, I actually have a couple of questions, too. Sounds good, thanks." He slides his phone into the pocket of his running shorts.

"So?" I ask, still waiting for an answer.

"So what?"

"What brings a city slicker like you here?" I ask again.

His mouth pulls into a side smile. "A few different things actually," he says thoughtfully. "But my kids were the number one reason. Some business opportunities were the second." There's a hint of melancholy in his eyes for a moment then it's gone in an instant.

"Where are your kids anyway?" I ask.

Adam turns his head, gazing back out over the town and stares. No response. I'm gathering that he really doesn't like to talk about his kids, which is surprising because he's such a doting father. At least at school he is—maybe it's just an act for all the single ladies. It's kind of like bringing a puppy to the park to attract the all young hotties.

I try a different tactic with him because he clearly doesn't want to talk about his kids. "Your children are great. Madison is such a sweetheart. And Luke, he seems like a good boy, even if he's a little wild at home," I tease, throwing his words back at him.

"I agree." He smiles. "They are great kids. They've been raised right."

"You should be proud of yourself then." I offer, thinking of my own childhood, remembering all the proud father moments my dad had.

"They've had to deal with a lot for being so young. They're amazingly strong kids." He inhales and scrubs his scruffy jaw with his hands before running them through his thick hair and then exhaling loudly. It's as if he's carrying the weight of the world and the weight has just been lifted. It must be hard to be a single father, raising two young children alone in this day and age.

Should I mention that I know about his wife? I can't even imagine what it would be like to lose the love of my life...again. I remove the elastic from my hair, readjusting my ponytail once again just so I could gather the wayward hair from my face. And I need to wipe away the tear without Adam noticing. I swallow the huge lump sitting there in my throat, just waiting to erupt and rob me of speech.

Again, we sit there silently, side by side, what seems like forever. Each of us lost in our own private thoughts. My mind drifts back to the first time meeting him, right here on the summit. Seeing him and Luke at the grocery store. His confrontation with me at the club. His constant flirting. Him walking and talking with his arm around Gina. That last thought makes me want to learn more about this man. It would seem that he's moved on pretty quickly after just having lost his wife, the mother of his children.

"I'm sorry about your wife. Madison told me she passed away recently," my voice whispers before I can stop the words.

His head whips around to face me, angry eyes bore into mine. "My wife? She wasn't my wife," he snaps. The volatile man from the club reappears briefly and then is gone. "I'm sorry," he apologizes with softer, pleading eyes. He runs his hands over his face and through his hair, leaving it sticking up in a sexy way. "That was extremely rude of me. Please forgive me." Suddenly I'm uncomfortable, wondering how things have taken such a serious turn. Adam's original request was a tour of the town, not a trip down memory lane of his loss and pain.

"It's okay, I understand." I smile timidly. "Believe me I know what it's like to lose someone you love very much. It's not easy to deal with, but everyone grieves in their own way."

The quiet resumes for what feels like an eternity.

In the distance, a low rumble of thunder breaks the awkward silence. Thick ominous grey clouds roll furiously into the town, promising one hell of a show. The pontoon boat is making its way back to the dock.

"Looks like a good storm's coming." I jump up, wiping the dirt from the back of my red Nike shorts. "I should get home before the sky opens up."

Adam looks troubled—his beautiful face marred by a serious frown and his brows furrow. He stands beside me, tapping out a text on his iPhone before turning to face me with his hand extended. Okay...I guess we're going to shake hands like a formal business meeting. I mean after all, I *am* his daughter's teacher, but why can't he just say, "See you later" or "Take care." *What's with always needing to shake my hand?*

"Mr. Lawson." I smile and I slip my hand into his firm grasp.

With a determined look on his face, his hand wraps around mine, pulling me close. Our locked hands caught between our chests. My heart flutters faster and my breathing hitches. My body goes on high alert.

"Miss Delaney," he breathes, stepping in closer, settling his eyes on my mouth. "I need to kiss you."

I gasp and try to release his hand, but he holds me in place, keeping me still. *He needs to kiss me?* My God, is this really happening? He is absolutely gorgeous and sexy, but me? He really wants to kiss me? My eyes wander of their own accord to his full lips and I release a breathy sigh. My tongue slips out to moisten my lips, giving him the answer he waits for.

"May I?" he asks and tilts his head as his free hand secures me at the nape of my neck. Adam leans in slowly, deliberately, controlled, waiting for the final okay. My eyelids close, my head tilts to the side. I feel his lips press slowly against mine. His lips are soft yet firm. A quiet moan escapes his chest and he places another chaste kiss on my mouth. I want to scream, *"Give me more! Open your mouth! Let me in!"*

Either Adam is a mind reader or more likely, he senses my reaction to him, because he pulls back to look at me and then goes in for the kill. The instant his lips touch mine again and his tongue slips through, I lose all sense of self control. His tongue is soft and warm and very much welcomed. My mouth opens, allowing his tongue to dance with mine, tasting me, desperate for more. I reach out to pull his head closer, my fingers tangle, grasping at his wavy hair. I moan into his mouth, surrendering to the pleasure of his kiss. I have never been kissed like this. So passionately. So needy. So full of pure lust.

His stiff erection pushes against my belly when his hands trail down my back, pulling me tightly against him. I can feel how hard he is. A thrill shoots through me knowing that I am doing this to him. His erection is for me. Adam's kisses become desperate, like time is running out and he'll never have this opportunity again.

"My God, I want you," he pants as he cups my face with his palms, he rests his forehead on mine. "Tell me that I can have you."

Wait! What? He wants me? Images of the Devin at the nightclub crash into my mind. My body is screaming "yes, take me now," but my heart tells me to run fast and far. I'm suddenly aware of where I am, what I'm doing, and who I'm doing it with.

I close my eyes and exhale loudly, answering him, "I can't."

Adam's eyes search mine while his thumbs caress my cheekbones, searching for a different response. "Can't? Or won't?" he asks. "Tell me."

"Both," I reply, trying to break away from his hold on me.

He brings his lips close to mine again, planting soft kisses along my jaw line. "Why?"

The ability to speak evades me, I have no words. So I close my eyes, conceding to the feel of his gentle kisses.

"We." *Kiss.* "Would." *Kiss.* "Be." *Kiss.* "So." *Kiss.* "Good." *Kiss.* "Together." *Kiss.*

A bolt of intense lightning followed by a loud clap of thunder startles me.

I struggle in vain to get out of his arms. "Please, stop."

"You feel this?" His hand squeezes mine. "You have to. There's no denying it." He circles his hips, pushing his erection into me again. "This is what you do to me. Every single, damn day."

The night at the club flashes before my eyes. Devin. His words. His actions. "I can't do this." I struggle against him. I need to find an excuse not to give into temptation again. I don't want to get hurt—I've had enough to last me a lifetime. "I'm...I'm your daughter's teacher. We can't do this." It's the only excuse I can think of at the moment.

"Why not?" he breathes into my ear. "You're attracted to me. I know you are and I'm so fucking attracted to you, I can't think straight." Those hips of his grind forward a second time. His hands palm my ass. "Are you wet just thinking about it? You would come so hard around me."

A wanton gasp escapes, my chest rising and falling with heavy breaths. "Please..."

"Please, what?" he asks, his teeth nipping at my ear, his warm breath tickles my neck.

"Please...STOP." I muster up the strength to push him away, turning my back to him. "I can't do this with you." My weak voice betrays my words.

Huge, heavy drops of rain pelt my face like the tears of my heart.

"Just think about it," he whispers in my ear so I know he's standing closely behind me. A hand touches my shoulder, turning me back around to face him. "We would be so good together. You can't deny what this is between us."

The heavy sky completely opens up, her floodgates opening without apology. Within seconds, we are both sopping wet. Looking around for shelter, Adam grabs my hands and pulls me under a tall pine tree. I crash into his hard body when he stops abruptly, pushing me against the tree. Adam's face is unbelievably breathtaking when he smiles. His fingers push the wet hair away from my face before tucking it behind my ear. I feel the pad of his thumb touch my earlobe, tugging it gently.

"Kiss me," he commands.

"No."

"Okay. I'll kiss you then."

"No."

"Why not?" he challenges.

"Because...I said so."

"Tell me you're not attracted to me and I'll leave you alone."

I want nothing more to tell him that he's wrong about the attraction, but I can't. I want him more than I've ever wanted anyone in my life. But he has trouble written all over him and I need to steer clear of trouble. It would never work. What the hell am I thinking? What the hell is *he* thinking?

My resolve is strong. "I won't lie to you. You are gorgeous and yes, I'm attracted to you, but I can't do this." I continue on, "I don't sleep around."

Adam reaches for my hand, drawing me away from the tree and into him. His dark eyes are serious. "Listen to me. I'm sorry if I came on too strong, but I won't apologize for wanting you. I've wanted you since the first time I saw you sitting in traffic behind me."

I stare at him, contemplating the words he's just said. What's he talking about? He saw me sitting in traffic? "I'm not sure I understand. When did you see me in traffic?" I feel his fingers stroke my cheek before he leans down to shower my neck with light kisses. My eyes flutter to a close as I angle my neck, allowing him better access. My God, I don't stand a chance.

"It was about a month ago. You blew your horn at me and when I looked in my rearview mirror, I *saw* you. You had a red ball cap on and...you were talking to yourself." He laughs. "You looked pretty pissed, but then your face softened when you looked over at your dog." We both glance at Brady. "There was something about the way you looked at him. It was intriguing."

I am at a complete loss for words. I remember the incident he's talking about—it was the day I drove home from Texas. Traffic was heavy because of construction and then the vehicle in front of me wouldn't proceed through the green light. It was him? Thank God I was in town. Who knows what hand gestures I would've sent flying his way if we had been on the open road.

A moment of lucidity strikes me and I straighten my head, denying the earlier access. "Maybe I should be flattered, but I'm not. You don't even know me and I'm not interested in having a one night stand with you."

"One night?" he asks with a sly smile on his face. "I couldn't do all the things I want to do to you in one night."

"Do you hear yourself?" I ask belligerently, anger starting to boil to the surface.

"I know what I want. I want you."

Again, Devin's words "I chose you" ring loud and clear. Goosebumps pebble on my forearms, sending shivers down my spine.

"Wait, so that's how this works? You 'want' me so I'm supposed to be so flattered that I drop my panties and spread my legs for you?"

I think I've stunned him because he says nothing in response. Dark eyes flash to meet mine.

"So what, no wining and dining? Straight to fucking?" I bark at him.

"That dirty mouth! The things I could do with that." Narrowed eyes smile at me.

Another flash of lightning hits the town below.

"Fuck this," I mumble under my breath. "I'm outta here." I step away from him, getting ready to leave.

"Stop. Come with me. Come back to my place."

"You stop! This," my hand waves back and forth between us, "whatever you think this is, isn't going to happen." My voice rises to be heard over the monsoon surrounding us. I push my wet hair back away from my face as anger wells up inside of me. "I'm not that girl. I told you! I'm not interested in being one of your 'fuck 'em and chuck 'em' girls!"

Adam stares at me as if he's trying to figure something out, his eyes blinking slowly. "But that night...you were at the club..."

Rain runs down Adam's body, showcasing his defined chest and hard abs. I want nothing more at this moment than to grab him and kiss him again. I'm sure he can see my pebbled nipples right through my shirt.

Adam steps forward again to pull me in, but I turn quickly,

calling Brady to follow and run as fast as my legs will carry me. The need to get away from someone has never been stronger than it is right now. My vision is hazy because salty tears and hard rain merge, soaking my face, blurring my eyes. I fall once, smashing my knee on a rock, leaving a line of blood dripping down my leg. How I manage to trek down with only a scraped knee surprises me.

Chapter Twelve

I SWITCH MY DISMISSAL DUTY FROM AFTERNOON TO THE morning arrivals just so I don't have to see Adam face to face. But that doesn't really matter because from my classroom window, I watch him every afternoon as he walks with his children to the black Escalade. I still see him in my dreams every night.

Later that day, I make phone calls to the parents, reminding and encouraging them to attend our upcoming "Meet the Teacher Night." During my lunch period, I manage to call half of the parents, but the others can wait until I get home. I don't think twice about calling from my cell phone—I've known most of these parents for years.

I dial. I hang up. I dial again. I hang up again. My heart pounds at the thought of having to talk to him. I know that as some point I'm going to have to talk to him again, his daughter is in my class after all. Thankfully, when I call the only number listed for Adam, a New York cell phone number, the recording says that the voicemail is full and cannot accept messages. Whew! Thank the Lord for small miracles! I look at Brady. "I guess I'll just have to write him a note. What do you think, boy?" He barks in agreement.

A beautiful spray of colorful wild orchids arrives at the office for me on Thursday. Flowers for me? I never get flowers. It's not my birthday and I don't have a special anniversary. Well, not one that I celebrate any way. It's not uncommon for Shelby to receive flowers from Mike. He's a romantic guy who's not afraid to show his love for his girl. He sends flowers for all the usual occasions, birthday, holidays and even "Just because" days. Oh, you should hear the terrible names she gets called when those get delivered. It's actually pretty funny.

I carry the beautiful arrangement back to my room. The white envelope boasts my last name, declaring that the flowers are in fact mine. I grin, letting a small chuckle escape, when I read the simple words written in block letters: "STOP AVOIDING ME."

Adam's messages via phone calls to the office have been in vain. I have no desire to talk to him. He crossed the line when he slipped a note into Madison's folder for me. That, too, was unsuccessful. I was avoiding him. He wants to fuck me and probably chuck me and he wasn't shy about it.

The flowers may or may not have softened my tenacity. After finally admitting that I am being ridiculous because I'm going to see him all year, I stand tall and remind myself that I am an adult, capable of having a conversation with him. I am determined to face him this afternoon and act as though nothing ever happened. No kissing. No touching. No wanting.

When the end of the day rolls around, I offer to fulfill my afternoon dismissal duty. I stand by the table, waiting for him to appear. My eyes stray to the door every few minutes. I hope to see him before he sees me. I feel like I'll be better prepared for the rush of energy that will no doubt course through my veins if I see him first. Unfortunately, the opportunity to see him or hear his sexy voice never comes because Gina picks up his children.

The walk back to my classroom is slow and quiet. The flowers perched on my desk mock me. I feel despondent—disappointment instead of excitement flows through me. Why would he send me flowers and then not come in today? Why would he pursue me if he's with her? Is this a game to him? I must be his new toy that will be discarded when he's done playing.

After I pack up my bags, turn off the lights, and tap out a response to Shane's text from earlier in the day asking to see me again, I nearly collide with a hard chest rounding the hallway corner. "Oh, sorry." I glance up from my phone.

Adam stands almost a head above me, dressed in a crisp, pale-pink button down shirt loosened at the collar, cuffs rolled up and grey dress pants. His hands reach out to steady me, grasping my shoulders firmly.

"Hi." He smiles tentatively.

"Hey." I smile sheepishly.

"Did you get the flowers I sent?" His eyes drop to my arms, carrying only my bag and phone.

"I did...thank you." I smile and drop my phone into my bag, ignoring the incoming text alert. "They're really beautiful."

We stand there in the hallway, staring at each other.

"Why do you keep running away from me?" he asks.

"I don't know." I lie, dropping my gaze to the tile floor. I know exactly why. I want to tell him how my heart has been shattered and that I'm afraid to let anyone in. I want to tell him that a guy like him is bad for a girl like me.

"You don't know?" His words are wary.

I don't answer, my eyes looking everywhere but at his. I feel my resolve quickly fading away when I finally look at him. He's beautiful and sexy and I want to have all kinds of wild passionate sex with him. I want to reach up and kiss his mouth fiercely, taking what I need from him. But at what cost? Are a few moments of lust worth the pain that will surely follow?

"Come for a drink with me." His dark eyes bore into mine. "One drink," he promises, holding up his index finger. He's so damn irresistible and just like that, I surrender the fight and wave the white flag, ignoring the red flags that are warning me away, telling me to retreat.

A huge sigh escapes me. "Okay, but you can't tell anyone. I do have a reputation to uphold," I tease.

I need to get home to let Brady out. I ask him where he'd like to meet, but he insists on driving. Adam follows me home so I can drop off my Jeep and let Brady take care of business. He drives closely behind me, talking on his phone the entire time. The curious part of me wonders who he's talking to. His face looks so serious, agitated even. Maybe it's the redheaded woman from the club or the blonde from the bar. Even worse, maybe it's Gina. Or maybe, just maybe, I need to mind my own damn business. The sensible part of me wants to jump on the highway and speed away from him. I'm sure he'll catch me—his SUV is way faster than my Jeep. What am I thinking? Am I really going to allow myself to be another notch on his bedpost?

I pull into my driveway, Adam follows. He cuts off the engine, steps out, and strides confidently over to me. "Nice place." I don't have to look back to know he's following me through the back door into my kitchen. Once inside, his eyes wander around my home, a small smile on his face. "It's...cozy."

"Umm...okay, thanks, I think." My lips tighten with reservation. *Cozy? What the hell is that supposed to mean?* My home isn't new; it's worn, showing signs of being well-loved. I can only imagine what the place Adam calls home looks like. I'm sure there are expensive luxury furnishings in every room. I bet he even has a housekeeper who keeps his place immaculate. I don't think I could live in a museum.

"I meant it as a compliment." He grins timidly. How the hell did he know what I was thinking? Maybe he is a mind reader.

"Okay. In that case, thank you." I nod and step back when I call Brady.

Brady yelps loudly as he crashes into and through my legs. I think he's happy to have me home.

"Can I get you something to drink?" I ask, hanging up my work bag on the hook by the door.

"No, thanks," he declines. "I'll wait outside."

Have I offended him in some way? He wasn't in my house for

three minutes and he bolted for the door. I move to change out of my work clothes. I kick off my black ballet flats and climb the stairs two at a time. Adrenaline courses through my body. My favorite pair of jeans fit perfectly, paired with an off the shoulder black top, complete with peep-toe heels. My hair falls into waves after running a brush through it. I reapply some blush and lip gloss. Five minutes flat, I'm ready to go.

Before I push the creaky screen door open, I stand there silently, gawking shamelessly at Adam throwing Brady's tattered tennis ball deep into the backyard toward the lake. Through his dress shirt, the muscles in his back show definition as he raises his arm to throw the ball. His legs, long and strong, strain in his dress pants. God, he really is a fine specimen. He turns around at my appearance, his eyes sparkling with delight when he sees I've changed.

"Wow. That was fast! You look great!"

Feeling slightly embarrassed at the compliment, I simply reply, "Thanks...you ready to go?"

"Definitely." He squats down to rub Brady's head one last time. "See ya, buddy."

I usher Brady back into the house while Adam washes his hands at the kitchen sink. The picture on the windowsill catches Adam's eye, prompting him to ask about it. It's one of my favorites; the picture was taken many years ago down at the lake. I think I was about eight at the time. My hair was in two, long braids like Pocahontas, my face tanned from the summer sun. I was missing my two front teeth so I grinned happily from ear to ear as I rode piggyback on Josh's back.

"Who's this?" he asks, taking the picture in his hand to look at it closely.

"Oh, God! Please don't look at that! That's so embarrassing!" My arm brushes against his when I retrieve the picture and place it back on the sill, mortification setting in quickly. "That's me and my brother. It was taken a long time ago."

"Yes, I can tell. You've grown up a bit since that picture." A sexy smirk greets me.

He guides me to the passenger side of his full-size vehicle with his hand placed on the small of my back, only releasing me to open the door.

The interior is beautiful, the soft black leather cradling me, screaming expensive luxury as music floats through satellite radio on the BOSE audio system. I turn to look at the spacious back seat. There's so much room to stretch out and...Oh, Lord, I mentally slap myself for my dirty thoughts when I realize that his *children* sit back there.

"Buckle up," he orders. Anxiety immediately races through my body as I reach over my shoulder to secure myself. He doesn't need to tell me to put my seatbelt on. I always wear my seatbelt; at least now I do.

I smile weakly at him as he begins to drive through my neighborhood. The summer sun is starting to set before us. The drive is filled with conversation about anything and everything, from the changing New England weather to his taste in music when Linkin Park comes on.

We arrive at Barcelona, an upscale bar, about twenty miles south of town. Insecurities creep up telling me that maybe he doesn't want to be seen with me, but I brush that thought aside when he reaches for my hand, lacing our fingers as we walk into the bar. He simply smiles when I give him a questioning look. A tremor of electricity races through me at his touch.

A pretty hostess, with a sleek dark ponytail and a short black dress, leads us to a small table in the middle of the busy bar before Adam requests something more private. Once we settle into our table for two in the back of the restaurant, I close the food menu, opting to peruse the drink menu instead.

"So, Miss Delaney..." Adam's voice is low and deep, "tell me something..." His hand straightens the silverware, his index finger running along the dull butter knife. "Why have you been avoiding me?" His eyes snap up from the silverware and stare at me, his fingers coming to a stop.

"What?' I reach for my water, suddenly feeling parched. "I haven't been avoiding you." I laugh as I lie, trying to hide my nerves, my voice an octave higher.

He glances around the room, sits up and then leans forward. "You have been avoiding me. I haven't seen you all week."

"I didn't realize you were looking for me." I grin.

"I kissed you. I told you I wanted you. Then I had to use every single ounce of restraint to keep myself from taking you right then and there in the middle of the damn woods...and then you...you ran away from me. Literally." I watch as his chest rises when he inhales deeply, shaking his head in disbelief at the memory.

A shiver shoots down my body, my eyes close, as I remember how it felt to have his lips on mine and his length pressed against me. I open my eyes.

"Are you cold?"

"No, I'm fine," I fib, reaching for my water glass.

A friendly waiter, dressed in standard black from head to toe, promptly takes our appetizer and drink orders then leaves.

"Tell me why you ran away," he demands, leaning in closer across the table.

I need to be straight with him, just tell him the truth. Adjusting myself to sit tall and confident, I lean forward, mirroring his posture. "Listen. You seem like a nice enough guy, but I know your type. I'm sure you have a bevy of beauties to choose from, willing and ready to drop their panties to please you in every way possible," my voice laced with sarcasm. "But, the reality is...that's just not me." I continue, "And if I'm being completely honest with you, I'm not interested in being one of your many conquests and I definitely don't share." My eyes glare at his as a particular redhead and a curvy blonde come to mind immediately. My confidence surprises me. I know I have his full attention; his eyes are completely focused on me.

Adam's response doesn't come swiftly. His words are chosen carefully almost deliberately. "You're right. I do have my choice of women, but that's my point, don't you see?" His voice now becomes firm. "I want *you*." His body relaxes as he sits back in his seat. "Are we not two adults who share a mutual attraction? Why not take advantage of that? Who says it has to be more than that?" *He's completely serious and completely crazy! He wants to be fuck buddies?* I should make a list of all the reasons this is wrong.

A sarcastic chuckle escapes my lips. "You're serious?" I ask with raised eyebrows. The throb between my legs begs me to say yes to his offer. "You're pretty confident, you know."

"Yes, I know." His lips pull to the side in a sexy grin. "I also know what I have to offer."

"My turn. Tell me why you want to go this route? It can't be just about sex since you said yourself that you have many willing women. So why fuck around? Why don't you just find someone to date?"

Two wine glasses are placed on the white linen tablecloth in front of us before the waiter opens the bottle, pouring a small amount into Adam's glass. He does that whole swirl, sip, and taste thing before nodding his approval.

Wine is poured into our glasses. I watch as Adam reaches for his glass and raises it. "Here's to no more running." His mouth opens slightly when he takes a long sip. I swear to God, if he does that again, I'll be sprinting into his bed, but I need to be sensible.

I clink my glass against his and then take a sip. This is good wine, not the cheap stuff I usually drink with Shelby. "You need to consider my point. I don't even know you and you're asking me to sleep with you. Not, 'hey, let's go to dinner and a movie.'" I raise my eyes deliberately. "You do realize that that's not how most men ask for a date, right?"

"First of all, I didn't ask for a date. I don't have the time or inclination to get involved with someone like that. Secondly, I would never subject my children to even the slightest possibility of getting to know someone and them losing her when things end between us."

When not *if! Wow!* I didn't expect that answer! Another piece of the puzzle revealed.

"Look," frustration evident in his voice, "I'm not in the habit of asking more than once." The man from the club is trying to rear his head.

With a cheeky grin, I pick up my wine and sip slowly. "Sorry to cause so much trouble, Mr. Lawson. I'm really not worth it."

The waiter returns with our appetizers, a sampling of the chef's favorites. I'm not the type of girl to be shy around food so I place a few things on Adam's dish and then on my own. I look at him and am surprised to see his brow is furrowed.

I pick up a cheese filled olive and pop it into my mouth. "What?" I ask, confused by his expression. Do I have something on my face? Maybe he thinks I don't have polished manners because I picked up the olive with my fingers not my fork.

"Why are you fighting this so hard? You're young, beautiful, and single. Why not indulge in something pleasurable with someone who finds you incredibly sexy?" He gulps back the rest of his wine and sets it down slowly.

Oh, God! Right then and there, I know that I'm giving in to this. He's right. I do need to relax, let go and enjoy some fun. I am a twenty-seven, single, independent woman with no one to answer to but myself. And I can only imagine what he can do with that body of his.

"Mmmm...so let me get this straight. You basically want to fuck me, but not date me. It's a *very* tempting offer, but I'll need some time to think about it." My eyes dance with humor. "You do realize that I am your daughter's teacher. That might complicate things, don't you think?"

"Why would it? No one has to know." His face is confident. "I do have another question for you."

"Oh wait, wait...let me guess..." I hold up my index finger, silencing him. "Are you going to ask how loud I'm going to scream when you fuck me?" Sarcasm seeps from my lips.

"No," he says arrogantly and shakes his head, "Pfff...I already know the answer to that." He looks up at me with hooded eyes, almost embarrassed. "What's your name?"

The sip of wine I've just taken goes down the wrong pipe and I cough. "My name? You don't know my name? You just asked me to have sex with you and don't know my name?" I'm not sure if I should be offended or not. But then again, it's not like he has access to my personal information like I have to his. That's just one of the perks of having his daughter in my class.

"I'm sorry. I don't." It's his turn to look uncomfortable. "Would you think less of me if I told you that I'm not exactly in the habit of knowing names?"

"Well, now, that would imply that I think about you at all, wouldn't it?" I set my fork down and reach forward, putting my outstretched hand across table and wait for him to return my handshake. "Hi. I'm Mia. Mia Delaney. It's a pleasure to meet you."

He shakes my hand firmly like we've just made a deal, his eyes crinkle with delight. "Mia." My name comes out like a whispered breath. "Mine," he whispers so softly I barely hear it.

My phone vibrates and both of our eyes look at the small clutch sitting on the table. I debate answering it, but I send it to voicemail instead. I'm sure it's just Pete or Shelby anyway.

"Is that your boyfriend? Is he calling to see where you are?"

"No."

"No, what?"

"No, that's not my boyfriend calling."

"How would you know? You didn't even look at it."

"For your information, Mr. Nosy, it wouldn't be my boyfriend calling because I don't have one." I continue, "And do you think I'd be sitting here with you, if I *did* have a boyfriend? I would never do that." The conversation suddenly feels serious, the tension heavy. "I'm not unfaithful. I told you already; —I don't share." My hushed words spoken so quietly, I'm not sure if he even hears them.

His face is serious, studying me and then he smiles. "Well, that's good to hear because I'd have to kick his ass and steal you away from him. I don't share either...at least I wouldn't share you." Humor displays itself through that roguish grin on his face. "I'd never be the other man. I AM the man." His laughter is infectious. I shake my head and roll my eyes, wondering how I'm getting involved with such an arrogant ass.

A little while later his phone chirps, signaling an incoming text. Checking his phone, he presses his lips into a hard line when he taps a response and then announces the time. "It's getting late. I have to get going soon." Our hands are joined after he reaches across and closes his hand around mine. "I needed to see you, to talk to you. It was killing me all week."

Butterflies dance around in my belly while the flashing alarm in my head declares, *"Abort. Abort."*

"Mia, there's something about you. Something sweet, sexy, refined, and feisty. You're a breath of fresh air." His thumb rubs across my knuckles.

In that moment, with his beautiful dark, soulful eyes staring at me, I know without a doubt that my decision is solidified. I want this man! I'll take whatever he's offering even if it is just his body. Just the thought of what this man will do, with me and for me, has me feeling wanton. A throb slowly builds up in my core, causing me to shift and cross my legs. I'm not a stupid person. I know this is probably isn't the best situation for my fragile heart, but at the moment, it isn't my heart that I'm listening to. So, my happily ever after is again put on the back burner to simmer until it's ready to boil over with years of endless love.

After Adam settles our bill, leaving a generous tip, he leads me by the hand out of the restaurant. No sooner do we round the corner towards the parking lot, he shoves me up against the side of the building, red bricks pressing hard against my back. His mouth crashes into mine, his sweet tongue begging for entry looking for its mate. My lips separate welcoming him. I feel his warm tongue, the taste of wine on his full lips. His body pushes into mine, his hands tangle in my hair. I am consumed.

I reach around his back to pull him in closer, letting my hand slide lower down his back until I reach his ass. He groans loudly in my mouth when I give it a good, long squeeze, causing him to circle his hips.

Without warning, he breaks the kiss and pulls back to look at me. "You do this to me. You make me crazy with want for you." He nuzzles my neck, running his nose up and down my throat, inhaling my perfume, lips licking and pecking. "God, you smell so good. I could feast on you forever."

My belly flutters with excitement. He's just so close, no space between our bodies. I close my eyes, turning my head away shyly, wishing I could believe those words. There's no such thing as "forever" with a man like Adam; there's only a "for now." I'd never be so foolish to think otherwise.

"Come on, let's go." His husky voice pulls me out of my daze and we walk hand in hand to his SUV. Adam drives with one hand on the wheel while his other hand rests above my knee, his thumb circles around and around. The ride back to town is quiet as I gaze out the windows, the dark highway offering little light. There's a shift in the atmosphere, an underlying tension between us. I am drawn to him—he's like a magnet pulling me in.

The name "Nora" flashes on the dashboard screen along with a distinct ring tone, indicating he's receiving her call. His finger freezes on my knee and then he hits the "decline" button.

"Why were you there?" he finally asks, breaking the silence.

"What? Where?" I'm not exactly sure where or what he's talking about. I've seen him all over the place so he's going to have to be a little more specific.

"A few weeks ago at that club...What were you—" his words cut short when his phone rings yet again. "Dammit," he says with a loud huff, tapping a button on the steering wheel with more force than is necessary.

"Hello?"

A woman's voice returns, filling the vehicle. "Hey, Adam." I recognize the voice immediately and my body tenses. *Oh my God, she is with him and I'm sitting here having just agreed to sleep with him. He is a pig!*

"Hi, Gina. What's up? I'm on the way home now." What? They live together? He's on the way home? I feel my heart pound hard in my chest. I look out the window and wonder briefly if I can survive a tuck and roll jump out of the car.

"Oh. Is everything okay? Did things go well with your last meeting?" she asks and waits for his response.

"Yeah, it did." He grins and looks over at me, placing his hand back on my leg. "I had to do some tough negotiating, but it all worked out. I think it'll be very lucrative deal for both parties." He winks at me and gives my thigh a little squeeze.

"Well, that's good. I know how persuasive you can be. I've seen you in action." She laughs seductively. My pulse quickens. I feel lightheaded and I think I'm going to pass out. *She's seen him in action?*

I reach into my clutch for a tissue to wipe my hands that are now clammy and wet. Anxiety races through my body. Oh God, please don't tell me that he's fucked her. I don't think I can handle that. That is an absolute deal breaker. I will never allow myself to cross paths with her again. Been there. Done that. Twice.

"Uh, Gina, were you calling for a specific reason? Are the kids okay?"

"Yeah, sorry," she stutters. "Maddie's been complaining about her stomach again. She sat out at dance and missed the new part of the routine. She'll have to work harder to catch up to the other girls. I'm not sure what's going on...is she always such a drama queen?" She's rambling now. Her words and laughter only seem to annoy Adam because his eyes roll and he tightens those luscious lips into a hard line.

"Is that so?" he says thoughtfully. "Alright, tell her I'll be there soon."

"Okay," her voice soft and sexy. "I made us dinner. I mean, I made you a plate. You can take with you or you can stay and eat it here."

"Thanks, but I've already eaten."

"Oh, I almost forgot to tell you that we have a meeting with Chris tomorrow. He has some good offers that he wants to discuss."

He disconnects the call, a questioning look on his face when he sees how tense I've become. "You okay? What's the matter?"

When I don't respond, he asks, "Does it bother you that I have kids?"

I am stunned. Where did that question come from and why would he even think that? His kids are great. I clear my throat and turn to face him.

"Not at all. I love kids!"

"Remember what I said. I keep my personal and private life separate. You'll never have to worry about them knowing about us or disturbing us. I *never* mix the two."

My spirit is crushed at his words. "Never?" I ask because I truly don't understand.

He shakes his head briefly. "Never." His answer is absolute. "It's not right. Most women are in my life for such a brief period of time. Why would I subject my children to that? Besides, they've lost enough already." I'm surprised by his honesty.

The green sign on the side of the road citing the town name and establishment comes into view a bit blurry. My eyes well up with unshed tears knowing that he's telling me right here and now that this...whatever this encounter, this affair, this hookup is, it will be brief. I'll be alone again soon enough and he will have moved on.

"Makes sense, I guess." I shrug and open the mirror on the sun visor. I tug lightly at my eyelash as though I'm trying to get something out of my eye. I don't need to explain the unshed tears. He'll think I'm a lunatic for getting teary eyed.

Closing the mirror, I angle my body to face him. "Can I ask you a question and you don't have to answer it if you don't want to, but..."

He looks at me curiously. "Go for it."

I swallow the quarter size lump in my throat before the words spew out of my mouth.

"Gina. How do you know her and have you slept with her?"

He chuckles. "First of all, that's two questions." With a playful grin, he continues, "I've known Gina and her family for a few years. Her brother, Chris, and I went to college together and are business associates and as far as your second question, do you really want to delve into each other's pasts or enjoy the present?" His eyebrows rise in expectation, a smirk on his face.

Oh Lord! I can only imagine his sordid past and the line of women who've shared his bed. Do I really want to be added to that list? No, but right now, my body isn't listening to my brain.

"No, I don't want to know about your past conquests," I say making air quotes, "but I do need to know about Gina. So have you fucked her?"

"Gina's a good girl." He smiles like he's thinking about his sweet old grandma. *Good girl, my ass! She's a backstabbing, life stealing whore!* "No, Mia. I never have nor will I ever fuck her."

I love the way my name rolls off his tongue.

"Her father and brother would have my balls on a silver platter with a side of marinara sauce." His laughter surprises me.

"But you do find her attractive? If it weren't for her family, you'd fuck her?" I prod further because I really do need to know.

"Wow, Miss Delaney. You have quite the dirty little mouth for such an educated woman. You like that word 'fuck,' don't you?" My core clenches tighter at his words. I need to keep it together until I get home.

"Yes, I do!" I shout playfully as my hand slaps his bicep lightly. "Now answer me!" I can feel the hard muscles beneath his dress shirt, and I squirm at the thought of those arms around me.

He turns those gorgeous dark eyes toward me, his mouth in a tight line. "Some men might say she's beautiful, but, no, I'm not attracted her. I am, however, attracted to you. In fact, I'd say very attracted to you. I'd even say stupidly attracted to you." He winks and his teasing words put me at ease.

Oh, thank God!

"Why the interest in Gina?" he asks as he pulls into my driveway, parking behind my Jeep that needs to be washed.

I debate for a second on what to say. "It's a small town, Adam. Everybody knows everybody." That's not technically a lie.

"Besides, I wouldn't want her sloppy seconds." I laugh, taking off my seatbelt to hop out, walking over to unlock the back door before whistling for Brady who hurries through the kitchen straight for the backyard.

"He's a good dog. My kids really want one."

"Then you should get them one. They'd love it." I nudge his ribs playfully with my elbow.

"Owww," he feigns injury and then he pulls me at the waist, bending to accommodate the difference in our heights. He stands almost a half foot taller and I'm wearing heels.

"Kiss me." He leans in to cover my mouth. His hands roam up and down my back squeezing my ass. Our tongues dance in each other's mouths, igniting a frenzied desire to find release.

"Fuck! I wish I had another hour or two right about now." His voice growls as his teeth tug at my earlobe.

"You like that word, don't you?" I hurl his words back at him.

"Oh, baby. I like to do a hell of a lot more than just say the word."

I put my hands up to his hard, firm chest and push him away.

"Go, Mr. Lawson, your children need you."

He argues, "But I need *you*." He pulls me into his erection, circling his hips slowly, temptingly.

"Go," I order him away. "I'll see you tomorrow at dismissal."

I yell to him before he climbs into the Escalade, "By the way, I never said yes!"

The driver's door closes. Maybe he didn't hear me. The passenger window rolls down slowly. "Oh, you will, Mia. You will."

Chapter Thirteen

FRIDAY MORNING I WAKE UP EARLY, BRIGHT AND EAGER to get my day going. A sense of excitement courses deep within me, something I haven't felt in what seems like long time. The dormant parts of my body which were buried beneath the sad reality of betrayal, heartache, and loneliness have been awakened and are on high alert. An unfamiliar throb between my legs makes me smile as I stretch my arms high above my head. Today is going to be an extra-long shower kind of day.

I'm no fool; well, I was at one time, but not anymore. I know not to get my hopes up that this, whatever this is with Adam, will ever become anything more than sex. He's gorgeous, sexy as sin, but he's careful and guarded, wanting to keep his private and personal lives separate. What he fails to realize though is that I'm already a part of his personal life through his children. Five days a week, six hours a day, a part of him, his beautiful and sweet little girl, is with me.

AFTER RECEIVING A TEXT FROM SHELBY TELLING ME that she's running late, asking if I could grab a coffee for her, I swing by Dunkin' Donuts like I do every morning and order. Pete greets me when I pull up to the drive thru window. I swear he drops any customer when he sees my Jeep pull in.

"Good morning, beautiful!" He pops through the small, open window to kiss my cheek. My seatbelt strains against my collar bone when I lean over to offer my cheek, my kiss floats in the air, never making contact with his smooth, after-shaved face.

"You look radiant this morning with that..." he peers in further to see what I'm wearing, "...pretty, green shift dress on. Is there any particular reason for that look?" He waggles his eyebrows. Pete thinks about sex constantly; he's quite the horny bastard, if you ask me.

"Peter Harris! You are such horn dog!" I smile, feigning offense. "Dude, it's FRIDAY, remember! It's only THE best day of the week!"

He passes me the cardboard tray with two large coffees. I look at the small bag wedged in between the drinks after I hand him my debit card. "Yeah, right! Something's up with you, Mia." His eyes narrow, a devious grin appearing as the small window slides shut. I peek into the bag and find a bagel sandwich and a donut. When the window reopens, I take my debit card and pass the bag. "I don't think this is mine. I didn't order a sandwich and a donut."

"That's on me. You're too skinny. You need to eat."

"I eat! Well, at least let me pay for it." I offer my card again.

"Babe, I'm the manager and my father owns the place. I think we can afford $4.00."

I sigh and thank him. "Goodbye, Peter." I emphasize his formal name. "Love you. By the way, I love the new haircut!"

"Me, too!" He runs his hand over his dark mane which hangs over his forehead.

Shelby and I pull into the school parking lot within minutes of each other. Shelby comes over to help me balance our coffees and workbag, and must notice my good mood, too. "You're awfully happy this morning." She eyes me suspiciously, searching my face for any clues. *What is it with her and Pete? Am I sullen all the time? They make me sound so grumpy!*

"It's Friday...you know, TGIF and all that shit," I say.

Heading into work, I use my fingers to wipe the tears of laughter from my eyes when Shelby blames Mike's "sunrise surprise" for making her run late to work. Let's just say that she'd be great romance writer; she's very descriptive and detailed!

I walk past her room into my own, drop off my bags, before heading back with my coffee in hand.

"So...spill it! What's going on? And while you're at it, tell me why you're wearing that dress. Did you forget about Dress Down Friday?" she demands.

I bite down on the inside of my cheek to keep from laughing and spewing out the words I want desperately to shout, "I had drinks with a certain fine fucker last night." I can't hold it in any longer.

"No, shit?!? Really...and???" Her green eyes are as big as saucers.

"And...it seems we have a common interest...drama-free sex. No strings attached." I grin convincingly, but Shelby knows me better than that.

Her smile fades immediately. "Uh, yeah...you don't really do the whole," she air quotes, "'drama-free, sex with no strings attached' thing very well, Mia." Her words are true and it stings.

"Well, I do now," I snap. My words are defensive and she knows it.

"And besides, I'm sure you'll be there to slap me straight if any drama comes my way." I grab my coffee and walk out ahead of her when the bell rings.

All day long I find myself smiling, revealing my great mood. I know that I need to be careful and guard my heart. It sometimes doesn't listen to my brain. Shortly after lunch, a text from an unknown number catches my attention. I open the message to find the words. "I knew you couldn't resist me." Oooh! That smug bastard!

I toss my phone back into my desk drawer with no response after adding Adam's name to my contact list as AL. Oh, what a name! I chuckle out loud thinking about how *Married with Children* was one of my dad's favorite TV shows. Al Bundy. YUCK! I might have to rethink a name for him. FF? Fine fucker? CS? City Slicker? JS? Just Sex?

Madison gives me a big, long goodbye hug at the end of the day before she sits down with her brother in the dismissal line. She was excited about spending the weekend with her grandparents because they are going to the Big E. Her mention of the huge state fair reminds me of going there as a kid with my family. The image of Josh walking around gnawing on a giant turkey leg makes me smile.

Adam doesn't have his children this weekend...I can't lie and say that the thought doesn't excite me. Just thinking about him, to look at his beautiful face and that hard body, knowing full well, without any doubt, what I will soon do with him and to him, has that throbbing back that will only dissipate with release.

The long line of parents seems endless today, my anticipation rising and falling with each face that isn't his. Even Gina's hateful glares and nasty muttered comments don't bother me. Finally, I look up to see to see stunning, soulful chocolate eyes. A sly grin spreads across my face.

"Hello, Miss Delaney," he says smoothly as he reaches for the pen, brushing my fingers lightly, scribbling his signature twice.

"Hello, Mr. Lawson," I say trying to appear unaffected although my heart is pounding feverishly in my chest.

"I'm dropping my kids off at their grandparents for the weekend." He smiles.

"Yes, your daughter mentioned that."

"Can I see you later tonight?" His voice is sexy, filled with unspoken promises of lust and passion.

I want to scream, *"YES!! Yes, please!"* But I don't. Instead, I tear off a corner piece of the sign out sheet and write my number down on it and hand it to him after my eyes quickly scan the area to make sure no one is watching. "Here. Text me later. I'm not sure where I'll be."

He looks at the small, scrap piece of paper thoughtfully, his eyebrows furrow as if he's confused. His eyes reach mine. "I definitely know where I want to be later."

"Mr. Lawson, could you move it along? You're holding up my dismissal line and I'd like to get home. Seems I might have plans tonight." I tease.

He slips the paper into the front pocket of his faded jeans, tips his head in a gentleman-like manner, "Miss Delaney."

I watch him as he collects his children, placing a sweet kiss on the top of their heads. Oh, that delicious mouth! I want that on more than just the top of my head!

I WALK DOWN TO THE LAKE SHORE AND WATCH BRADY splash and run through the shallow water. Several people are there unloading their boats by the dock, trying to draw out the last, few warm summer days before the chilly autumn New England weather sets in. My work bag was packed, my errands to package store and grocery store could have all set world records. One might think I'm a little anxious to get home.

After showering and throwing on my favorite ripped jeans, a white tank paired with a light cardigan, I send Pete a quick text telling him that I would go to see his cousin's band tomorrow night. He doesn't respond right away, but I receive a text from Adam asking if he's able to come over around 9:00. I tapped out a response letting him know that 9:00 works for me.

Chapter Fourteen

I<small>T'S</small> <small>A</small> <small>GORGEOUS</small> <small>LATE</small> <small>SUMMER</small> <small>NIGHT</small> <small>WITH</small> <small>A</small> <small>LIGHT</small> breeze. Dried kindling sparks in the fire pit, casting a pretty orange glow. I sit in the worn Adirondack chair, trying to relax while drinking my glass of wine, but my body is on high alert knowing that Adam is on his way over. I sync my phone to play music on my outdoor speaker system. Colbie Caillat sings about realizing what's right in front of her.

The loud, deep purr of a car's engine startles me, causing me to turn in its direction. Oh, the Longos will not be happy with this noise. I'm sure the whole neighborhood can hear this car. Where's the vehicle he usually drives? I don't think I like this car. The sleek black Camaro is way too loud, drawing too much attention and it's the car he was driving the night at the club. Oh no! I hope he doesn't have a Napoleon Complex or anything. You know, big car, small dick. I chuckle at my private joke, although what I felt pressed against me was far from small.

The engine quickly cuts off and Adam steps out into the light from the garage's motion-sensored light. I walk over to greet him. He's looking incredibly sexy dressed in dark jeans and a black, fitted v-neck Henley. I am taken by complete surprise when he strides over, grabs my face, and crushes his mouth to mine. His lips are warm, his tongue sweet and begging entry. My free hand pulls at the back of his head, needing closer contact. I inhale his freshly showered scent mixed with his own woodsy manliness.

"I have waited all day long for that. It's all I've thought about," he mumbles the words against my lips. "How are you tonight?" he asks nipping at my lips, smiling down at me. The ability to speak has momentarily escaped me so I look up his beautiful face and just smile. *Breathe, Mia. Breathe.*

His nose skims my jaw line descending further to my neck. "Mmmm...you smell so good." The heavy stubble of his chin and his moving lips tickle me, making me a squirm, closing the gap between my jaw and my neck.

"Ticklish?" he asks. His nose skims the other side of my now exposed neck.

"Extremely." I giggle.

"I'll have to remember that." He exhales a deep breath and looks beyond me towards the fire pit.

"Would you like a drink?" I hold up my glass of wine, swinging it side to side.

"Are you trying to get me drunk so you can seduce me?"

"No! I'm simply asking if you want a drink." I smirk, turning and walking back to sit down. He follows my lead and sits in the other chair closest to mine.

"This is really nice out here. Do you know what the value of property like this would go for?" He scans my yard, probably seeing dollars signs in his head.

"I agree, but I'd never sell this. Although it is easy to take it for granted when it's there all the time, you know?"

I watch him settle in, lean his head back and look up at the stars. He has the most perfect profile I have ever seen. His eyes close and reopen, blinking several times with purpose.

"There are some things that I could never tire of seeing all the time."

His remark catches me off guard. Surely he can't be talking about me? I *am* a fool for even thinking that! Surely he is talking about his children or his car or a woman's breasts.

I pass him a glass of wine after refilling my own. Our glasses clink. "Here's to not taking things for granted!" My smile beams at him. "Cheers!"

We sit there for the next hour or so talking about nothing really. I find out more about the man who is Adam Lawson. He's a real estate developer with several projects going on, some in the area, some farther away. We make small talk with lots of sexual innuendos. He's a brilliant flirt and with the liquid courage I've gained, I give it right back. The sound of an incoming text interrupts the music for a moment. I ignore it, knowing it's probably just Pete or Shelby.

"You don't want to see who that is?" he asks with some curiosity in his voice.

"No. I'll check it later."

Adam follows me into the kitchen when my stomach growls in need of food not more wine. I quickly realize that I haven't eaten since lunch so I grab a bowl of red grapes, some Asiago cheese and bruschetta to tide my stomach over. As I reach up to the cabinet to retrieve a dish, I feel Adam's chest press into my back, his strong arms reaching around. One hand grabs my waist, the other around my jaw, angling my neck. His firm erection thrusts against my ass. I gasp and then moan.

My long hair is gathered and pushed over my shoulder. I feel his breath in my ear as he murmurs the words, "Turn around." I do as he commands.

Instantly, he kisses me hard and long, his hands travel over the swell of my breasts, down to my stomach before finally settling between my legs. The kiss is loaded with such passion, such need, such desire.

His skilled hands massage me through the layer of denim, searching for that sweet spot. "I can feel how wet you are. Is this for me?"

I open my eyes to look at him and smile. I reach down between our bodies to stroke his length tenting through his jeans. "I can feel how hard you are. Is this for me?" I smirk, throwing his question back at him. Good Lord, who is this person I've become? I'm not usually this forward. Shelby would clap or wave pom-poms and tell me how proud she is of me.

"It is most definitely for you." His erection is pushed further into my hand.

The button and zipper of my jeans are quickly undone before he slides his hands down, over the bare flesh of my skin, circling my swollen nub with his fingers. *I am going to come in like 3.5 seconds if he doesn't stop. I will die of embarrassment.* He must sense my impending orgasm because he removes his fingers and slides one and then two into my wet core. *He does want to kill me!*

"Adam," I pant, "please stop. I...I don't want to come yet."

"Mia...you're going to come *now*. And you're going to come again *later*." He promises. His fingers continue their relentless, sweet torture until my knees nearly buckle and I find my release right there in my kitchen against the cabinets.

"Oh my God!" I bite into his shoulder to prevent myself from screaming and waking up the Longos. My hand continues to stroke him, but I want to feel his flesh so I quickly work to release him from the restraint of his jeans. His erection falls hard and heavy into my hands as I begin stroking again from base to tip. He hisses in my ear, "Where's your bedroom?"

"Not yet." I shake my head and smile coyly. Instead, I drop to my knees and take him into my mouth. He fills my mouth completely. I have never EVER in my life been so brazen and bold with a man. I stroke and suck, looking up to see his face in appreciation. I am relentless in my pursuit.

"Oh, fuck. Mia, stop. I don't want to come in your mouth. I need to be in you. NOW." He pulls me up by my arms and kisses me. He follows me up the stairs to my bedroom. Our clothes are shed immediately and tossed haphazardly on the floor. Each article of clothing ripped from our bodies. I knew he was in amazing shape from what I'd seen of him, but I wasn't prepared for the god who stands before me. His entire body is pure perfection from his sculptured chest, washboard abs, narrow hips to his very, *very* impressive length. If I didn't know that a vagina has to stretch to accommodate childbirth, I'd be afraid to have that in me.

He appraises my body the same way I do his. I feel like Michelangelo's sculpture of David in Florence as he studies me. His eyes sweep from the top of my head, to every part in between, his face thoughtful, appreciative. I work hard for my body and I am happy to share it with him.

"Do you know how beautiful you are?" he asks.

Choosing not to respond with spoken words, I pull him into me and kiss his stubble covered jaw, his hard chest, strong arms, tight abs, and his manhood. I want him to know the feeling is mutual.

He walks us backwards until I can feel my bed behind me, my legs finding its resistance. Gently, almost lovingly, as if I were precious, Adam lowers me down. *Almost lovingly? What?* Scratch that...not lovingly. Adam doesn't do love and I'm not interested in love. *SEX! Hot, sweaty, off the charts SEX! That's what this is about!*

Using his long legs, he spreads my thighs open as he kneels between them, ripping open a condom and rolling it on. My body, anticipating his entry, prepares for him. Nothing in this world can compare the feeling of Adam looking down at me as he surges forward slowly and slides into me. That first thrust! "Ahhh..." my eyes feel heavy and close. The feeling is almost indescribable. The fullness of him. The connection between his body and mine. We begin a slow sensual dance, our naked bodies moving together as one. My body ignites, a slow rumble begins deep within my core. Up and down. In and out. Around and around. Over and over again. Lowering himself to kiss my lips, my neck, and my breasts, Adam continues his wonderful, sinfully delicious barrage.

Abruptly, he stops. Everything just stops. I'm on the precipice of a universe shattering orgasm and he just stops. My veiled insecurities race to the surface. What if this isn't good for him? What if I'm doing something wrong? Memories of years ago invade my thoughts. Awful memories of not being good enough tear through me.

I move to untangle my legs which are wrapped tightly around his waist, but his arm shoots out, holding me still. "Don't move," he commands.

"You feel fucking amazing. I don't want it to end just yet." The words are growled in my ear. Crisis averted. Insecurities pushed down. And so again starts the slow thrusting, the circling of his hips. I've had sex plenty of times, but never has it felt like this. I feel a slow, deep build up in my core with each thrust as I squeeze my legs tighter around him, trying to find the right angle and pressure to release that tension.

Adam must sense my need because he pushes up on his arms, bearing his weight and thrusts into me longer, deeper, and harder. My eyes close as the incredible and unfamiliar sense of freefalling overcomes me and I let go. *Holy shit!* His thrusts become urgent, pushing deeper than before. "This...this is what you do to me..." he says through gritted teeth as his final thrust gives him the release he desperately seeks. His body, veiled in sweat, collapses on top of me.

"Holy shit," the only words I can manage to utter, fall breathlessly from my mouth. My nails rake up and down his back, his full weight pinning me down. "That was incredible."

Adam still doesn't say a word. His face is buried in my neck, his breathing ragged, trying to slow down.

"Hey, you okay?" I tug at the back of his head, wanting him to look at me.

"Give me a minute," he mumbles, pecking my neck with tiny kisses which makes me squirm and giggle. My awakened body is on fire, ready for round two.

My room is illuminated by the bedside lamp; the light casts a serene glow, making everything warm and inviting. I welcomed

Adam into my bed but I cannot, I will not, welcome him into my heart. Not that he'd want to be there anyway.

So I just lie there, with Adam on top of me, giving him the time he's asked for. My fingertips circle random patterns on his back until my stomach growls in protest of having been denied sustenance earlier.

Adam raises his head, a wide, satisfied grin across his unshaven face and says, "Somebody's hungry."

I smirk. "Yeah, I was rudely interrupted earlier."

His weight lifts off me as he rolls to the side. He knots the condom before propping himself up on his elbow so he can look at me. His finger circles around my navel slowly, traveling upward toward the swells of my breasts before pinching my taut nipple playfully.

"Ouch! That hurts!" I slap his hand away, narrowing my eyes, trying to conceal my amusement and pleasure. "Oh shit! Please tell me you're not one of those guys who find pleasure from that BDSM crap! I am so not going there!" I look at him, expecting a reply.

"What's the matter? Are you afraid of a little pain? Pain and pleasure do go hand in hand, you know. It's a very fine line." His deep voice mocks me. "No pain, no gain." He's teasing me! Bastard! With his index finger, he traces the small, very faint lines down my lower abdomen. "What are these?"

I pull the sheet over to cover my nakedness. Suddenly, I feel very apprehensive. Dammit! I didn't think he'd ask me about these marks. Most guys aren't in the habit of inspecting my belly. Their attention is usually a little lower. "Uh...stretch marks?"

"Yes, I can see that. How'd you get them?" I notice he swallows hard and waits for an answer. "Tell me."

My shoulders shrug, trying to pass for nonchalance. "How do most people get stretch marks? Weight gain. Weight loss. I like to eat." I'd rather he just drop the subject altogether; they're just stretch marks after all. He doesn't need to know about the pain these stretch marks represent.

My curiosity gets the best of me as I continue, "Why do you ask?"

"No reason, really." He smiles, his dark eyes sweep up to look at my face. "I just want to know every inch of this beautiful body of yours."

My stomach growls again. I throw my arms over my eyes to hide my embarrassment.

"Let's go. Up you go." He's off the bed instantly, standing gloriously naked, pulling me up to follow. "You need to eat a proper meal."

"It's too late to eat a 'proper meal,'" I protest, deepening my voice to mock him. "Besides I'm always hungry. You have no idea! My stomach is a bottomless pit." I laugh quietly, grabbing my short red robe from behind the bedroom door.

Adam slips on his jeans and shirt then follows me downstairs to the kitchen where my deserted cheese and bruschetta have somehow, inexplicably found their way into Brady's belly. My dog sits on the couch, looking guilty as sin, probably hoping his "puppy dog eyes" routine will earn him some mercy and forgiveness.

"Brady! Bad dog!" I scold him. I scold him. He lowers himself from the couch with his tail tucked between his legs, lies down, turning away from me on his oversized, plaid doggy bed.

Adam walks over to the door that separates the kitchen from the living room and squats down, angling his head to look at the writing on the white trim. "Josh age 5. Mia age 2." He smiles and runs his finger over the thin, black permanent marker line. "Josh age 8. Mia age 5." He continues to look at every line that bears my name, age and height until he reaches the line marking my age at 15. That's when I finally put my foot down and refused to be measured any more. *God, I would give anything for my dad to be here and force me to stand against the thick, white trim to record milestones in my life.*

My private thoughts are interrupted when he asks about the

other name recorded. I tell him about my older brother, Josh, his wife, Araceli, and my adorable niece, Ashley, and nephew, JJ. He listens intently. I tell him about my plan to visit them again for Thanksgiving and about the crazy adventures we've had together. He nods thoughtfully. "That seems nice, you know—to be close to your family." His mood becomes sullen after that comment so I decide not to pursue the subject of his family.

Adam's interest in my family seems genuine. It surprises me actually that for wanting only a casual, sexual relationship, he asks a lot of questions. I answer his questions about Josh and our relationship as siblings. My brother, with light brown hair and blue-grey eyes, is tall, smart and athletic. He was always my hero and my best friend. Adam smiles when I tell him that I was that annoying little sister with skinned knees, the dirty little tomboy who wanted to tag along no matter what my brother was doing. Josh was usually pretty good about it. That is until he discovered girls.

I recant the story of when we were kids and Josh called me "PIA" in front of his friends because he hated that I was always following him around. I ran all the way home with snot running down my face and cried in my mom's arms like a damn baby. I was completely humiliated and heartbroken when my brother stood by silently while all of his friends taunted me, telling me that I was nothing but a pain in the ass.

"That's terrible!" Adam teases me, but concedes that Josh was a good brother when I tell him how later that night Josh came to my room and apologized, explaining that he's older and likes to do things with his friends. But my feelings were hurt so it was then that I decided to find other things to do that didn't include my brother. I started running that year and haven't stopped since. Why I've just told Adam this story about Josh is beyond me. Talking about my family isn't something I do that often anymore.

A loud yawn escapes me and I realize it's late. I don't want to start cooking at this late hour, so I settle on a bowl of cereal instead.

Adam's laughter fills my kitchen when I pull out a family-sized box of *Fruity Pebbles* from my pantry and set two bowls on the island.

He looks dubiously at the cereal box.

"May I offer you a bowl of our finest cereal? It's a wonderful blend of fruity goodness and pure sugar. It goes wonderfully paired with cold milk, sir."

He laughs, finding my attempt at sophistication humorous. "Sure. *Fruity Pebbles* it is."

I feel like we're playing twenty questions, but he's the only one doing the asking. When I ask about Madison and Luke, he immediately shuts down or tries to divert my attention with playful kisses. It feels like I've known him for such a long time—we're comfortable with each other which can be a good thing, but it also feels like I could lose myself in him, be consumed by him, and I will never let that happen again.

When our bellies are full and our bowls empty, Adam takes them to the sink and washes them quickly. I can't help but stare at him in disbelief. His phone dings with a text alert. Pulling it out of his front pocket, he shakes his head and grimaces when reads the name, shoving it back in without responding.

Oh, crap! My phone is still outside! I push the screen door open to retrieve my phone and see several texts from Shelby, Pete, and Shane and two missed calls from my mom.

"Who are Pete and Shane?" he asks indignantly. I literally jump because I didn't realize he was standing so close behind me or that he'd seen the names on my phone.

"No one. Just my friends." I pick up the two discarded wine glasses and the empty bottle and head back inside. All of a sudden, there's a strange tension radiating from Adam and it's directed at me.

"Are you okay? You seem a little tense all of a sudden."

Instead of answering with words, he crushes his lips against mine, pulling me close, his hands squeeze my ass under my robe. "I won't share you. I told you that."

Whoa! What? He sounds a little possessive and I'm not his to possess. *Reality check, my friend.*

"Adam, what are you talking about?" I break the kiss and push back against his chest. "I have friends, lots of friends, some happen to be guys. You need to chill out." My eyebrows rise in expectation, a look of disdain crosses my face, "You're not going to be all alpha male, 'me man, you woman,' are you? I kind of got the impression that this was going to be…" I search for the right word, "casual."

His eyes search my face, seeking forgiveness and then he murmurs, "You're right. I'm sorry. It's just…you…never mind."

"Let's not confuse what we've agreed to do with anything other than what it really is. A booty call. Friends with benefits. You know," I air quote, "fuck buddies." Shelby would be so proud of me right now. From the sounds of it, one would be convinced that I'm really in control of the situation.

"Okay! Okay. I get it!" He backs away from me. "Listen, I had a really good time with you tonight." His next words are spoken quietly, yet demanding. "I want to see you again tomorrow night."

Adam is a man who knows what he wants and is clearly used to getting it. I glance over my shoulder to look at the digital clock on the microwave which indicates it's already tomorrow in bright green. "Well, it seems that you're in luck, my friend." I smile. "Apparently, it's already tomorrow and you're seeing me."

He steps forward, wraps his arms around my waist. "You *are* a wise ass, aren't you, *friend?*"

"Better than a dumb ass." I smirk and then laugh, pulling at the nape of his neck, angling his head for a kiss.

Once again, his phone chirps and I can feel the vibration against my hip bone. Holy crap! He's a busy man. His lips cover mine in a slow, sensual dance, not with the intensity or need of earlier. I can't even imagine who is texting him so late on a Friday night. Something tells me it's not work related. It's probably one of his many women. Adam Lawson doesn't do monogamy—he's a virile

man who can have any woman with the snap of his fingers. HOLD
UP! What am I saying? Oh, hell no! I refuse to share him while
we have an agreement to be friends with benefits, fuck buddies or
whatever label is more acceptable these days. No way! Absolute deal
breaker!

"Are you going to answer that?" I ask boldly.

"No."

"Is that your girlfriend? Is she calling to see where you are?" I
toss his questions from the bar back at him.

He grimaces. "I don't do girlfriends."

"And I don't share."

He narrows his eyes on me.

"You should go—" I clear my throat, suddenly I'm parched and
my mouth is filled with cotton.

"I should probably get going—"

The words spill from our lips at the same time, sheepish smiles
appear on both our faces.

I need to play this cool. Thank God he can't see how fast my
heart is beating or how wet I've become again.

"Yeah, that's probably a good idea," I mumble against his lips
before stepping back to retie my robe which he loosened with
roaming hands.

Adam leans down for a final kiss goodbye, letting out a quiet
growl. "I'll see you later."

"See ya." Holding the screen door open, I watch as he walks to
his beast of a car as he pulls his phone out of his pocket.

"Hey," I call to him with a whispered shout. "Could you maybe
roll that thing out into the street? I do have neighbors, you know."
My grin is playful.

"Goodnight, wise ass." He smirks before sliding into the driver's
seat to start his sleek, sporty vehicle. Listening to the sexy, deep
purring sound of his car backing slowly down my long driveway,
I'm startled when the engine revs loudly before speeding away. I

rush back inside, grabbing my phone to send him a quick text, "And you call me a wise ass?"

His text makes me laugh. "Me man, you woman." Adam Lawson has a playful side.

Chapter Fifteen

"HEY, DADDY." I LOOK OUT OVER THE TOWN, MY LEGS dangling carelessly over the edge. Brady has taken his usual spot under the trees for some rest. My father and I have a one sided conversation, but I know he's listening, always looking out for his baby girl.

The cool, bottled water doesn't do anything to quench my thirst today. I know the reason. I'm not thirsty for water, I'm hungry for Adam. My thoughts have been consumed by him all night and all morning. His lips. His eyes. His body. His...I suddenly remember where I am and that I'm *supposed* to be talking to my father. He would be just as mortified if he knew my deepest desires.

After my run and chat with my dad, the better half of the morning was spent lounging around, returning missed texts and calls from last night. Pete's cousin, Ryan, is the lead singer in a new, alternative band and they're playing tonight at Whiskey's, this awesome dive bar just a few towns over. I promised Pete I'd go with him to check it out. Hopefully, Shane is finally getting the message that we will never be more than just friends ever again. And I mean EVER! I'm mad at myself for mentioning that I would be out and about at the bar. He said he might stop down for a few drinks. *GREAT!* I guess he didn't get the message after all.

Several times during the day whenever I got an incoming text, my heart skipped a beat with anticipation before turning into disappointment. I thought they might be from Adam, but they never were. What did I really expect? It is what it is. Sex. Nothing more. Nothing less.

"Damn, girl. You look good! Maybe I'll play for your team tonight." Pete eyeballs me, spinning me around. "I like the whole 'fuck me pumps,' ripped, tight ass jeans, and tight shirt thing you've got going on. Your tits looks great!"

"Oh my God, Peter!" I slap his arm. "Are you sure you're gay?" I tease.

He jumps into the passenger seat, cranks up the satellite radio as we head toward the bar.

The weight of Pete's stare is heavy even though he's singing along to the music. "What?" I snap. "Why are looking at me like that?"

"You got laid," he blurts.

"What?" I sputter.

"You totally got some! I can see it all over your face. You're like fucking glowing!"

Pete knows me too well and I'm not a very good liar. I nod at his smiling face.

"Who's the lucky bastard? Shane? God, what I wouldn't do to have a piece of that!"

"Ewwww. Gross! You can't have my sloppy seconds!" I laugh and let out an exaggerated gag.

My phone vibrates and the chirp comes through over the music. I'm almost afraid to get my hopes up...again. As soon as we pull up to the red light, I check the message.

AL: I can still feel you wrapped around me. Can you feel me?

OMG! No "Hi. How are you?" Hmmm! Okay friend, so that's how it's going to be?

Me: Sorry. I think you have the wrong number.

A cheeky grin spreads across my face as I slide my phone onto the dashboard. *There! Take that, arrogant man!*

"You gonna go? Or just sit there with that 'eat shit' grin on your face?" Pete points to the green light.

Another chirp and I ignore it for the time being.

There's an excitement buzzing throughout the bar, a loud murmur of people talking and laughing over the music. The bar is pretty packed tonight, some faces are familiar, and others are not. Pete and I make our way to the bar to order our drinks. The first cover band is playing a decent version of "Sex on Fire" by Kings of Leon and my thoughts immediately go to Adam.

Ryan and another band mate, Will, stop by to have a beer, thanking us for coming out tonight. "Hey. Nice to meet you." I smile at Will, who is tall and lean, his arms covered in colorful, intricate tattoos of every design. His eyes rake over my body when we're introduced. Drinking his beer and telling us about their music, I'm slightly uncomfortable with how close he's standing, pressing into my side.

"I'll be back." I grab my beer and push my way to the back of the bar in search of a bathroom. As usual, the line is ridiculously long. Silly drunks want to talk about their problems, I just want to pee. Reaching into my bag, I retrieve my phone and check my messages, smiling when I see that Adam sent three messages. I remember that I never responded to his earlier text about me feeling him. Hell, yes, I can still feel him!

His second message simply says, "Free after 9." The third, "Playing hard to get? I believe I've already had you. I want more." *What? More what? SEX, Mia! Get that through your thick head!*

As the line moves up, I send him a quick text telling him that I'm out with friends at a bar. Almost immediately he responds. "Which bar?" Crap! I'm not sure I want him here. Pete will most definitely pick up on something and I'm not willing to share this with him, at least, not yet. Against my better judgment, I tell him where the bar is and that I'd like to see him.

Pete stands close behind me, swaying from side to side while my hands reach high into the air, fingers snapping along to the music. I feel his breath in my ear as he sings along with the band. Anyone looking at us would think that we're together. I glance up at the band as Ryan belts out Neon Trees' "Your Surrender." Will keeps the rhythm on the drums. When he catches me watching him, he smiles and winks.

Over an hour and three bottles of beer later, my buzzed body goes on high alert. I know he's here, I can feel him. There's a charge in the air when he's near me. How did I not notice that before? Thinking about it, I felt it the first time I ever laid eyes on him on the summit. Again I felt it at school and most recently in my bed. Scanning the packed bar, I search for him not knowing exactly where he is. When I finally catch a glimpse of him, he's across the bar, his eyes focused on me like we're the only ones here in this noisy bar. His dark eyes light with excitement like a predator closing in on its prey. I am a little bunny to his big bad wolf!

There's a battle raging deep within me. Do I go over and meet him? Do I let him come to me? Decision made, I stay where I am. If the big bad wolf is going to devour the little bunny, I'm certainly not going to offer myself up on a silver platter!

Minutes go by and anxiety creeps up when I can't see him anymore through the horde of people. Maybe he saw me and changed his mind. Maybe he's with someone. Maybe...I startle, my shoulders tensing when I hear, "Hello, gorgeous." Adam's voice vibrates against the back of my head close to my ear. He leans forward, his body pressing into my back. "You look beautiful. But then again, you always do."

I turn around to face him with a huge smile on my face. "Hey, my friend. What's up?" That's not the question I really want to ask. I want to know why he's here. Why would this gorgeous man, who garners the attention of so many people, want to be here, in this noisy dive bar, with *me*? His eyes, dark and expressive, a perfectly imperfect nose and those full lips call to me. I resist the urge to run my fingers through the thick hair covering the lower half of his face.

I'm sure we look like idiots because we're just standing there facing each other, our eyes speaking a language of their own, making unspoken promises of what's to come. The tension radiating between us is incredible. This attraction is not one sided—I know he feels it as much as I do.

"Ahem," Pete clears his throat and elbows my ribs lightly. "And who's this?" He ogles Adam, looking at him like he's a scrumptious dessert that he wants to sink his teeth into.

"Peter, this is Adam Lawson. Adam, Peter Harris." They shake hands and nod their heads. I notice Pete's eyes shine a little brighter than they normally do. I quickly give Pete the "PG" version about Adam's daughter being in my class and how we've run into each other on the trails at the park from time to time. Pete purses his lips and roams his greedy, little, lustful and very disbelieving eyes over Adam's body from his dark, wavy hair down his long-sleeved shirt and snug jeans all the way to his black combat boots. I know Pete doesn't believe me, but what am I supposed to say? "Hey, this gorgeous man and I have just basically met and he thoroughly screwed my brains out and I'd like more, please?" Pete knows about everything that happened years ago...well, almost of all of it anyway.

Before I realize it, the band finishes playing their set and Ryan and Will make their way back over to us. Adam's body becomes noticeably closer than before when Will asks what I thought of the band and then suggests that I come watch them play again next weekend. Adam's fingers and then his palm slide under my hair to the nape of my neck, massaging me gently with his firm hand. It feels as though he's staking his claim, apparently letting everyone know that I'm here with him.

I smile at Will and tell him that I don't have any specific plans yet for next weekend, but that I'll keep it in mind. The massage gets deeper on my neck. I angle my head to look back at Adam, surprised to see his beautiful face marred with a serious glare, causing his brows to wrinkle. My "go to" resolution to diffuse a tense situation is to talk about it.

"We'll be right back." I pull his hand from my neck, keeping our fingers laced. Using my free hand, I reach for my wristlet and phone then lead us out of the bar into the alley, not stopping once along the way.

"What's wrong with you? Are you mad about something?" He can't be mad at me because I didn't do anything. My voice comes out harsher than I intend, my eyes looking up straight at his.

"You..." he murmurs. Stepping away from me, he covers his face, running his hands over his eyes. "You're driving me fucking crazy!" In an instant, he's on me, smashing his lips against mine, kissing me furiously like a ravenous animal. "You have no idea what you do to me." His nose skims my jaw line, inhaling long breaths.

Holy shit! That is so unexpected, I don't know what to say! He can't go around saying things like that to me and not expect me to feel something. That's just wrong, cruel even. If he only knew what his words do to my body. And my heart.

"Listen. I'm not sure what you're talking about exactly so you'll need to clarify things for me." I reach up to caress his unshaven face, my thumb runs along the seam of his lips. His eyes close and his body relaxes at my touch.

"Adam? Talk to me. What's going on with you?"

"I don't think I can do this." My heart is in my throat when he says those words, my mouth is like cotton and I can't swallow.

"When I'm with you..." he starts, "it feels so good. I want things that I have no right to want and definitely don't deserve. And my life is so fucked up right now." He wants me? He feels things? Oh, shit! I didn't see that one coming. Why would he say his life is fucked up? Looks pretty perfect if you ask me, but then again I know all too well that looks can be deceiving.

"You really have no idea what you do to me, do you?" His hushed words are mumbled onto my lips.

I smile, tugging at the back of his head to bring him closer. "I guess I don't, but I know what you do to me."

Chapter Sixteen

I WAKE WITH A JOLT. MY HEART IS POUNDING AND MY naked body is on fire, tangled in a mass of long arms and heavy legs while small beads of sweat dot across my forehead and drip down my neck. My breathing regulates as Adam nuzzles into my neck, his tanned arm drapes across my stomach, pulling me in closer to him. He is sound asleep, only his soft breathing can be heard. I want so much to run my fingers through his messy, dark hair, but I don't want to wake him. My eyes scan the room, blinking rapidly as I remember last night. He came to the bar. I texted Pete to tell him I was leaving and that I would leave the keys under the floor mat so he can drive himself home. Adam sped through town as he drove us home in that fast, black Camaro of his. I was pretty buzzed, but I remember laughing about how the Longos were going to file a noise violation complaint against him.

I remember the kissing. Oh, God the kissing! He kissed my mouth, my neck, and my breasts before dropping to his knees and kissing me everywhere while I stood in my kitchen against the wooden island. He is a man of many, many talents. I remember kissing our way up the stairs to my bedroom, the rest of our clothes ripped off and then he pounced on me, taking me hard and fast as though he couldn't wait any longer.

I lie there staring at Adam, who is on his side with one arm tucked beneath the pillow, and smile. Oh, crap! I know myself and I know what I'm feeling and this is NOT good. I know in the end, my fragile heart will get splintered into a million shards by him. Am I willing to take the risk with what's left of my heart? Asking my heart, body, and mind to work cohesively has never been an easy task for me.

Brady's appearance in the doorway lets me know that he has needs, so I carefully lift Adam's arm from my breast and ease my way out of bed. I don't want to wake him just yet. I need a few minutes to myself to gather my thoughts and have a chat with my heart. Throwing on my robe, I tiptoe downstairs, let Brady out, and make a cup of coffee. I wash my face and brush my teeth while my coffee brews. There are two things I need every day—a good run and strong coffee.

From the back door, I watch as he runs deep into the thick trees following the trail that leads down to the water to greet the early risers who walk the shore every morning. Making my way over the patio table on my deck, I'm thankful for the row of tall arborvitaes that separate my backyard from the Longo's, shielding me from prying eyes.

I sit there drinking my coffee while taking in the beauty of the quiet morning, knowing that a gorgeous, unattainable man lies in my bed. Thoughts flood my mind of why he's so guarded, unwilling to let anyone in. Different scenarios dance around my head trying to figure out what he meant about his life being fucked up. I know what he wants, what he's offering, but is it really enough for me? Maybe Shelby was right. I don't do casual sex.

When Brady finally reappears, he runs past me, causing me to turn and look over my shoulder. Adam is standing just outside the screen door, his eyes are fixed on me. I smile when I see him lower into a squat to give Brady's belly some love.

"Hey, buddy," he says in the goofy dog-talk voice. "Where's your ball? You wanna play?" Brady jumps up in search of his tattered tennis ball.

"You've made a new best friend, you know," I tease. And here's that awkward moment when I'm not sure if I caught him while he was trying to leave without saying goodbye or should I be polite and offer him coffee.

"He's such a great dog. How long have you had him?" Adam rises and walks over.

"I got him when he was just a puppy." I smile sadly. I hadn't planned on rescuing him, but in reality, he rescued me.

The apprehension between us is thick. He seems uncomfortable, wanting to say something but not sure what exactly. I offer him a cup of coffee, but declines with a simple, silent shake of his head. So I wait. And wait. And wait.

"I'm sorry about last night," he finally says, his eyes looking ashamed. *He's sorry about last night? What's he sorry about?* Last night was fantastic—at least I thought it was. I sip my coffee, hoping and waiting for an explanation of some sort.

"I really didn't mean to go all cave man at the bar," he says apologetically, rubbing his palms over his eyes in circles before pulling out a chair to sit in. *Whew! Thank the Lord, sweet Baby Jesus!*

"I'm not usually like this." My look must be one of disbelief because he continues on, "Seriously!" His voice drops to a whisper, "I don't usually care. I'm not really sure why I did that."

My eyes widen at his honest confession.

"It's just...seeing that guy hit on you...I don't know...it kind of pissed me off." He exhales loudly.

"Who was hitting on me?" I ask, tipping back the last of my coffee.

"That guy in the band. What's his face? Will?"

"He was? I didn't notice." I am such a liar! Oh, I noticed alright. The way Will's tatted arm kept rubbing against mine or how he would look at me instead of listening to whoever was talking.

His eyebrows rise. "Are you serious? He definitely wants you."

This makes me laugh. "Adam, he can't possibly 'want me,'" I air quote, "he just met me."

Again, he sits quietly, thoughtfully and then his eyes flash to mine before he murmurs something that sounds like "I did."

I need another cup of coffee, and Adam finally agrees to a cup so I walk into the house and pop a medium roast K-cup in the Keurig. I rummage through the fridge to get some fruit and cream cheese for bagels.

A voice from outside causes me to straighten to attention, drop the untoasted bagel and look out the kitchen window. *Oh, shit! What the hell is she doing here?* Her voice is high-pitched, oozing curiosity. "Oh! Good morning, young fellow. And who might you be?" she sings. Adam responds quickly, standing up to introduce himself.

Double shit! I race upstairs to throw on a pair of shorts, a bra and an old ragged t-shirt. I pull my hair into a messy bun before placing the food and cups of coffee carefully on a breakfast tray. *I can do this. I am twenty- seven years old. This is my home and...she can...mind her own damn business!*

I set the tray on the table and greet my nosy neighbor. "Good morning, Mrs. Longo. And what brings you over so early on a Sunday morning?" I smile sweetly while silently cursing the old woman. "I thought you'd be in church by now praying for the sinners of the world."

"Well, it is a good morning indeed." She smiles back, eyes bouncing back and forth between Adam and me. She places a loaf of her famous banana nut bread on the table before us.

"Seems I didn't sleep too well last night. Some car's loud engine woke me up out of a sound sleep right in the middle of a dream." She smirks at Adam who hasn't said two words since I've returned with food. When Mrs. Longo reaches down to pet Brady, I look across at him and mouth the words, "Told ya!" His mouth is full of food, but he manages a throaty laugh, nodding his head in agreement.

My hospitality overrides my annoyance when I ask if she'd like a cup of coffee, but she declines. "No, thank you. I just wanted to drop this off. I know how much you love my banana bread especially when I add extra nuts." Her eyes rake up and down Adam in approval.

"Thank you, Mrs. Longo. That was really kind of you to bring it over this morning." I give her a knowing look and smile.

Adam, with his wrinkled shirt and messy hair, rises and extends his hand to say goodbye. "It was a pleasure meeting you." His wide smile is genuine.

Mrs. Longo returns the gentle handshake before narrowing her sky blue eyes. "Be good to her," she says with a tight smile on her face.

Dear God! Please open up the Earth and swallow me now! Embarrassment floods my face, a red blush on my cheeks. "Goodbye, Mrs. Longo. I'll see you later."

"Oh, Mia, dear. Let me know if I'm watching Brady next week. I know you're probably going to the game."

"Game?" Adam asks as he reaches into his pocket and pulls out his phone, rolling his eyes when he looks at the screen. I can only imagine who's calling him. An ex? A girlfriend? A lover? He notices me watching him.

"Everything okay?" I ask, imagining all the women who have his number and use it frequently.

"Yeah, it's fine. Some people can't take no for an answer." His words are abrupt as he slides his phone back into his jeans. "Listen, I've got go." He looks at me hesitantly, with hooded eyes. "I have a couple of things I need to do before I pick up my kids and take Luke to his game," he says sullenly, the laidback humor now gone.

This is the first mention of his children, Madison and Luke. It makes me wonder why he doesn't talk about them often. Although he did mention that he doesn't combine the two parts of his life. Maybe most of his women don't even know he has kids. I get the whole separation thing, I guess. They really are great kids. I would love to have kids like that someday—they would be the center of my universe.

We both rise to clean up the table and walk inside. We move effortlessly, putting things away around my kitchen, not speaking many words.

And here's that awkward moment that I knew was coming.

"What are you doing later?" he asks.

I shrug. "I'm not really sure. I might head down to the lake. Go paddle boarding, kayaking." I open the fridge to put the creamer away and notice that I'm running low on the essentials. "Probably go grocery shopping. Why do you ask?" For a moment, I think maybe he's going to ask to see me later. Maybe I should have said, "I'd be at the park," so we can meet up there and he can bring his kids along. What is wrong with me? Bring his kids? He's made it perfectly clear what this is and isn't. *Settle down, Mia. Settle down.*

Adam strides over to me, pulling me close and whispers in my ear, "Thank you for this weekend. I had a really good time." He nips at my diamond-studded earlobe. I can feel his lips flatten—I know he's smiling. *A good time?* Suddenly, I feel like a cheap whore whose name and number are written on a bathroom wall in a sleazy bar.

I push him back. "Yeah, I did, too. Thanks. Hit me up sometime." A wink and a cheeky snap of my teeth escape me like I'm a cheesy, used car salesman. *Oh my God! Did I really just say the words, "Hit me up sometime?" What an idiot! Who the hell says that?* He must sense my unease, his eyes narrowing with concern as he opens the distance between our faces to look at me. "You okay?"

"Uh, yeah. I'm fine. Why wouldn't I be?" I lie. I just had two of the best nights of my life and I feel like a whore for it. *Drama-free sex, Mia! Remember?*

"I'll text you later," he says before planting a chaste kiss on my lips then walking out the door into the driveway.

I stand at the sink, washing our coffee cups, listening to the roar of his car race down the street. I'm pretty sure that's the last time the Longos will ever hear that sound. I'm surprised that I feel a little disappointment at the realization.

Adam got what he wanted this weekend—I'm out of his system for sure. Unfortunately, he's not out of mine. Not even close.

Chapter Seventeen

Even though the weather has been unusually warm for this time of year, the full green trees are beginning to change, their leaves turning into hues of red, orange, and yellow. The mild temperatures have provided an extended summer, welcoming people to enjoy the outdoors before the long, cold, harsh winter sets in.

It's already midweek and I'm looking forward to the weekend with my friends. We're heading up to Foxboro, Massachusetts to watch the Patriots game and it's a guaranteed fun-filled day with football, music, beer, and food as rowdy tailgaters and fans from opposing teams all share their love of the game.

I've seen Adam every day at dismissal, but he's never said more than a clipped, "Miss Delaney." No smile. No flirting. Nothing. So I simply return his greeting, "Mr. Lawson." What the fuck? Maybe the whole encounter last weekend was some strange hallucination. Well, damn. I must have a pretty good imagination because parts of my body were sore for days. Maybe I need to make an appointment with Gail and get my prescription refilled.

After Brady and I hike the trails instead of doing our regular run, we make our way toward the group of people by the football field when Shane waves us over. I secure Brady's leash because I know how excited he gets when he sees the football being tossed back and forth.

Shane leans down and kisses my cheek, pulling me into a side hug. "Hey, I'm sorry about the other night. I really wanted to see you, but my sister called and needed my help with the baby. You know how that goes, family first and all." Shane removes his ball cap, runs hand through his blonde hair, before readjusting his cap backwards. He really is hot. I wish I could feel something other than betrayal and find a way to forgive him, but after last spring, there's no going back and I think he knows it.

"C'mon, Coach!" I hear voices whine, calling him. We both turn to look at his players, but my eyes widen and my heart skips when I see Adam standing there, with a cup of coffee in one hand and holding Maddie's hand with the other. He glares at us. He looks so irritated. His tall, lean body is stiff and angry. Madison is by his side, tugging at their clasped hands.

"Come meet the kids. You probably know most of them," Shane says.

"Uh...sure, but just for a minute." I smile hesitantly and follow him.

"Hey, guys. Say hi to Miss Delaney."

I smile. "Hi guys. How's it going?"

"Good." "Fine." "Hi." Their words echoed in response as they all hover around Brady who loves all the attention.

Madison runs up to me and wraps her arms around my waist. "Hi, Miss Delaney!" I return the hug and smile down at her. "Hi, Maddie! What are you doing here?" I ask.

"My brother has football practice," she answers. "I'm here with my dad." She turns to face her father who is still glaring, his strong jaw now ticking. *What the hell is his problem? He's acting like a complete lunatic.* First he fucks me senseless, then he doesn't talk to me all week and now he's mad at me?

"Come on, Madison. Let's go," Adam calls to her sternly, his eyes fixed on me.

"But Dad, you said I could play on the jungle gym!" she protests, her big eyes revealing her disappointment.

"No. We need to go. We'll come back later for your brother."

"Daddy, you didn't even say hi to my teacher." Madison pulls on my hand dragging me toward her father.

"Hi," I squeak and offer a smile.

With his jaw still ticking, Adams greets me stiffly. "Miss Delaney." His dark eyes bore into mine. I'm not sure how to read him. He's obviously upset with me about something.

Shane walks over to us and says that he's got to get back to practice, but that he'll call me so we can make some plans.

Madison begs her father to let her go play in the playground for a few minutes, and he reluctantly agrees. We stand there awkwardly watching his daughter run off, neither one of us says a word, but our eyes speak volumes.

"So, you're going to go out with him?" Adam stares straight ahead watching Luke practice. Anyone looking at us would never suspect his question.

"What?" I turn to face him, confused by his question. He has the most beautiful profile and his jaw only covered by a light scruff. He looks good enough to eat.

"Isn't he the guy from the pizza place? You're going to go out with him?"

My eyes roll involuntarily and quite dramatically. *What business of his is it what I do and whom I do it with? Why the hell does he care what I do?*

"You're with him?" He continues badgering me with stupid questions.

"Not that it's any of your business, but no, I'm not with him. I'm not with anybody," I answer, swallowing back my emotion.

"What's that supposed to mean?" he snaps, finally turning to face me with serious eyes. His phone buzzes signaling an incoming text or email.

I turn to face him and meet his angry glare. "Just what I said. I'm not with anybody."

"You're with me!" His words come out through gritted teeth. He reaches into his pocket and responds quickly with a text. I know I shouldn't care, but I'm curious so I glance at his phone and see the name Nora. Nora? How can he say I'm with him when he's clearly with her? Maybe they're lovers? Irrational jealousy surges through me at the thought.

I laugh out loud bitterly. "The hell I am! You never even texted me! You barely look at me when I see you at school!" I'm pissed now so the words fly out of my mouth. "So no, my friend, I am *not* with you!" I know I'm a little naïve when it comes to drama-free sex, but I never expected Adam to think that I was with him. Does that mean that we're exclusive? Are redhead and blonde out of the picture? What about "Nora"? I guess deep down inside, I "hoped" that we could be exclusive, but a man like Adam doesn't exactly have monogamy written on him.

"This is how we said it had to be. Keep things on the DL?" he retorts, answering between gritted teeth.

"Keeping things on the DL and treating me like a cheap whore are two different things!" My emotions are beginning to surface and I know I need to get out of here.

Adam's body whips around completely facing me. "What are you talking about? I didn't treat you like a whore! I would never do that!" He adds, "Not to you." His hand moves as if he's reaching for my face and either realization of where we are or he just changes his mind, because he pulls back and lowers his hand.

Oh, man! I can feel the tears start to surface, filling my eyes.

"Whatever. I have to go." I turn to leave, but his hand reaches out and grasps my forearm. "Mia, I would NEVER do that to you," he whispers.

"Yeah, well, too late. You already did." I shrug out of his grasp.

I'm so angry with myself for getting involved with him. Regret surfaces immediately. He has heartbreak written all over him. I don't think...no, I *know*, my heart can't handle that. The tender stitches mending my heart are already stretched thin. I should walk away. I should just leave, but I don't. He's like a magnet holding me in place.

Shane and Luke walk over to us as practice ends. "Dad, did you see that catch I made?" The little boy who is a carbon copy of his father looks up hopefully.

"I'm sorry, buddy. I didn't see it. I'll get the next one." Adam reaches down and tousles the young boy's short hair. Luke asks if he can join his sister and runs off to play.

"Hey, you okay?" Shane asks when he notices my flushed cheeks and glassy eyes. "Yeah, I'm good. There was something in my eye, but I got rid of it. I think it's out." I smile and flick my glance quickly at Adam. I swear he just growled deep within his chest.

"Let me drive you home," Shane offers kindly. "We could grab a bite to eat or go through a drive thru since you have Brady and hang out at the lake. It's been forever since I've been there. Whatever you want—it's up to you." Shane's blue eyes beg for any sign that I'll accept his offer. I wish I could, but I can't.

Although I don't look at Adam, I could feel the holes he's drilling in my head like he's about to explode at any moment.

"That's sweet, Shane. But I'm good, really. Thank you for the offer." I step forward and give him a quick hug before he turns and walks away. *Yes, I'm being a jerk! But right now, I'm mad and Adam deserves it.*

Maddie and Luke bring Brady over to us. "Dad, can we get a dog? Please? C'mon, Dad, please? You said maybe when we turn seven and our birthday is coming up..." They gang up on their father who just rolls his eyes with mock amusement and says no.

I try to appease them by telling them that they're more than welcome to play with Brady if I see them again at the park. Everybody seems happy—crisis averted.

I say goodbye to Luke and Maddie quickly while avoiding their father's gaze. I walk with Brady towards the park exit where the sun is setting, painting a gorgeous pink and purple sky. I look back to see Adam staring at me while his kids climb into the back of his black Escalade.

I KNOW THAT I WON'T SEE HIM AGAIN UNTIL FRIDAY because the Wicked Witch picks up his children every Thursday to take the girls to dance class. The day goes by rather quickly as I get ready to greet a roomful of parents interested in their children's progress and to meet the teacher. Adam is the only parent who does not show up for "Meet the Teacher" night. Why should he, really? He already knows all he needs to know about me. He knows the teacher better than anyone, even better than he should. What really pisses me off is that even though I know he has said he works late on Thursdays, his children and their education should be priority— at least, it would be for me.

After conferences wrap up for the night, Shelby and I head out for a quick dinner and drinks. I glance down at my phone when I get a text alert. Sure enough, he decides to text me now after I haven't heard from him all week.

> AL: Can I see you tonight?
>
> Me: Hello to you too.
>
> AL: Sorry. Hi.
>
> AL: So can I see you?
>
> Me: I don't think so. I'm not going to be home for a while.
>
> AL: Why?

Me: Because I'm not home.

AL: Where are you?

Me: At a bar...with Shelby.

AL: Who's Shelby?

Me: Your son's teacher.

AL: Ohhh, Mrs. Matthews. Got it. Anyone else there?

For wanting to keep things casual, he sure does have some jealousy issues. I'm going to have fun with this.

Me: Yes. Tons of people.

AL: Who? It better not be Shane.

Me: Wouldn't you like to know!

AL: Not funny! Tell me where you are. I'll meet you.

Me: No.

Shelby asks about the "take that" grin I'm wearing as I text, but I just shake my head and laugh.

AL: You're wasting time!

Me: Excuse me? I'm wasting your time? Sorry about that!

AL: No. You're wasting time that I could be buried deep in you making you scream my name as you come.

I feel moisture pool between my legs with his simple promise.

Me: Tempting as that is, I'm going to have to pass.

AL: Pass? Are you serious?

Me: Very.

AL: Are you upset with me?

Me: Nope. Not at all.

AL: Why won't you see me then?

Me: Because I'm out to dinner, trying to enjoy my company.

AL: You don't want to enjoy my company?

Me: Oh, I've enjoyed your company all right.

Me: Food's here. Gotta go. Night.

Chapter Eighteen

OUR TREK UP TO GILLETTE STADIUM IN FOXBORO TO watch our beloved Patriots play is always a good time. Days like this are when I miss my dad the most. He was a lover of the game of football, but he was a diehard New England Patriots fan. I remember Sunday afternoons sitting on the flowered couch with my dad and Josh, each of us wearing our Pats gear from head to toe. It's where I learned the game and fell in love with it. While some girls loved football for the tight pants and cute players, I was all about the game. The tight pants and cute players were definitely an added bonus, though.

We didn't have much money growing up so when my dad won money from a two dollar scratch off ticket, he purchased Patriots season tickets for our family of four. Instead of watching the game on the couch, we sat in the nosebleed section and cheered. Since Josh moved away to Texas, I get to go to all the home games. If the team makes the playoffs, he flies up and we go together. It's a win-win for everyone.

A few years ago, when the team moved to a new stadium, I was able to upgrade our tickets to the 50 yard line. Needless to say, I made a lot more friends with that. But it's always the same group of close friends: Pete, Shelby, Mike, Shane and me. Pete and Shane sometimes had to compete for the fourth ticket.

Since Adam has his kids this weekend, we text back and forth sharing little details, building anticipation for the next time we see each other. To say he wasn't thrilled that I didn't give in and let him come over Thursday was an understatement. Adam Lawson isn't a man who usually asks for things. Women are probably wrapped up nicely with a pretty bow, willingly offering themselves to be taken. I have been alone for a long time, counting on no one but myself. I'm not about to fall to the ground and worship at his feet. I might fall to my knees on the kitchen floor and worship something else, but you get my point.

The time I see him at work is brief. A spoken, cordial "hello" can be heard, but silent, lustful promises are made with our eyes. We text a lot—sometimes it's during the day and I have to remind him that I'm supposed to be teaching. Other times it's late at night when I'm relaxing with Brady.

I text him from the game, telling him where my seats are, and suggest that he should look for me on TV. My eyes blink in confusion when one of his texts included a selfie of him and the kids watching the Pats game on his gigantic, plasma TV. I was thrilled that he did that; he did what he always said he wouldn't. He combined his kids and his flavor of the month which happens to be me at the moment. Granted it was only in a picture, but still, it made me smile, causing my heart to get all warm and fuzzy. Stupid heart.

His response floored me because not only did the picture stir my heart, but his words that accompanied the text brought tears to my eyes. "I would find you anywhere. You stand above the rest."

Pete harasses me about texting my lover boy during the game, insisting that I put my phone away or he'd take it and hide in down his pants. Ewww, that's just gross, but knowing Pete, he wouldn't be turned on by *my* hands in his pants. I smile at Pete as I do what he's asked, but then a probing feeling comes over me as I think about his words—"You stand above the rest." The rest? What does that mean? The rest of his women? The rest of the crowd? I'll have to sneak up to the bathroom during half time so I can ask Adam what he meant.

It's pretty late by the time I arrive home that night and I'm exhausted. Tailgating, beer, and cheering make for a grueling day. After I walk over to get Brady back, I thank Mrs. Longo for keeping him for the day. I hand her an envelope with cash, which she refuses, as usual. I make a mental note to bake her some cheesecake brownies this week instead. Or maybe I'll pick up one of the newest erotica novels for her. She often mentions that although Mr. Longo is well beyond his years, he's still a young man at heart. I wouldn't want to give the ol' boy a heart attack or anything.

After showering quickly, I climb into bed and plug my phone in to charge on my nightstand. The battery died before I had a chance to text Adam back and ask him what he meant. Unfortunately, no one had a car charger. How we managed to travel out of state without a phone charger is beside me. Not that it mattered really since I pretty much passed out in the back seat next to Pete. The combination of drinking and not sleeping well is a lethal combination for me. This girl needs a solid eight hours of rest.

Holy shit! 14 text messages, 8 missed calls, and 4 voicemail messages. With the exception of one call from Mrs. Longo, one text from Shane and two from my brother, every other message was from Adam. Wow! I'm not really sure how I feel at the moment. I read all his text messages which varied from casual, "Your boy, Brady, is kicking some ass!" to "Where'd you go?" to pissed off "Why aren't you answering me???" His voicemails were of the same tone: casual to concerned to angry. He said he was about to call around to get Shelby's number just to make sure that I was alright.

The time on my digital clock reads 12:46. It's really too late to call him so I decided to send a quick text letting him know that I'm home and that we'll talk tomorrow. Within two seconds of hitting "send," my phone rings and the name AL appears on the screen. I answer immediately, wondering why he didn't just text me back. I wasn't prepared for his response.

"Mia! My God! What the hell happened to you?" His voice booms through the phone, causing me to wince and pull the phone away from my ear. It takes me a few seconds to respond. "Are you alright?" He fires away with another question.

"Hi," I stammer. "Adam, I'm fine," I add quickly, yawning loudly into the phone.

I can hear him exhale loudly on the other end of the phone. I can only imagine how his body must look, tense and hard.

"Are *you* okay?" I ask because I'm really puzzled by his reaction.

"I'm fine. Now." I can hear a sense relief in his words as he exhales loudly.

What I thought was going to be a quick conversation of hushed "good nights" turns into a detailed play by play of my day at the game and how my phone died. With each word of my explanation, I can tell that I've put his mind at ease, but I'm left wondering why he was so upset. What's the big deal anyway?

IT'S ONLY MONDAY AND I'M ALREADY LONGING FOR THE weekend. I want nothing more than to crawl back into bed and sleep. Adam's early morning texts were bright and cheery, wishing me a good day or telling me that he can't wait to see me again.

After lunch I ask my class to write a journal entry about something fun they did over the weekend. When I read Madison's, I literally have to sit back and take a breather. With her neat, primary handwriting, she writes about going to the movies and out for pizza with Daddy, Luke, Sophie and Gina. Well, isn't that nice? What a happy fucking little family outing. Adam did tell me that he was taking the kids to a movie, but he never mentioned having extra company. What's the deal here? Am I being completely naïve in thinking that I'm the only person he's sleeping with? A man like Adam doesn't do monogamy, I'm sure. I know this and yet it's so hard to walk away. It's like taking a hit of a toxic drug and getting addicted after the first time. I know it's bad for me, but I want more. I think I might need Adam-rehab.

By the end of the day, I'm anxious and antsy. I probably shouldn't have had that third cup of coffee. I watch as Adam holds the door for Gina, ushering her into the building. My green-eyed monster rears her ugly face, watching them talk together as they wait at the end of line. Adam listens intently to whatever she's saying, but his eyes always find mine.

When Gina signs her name, she looks at me with disdain, and then steps aside so Adam can sign for his children. She waits for him to finish.

"Good afternoon, Miss Delaney," he says and smiles.

"Mr. Lawson," I answer plainly, causing his brow to furrow.

"All set?" Gina chimes in, stepping closer to his side.

I want to jump over the table and bitch slap her.

"Gina, you know Miss Delaney, don't you?" Adam asks, diverting his attention between the two of us.

Blue eyes glare at me. "Yes, I know exactly who she is."

"I thought you might since you're both from here," he adds.

"We went to school together." Gina's voice feigns interest, but I know better. I wonder if she's trying to figure out how he knows that I'm from here. Where your daughter's teacher is from isn't exactly common knowledge, now, is it? Or is she trying to dodge the inevitable bullet that will show him what a bitch she is by downplaying our relationship.

"I bet you two would have a lot in common, funny stories to tell, huh?"

Oh, beautiful, sexy Adam, please shut the fuck up! You have no idea what you're saying or the wounds that you're reopening.

I finally speak, "You could say that again. We did have a lot in common, didn't we?"

Gina's eyes narrow at me.

Needing this brief encounter over, I call the kids over to their waiting parents.

Maddie and Luke jump into Adam's arms, each receiving a kiss on the top of their head. Sophie, with her big green eyes, stands beside her mother who is now talking on the phone, and watches longingly at this display of affection.

I watch all five of them leave together like one big happy fucking family.

Chapter Nineteen

BY THURSDAY NIGHT, I AM DESPERATE. I NEED ADAM TO release my tension—I need him in my bed. He responds quickly to my invitation to come over after work.

About an hour later, Adam pulls into my driveway quietly, the purr of his SUV barely heard unlike his car. He knocks lightly at the back door before walking straight in like he's done it a million times. His eyes find me immediately and they are serious, filled with lust for me. I am drawn to him like I've never been drawn to anyone in my life. He will consume me, of this I am sure.

His arms wrap around my body, pulling me flush against him, his hands pull my hair free, letting it fall over my shoulders. Through his beautifully tailored dark pants, I can feel his length harden and twitch. My lips are crushed against his, our tongues begin an erotic dance around and around, tasting, desperately savoring one another. My fingers work quickly to unbutton his shirt and then pants, just low enough for him to spring free. Our lips separate for a split second while he lifts my burgundy shift dress over my head, dropping it to the floor as he walks me backwards to the living room where the sofa welcomes us. The telltale sound of crinkling lets me know what's about to happen.

He enters me forcibly, pounding into me without apology. It's what we both want. It's what we both need. I yank his wavy hair with one hand, pulling him in closer, while I use my other hand to rake my nails down his back. I know those marks will take a day or two to heal just as my body will need some time to recuperate from this. God, he feels so good. With the perfect angle, he gives me a much needed release before thrusting one last time and finding his own.

"Hi there." I smile when he pulls his face from my neck.

"Hi." He grins back.

"Thank you for that." I lean up to kiss his neck.

His eyes search mine, and he smiles. "Thank *you*. Thank you for saying yes."

"And how was your day, Mr. Lawson?"

"Busy. I've got so many things going on right now, it's hard to see straight. Hopefully some things will be over sooner rather than later," he responds seriously. Some things? I hope what we're doing doesn't qualify as "some things."

Our conversation is comfortable, although the weight of his body on mine is not. "Did you eat dinner?" I ask, guessing that he didn't since it is still dinnertime.

"Actually, I haven't. Are you going to feed me?" He growls into my ear. "My appetite is insatiable, you know."

"So it seems."

"I could whip something up. I don't mind," I suggest carefully. I'm not really sure if having dinner together would be appropriate for our "friends with benefits" package. Maybe I'll need to apply for an upgrade soon.

"Really? You'd cook for me?" He's surprised by my offer.

Between my legs, I feel him soften and slip out of me. "Sure, why not? I wouldn't want you to wither away or anything." I smirk.

Almost immediately, I'm flipped over onto my front, my face planted on the couch cushion while my ass is yanked into the air. I feel his weight shift briefly when he moves to retrieve something. I hear another crinkle.

"I'll give you wither away," his voice, deep and sexy, fills with amusement as he begins round two, taking me hard from behind.

I STAND AT MY STOVE, SAUTÉING GARLIC AND ONION IN olive oil, tossing in some sun-dried tomatoes, fresh basil and grilled chicken to serve over linguine. Before sitting down at the island to eat, Adam sets out our dishes and silverware, choosing a chilled Riesling from the fridge.

Glancing back at him, I notice he's on his phone texting. Gone is the relaxed, satiated Adam replaced by a serious man, looking contemplative.

"Is everything okay?" I ask, spooning pasta onto his dish and then mine.

Adam clears his throat. "Yeah, it will be."

I can't help but feel that things aren't exactly "okay" with Adam. For a man in his early thirties, he's got a lot going on. How do I know his age? Oh, I may or may not have looked at Madison's file in the office.

Adam raises his glass of wine, turning to look at me. "Here's to not letting things wither away." That smirk appears accompanied by a wink.

"Cheers." I grin, bringing the glass to my lips, sipping slowly.

"Do you have any plans for Saturday?" Adam asks hesitantly, while spooning a second helping of pasta.

"I'm not sure, really. I guess I don't have any specific plans. Why?" I'm curious.

He stares at his plate of food pensively and then tells me that he has to go into the city to look at some properties and asks if I'd like to join him for the day.

I eye him suspiciously. "Are you serious?"

"I am." He nods in approval.

The package upgrade must have been approved during dinner because we would be in public together not engaging in any kind of sex. I'd be foolish not to be skeptical.

Oh God, the last time I was in the city, I was with Kate at the club and she abandoned me. I punched Devin in the face for manhandling me and Adam was mean to me, warning me away, telling me never to return. I'll have to ask him about that sometime.

"Are you going to the city for business or for pleasure?" I ask as I clear our empty plates and wash them quickly, wondering if he understands my implication about going to the club for pleasure. I can't imagine him wanting to take me there after he warned me away.

"Well, that depends. If you come with me, it'll be both. If you choose not to come, it'll only be business."

That little bit of information makes me sigh in relief. No Mia equals no club.

"What will I do while you're working?"

"You'll be right beside me," he answers as though it's common knowledge that I would be with him.

"I'd have to make arrangements for Brady, but I guess I can go."

"You *guess you can go?*" An arched eyebrow raises, his hand clutching at his chest in mock horror. "You don't want to spend time with me?" All humor is erased from his face. He's completely serious.

"That's not it!" I roll my eyes. "I just didn't think we'd be spending any time together...you know...apart from when we're having sex." My face turns bright red with embarrassment at having to say those words out loud. It's one thing to do it; it's another to talk about it.

"I happen to like spending time *with* you as well as *in* you." He tucks my hair behind my ear and leans in for a kiss.

"Okay, I'll go." The butterflies reappear in my stomach, doing an intricate dance, fluttering every which way. My heart pokes her head out for a moment, before my brain shoos her away.

I SPEND ALL DAY FRIDAY THINKING ABOUT OUR TRIP TO

the city. I'm excited about spending the day with him. I wonder if he'll hold my hand or kiss me senseless on the busy sidewalks. We've never been on a date other than dinner. I guess that makes sense because we're not dating; we're just having sex. I need to be careful and not mix things up. My fragile heart is on alert.

Early Saturday morning, I'm dressed and ready to go when my phone alerts me of a text.

AL: Something's come up. I have to cancel. I'm sorry. Call you later.

He never called.

Chapter Twenty

I DIDN'T CONTACT ADAM NOR DID HE CONTACT ME. When I see him at dismissal time, I treat him like any other parent. He receives a cordial greeting, a simple smile, and his children. That is all.

I spent a lot of time on Sunday thinking about how I should handle this. I knew better than to get excited—Adam had made his intentions clear from the very beginning. Why he asked me to go with him into the city is something I can't figure out. That's not something fuck buddies do. Part of me, the emotional side, wanted to call him out on what he did, but then I would appear as some whiny, needy chick. The intelligent part of me told me not to worry about it...it is what it is. Brain scolded Heart for getting her hopes up—she knew what we were getting into when I agreed to sleep with Adam Lawson.

I run harder and longer every day all week, morning and night. Wednesday afternoon when I see Shane at the park for football practice, I wave a quick hello but ignore his hand gestures to call him. I know Adam is nearby, I can feel him. My eyes dart around, looking for any sign of him or his kids. Luke is on the field with the other boys, but Adam and Maddie aren't here. I turn up the volume on my iPhone, blasting Fall Out Boys in my ear, urging me to pick up the pace as I trek toward the "expert" trail.

Panting heavily, I lean over, trying to catch my breath when I sense a figure approaching me. I don't have to look to know it's

Adam. The tingling in my body tells me it's him. I straighten myself, remove my earbuds and readjust my ponytail before meeting his eyes.

"Hi," he mumbles, walking over to close the space between us.

Play it cool, Mia. Say hello like it's no big deal. Do not let him see how he affects you.

"Hey, what's up?" I say casually trying to hide my nerves.

Adam's eyes narrow, assessing my reaction or lack thereof to his greeting.

"I've been waiting for you." He looks at me seriously.

"Really? Why?" I ask, puzzled.

"I needed to see you."

"Uh, you see me every day, Adam." I chuckle, nervously.

He says nothing while searching my face.

"I needed to see you to explain myself."

I look down and kick the dirt under my feet. "No explanation needed. It's all good."

"Mia..." he pleads, reaching out to touch me. "You're upset. I can tell. Please let me explain."

"Seriously, Adam. It's no big deal," I say, trying to convince both of us before stepping back away from him. The hammering of my heart gets louder. I want to scream, *Is this some sick game? Reel me in and then cast me back out?*

"Damn," I say as I realize that I left my water bottle at home.

"Here. Drink." He holds up his own bottle of water, offering it to me after he takes a quick drink.

"No. I'm fine. Thanks." I decline his offer. My body kicks into overdrive when his tongue darts out and licks the moisture from his lips. *God, that tongue and those lips have been everywhere on me.* A quiet, wanton sigh escapes me.

"Take it," he insists.

I unscrew the bottle and raise it to my lips and drink. And drink. And drink until it's all gone. "Ahhhh, that's so good," I smirk.

"Thanks."

Adam snorts and chuckles when I hand back the empty bottle.

The familiar sound of his phone interrupts us. He reaches into the pocket of his running shorts, grimaces and responds to the text.

"Can I see you tomorrow?" He looks at me with uncertainty.

"Actually, I'm not going to be around tomorrow night." I lie.

"Oh, okay," he answers dejectedly. "I have my kids this weekend so I probably won't get to see you."

"No worries. Like I said before, it's all good."

"What the fuck! This fucking phone," Adam mutters with annoyance before swiping his finger to take a call. "Hey," he answers.

"Fucking phone" is an understatement. At least he and I are on the same page about the constant interruptions by his phone. I listen intently as he continues his conversation. "Yeah, I'm almost done. No, you don't have to come over. I'll swing by your place after." He disconnects the call.

And now, ladies and gentlemen, making her appearance once again is...the green-eyed monster. I stand there, wondering who wants him to come over and whose house he'll be swinging by later. I swallow the lump in my throat. Then it dawns on me. This woman is probably the "something" that came up. God, I'm such a fool for thinking that he would want to actually spend time with me outside of the bedroom. Maybe she's prettier, thinner, or sexier. Maybe she's got exceptional skills in the bedroom. It wouldn't be the first time I came in second place.

"Sorry about that."

"It's fine." I glance at my phone that's secured on my bicep, checking the time and see a text from Shane. Oh my God. He's relentless. I think I'm going to have to go the "bitch" route with him since he clearly doesn't get the hint. "I've gotta go."

Adam's eyes narrow when he sees Shane's name on my phone, but he doesn't say anything.

"I'll see you around." I turn away before starting the run downhill.

JUST BEFORE I CRAWL INTO BED, I GET A SIMPLE, THREE word text: "I won't share." Oh, Adam Lawson, what am I going to do with you?

Chapter Twenty-One

OVER THE NEXT WEEK, I SPEND AS MUCH TIME AS possible doing things outside. I cut the grass, wash my Jeep, and store the paddleboards in the garage. There's a chill in the air each morning—a sure sign that fall is upon us, needing to spread her colorful wings. At night, I read or bake and rearrange my closets and drawers, putting away summer clothes and pulling out my warm sweaters.

Adam and I text back and forth all week, but I don't see him much except for in the afternoons when he picks up his children from school. I miss him. My body misses him.

On Wednesday night, Pete and I grab a bite to eat before we drive over to hear his cousin's band play. The bar is packed and the music is loud. A few beers later and a full set by the band, Ryan and Will order drinks and sit with us. Will sits next to me, brushing his legs against mine.

"Hey, you! What'd ya think?" Will leans into my ear so I can hear him over the music.

I hit send as I respond to Adam's text and set my phone down. "It was great. You guys are really good!" I'm honest in my answer. They are good.

For the next hour, we drink and talk while I nonchalantly and discreetly text Adam. I yawn loudly. It's getting late and I need to head home, but Pete doesn't want to leave yet. He's mending a broken heart since his boyfriend has moved on to "bigger and better things." Yes, those were his *exact* words. Rat bastard!

As I say my goodbyes, I watch curiously as Will leans over and whispers something to Ryan. He turns to me and asks if I could give him a lift because he's got to get up early for work. I didn't realize that Will has lived in town for a few years—my mind has been a little preoccupied, I guess. They all stand up, do that weird guy handshake, half-hug thing before Will walks with me to my Jeep.

"You okay to drive?" Will asks.

"I'm fine. Didn't you notice I've been drinking water for the last three rounds?" I laugh, noting how glassy his eyes are.

"Well, that's good to know." He slams the door and buckles up.

"You're not going to throw up or anything, are you?" I look at him anxiously.

Will just laughs—he's got a nice laugh. He tells me about the band and their plans. I find out he works at an adult group home during the day.

I park alongside the curb when I reach his apartment, noticing that it's after midnight. I'm so going to pay for this tomorrow.

"Hey, thanks for the lift, Mia. I appreciate it." Will smiles and runs his hand through his hair.

"Yeah, no problem. It's on my way home anyway."

Will hesitates before opening the door. "Can I take you out sometime?" His question is met with silence.

"Um, wow," I whisper because I so did not see that one coming. Okay, well maybe I did a little. "Here's the thing, Will," I stammer, "I'm kind of seeing someone."

"You are?" He looks at me suspiciously.

"I am." I nod apologetically.

Will pushes the door open, turns around and leans back in to say, "Well, if it doesn't work out, you know where to find me."

Once I get home, I let Brady out and text Adam to let him know that I'm home safe and sound. I brush my teeth and crawl into bed, hoping that sleep will come soon, but Adam doesn't yield with his bombardment of texts—some sweet, others, not so much. Sleep does eventually find me with the lights still on and my phone in hand with unanswered messages from Adam.

AL: Glad you had a good time.

AL: Hey, where'd you go?

AL: Guess you fell asleep.

AL: Good night. Sweet dreams.

THURSDAY AFTERNOON, MRS. CHAPMAN, MY PRINCIPAL, calls me into her office, asking to speak to me. Oh, shit! I feel like a kid being called into the principal's office. That's something Josh was used to but not me. A million thoughts race through my mind about what she could possibly need to talk to me about. *It has to be something serious or else she would've left a note in my box or emailed me.* Panic starts its ascent through my body. *Maybe someone found out about Adam and me. Maybe I'm violating some Board of Education policy. I'll have to look at my contract to see if it says anything about sleeping with parents of students in your class.* I can't imagine that a school can dictate what their staff does or doesn't do, but you just don't know anymore. I've heard about people getting fired over Facebook posts.

"Come in Mia. Please, have a seat." I walk hesitantly into her office and sit in one of the two upholstered chairs across from her desk. I wait for her to speak. She reaches into her file cabinet and pulls out a manila folder, placing it on the desk between us. Her soft, curly grey hair does little to hide the seriousness of her face as she sits there in her navy-striped polyester pantsuit. Her beady eyes watch me.

"So, how are things going, Mia?" Her high-pitched voice asks, laced with concern.

The phone on her desk rings. She raises her long index finger, smiles tightly and then answers the call quickly. I listen patiently as she answers some questions and then disconnects the call.

Before I can respond, she smiles, her demeanor changing, and says, "You seem to be in a good place this year." Mrs. Chapman, like many of my colleagues, knows that I dealt with some serious shit years ago. They don't know the extent of it, but I know that people talk. It is a small town, after all.

"I'm good. Thank you." My eyes are glued to the folder, wondering what its contents may reveal. My blood pressure is through the roof.

"Well, I'm happy to hear that."

I smile waiting for the bad news to hit me.

"There is something I'd like to talk to you about." She fingers the folder.

"Okay..." My heart starts to beat even faster. I feel a bead of sweat form above my right eyebrow. Am I about to be busted? Teaching is everything I have; it's who I am. I can't lose my job. I can only imagine the rumors that are sure to swirl around town once I'm unemployed. It will be unbearable.

"I know you were out of sorts last spring and I don't need to know the details. I also know you've got a lot on your plate with coaching and all, but I was wondering if you'd like to chair the Harvest Festival this year?"

Chair the Harvest Festival? Are you kidding me? That's what this is about? I'm not being fired? I haven't been outed about sleeping with Adam? A disbelieving laugh escapes my lips and earns me an odd look in the form of a raised eyebrow from the rail-thin woman sitting in her oversized leather chair.

"Well, I'm not quite sure yet if I'm going to be coaching this year, but I'd love to serve as chair. The kids love this event. Just tell me where to sign up." I smile, letting out the breath I was holding.

The folder is opened and a sheet of paper is slid across the desk, listing names of parents and faculty who've volunteered to help out with the event. There is contact information for vendors and volunteers. I scan the names quickly. My breathing hitches when I see Gina DeGennaro's name highlighted in fluorescent yellow.

"Actually, would you mind very much if I give it some thought?" I ask ruefully. "I've just started taking a class on-line and I don't know how demanding it will be." *What the hell is wrong with me? Why should I let this viper deter me from doing something I love?*

She eyes me suspiciously before looking down at the paper I hand back.

"Mia, what degree could you possibly be going for now? Don't you have two Master's degrees *and* a Sixth Year degree in Administration?

I shrug my shoulders and smile sheepishly at her words. She doesn't need to know that the only reason I kept pursuing degrees is my therapist told me to keep my mind busy. I was in a bad place, constantly living in the past and dealing with all the "what ifs."

"Sure. Can you let me know by tomorrow? I'd like to get things rolling as soon as possible."

I smile and turn to leave.

"By the way, I have that letter of recommendation for you, if you still need it."

"Okay, thank you." I don't know if I'll need it, but it's always a good idea to keep my options open. Who knows what the future holds.

THREE O'CLOCK SHARP.
"Hello, Miss Delaney."
"Hello, Mr. Lawson."

SIX THIRTY-THREE, ADAM PULLS INTO MY DRIVEWAY,

198 - L.M CARR

and saunters into the kitchen after a hard day at the office. I can't imagine what's so hard about an office job. It's not like he's teaching nineteen second graders all day.

"Hello, beautiful." His arms wrap around my waist, embracing me. "Do you have any idea how much I've missed you?" I pull back and eye him skeptically.

"Who are you and what have you done with Adam Lawson?" I grin, kissing him, inhaling his scent.

"He's right here, baby." His erection is pushed into my belly, causing me to squirm.

"I've missed you," I confess honestly. I have missed him. This constant roller coaster of emotions is exhausting.

"I made dinner. You hungry?" I nod towards the oven where chicken marsala simmers on low.

"I'm always hungry for you." Adam pulls my dress up, slips my panties off, lifts me up onto the island, and then slides the salad bowl out of the way as he proceeds to feast on me for an appetizer. What is it with this man and my kitchen, specifically, my island?

We sit side by side, rather than across from each other, while we enjoy our dinner which had to be warmed up for obvious reasons. I scold him when he feeds Brady scraps from the table. He asks about my week and tells me about his. We've become so comfortable with each other in such a short amount of time. The arrogant man I met at the park and the harsh man from the club are tucked away beneath this kind, gentle, sexy man beside me.

"Mmmmm." Adam bites into the homemade apple crisp, declaring it to be the best he's ever eaten in his entire life.

"Well, you know what they say, 'the best way to a man's heart is through his stomach.'" I laugh and then freeze, immediately realizing how that came out. *Oh crap! Why did I just say that?* He's probably thinking of any excuse to get up and leave, running as far away from me as he possibly can. I don't ever want to be that woman. You know the woman who *says* she's okay with casual sex, but is secretly hoping the guy will fall in love with her, get married and live happily ever after. I *definitely* don't want to be that woman. Brain smirks at Heart.

I sip my coffee quietly, praying for the awkwardness I've created to pass quickly.

Adam stops chewing, sets his fork down and looks at me. "Is that so?"

He wipes his mouth with the napkin, his eyes never straying from mine.

"Are you trying to get to my heart, Miss Delaney?" he asks seriously, although his eyes dance with amusement.

The cup is taken away from me and placed on the table, freeing my hands completely. The loud scraping noise from his chair as he moves closer makes me wince. Here it comes...the BIG goodbye, the inevitable "I don't have time or the inclination to date" speech to let me go, ending our arrangement.

"Come here. Sit with me." Adam pats his lap, tugging on my hands so I can shift from my chair to his.

"I'm sorry I said that. I was just trying to be funny." Ashamed and embarrassed, I hang my head and bury my face in the palm of my hands.

"Hey, look at me." Adam waits for me to look at him. "I asked you a question and I'm still waiting for an answer."

I wonder if he's enjoying this torment of seeing me humiliated. I might as well get this over with so I can go back to mending my fragile heart.

"Look, I know what we agreed to and I really am okay with it, but sometimes, I wonder what it would be like if we could be more." Why on Earth did I just blurt that out? I am such a damn fool! He starts to speak, but I put my finger up to his lips, silencing him. "Can we just forget about what I said? I don't want to ruin a good thing. I like spending time with you and I'm not ready for it to end just yet." I feel his lips move so I press harder. "If this is goodbye,

200 - L.M CARR

I'll understand. We'll keep things cordial at school and it'll be as if nothing ever happened. Okay?"

My hand is pulled down from his mouth. "Can I talk now?"

I nod.

"First of all, you still haven't answered my question. Are you trying to get to my heart?" His fingers trace a line down my jaw.

I wish at this moment that I knew what the right answer was. *Am I trying to get to his heart? No! Maybe? Yes*...God only knows he's already in my heart. When I began this "arrangement," I thought I could handle it, but truth be told, I don't think I can. I am without a doubt falling in love with Adam.

"I wasn't *trying* to do anything," I admit honestly.

"Secondly, I like spending time with you as well, but I'm not that happy anymore with our arrangement." His face is unreadable as he exhales a deep breath.

Here it comes...wait for it...wait for it. My body goes into defense mode, ready to bolt out the door.

"Lastly, I don't have any plans of saying goodbye or letting you go because whether you tried to or not, you have found your way into my heart."

Wait, what? He's not letting me go? He wants to keep me? But he's not happy with our arrangement, he said so himself. I have his heart? Holy shit! I want to scream out loud.

Adam gently cradles my face between his hands and kisses me reverently, treating me as something pure and precious. As our tongues begin their slow waltz, hands join in, caressing each other, slowly removing any and all obstacles in our way except his dress pants. The half-eaten dessert abandoned because now we are only hungry for one another.

I wrap my legs around his slim waist as he carries me quickly up the stairs into my bedroom, wishing that I had finished the task of putting away my summer clothes which are still strewn all over my unmade, rumpled bed. "I'll never have enough. I'll never let you go,"

Adam's murmured words of promise and desire invade my ears as he kisses along my throat, sucking and tasting.

Chapter Twenty-Two

FOR THE FIRST TIME, ADAM AND I MAKE LOVE. IT IS more than just "drama free sex" more than a casual encounter. This union is a display of a deeper emotional connection—the joining of his heart with mine. Adam knows my body, my wants, and my needs. His weight on me, his body stretched out against mine is a warm, welcomed blanket in the dead of winter. My hands fist his wavy hair, my eyes memorize the features and angles of his beautiful face while my legs wrap tightly around his body. I need to feel as if we are one. His thrusts are slow and deliberate—he's giving all he can to me until there is no more to give.

Sated and weary, I snuggle into the crook of his neck and smile, finding it to be a tiny piece of Heaven on Earth. I inhale his scent. It's unique, all Adam. It's the perfect combination of strong masculinity mixed with a hint of earthy cologne. If I could bottle it up, I would. Our labored breathing and pounding hearts resume their natural rhythm, slowing down after we both achieve release.

And then his phone chirps. I reach down to the floor on my side of the bed to retrieve his phone, handing it to him quickly, but not before I see the name. Adam catches my eye roll, smirks and leans over to kiss my forehead. My eyes roll again. As much as I don't want to bring up the subject, I know that I have to. It's an absolute deal breaker. I need to find out the basis of their relationship and I need to know why Gina calls him constantly.

I watch as he responds quickly to the text, setting the phone down on my nightstand.

"Can I ask you something?" I ask as I prop myself up on an elbow, tracing circles between his chest hair.

"Of course," he replies sweetly.

"I asked you once about her and, for the most part, I believe you." I swallow loudly. "Why is she always, and I mean like *always*, calling or texting you?" I know sound like a jealous person, but what she did to me was unforgivable and I will never trust her. "She could be a problem for me, Adam."

Adam pulls me across his chest, our faces inches apart, and then pushes back my wild hair. "Miss Delaney, are you a bit jealous?" He grins.

Yes! No! "Maybe. A little."

He kisses my lips. "There is no reason to be jealous. I want you. Only you."

"Okay, but can you explain all the calls and text messages? Even you have to admit, it's incessant." I raise my eyebrows to prove my point.

Adam searches my face, perhaps deciding how to best answer my questions. "I agree with you she does call me a lot and it can be annoying, but it's not like I can just cut her off entirely. She's helped me through a lot and she's great with my kids." She helped him through a lot? What in the world could Gina have possibly helped him out with? "She's like family."

Oh, for the love of God, go figure. I get involved with someone who's involved with her. His next whispered words send chills down my spine. "I've been part of that family for a long time. They were there for me when no one else was. I owe them a lot." I swallow hard. The DeGennaros are not a family you want to owe anything to.

"Are there any other women that I need to be aware of?" Immediately I think of the redhead from the club and the blonde from the bar.

"No." He shakes his head quickly. "It's just you."

"How about you? Are there any guys who need an ass kicking?" Dark eyes narrow playfully. "I know I'm just one of your many suitors."

I laugh at his response. "Suitors? What are you like 75? "

"Nope...31. And don't change the subject." His hand reaches down and squeezes my ass, admonishing me.

"I, unlike, you don't have a horde of people vying for my attention."

"What? Are you insane? Let's see...there's Peter." He looks up like he's doing a challenging math problem. "There's what's his name, the coach, Shane...that lanky, tatted dude from the band, Will...give me a minute, I'm sure I can think of some more."

He's been paying attention and he's pretty much on target except for Pete. Thank God he doesn't know about Luis, Max, or Devin. But come to think about it, we can cross Devin's name off the list—he didn't want to date me, he just wanted to fuck me.

"Oh, and don't you notice all the other dads checking you out when you're at the park running?" He continues on, shaking his head.

"You are the insane one." I lean down to kiss him. "Besides, the only *dad* I'm interested in is you!"

Adam tenses immediately beneath me, apprehension mars his face.

Did I say the wrong thing? Maybe I shouldn't have brought up the fact that he has children.

"I wish we had met at a different time or place. Things could be different. If I didn't have kids...""

I cut his words off immediately as if he'd spoken blasphemy. "Oh my God! Don't ever say that!"

Confusion spreads across his face, trying to gauge my reaction. "Mia, I love my kids. Don't get me wrong—those kids are my entire world, but I'm more than just their father." He continues, "But it's not about me. They are my priority and I would never allow anything or anyone to hurt them again."

"I would never hurt them," I whisper.

Adam pushes back and pulls me to straddle him. He looks at me with those incredible eyes like I'm the most beautiful thing he's ever seen. His thumbs circle my face, my lips, and my eyes slowly before pulling my face down to kiss me.

"I know you would never hurt them...intentionally." He smiles warily. "Unlike their mother," he whispers so quietly I'm not sure I heard him correctly. Their mother hurt them? I wonder if she had been abusive toward them. My heart breaks just thinking about the day Madison proudly displayed her mother's tattered ballet slippers. It was obvious that Madison loved her mother, how and why would she hurt her children? A mother is supposed to love and protect her children, not harm them.

"Adam, I'm so sorry," I sigh.

Adam's eyes close and he inhales and exhales. Silence fills the room, time ticks on slowly.

"I never thought I'd say this, but I love spending time with you." He searches my face, his words reaching deep into my heart. "I want to spend time with you and not just in your bed. I want to take you places and do things with you. I want to enjoy your company as well as your body." His eyebrows waggle playfully. "This is what I can give you, Mia. You know my time is limited, but if you're willing to wait and work around my life, I want to see where this goes. I'm not making any promises, though." His hands stray to run the length of my hair covering my naked breasts. The smile on my face widens and then falls at his last comment. He's not making any promises. What's that supposed to mean?

"I'd like that very much," I kiss his lips, answering honestly.

"I told you once that I won't share you. I meant that. I don't want you hanging around Shane or Will. They want what's mine."

Ohhhhh, so I'm his, am I? So then that would make him mine?

I narrow my eyes and smirk. "One might say that sounds a little bit like a relationship." My words hang in the air, waiting for his response. "You know the whole, 'you're mine' thing," I air quote. "You think I'm yours, huh? So, I guess that would make you mine, then?" I smirk, my eyebrows expecting an answer. *So what about all the late night texts?*

His face is still, displaying no emotion or expression. Finally, a small twitch of his lip gives way to a grin. "Absolutely. You have as much of me as I'm able to give you."

And...his phones chirps, interrupting us. AGAIN! I have never felt such animosity toward an inanimate object. I literally want to take a sledgehammer to it.

We both reach over to the nightstand to retrieve his phone. There is no need for words as I smirk seeing the name "Nora" and hand him the phone. A surge of heat shoots through my body. I recognize this feeling. It's anxiety. Wordlessly, he takes his phone out of my hand, enters the password, his eyes flashing back to mine, waiting for me to speak. I chew the inside of my cheek so I don't say something I'll regret. My chest rises and falls as I take a deep cleansing breath and start to climb off of his lap, but his hand reaches out, holding me in place by my thighs. Two seconds ago, I was riding high on cloud nine and I've just crashed landed without warning.

"I won't share either," I say, reminding him of his words earlier. He simply nods and taps out a quick response, then sets the phone down on the bed. I would love to know what he's thinking at this moment as he stares at me, his eyes blinking thoughtfully until he slaps my ass twice lightly so he can get up.

The music streaming through the BOSE fills the room with Adam Levine singing about never wanting to leave this bed.

I grab the fitted sheet and wrap myself up as he gathers his pants, redressing quickly, shoving his phone back in his pocket. I know he has to go and I know he's doing the best he can. But it still sucks! I wonder briefly what it would be like to make dinner for him, tuck his kids in at night and then crawl into bed with him beside me. A "slap, punch, slap" combo snaps my brain back to reality for even allowing those thoughts to form in my mind.

"It's getting late," he says quietly, walking toward the bedroom door. "I need to get the kids home and into bed. Gina's got an early morning meeting."

"Gina? What's she got to do with anything?" My voice sings like a soprano.

"My kids are at her place. Every Thursday. I told you she helps me out a lot." He looks at me as if we've already clarified this. *Hmmm...I wonder what else she's helped him out with. Stupid slut!*

"Ohhh...that's right. You did mention that." I smile and carefully walk down the stairs, wrapped up in my toga like a Greek goddess. "It's okay that you came over for a 'slam, bam, thank you ma'am.'" I tease and wink, walking into the kitchen.

"What? You know it's not like that." Anger seeps through his voice. "It's not like that with you," he says quietly, hugging me tightly.

"You've got to lighten up, babe. I'm just kidding." Untangling my arms from the warmth of his cocoon, I smooth down his shirt over his chest.

"If I could stay here, you know I would. Tonight was perfect." Adam wraps his arms around me again, burying his nose in my hair, inhaling deeply.

Tender, chaste kisses are shared between us. My eyelids grow heavy and close as his little pecks trail all around my face, down my neck, and finally back to my mouth. If we don't stop now, he'll never leave. He'll have his way with me right here.

"Adam," I pant, pushing him back just far enough so I can see his eyes. "You need to go." I reach up and smooth the lines of his face before giving him one last kiss. His throat bobs as he swallows hard, his head nodding in agreement. "You're right. I do."

I don't want him to leave with a look of melancholy written across his face. My hands fist his hair, and I kiss his mouth feverishly, ravishing him so he'll have something to look forward to. "Let's call that a little preview of what's to come when I see you again. Will I see you this weekend?"

He nods his response, tossing his head back laughing. "Is that supposed to make me want to leave or stay because you're not helping." His bulge is pushed into my belly, making me second guess my choice. "Go!" I open the back door and watch him slide into the driver's seat of his SUV.

Chapter Twenty-Three

Early the next morning, I get a text from Shelby telling me that she's heading into work early and that she's picking up coffee for us. She walks into my room, carrying two cups of coffee and sits on my reading table. The look on her face is one of apprehension and she looks a little green, too. I take the piping hot coffee from her, but she quickly grabs it back. I don't see what the big deal is because we take our coffee the same way.

"Sorry, I gave you the wrong one." She looks at the side of the Styrofoam cup labeled "Decaf" and smiles sheepishly.

"Okay..." I eye her suspiciously, knowing something is off with her. "What's up with you?"

She blows on her coffee and hesitates before speaking. My anxiety shoots to an unusually high level, wondering what could possibly be wrong. She's a newlywed with a husband who is absolutely, positively, madly in love with her. How bad could things be?

"Shel, you're making me nervous here. Tell me," I demand.

"Promise me you won't be mad."

"Oh shit, it's that bad?" I ask, hoping she didn't do something stupid.

"I'm pregnant," she mutters the words so quietly, I'm not sure I hear her correctly.

"You're pregnant?" I inhale deeply, swallowing the sip of hot coffee and then plastering a massive smile on my face. I'm beyond thrilled for her.

"I know this is tough for you, Mia. Please don't put on a brave face for me."

Shelby is completely right; this is tough, but this isn't about me.

"Shelby Matthews!" I place my coffee down and pull her into a tight embrace. "I'm so happy for you! Seriously! You're going to be a wonderful mother."

Her arms don't let me out of the embrace. I feel her petite body shudder and she exhales loudly. "I've been meaning to tell you for a few weeks now, but you've been busy."

"Bullshit! I am never too busy for you," I tease, pulling out of her hug.

"So, gimme the details. How far along are you? When are you due? Boy or girl? And most importantly, who's the father?" I laugh as I bombard her with all these questions.

"I think I'm about six weeks. First appointment is in two weeks. I don't care as long as the baby is healthy and I sure hope to God it's my husband's." She throws her head back in laughter as she gives it right back to me.

"Holy shit, Shel, you're having a BABY!" I squeal with excitement like a little school girl.

"Hey, Auntie! Watch your mouth!"

Shelby's news is a double-edged sword. I really am happy for her and Mike, they are going to fabulous parents. While my heart is happy for her, those dormant feelings of loss and sadness try to break through. I refuse to let them. Perhaps good things come to those who wait. Perhaps not.

Two things happen later in day. First, I walk into Mrs. Chapman's office and tell her that I would be happy to chair the Harvest Festival. Fuck Gina.

Second, a small pink envelope sitting on my desk catches my eye when I return from lunch. It has my name scribbled across it. I know the handwriting belongs to Madison. It's not uncommon for my second graders to write me notes or make cards, but for some reason, I decide to open it now. A cartoon ballerina graces the front of the card and the words "You're invited..." are written in a swirly, glittery font. It's an invitation to her birthday party at Adam's house in two weeks. Our weekend. A million thoughts run through my mind in that instant. Does he know she gave this to me? Should I go? Would he really want me there? Was he going to tell me about it? Why would he plan this on our weekend? I stuff the card into my workbag and pull out my phone, sending him a quick text about having received her party invitation.

AL: I know she gave it to you. She asked me this morning right before we left.

Me: And you're okay with this?

AL: I'm in a meeting. Talk later?

Me: Sure.

After recess, I pull Maddie aside and thank her for the invitation. My heart breaks when she wears a look of disappointment when I tell her that I'm not sure if I can make it.

"That's okay. Daddy said you probably wouldn't come anyway."

"Oh...well, I didn't say it was a definite 'no.'" I smile. "I'll let you know, so for now, it's a 'maybe.' I'll try to come."

The smile beaming from her beautiful face is enough to light up our town in a black out!

Dismissal is the same as always, cordial greetings and nods.

"Hello, Miss Delaney."

"Hello, Mr. Lawson."

Adam arrives later than usual after dropping his kids off at their grandparents' for the weekend. We've made plans to head north early Saturday morning. I was a little apprehensive when he called me and said that he wanted to take me away for the day. Dreadful images of me waiting for him the morning he cancelled our day in New York swirled around in my head, taunting me, telling me not to get my hopes up.

I don't hear him come in over the music that's playing, but I feel him as soon as he comes in through the kitchen door. I can always sense when he's near. He's still wearing a navy suit, a patterned tie loosened at the collar and he looks utterly exhausted, his face gaunt.

I turn down the music and walk over to him. He wraps his arms around me and holds on for dear life. It's not unusual for him to be affectionate with me, but this embrace feels different—like it's the last one he's ever going to give me, the kind you give when you know you won't see that person again. I am spun around and pulled into his chest. He sweeps my hair over my shoulder, glides his nose back and forth slowly, gently, over the nape of my neck, inhaling and exhaling deeply several times. When with a final inhale and exhale, Adam turns me to face him once again, he rests his face in the crook my neck. Hmmm...wonder what's up. I rub large circles on his back, trying to ease some tension.

"God, I've missed you," his words mumbled, his lips pressed against my ear.

"I missed you, too."

"I'm so tired," his muttered words are a sign of his weariness. "By the time I got the kids into bed, it was almost ten o'clock." He shakes his head. "They were exhausted and then Maddie woke up from a nightmare screaming, calling out for her mother. It's just not right." He shakes his head again. "Needless to say, I didn't sleep well last night...I kept thinking about you. About us." His lips press together, frustrations mars his face.

"I'm sorry." I run my fingers through his hair, thinking he needs a haircut. "I wish I could help you somehow."

He smiles, leaning down to kiss me. "You help me more than

you know."

"Come with me." I grab his hand, leading him upstairs and into the bathtub. He sits on the closed toilet while I fill the small bathtub with water and pour in some melon-scented bubble bath to which he just laughs.

"What? It smells nice!" I laugh, feigning offense at the disgusted, yet playful, look on his face.

Our clothes are shed and we lower our naked bodies into the hot water, facing one another. His eyes close and he tips his head back, resting it on the edge of the tub. His shoulders look tight, full of stress. I watch him quietly and carefully, imagining the gears shift in his head, all working at the same time causing an overload.

I lather up my hands, pull his foot up from underneath the water and begin to massage it, running my thumbs up and down the arch, hoping to relieve some stress. His breath hitches and then exhales, his eyes never opening. I switch to the other foot and he obligingly lifts it up from under my leg. I can see the tension in his body begin to dissipate. Still he says nothing, but the gears are slowing down as relaxation overcomes. I grab the loofah sponge and soap and begin to wash him from bottom to top, paying close attention to his sensitive areas in between. He looks like he's fallen sound asleep, but his mouth pulls into a side grin when I run the sponge over his semi-erect length and between his legs. Even at half mast, he's impressive.

"You're good for me," he croaks, his voice raspy.

"I am?" I ask.

"You're like my own little oasis, my private tropical island. You're my respite from the world." He opens his tired eyes, smiling at me.

My heart softens at his words and another brick from the wall surrounding and protecting my heart loosens and falls.

His words reveal the mounting pressures. Raising his children on his own, working long hours to build his company...and me.

Me? I don't want to be a "pressure." He must sense my hurt

because he sits up quickly pulling me to straddle him, soapy water dripping from my body. "This is all new to me. You are what keeps me sane, Mia. There's only so much pressure a branch can take before it snaps and breaks." His words filled with sadness.

Tears fill my eyes. I want so much to help him and be there for him *and* his children. Would he allow it? Would he let his two lives become one? Would he let me love him completely? *Love him? What the fuck? I don't love him. Do I? Oh shit, I think I do. Yep, I do love him with all my heart. How did I let myself go and fall in love with him?* I know from experience that the things I love are always taken away from me. *I guess the more important question I should ask myself is whether or not Adam would ever love me back?* I shiver.

"You're getting cold. Let's get you out." Adam wraps a towel around his waist, before drying me with a fluffy towel. He lowers his head and kisses each one of my breasts, sucking my taut nipples into his mouth. "Mmmm. So sweet."

Hands roaming, mouths kissing, we walk backwards into my room, landing on my bed. Adam worships every part of my wanton body with his late into the night and again the next morning. He is a very, very generous man.

As WE WANDER AROUND THE COASTLINE ON A BEAUTIFUL autumn day, Adam holds my hand. We share chaste kisses and passionate kisses all without the worry of prying eyes. It's absolutely perfect. The pressures are gone, left back at home under the covers of my bed. We sit on a park bench on the boardwalk and take notice of a young family of four playing on the swings. Laughter is heard, their joy is unmistakable by the smiles on their faces.

"Tell me something." He takes a sip of coffee, keeping his eyes on the family.

"What do you want to know?" I ask before taking a sip of warm apple cider, angling my head to look at his profile.

"Tell me why you're not married with children?" Adam turns his head slowly to look at me.

Shit! I wasn't expecting that! I don't answer. I don't want to. *Do I tell him the truth? Do I tell him that I should be married with at least one child, but that in one night, one fateful, winter night it was all taken away from me?*

"You are incredibly beautiful. You're sexy, smart, funny, and you're great with kids." He rattles off my qualifications, twirling a lock of my long hair around his fingers. "I can't believe some lucky guy hasn't come along and snatched you up."

I shrug, not really wanting to have this conversation and ultimately ruin the great time we're having. I don't want to think about the past or even the future. I just want to think about the present. I clear my throat, offering my reply. "I don't know. I guess my time hasn't come yet. You know the saying, 'It'll happen when it happens.'" I give the most generic answer possible.

"It'll happen, Mia. Just you wait." He smiles and turns back to look at the family of four who have moved onto the slide.

What's that supposed to mean? "It'll happen?" When? With whom? He can't surely mean with him? The realization of his words finally hit home. *Oh, I get it.* This is his way of saying we're not permanent. I'll find someone when he's done with me. *Right, got it!*

We spend the rest of the day milling around, window shopping, looking and people watching. He makes some funny observations about the locals in this little seaside town. We find a little shop decorated for Halloween that is sure to scare the town's kids and their parents. It reminds me that I have a meeting this week about the Harvest Fest and then I need to start working on my annual Halloween Party. Maybe I can get Ryan, Will and the rest of the band to set up in the backyard and play for us. It'll be great to have live music and it would get their band's name out there.

During our drive home, I find out that Adam is an only child who, after his parents divorced, lived with his mom in New York and travelled almost every summer to see his father in Southern California. I smile as I wonder what he was like as a boy. I imagine he looked just like Luke and was probably just as rambunctious. Lost deep in our own private thoughts, our fingers are laced together on my lap. John Legend croons softly about giving everything to his lover. We exit the highway and begin the drive through a nearby town. A house with colorful birthday balloons tied to its mailbox reminds me of the birthday party invitation I received from Maddie.

"What can I get Maddie and Luke for their birthday?" I ask. His circling thumb stops abruptly and then resumes slowly.

"You don't have to get them anything." He shakes his head, swallowing hard.

"Why not?" I ask with incredulity in my voice. "It's their birthday! Everybody loves birthday presents."

Adam slows to stop at the traffic light and turns to face me. "I have to tell you something and I don't want you to get upset."

Oh, crap. I am so not going to like this. "What?"

"I don't think you should come to the party."

I try to pull my hand away, but he tightens his hold.

"Let me explain."

I suddenly feel like his dirty little secret and he wants to keep me hidden away. I wouldn't be there as his lover, I'd be there as his daughter's teacher.

"Go on." I urge, reaching for my silver necklace, flipping the pendant between my fingers.

"You know how busy I am, right? You see how crazy my schedule is."

I nod a curt "yes" response, not liking what he's going to say I'm sure.

The light turns green and he proceeds. "Well, Gina offered to do everything for the kids' party and I know you don't like her. I know you have some issue with her, but she's like family to us." I know he probably doesn't mean to, but his words are hurtful. He must think that I'm immature and have never gotten over some petty high school drama. God, if he only knew the truth.

My lips purse and I turn to look out the window. He has no idea what my issue is with her and I'd rather keep it that way. If she had any clue that I was sleeping with Adam, she'd be after him, all over him in a heartbeat. Just like before. Twice before.

"Are you sure that's the only reason you don't want me to come?" I ask, looking back at him.

"What's that supposed to mean?" He sounds annoyed.

"Adam, I wouldn't be going to your daughter's party as your lover. I got an invitation as her teacher. There is a difference." I give him a look that implies I think he's dense or stupid, even.

A call comes through over the vehicle's Bluetooth system, cutting into the music. I swear this woman has a mental GPS or something. "Hey, Gina," Adam answers, pressing a button on the steering wheel. I roll my eyes when he gives me an apologetic look. Mentally, I yank at my hair and scream, *"AHHH....WHAT. THE. FUCK! Go away, stupid bitch, go away!"* But the reality is that I just sit there.

"Hey, yourself. How's your weekend?" Gina's voice is sweet like sugar and I want to vomit.

"It's good. What's up?" The only consolation I have is that he sounds a little impatient with her.

"Oh, I wanted to tell you that I've secured the caterer for the party and the..." I tune her voice out.

Not really wanting to subject myself to their conversation, I reach down into my bag to check my phone and I see that I've missed a call and have a voicemail from Mrs. Longo along with two texts: one from Pete, the other from Shane. I quickly reply to Pete's and delete Shane's. I don't want to have to explain to Adam about how Shane has still been hounding me relentlessly with his pleas for a second chance. *Stubborn ass! He doesn't get that "no means no"!* I cover one ear to drown out Gina's voice still rambling on and on about the arrangements for the party. I listen to Mrs. Longo's voicemail telling me that Brady was behaving strangely but now is fine and that I shouldn't worry about him.

Our calls end at the just about the same time. Adam asks if everything is okay with me, nodding in the direction of my phone. I ask the same of him and he replies that all is well.

I<small>T'S</small> <small>LATE IN THE AFTERNOON WHEN WE FINALLY PULL</small> into my driveway and again, the ringing comes through, but this time, the ringtone is a familiar pop song. "Hi, Maddie girl." Madison has a cell phone? She's just six years old! There is no need for her to have a cell phone. That's just ridiculous.

"Hi, Daddy." Her normally sweet, happy voice is low and sad.

"What's up? Are you having fun at Gramma's? How's your brother? Is he in trouble again?" He asks the last question hesitantly, his eyes narrow at the screen.

"No, he's good, but I want to come home. Can you pick me up early?" she asks softly.

Adam turns his head to look at me as if I can offer words of wisdom. "Sure, honey," he replies hesitantly. "But, why? What's wrong?"

"My belly hurts and I miss you." Her voice hiccups as though she'd been crying.

"Maddie, let me call you right back, sweetheart. Okay?"

"Okay."

He turns the key, silencing the engine while his other hand grips the steering wheel, turning his knuckles white. "I'm so sorry, Mia. I *have* to get her. I know this is our weekend, but she needs me." His expression is forlorn.

"Are you kidding me? Adam, she's your daughter! You better go to her!" I can't believe he's even worried about me. I would be half way there if my daughter needed me. I would do *anything* for my daughter.

Adam carries the shopping bag into the house. I couldn't help but purchase a few eccentric things for my mom. "Thank you." He pulls my face, kissing me appreciatively. "I lo– I'll call you later." He smiles, a look of revelation on his face and it's immediately replaced by a look of surprise.

The last text message of the night that I receive from Adam is a picture of me. I'm asleep across his chest, my hand spread across his neck, my hair draped down over my shoulder leaving my full breast exposed. I was stunned at the intimate image because I looked so peaceful, so in love. The words he sent to accompany the picture were simple. "My sleeping beauty."

Chapter Twenty-Four

I ARRIVE FASHIONABLY LATE AT ADAM'S HOUSE FOR Maddie and Luke's birthday party. Over the years, I've been invited to birthday parties, sporting events and even a bar mitzvah, but I've never been as nervous as I am today. My bedroom floor is littered with clothes that I've changed into and out of a hundred times. I finally decide on black capris, ballet flats, a ¾ length red cotton jersey top paired with a cardigan and a thin scarf since it's unusually warm for this time of year. My hair still drapes down past my shoulders, even though I've cut some layers into it again.

Seeing Adam's house for the first time up close is daunting. It's a sprawling, magnificent grey farmhouse colonial with a wraparound porch. The landscaping is impeccably well-mannered, with shrubs and low bushes spreading throughout the multitude of flower beds. Colorful trees encase the large yard. A rock fountain streams water down into a small fish pond.

I never noticed how beautiful it was before—you can't exactly see it from the road because of the tree lined driveway. This house makes mine look like a dollhouse. I chuckle as I get out of the car when I remember how Shelby was absolutely mortified the night I made her stalk his house with me while we were out and about. It's amazing the amount of information one can gather from a student's file in the office. Employment information. Date of birth. Address. Phone number. Shelby said I was stalking, I called it research.

Walking around the house toward the backyard and the sound

of children's laughter, I see Adam. He's dressed casually in dark jeans and a burgundy, long sleeved shirt pushed up at his forearms, exposing the remnants of his summer tan. I recognize many parents and children from school, all milling around playing various games. There's an older couple standing off to the side whom I don't recognize; they look about as out of place as I feel. It looks like a child's dream birthday party, from the carnival games, cotton candy machine, and bounce house complete with a huge slide. This is one extravagant birthday party. There has to be at least forty kids and all their parents. I don't think I knew that many kids growing up.

Along the way to find Madison, I'm stopped several times by parents and students telling me how sweet it is that I came. My smile widens when I see Adam's broad shoulders and lean body standing there, talking to a small gathering of parents and a man that looks very much like Chris, Gina's older brother, but I'm not completely positive. I haven't seen him almost five years. Chris and Josh had been good friends growing up, but so many things have changed. When those piercing blue eyes lock with mine, I know for sure it's Chris. His eyes seem to narrow with a look of interest combined with curiosity. There's something else in his eyes as he stares at me, but I can't quite place my finger on it.

Adam follows Chris' gaze and turns towards me, his dark eyes meeting mine then crinkling when he grins. It's not like I can just walk up to him and plant a big ol' kiss on his lips. I'm here to attend a student's birthday party. I want to acknowledge him so I smile, nodding slightly, and then proceed to wander around looking for Madison amongst all the laughing children.

I spot Madison by the cotton candy machine and that's when I feel the daggers being launched in my direction, possibly even at my heart. Gina is making her way through the crowd carrying a tray of food, a disgusted look flashes across her face before she plasters on a big fake smile. I have to give it to her; she knows how to play it up for an audience just like she did at our planning meetings for the Harvest Fest.

"Miss Delaney! You made it!" Madison cries, giving me the biggest hug imaginable, causing me to drop the two gift bags that I've brought so I can wrap my arms around her little frame.

"Hi, Birthday Girl! I told you I would try to come and here I am." I hug her back.

Her eyes look down at the gift bags. "You didn't have to bring me a present. YOU are my present." Her brown eyes crinkle just like her daddy's.

"You want some cotton candy?" Her little hands with pink painted finger nails offer me some sugary heaven on a stick.

"I'd love some." I smile and pull a piece off. "This is delicious!"

Her name is called by another little girl to join her on the bounce house. I urge her to go on. Madison smiles, takes her gift and runs off to set the bag down with the mountain of others before heading to the inflatable house, leaving me to finish the cotton candy.

Adam's backyard has been transformed into a kids' carnival. He's really outdone himself. The loud sound of balls crashing into pins complete with hooting and hollering draws my attention and it's where I find Luke playing a game with his friends.

"Hey, bud. Happy Birthday!" I tap the brim of his Yankees ball cap, causing it to drop low over his eyes. "Hey! Cut it out!" he readjusts his cap, realizing that it was me who tapped it. "Oh, Miss Delaney! I didn't know you were coming." The look on his face is priceless—it's covered in confusion, surprise, and amusement. "Is Brady with you?" His dark eyes dart behind me, looking for his four-legged playmate.

"No, bud, sorry." I laugh. "Brady's at home. Here." I hand him his gift. "It's just a little something for you from me...and Brady, too." I wink.

"Thanks. Wanna try?" Luke holds out a dirt-stained, white baseball. "You just throw and try to knock down the bowling pins." He points to the pins he's already knocked down. "It might be kinda hard 'cuz you're a...you know...a girl."

What a little sexist! I wonder who he's learned that from. "Luke Lawson! Why, I can't believe you just said that!" My head falls back in laughter. "Gimme that." I take the ball out of his hand and tell the game attendant, a young, long haired gangly kid, to stack them up again. "Watch and weep, buddy." I warn, looking down with narrowed eyes. I wind up like I'm on the mound and let it rip, smacking all six pins down on the first try.

"No way! How'd you do that?" Luke's jaw drops and he yells, turning a few heads in our direction.

"What do you mean, Luke? Boys can't do that?" I tease in my best "I don't know what you're talking about" voice. "You know girls do play this little game called softball." I wink, slapping the brim of his hat again before I walk away.

As I sit with a few parents and munch on some fresh fruit, I offer to hold Kim Cumming's baby girl who is absolutely beautiful with a head of strawberry blonde ringlets. I listen quietly as I engage in my own conversation with the baby. I overhear some mothers whisper to each other about the party, gossiping about how sexy Adam is, about how lucky Gina is and what a great couple they make. Boy, that rumor didn't take too long to start.

I can't stand gossip. Get your facts straight before you open your mouth and spew your half-truths. Needing to get away from the women and their shallow conversation, I hand the little one back to her mother and walk over to get a drink.

"You're amazing. I'm adding that to my list." Adam's voice comes up behind me as I open a bottle of water. I turn in his direction and smile. "Oh, hello, Mr. Lawson." I extend my hand to shake his. I need to touch him. I need to know he's mine regardless of what I hear. All these women want him, but he's mine. I want nothing more to climb to the top of the bounce house and scream at the top of my lungs, *"Back off bitches, he is MINE!"* His hand closes around mine, an electric current of energy flowing between us. "I'm happy you're here. I've missed you." An outsider would think we're having a conversation about the lovely New England weather. We maintain a certain distance and appear to be professional.

I pull my hand from his and look around at all the people gathered here to celebrate his children's birthday. I want to keep things looking casual like a teacher and parent having a conversation about the party, not two lovers needing more than a brief touch.

"You sure know how to throw quite the party, Mr. Lawson." I smile.

He looks at me sheepishly. "I can't take credit for any of it, you know that."

Ahhhhh, that's right. This is all Gina's doing. "Well, the kids are having a great time and that's what really matters." I shrug, hoping he doesn't sense my annoyance or jealousy. I'm not really sure which it is that I'm feeling at the moment.

The party continues with deliciously catered, gourmet food, sweet cakes from a New York bakery and games to rival those at a real carnival. It's all a little over the top if you ask me, but then again, this was all organized by Gina. I'm sure she had a field day with Adam's credit card.

All afternoon, Adam and I steal glances, filled with lustful promises of things to come. It's getting late and I need to get home to Brady, but Maddie begs me to stay while she opens her gifts.

I look at the huge pile and worry that we're going to be here for a very long time. Many girly, sparkly gifts are opened, wrapping paper tossed aside. Apprehension begins to set in, wondering if maybe I've overstepped in selecting this gift for Madison.

Her eyes light up when she lifts the lid and discovers the wind up ballerina that twirls inside of the pink and purple musical jewelry box. Her smile falters momentarily before she jumps to her feet, running over to hug me. "Thank you, Miss Delaney. I love it so much. I really do."

I'm a little embarrassed at her display of affection since most people got an Adam-prompted "thank you," but all eyes are on us at the moment. "You're welcome, sweetheart. I know how much you love ballerinas."

Gina's voice rudely interrupts, "Okay...back to presents, Madison. You have lots to open." Her voice is all sugar and spice, but I know better. I wish Adam could see right through her like I do.

I bend down to look Madison in the eye. "There's something else in the bag, too. I have to get going. Thank you so much for inviting me to your party. I had a lot of fun." Her little arms wrap around my neck, quiet words whispered, "Miss Delaney, I love you." I feel my traitorous eyes start to tear up. "Bye, honey. See ya Monday." I stand up quickly, pulling my sunglasses down to shield my watery eyes.

"Cool! Look, Dad! Miss Delaney got me science kit and a Frisbee from Brady. Awesome!" Adam looks over at me and mouths sarcastically, "Thanks a lot." I chuckle because I'm sure he'll be cleaning up plenty of science experiments gone wrong. I wave goodbye to Luke as he waves back and shouts "thank you." Goodbyes are said to the rest of the party goers and an older woman, probably in her early sixties, watches me carefully before I walk down the long driveway to where I parked my Jeep.

The sound of hurried footsteps stops me. "Hey!" Adam's breathy voice closes in behind me. "I wanted to thank you for coming today." He looks around at the rows of cars parked, scanning for prying eyes. "And I wanted to give you this." He grabs my face and kisses me fast and hard, his tongue invades my mouth. "You really are amazing." He pulls back and then gives me another hard peck. "Drive safely."

He begins to walk backwards, and tells me to text him when I get home. He shoves his hands into the front pockets of his jeans, watching me climb into the Jeep as I begin to back out.

Chapter Twenty-Five

TUESDAY OF THE FOLLOWING WEEK, I BUMP INTO ADAM and his kids at the park because Luke's football practice had run a little later than normal. I have no choice but to make good on the promise that they could play with Brady especially since Adam did not get them a dog for their birthday.

Adam and I sit there, side by side on a park bench, watching his children run happily, as they scream and play with my big, goofy dog. He stretches and rests his arm on the back of the bench, his thumb lightly circles my shoulder. I would love to lean in and inhale his scent. He always smells so good.

His question catches me off guard, "Why did I overhear Shane telling one of the dads that you guys text all the time and that he's hoping you'll give him another chance?" I choke on the sip of water that goes done the wrong pipe. *What? Why would he do that?* I mean, it's true, he does text me, but I don't usually respond or if I do, it's always a curt response. He knows I won't give him a second chance. *What a damn liar!* He's really starting to piss me off.

I wipe my chin and angle my body to face him. "I could ask you the same question. Why did I overhear a bunch of gossiping mothers at the birthday party say how lucky Gina is and what a great couple you make? They all think you and Gina are together."

"What? Who said that?" His face scrunches and he looks as though he doesn't believe me.

"Adam, it doesn't matter who. It's what they're all saying. Or what Gina is telling them." I wave and smile at the kids playing with Brady.

"But you know that isn't true!" he counters.

"Just as you know that I'm not with Shane. He could call, text, and beg me to go out with him, but I'm with you. *Always* with you."

Madison and Luke come running over frantically, blood dripping from Luke's nose, sobs coming from Maddie. "Dad! Daddy!" They cry in unison.

Adam and I both jump up and rush over to them. Maddie explains through tears that she threw the Frisbee and hit him in the nose. I comfort her as Adam tends to Luke's nose, pulling off his own t-shirt to stop the bleeding. I can't help but gawk at Adam's body—it's perfect.

Without giving it a second thought, I suggest that we head back to my house to get him some ice especially since it's already starting to swell. Adam is hesitant, but he agrees before we pile into his Escalade while Brady rides in the trunk. I refuse to let him ride in the back with the kids. A big slobbery dog and luxurious leather seats aren't exactly a good combination. Adam and I each hand the kids our phones so they can play a game on the ride to my house. Maddie is still too upset to play, but Luke plays on my phone and inadvertently hits a wrong button, making a call. Over the Bluetooth system, the sounds of the Neon Trees' hit song "Sleeping with a Friend" blasts throughout the car, revealing my name on the screen. Watching Adam's face turn ten shades of red as he scrambles to turn it off, has to be one of the funniest things I've ever witnessed. He looks embarrassed, his eyes glance around everywhere but at me. I can't help the wide grin on my face. Adam Lawson has a sappy side.

Luke sits on the island with a tear-stained Maddie next to him. I reach into the freezer and grab a bag of frozen peas for his bruised nose. Then I take a wet, warm washcloth to Maddie's face, wiping away the sweat and tears, all the while reassuring her that Luke will be fine and reminding her that accidents happen.

After inspecting Luke's nose, Adam watches me with Maddie, his eyes thoughtfully looking at me.

"What?" I ask.

"Nothing." He smiles.

With lots of prodding from me and begging from his children, Adam relents and agrees to stay for dinner. Our pasta and meatballs are ready in less than twenty minutes. I'm so glad I follow my mom's habit of keeping sauce and meatballs in the freezer. I grab one of my brother's old t-shirts for Adam and toss his bloody one in the hamper. Since I don't have a kitchen table, the kids wash up and help Adam set the table in the dining room which is rarely ever used any more. We sit like a family of four, Adam and Luke at each end with Maddie and me across from each other. We eat our pasta and talk about everything, laughing about nothing all at the same time. *Family?* No, Mia. Not a family. His family. The one you're not a part of, silly girl.

That familiar sense of loss creeps back as I watch them back out of my driveway after we loaded the dishwasher and each had an ice cream sundae. I hate that I feel this way. I just had the best time with Adam and his kids and yet I wish it didn't have to end.

AL: Thank you for dinner and for taking care of Luke and Maddie tonight.

Me: ANY time. You know that! I love those kids! ●

Crap! I palm slap my forehead. I used the "L" word. Damn, I hope he knows what I mean.

AL: I wasn't sure how to feel about it.

Me: Uhhhh...okay...I guess. Not really sure what that means.

AL: I've never had that with the kids. It's always just been the three of us.

Me: You have a beautiful family.

AL: Thank you.

Me: It's late. I'm going to bed. Good night.

AL: Sweet dreams.

Me: You, too. XOXO

I'm dreaming about running through the woods and I hear voices, but I can't get to the voices fast enough. It sounds like Maddie and Luke are crying, but no matter how fast I run, I can't find them. I wake with a jolt. I reach for my phone to check the time since it's still completely dark out. I see an unread text from Adam.

AL: And for the record, my kids love you, too.

Chapter Twenty-Six

ALL DAY LONG INSTEAD OF THINKING ABOUT LESSONS I'm supposed to be teaching, the words from his text come back to me. "My kids love you, too." What does that mean? They love me back? Or they love me as well as he does? Why am I torturing myself? Why am I getting my hopes up? He can't possibly mean what I think he means, can he?

Shelby and I stay after work to finish preparations for the Harvest Fest. She reluctantly agreed to chair the event with me so I wouldn't have to deal with Gina on my own. She knows what a nasty bitch Gina can be. At our last meeting, I quickly and quite happily, put Gina in her place when she tried to take over saying she'd use her contacts in New York to get us a better deal on things we needed. Shelby politely reminded her that we like to use our local markets which only pissed Gina off even more. Things remained strained but professional and we kept our personal issues out of sight.

Hosting an event with 350 people in attendance went off pretty much without a hitch. Adam's offer to help me find some extra materials in the supply closet gave us just enough time to get our clothes off and back on without raising suspicion.

Adam loved my nurse costume which I chose intentionally to pay homage to our retiring nurse who was notorious for sending sick kids back to class only to have them vomit on their desk. When Adam requested that I keep the costume, he was met with my raised eyebrows. "You can be my naughty nurse any time," he growled and bit down on my earlobe as he helped me slip back into my costume.

"Your lip gloss is a little smeared and you're misbuttoned." Shelby smirked at my appearance once we returned. "And *your friend* was looking for you," she said to Adam, nodding in Gina's direction. Adam rolls his eyes before heading off to find his kids. All the kids had so much fun decorating pumpkins and playing games. I may even serve as chair next year, if I'm still here.

THERE'S A BUZZ OF EXCITEMENT AS HALLOWEEN DRAWS near. Jack-o-lanterns are carved, homes decorated and haunted houses abound. I'm happy it falls on a Friday this year. The kids at school are insane the day after Halloween. I'm happy I don't have to deal with cranky kids who were up too late and ate too much candy.

I decide not to host my annual Halloween bash because Ryan and Will's band is playing at a local bar tonight. Adam has his kids so I won't see him. Aside from seeing them at the park and having them over for dinner, as far as the kids know, I'm still just "Miss Delaney, Maddie's teacher" not "Mia, Daddy's girlfriend."

Pete called and asked if I needed help passing candy out. He insisted that no kids ever stop by his apartment, but I think he just wanted to eat the full size candy bars that I hand out each year. I swear he's eaten more candy than he's given out to the kids.

Later that night, my doorbell rings nonstop with clowns, superheroes, princesses, and ninjas, all causing Brady to bark loudly and continuously. He looks adorable in his cow costume this year. Pete laughed when he took a picture of me with Brady. "You know that poor dog of yours is probably humiliated that you dress him up. First, you chop off his balls and then you dress him up for Halloween. It's not right, Mia. It's not right."

He squats down and holds his hand out. Brady lifts his paw and puts it in Pete's hand. "Time to turn in your man card, dude." A curious look passes over Brady's face as his head tilts to the side. I think my dog agrees with Pete, but I'll never admit to it.

"Oh, shut up! He loves it. And he looks adorable." I shower the top of Brady's head with lots of kisses.

An hour later, the candy bowl is running low so I head into the kitchen when I hear the doorbell ring again. "Pete, get the door." I call out.

"I can't. I'm in the bathroom. I think I ate too many Snickers." He answers back. Good! I hope he has the shits for days for eating all that candy.

"Coming," I yell over Brady's bark. My eyes widen in surprise when I open the door to see a group of five people standing there. It's not just any random group of candy seekers. It's Adam, Maddie, Luke, Gina and Sophie. *What the fuck! Really, Adam?* All at once, my body is suddenly attacked by a barrage of feelings which flash through me: embarrassment, humiliation, jealousy, and anger. I want to slap that smile off his face and make him realize what he's done by coming here with her. He never mentioned that he was planning on stopping by when we talked earlier.

"Uh...hi! Well, isn't this a surprise." I look down at the kids quickly before Adam catches the anger in my eyes. Maddie and Sophie are dressed as ketchup and mustard while Luke is dressed up as a mad scientist. Gina just stands there in tight jeans, a fitted sweater, and tall leather boots. She wears a wicked grin on her make-up plastered face.

Just then Pete comes around the corner from the bathroom telling me to close up shop because Ryan texted and said the band is going on sooner than expected. Pete catches my "shut the fuck up" glare as Adam stands on my front porch. *Crap! I hope Adam didn't hear that.*

Maddie is the first to speak, her sweet little voice uttering the familiar phrase, "Happy Halloween." "Trick or treat," Luke chimes in while their father stands there brooding, anger starting to seep from his hard body. I don't dare a glance at his handsome face.

"Hi, guys! Happy Halloween!" I quickly transform from jealous lover to happy teacher in an instant. Knowing that I've got to get going soon if we want to catch Ryan's band, I give each child a huge handful of candy, never looking up at Adam because I know what I'll see and it definitely won't be pretty.

Sophie hesitates before opening her bag, looking at her mother for reassurance. "Whatever. I'll check it later," Gina mutters.

The nerve of this bitch! Coming to my house and insulting me.

I chat quickly with the kids about all their candy and laugh about which houses gave them raisins. *Raisins? Come on, people. It's Halloween!*

Sophie tugs on her mother's arm, whispering in her ear. "No, Sophie. Absolutely not. You'll just have to freakin' hold it." I hear Gina spit out. Sophie protests again saying that it's an emergency.

Oh, God. I do not want to welcome this wench into my home, but I'm not heartless. "Do you need to use the bathroom, Sophie?" I ask, looking at the daughter, ignoring her mother.

"No! She's fine," Gina bites out.

"Mommy, please! I have to go! Bad!" Tears well up in Sophie's eyes.

Adam and his kids stand there awkwardly watching the scene unfold.

"It's fine. Just let her use the bathroom. You know where it is." I glare at her then stand back to make way for them to come in.

"Oh. My. God. Sophie, you're such a pain in the ass sometimes." She grabs her by the arm and takes her to the bathroom around the corner. Maddie and Luke take the opportunity to play with Brady. I finally meet Adam's angry eyes. *What's his problem? I'm the one who should be pissed!*

"You're going to the bar?" he asks.

"Yep." I nod, responding. I want to scream and tell him that I'm going to get stupidly drunk and dance on the bar and get wild and crazy.

"What if I don't want you to go?" he challenges.

"Uhhh...I'd say you're crazy!" I laugh without humor.

"Is Will going to be there?"

"Probably! He *is* in the band," I say slowly, giving him a look that says, "You already know this." What a double standard! He can parade around with Gina, knowing damn well about the lies she's telling people, but I can't go listen to a friend's band. Fuck that! Something is seriously wrong with this picture.

I'm on a roll, the words spill from my mouth before I can stop them. "Wait? Um...who are you at my house with? Oh, that's right... Gina!" Sarcasm stains my words as I point my finger at him and snap my teeth. "Adam, do you realize how absurd this is?" My head shakes and my eyes roll involuntarily at the ridiculous situation we find ourselves in.

He stares at me with angry eyes, swallowing hard, his teeth clenching, making his jaw tick. "Don't start with this again, Mia. I've already explained this to you. I have to be close to her." What? He has to be close to her? What the hell does that mean? He must realize what he's said because he quickly utters, "She's like family."

"Whatever," I blurt.

Gina walks around the corner, dragging Sophie behind her. "Let's go," she snaps. "Wow...Nice to see you've fixed the place up, Mia." Her voice oozes derision as she walks past me and out onto the porch.

"Fuck off," I mumble, hoping it was loud enough only for her to hear. I wouldn't want the kids to hear my foul mouth. I'm not sure if Adam caught that brief interaction, but he doesn't say anything if he did.

"I don't live off my *father's* money." I glare at her.

She snorts. "You've got that right! You live off of *mine*." Her blue eyes narrow at me, raking up and down my body.

I say goodbye to the kids before looking at Adam, his face

unreadable now. "Thanks for stopping by. It's always a pleasure to see you two. Have a wonderful night!" I close the door harder than necessary. Remember that brick that fell from the wall surrounding my heart, well, it's back in place sealed this time with thicker mortar.

I ignore the many texts that I get from him. I don't want to talk to him right now. I choose to leave my phone in Pete's car when we go into the bar. I just want to drink, dance, listen to some good music, and have a good time. I don't need this drama. It will only lead to heartache.

It's after two in the morning when I stumble to Pete's car and climb into the passenger's seat. I roll the window down for fresh air, hoping to quash the contents of my stomach from rising up. I remember my phone is in the glove box. Pulling it out, I see that I have 31 text messages and 26 missed calls all from Adam. Uh oh, I think he's either really pissed or desperately needs to get laid.

Scrolling through them quickly, he's mad at first, then he's sorry for coming over with Gina, then he's pissed because I'm not answering, and then he's worried. He's like a roller coaster of emotions. I can't even bring myself to listen to his voicemails.

The next morning, the rising sun shines through my bedroom window. My sheets are a tangled mess around my fully-clothed body, a pounding noise throbs in my head like freight train. Holy shit! I feel awful. As I make way downstairs to let Brady out, I carefully grip the railing, taking each step slowly. I think I might still be drunk. A combination of caffeine and Excedrin are always my "go to" hangover cure. The time on the microwave tells me it's only 6:42. Damn, why am I up so early? I need to shower, crawl back into bed and sleep this hangover off. The coolness of the refrigerator offers little relief for my pounding head. I finish my cup of coffee just as Brady barks at the door to come in. I scold him for barking so loudly and he runs off to hide behind the couch.

Hours later, a loud knock at the door and Brady's bark wake me from my deep slumber. Keeping my eyes closed, I lie there in my bed, hoping Mrs. Longo will just go away. But the knocking and barking begin again and then stop. The sound of glass breaking and heavy footsteps put me on high alert. I sit up quickly, my eyes settling on my nightstand which houses my gun.

My bedroom door is pushed open by a frantic Adam, who is breathing fast and hard as if he'd just run a marathon. His wide eyes look around the room and fall back to me. "Where the hell have you been?" he yells.

"Shhhhh...please don't yell. My head is killing me." I lie back down, throwing my hands over my head.

"Answer me! I've been going fucking crazy all night, worrying about you." He tugs at his hair, and then scrubs his face with his palms.

"I told you to stop yelling!" I wince at my own loud voice. "I'm fine. Just a little hung over, that's it."

Adam walks over and sits on the edge of my bed, looks at me and shakes his head. "Why did you go to the bar last night? Were you trying to make me jealous?" His voice is eerily calm.

"No! Why would I do that? I didn't think I was going to see you last night. It wasn't a big deal. And besides that, while we're asking questions, why don't you answer one for me? Tell me why you're always with her. Maybe there's more truth to the rumors than you're telling me." I shout even though my head aches and I want to cry.

"Move over," he says, wrapping his body around to spoon me. His lips whisper in my ear. "Listen to me. You...are all I think about. The thought of some other guy hitting on you, touching you, wanting you...it kills me. It absolutely shreds me." His arms pull me closer to his chest. "You don't know how much you mean to me. How much you mean to my kids. And that scares the shit out of me, Mia. This is exactly what I was trying to avoid. You have the power to hurt me and my family."

The desperation in his voice brings me to tears, quiet sobs rack through my body. "You're all I think about, too. What you have...it's all I've ever wanted." His chaste kisses are placed on the back of my head. "But you won't let me in. You keep me tucked away and that hurts—especially when that nasty bitch gets to enjoy you AND your kids at the same time."

His fingers stroke my hair from my forehead to the end of the long layers. "Things need to change. I can't do this anymore. We can't do this anymore. It's not right." Oh, God! I want to scream at the top of my lungs, but nothing comes out. "You're breaking up with me? Oh, fuck! Please just go. Don't make this any harder than it already is, Adam. Please." I beg him, hot tears drop from my eyes, rolling down my face.

I'm fine. I'll be fine. Believe me I've been through much worse than this I want to tell him. "I promise I'll be alright. Just go." I bury my face in the pillow. One would think that he's left the room, but I know he hasn't. His breathing is slow and controlled.

"No, Mia. I'm not leaving you."

"I'll be fine, really." My words choke out.

"I can't leave you even if I tried. I'm in love with you." His whispered words spoken so softly, I almost miss them. "I think I have loved you from the first day I saw you." My hair is pushed away so he can see my face. "Did you hear me? I. LOVE. YOU."

His words make me cry even harder, loud sobs fill every inch of my room. I want so much to wrap my arms around him and tell him that I love him, too, but instead I say, "You can't love me. You don't know me. I've done unforgivable things."

"I do know you. Whatever you say or think, I know you. I know you're beautiful, kind, generous, loving, and compassionate." Adam pulls me up to hold me against his chest. "I love you, Mia Delaney. I'm tired of holding back. I'm tired of keeping you at arm's length away from my kids and away from my heart. I'm tired of hiding our relationship. I don't want to hide what we have."

He loves me? Adam Lawson *loves* me! He wants a real relationship! Heart sticks out her tongue at Brain because never in my wildest dreams did I imagine that from the lips of this gorgeous man, these words would be spoken. Maybe he's what I've been waiting for. What I need. And Maddie and Luke are incredible children whom I've come to love so much already. The bond I have with Madison strengthens every, single day.

I wrap my arms around him tightly, pouring every ounce of love into it. "I know this is going to sound crazy because I do love you. I love you so much, but I'm also terrified to love you. I'm afraid to love your kids."

Confusion is written across his face as he looks down at me. "Why? Why would you say that, Mia?" His deep voice laced with hurt.

"Remember what you said when we first got together about not wanting your kids to get hurt? I get that completely. You see, in the past, the ones I've loved have been ripped away from me. It's happened too many times already."

Adam's arms pull me closer, offering his body as a shield to protect me from the pain he cannot see but knows is deep-rooted. "I'm sorry you've had to endure pain and loss."

"I don't want to tell you everything because it serves no purpose. I can't change the past. But please just know that how I feel about Gina is legitimate and that I have never, in my entire life, hated anyone ever as much I hate her. It's not some petty high school jealousy or rivalry—it goes way beyond that." I wipe my nose with the back of my hand. "What she did to me is unforgiveable and irreparable." Loud hiccups shake my body. "She's a huge part of the reason why my life is what it is."

"Okay. You don't have to tell me right now although I would like to know someday so I can fully understand." My chin is raised, met by his lips. "I'm not going anywhere, Mia. You have me. You have us." I close my eyes, tears streaming down, staining my face even more.

Chapter Twenty-Seven

NOVEMBER BRINGS A PICTURE PERFECT, BRISK NEW England autumn, colors arriving fully with beauty and welcoming scents. Since Adam and I have begun a real relationship that includes his children, we spend nearly every evening together. He doesn't come in to pick up the kids from school anymore, I just bring them home with me and he meets us at the park for Luke's football practice and they stay for dinner afterward. I bring Maddie to dance class on Thursday but choose to wait in the car with Luke. Sometimes I play catch with him or listen to him ramble on about weird science facts. The kids are beyond thrilled to be able to play with Brady everyday while I watch them or get things ready for dinner. I do miss our Thursday night rendezvous. Without the need for Gina to take Maddie to dance class, we don't have that planned time together—just the two of us.

Mrs. Chapman wasn't too pleased when my name was added to the children's file as a contact person. The conversation in her office about my personal life didn't go over very well; she said she was concerned and suggested that I should be careful. I thanked her and reassured her that I would be fine.

"Mmmm...smells and tastes delicious." Adam's nose skims my neck, his tongue peeks out to lick me. "And I'm not talking about whatever you're making for dinner." His mouth quickly finds mine as he pulls me into him. "I want to feast on you all night long. I miss you. We miss you." He circles his hips, pushing his erection into my belly.

I shoo him away before the kids come in to wash up for dinner. I run my hand along the seam of his tented pants with a promise of a sinful dessert. The four of us enjoy a succulent steak and mashed potato dinner with brownie sundaes for dessert. Adam tells the kids to get their homework started while I show him where the shower needs to be fixed in the upstairs bathroom. His chocolate eyes dare me to question the leaky shower in need of fixing.

"We'll be right upstairs, kids. Call us if you need anything." He shouts over his shoulder as his hands are already all over me like a desperate man.

As soon as the bathroom door is shut, I am shoved up against the sink, my pants dropped to my ankles while my leg is thrown over his shoulder allowing him to ravage my swollen nub with his mouth. I look down at his dark head as it is raises and lowers, pushing in and out. His fingers are added, plunging one and then two deep into my core, making me yank his hair harder as I come.

"Turn around and hold on to the sink." His pants are unzipped and lowered just before he plunges deep into me, taking me harder than he has in a long time. Our eyes meet in the oval mirror; his expression full of lust and love. His hands travel all over my body from my breasts, to my hips, back to my sensitive spot. Several more deep thrusts and his body tenses and then relaxes as he finds his silent but forceful release in me. Thank God for birth control pills.

"God, I love you." His body bends over me, kissing my shoulders and back.

"Mmmm...I love you, too." I feel empty the moment he slides out of me, redressing quickly. He reaches for a washcloth, running it underneath the hot water before wiping me clean.

"I think your shower is all set, ma'am. Let me know if it leaks anymore." He smirks and kisses my cheek.

"You're quite the handyman, aren't you?" I slap his ass when he turns to open the door.

We walk downstairs to find Maddie sitting at the kitchen table and Luke rolling on the floor with Brady. Uncontrollable fits of laughter come from both of us when Luke asks what all the noise was, saying it sounded like his dad was banging something with a big hammer. Oh, God! If they only knew what an incredible handyman their daddy is, especially with that big hammer of his.

We say our goodnights with hugs and kisses before Adam takes his children home to get ready for bed. Gina's name appears on the screen of his phone just as he steps into the Escalade. Once again, he kisses me and apologizes. I wonder what she's calling for now. It's obviously not about the kids since they're with me all the time and it's a little late for a business call.

Sitting on my couch, curled up under the red and white plaid blanket, I close my eyes and think. I'm filled with such mixed emotions. I feel completely satisfied with our relationship now that we don't have to hide. The bond that is forming between his children and me is incredible and I feel grateful for them. But there's a little nagging feeling that makes me shiver. Brady jumps up and cuddles at my feet.

As I stroke Brady's back, I close my eyes and let my thoughts wander. I wonder how Adam became so close to the DeGennaros and then I consider the disturbing fact that Gina will always be in the picture, either lurking in the background or playing the damsel in distress, in need of his help. Although they have a professional business relationship, I know she would love to have a sexual relationship with him. I can't say I blame her on that one. Since Adam's company does a lot of work with Gina's family and their many businesses, it is only a matter of time before all of our paths cross.

Carl DeGennaro, whom I loved like an uncle, has not spoken to me in nearly seven years. Twelve days after the plant explosion that killed my father and led to the consequently devastating events of that night, we said goodbye and buried what was left of him. Carl, wearing all black from head to toe, kept his head hung low and eyes hidden from me beneath dark sunglasses. I was frozen like a statue when he hugged me, stroked my hair, and kissed my cheek before telling me how sorry he was and that my father was a good and honest man.

My father had had suspicions that things weren't right at the plant for a while, but being the good foreman and friend that he was and, more importantly, needing the job to support his family, he kept his mouth shut. Dad knew about Carl's other "business investments" and knew that money had become tight for him. My father was a hard worker who basically lived paycheck to paycheck like so many other people. I remember overhearing my mom complain a few times that his paycheck was overdrawn; there was no money so they had to struggle to make ends meet for a few weeks. My mother offered to get a job but he said no, insisting that she continue to stay home and raise us kids.

There are certain people in this life that you don't want to ever owe money to and apparently the DeGennaro family owed them a lot.

That fateful night as I talked to my mother on the phone, letting her know that I was driving into town early for a doctor's appointment, she told me that my father had gotten a call about some emergency alarms going off at the plant and because we lived closer than Carl, he went alone. I laughed at my mother's constant warning to drive carefully; we lived in New England and endured Old Man Winter's brutal blankets of snow and ice year after year.

Within mere minutes of my father arriving at the plant and searching for the source of the emergency, the building erupted into a mass of flame and fire, a huge orange and yellow mushroom cloud could be seen for miles, rocking the surrounding buildings from their foundations, shattering house and store windows alike. The fire department said there was nothing they could've done for him even if they had gotten there sooner. My father never knew what happened, for that I am grateful. The chief fire investigator ruled the cause of the explosion as inconclusive and took an early retirement a month later, having received a very generous severance package from an outside source.

Although no one was ever convicted, everyone in town knew who the guilty party was. Carl DeGennaro became a quiet and sullen man who agreed to the deal his lawyers hashed out. My mother was awarded a very large settlement from the wrongful death lawsuit of my father, but she didn't want the money; she just wanted my father back. She'd lost the absolute love of her life which led to her losing touch with reality. The money had been divided between Josh and me. My brother set up a college fund for each of his kids. My share was placed with an investment broker in California and hasn't ever been touched.

AT SOME POINT I FOUND MY WAY INTO BED, BUT I tossed and turned all night long. I was awakened by dreams of loud explosions, barking dogs, and mops in storage closets.

Chapter Twenty-Eight

WHEN ADAM INFORMS ME THAT HE HAS TO GO AWAY FOR a planned business trip to meet with investors for some property which, if handled correctly, could be *extremely* profitable for him, I am in awe. To watch him transform from sexy dad to savvy businessman is something amazing. The way his hands move in front of him, the way his face grows serious and his eyes sparkle when what most people see as a dilapidated building in need of being torn down, Adam envisions its potential and worth. I love to watch him work. It is his passion.

He'll be gone all weekend and the kids will be with their grandparents so I'll have the weekend to myself. I do feel a little guilty for wanting some quiet time, but truth be told, I'm not really used to all of this. I've been alone for so long. I make plans to hang out with Shelby and Mike and Pete agrees to tag along. We have big plans for the night. Pizza and Pictionary.

Shelby and I are in my classroom talking before school starts when I get a phone call from Adam. I'm a little surprised because he said he'd be in a meeting all morning and we'd already had our morning round of naughty texting. If my man needs a little incentive to get him through his stressful day, then I am more than happy to oblige.

His voice is rushed, panicked even when he tells me that the grandparents are unable to watch the kids this weekend and he really needs to be at this meeting. I don't hesitate when he asks if

I would watch the kids for the weekend. I agree immediately. But then, I want to reach into the phone and strangle him when he offers to pay me for "babysitting" them. Not cool, Adam Lawson. Not cool. He hurries off the phone after thanking me.

"Change of plans, Shel...pizza and Pictionary at my place." We walk out to pick up our classes as the bell rings.

A bouquet of flowers arrives in the office for me shortly after lunch. A huge vase filled with wild orchids, yellow sunflowers, red and orange mums brightens my desk. They're all my favorite fall colors. I read the neatly typed words on the simple white card, the seven little words touch my heart. "You are simply amazing. I love you."

Madison, with red-rimmed eyes, is not in a good mood this morning when I greet her along with the rest of my class. It's hard not to treat her differently when she's become so close to me. Before recess, I ask her to stay in and talk to me. She tells me that her feelings are hurt because of something that Sophie said to her.

"She said I don't have a mommy because me and Luke killed her. And that it's our fault she's in Heaven." Loud sobs wrack through her body.

"Oh, Madison, sweetheart!" I hug her tightly, pulling her onto my lap. "I don't know why Sophie would say such a thing, but that's not true. You know that, don't you?" I silently hurl every foul word I can think of at Gina because I know she's the source of these lies.

"Maddie." I swallow the lump in my throat. "Your mom loved you and Luke so much. It's not anyone's fault that she went to Heaven. People get sick all the time." Circling her back with my palms, I try to quell her tears and mend her broken spirit.

"Do you want me to talk to Sophie for you?" I ask.

She shakes her head, "No, I don't want to ever talk to her again. I hate her."

And *"I hate her mother,"* I want to say but don't.

I reassure her that Sophie wasn't trying to be hurtful with those words and she was probably just repeating what she thought she heard someone else say.

"Do you want to call your dad?"

She sniffs her nose, nodding a yes.

I call Adam quickly and tell him what's going on. I can't hear what he's saying to her, but she nods and says, "Okay. I love you, too." She hands the phone back to me.

"Sorry to bother you at work, but I thought it was important."

"No, you did the right thing. You and my kids are the most important things to me. I'll make this right." He disconnects the call.

Walking up behind her angrily, I grab a fistful of that long, blonde hair and smash her head forward on the table over and over again, leaving her in a heap of bloody bruises. I scream words of rebuke and hate, as everyone watches, but no one comes forward to intervene. I hurl words of disdain as I tell her what a horrible mother she is and that she doesn't deserve her daughter. Evil laughter spews from my belly.

As she lies in a bloody heap, her body mangled, I kick her hard one more time, "That's for the past, bitch!"

At least that's what I want to do when I see Gina come in at dismissal time. I shake my head briefly and release a disbelieving chuckle, bringing me back to reality because the scenario that just happened was all in my head. I have no idea where that violent episode came from.

Madison sits at the table alongside me, coloring a page from her new coloring book, rather than sitting with the other kids waiting to be picked up. Gina glances at Madison and then glares at me, asking her why she's not sitting with all the other kids. I reach down to gather Maddie's long brown hair in my hands just like my mom used to do to mine then smile and wink, ignoring Gina completely.

"I'll be right back, Maddie," I say as I follow after Gina and her daughter.

"Gina," I call after her.

She turns around, rolling her eyes at me. "What?"

"Can you tell me why Sophie told Madison that it's her fault that her mom died?"

She snorts loudly. "How would I know?" She continues, "And besides, how is Madison any of your business? You do realize you're just one of the many women he's fucking. There are others, you know."

What? How dare she? That fucking lying bitch! "Well, it is my business because I'm her teacher," I retort.

"Well, you're acting like you're her mother. Newsflash, Mia. You're *nobody's mother.*"

By the time Adam gets to the house that afternoon, I'm emotionally exhausted. I start dinner and from my kitchen window I watch Luke and Maddie run and play with Brady. For some reason, my mind wanders to thoughts about their mother, Johanna.

The conversation I had with Adam a few weeks ago about why he always has to answer his phone, never letting it go to voicemail replays over and over again. I wasn't prepared for the answer I'd received. The guilt that he carried, and still does, about that awful night when he told me how Johanna had called him relentlessly, but each and every time, he chose to ignore her. He didn't realize at the time that this was her most desperate and final plea for help. Too many of life's pressures consumed her. The pressure of raising her children as a single mother, the pressure of needing a perfect body to restore her dance career, and her lifelong battle with depression were all just too much to bear for her. That night, as her babies slept soundly in their bed, she called Adam one last time before taking her own life.

I held Adam that night as silent sobs vibrated through his body and tears of guilt and shame coursed down his face, his whispered words repeated, declaring it to be *his* fault that his children were motherless. "If only I had answered, I could've saved her." Through unrelenting tears, Adam repeated those words like his words could bring her back. Some people don't want to be saved, others are beyond saving.

I had drawn a bath later that night, hoping I could help wash away some of the guilt he felt for her death. The story that unfolded before me was one that I never expected. It was the story of Adam and Johanna.

Johanna had been a ballerina for a dance troupe in New York City. Her face and body were beautiful; her long brown hair cascaded down her thin back, always shielding her tall, lean, but strong body. Adam was immediately drawn to her, but not just because of the beauty she possessed, it was her innocence. Moving from her suburban home, she was innocent to the ways of the world, having lived a sheltered life with only her parents, a conservative cardiologist and his wife. To be a prima ballerina was her dream.

They never really dated or became a couple, but they would always end up at a hotel after a night of partying. Johanna had hit the party scene fast and hard, experimenting with drugs and alcohol.

When she found out she was pregnant, she told no one—she just disappeared, telling her parents that she had joined a troupe in France. Adam didn't really think much about it since they hadn't hooked up much lately anyway. He continued working to build his company, buying and selling property all over the tri-state area, partying with Chris, and bedding a different woman pretty much every night.

Johanna rocked his world three years later when she showed up on his doorstep with twins, claiming them to be his children. Of course Adam denied it, and demanded a paternity test, but he knew it was true the moment he saw Luke. It was as if he were looking in a mirror—his own face staring back at him.

Adam was hurt and angry at her for never revealing the truth and keeping his children away from him, although he wasn't ready to become a father at the time just quite yet. Adam's attempts to see his kids were unwelcomed since she only wanted child support from him. He even offered to marry her. That was a hard pill to swallow for me even though it all happened before I knew he existed, but still, he would've married her for the sake of his children. Eventually she relented after a judge issued him visitation rights.

They were always at odds, never agreeing on what was best for the children. Johanna wanted to keep them in Connecticut, where she lived with her parents, but Adam wanted them in New York. Since she turned down his offer of marriage, he then offered to buy her an apartment so she could be close to the theater district because her dream of being a prima ballerina never waned. The mounting pressures of life and her battle with depression consumed her; desperate pleas for help went unnoticed by everyone around her, especially by the father of her children.

THE BEEPING OF THE KITCHEN TIMER AND THE DELICIOUS aroma of lasagna calls us in for dinner just as Adam arrives from work. His arms wrap around me, pulling me in like he's a desperate man. His face is buried into the crook of my neck, inhaling my scent. I feel the tension of his stressed, hard body dissipate almost immediately.

"I can't ever lose you." His words are spoken sincerely, but there's an undertone of something—fear, maybe.

My hands run through the back of his hair, pulling his face down for a long kiss. "I'm not going anywhere. You and these kids mean everything to me." I smile, searching his weary face for a reason behind this demeanor.

The four of us sit together, say grace and enjoy our dinner. The kids compete for attention, telling their father all about their day which includes the upcoming second grade field trip and their parts in the chorus program.

"I need to be deep in you," Adams growls in my ear, nipping at my earlobe as I load the dishwasher.

A smile spreads across my face, needing more than just his words. I also need him buried deep in me. We quickly step away from each other when Luke comes back into the kitchen to complain that Brady doesn't want to play with him. Poor Brady, my boy is getting old and he can't hang with the young ones as much anymore. He has been a little off lately, barking to go outside at all hours of the night, waking me up constantly.

I promise Adam that I will see him at his place tonight after I've finished taking care of a few things at home. We don't do sleepovers during the week when the kids are home, but tonight might be an exception. We're desperate for each other.

Chapter Twenty-Nine

AFTER I GET BRADY ALL SET FOR THE NIGHT AND I'VE got my bag packed, it's pretty late when I finally lock up my house and drive to Adam's on the other side of our sleepy town. The soft sounds of O.A.R. singing "Peace" keep me company.

A thin layer of snow covers the quiet, dark roads. Jack Frost wants to make an early appearance, I guess. Most families are already settled at home for the night while children are tucked into their beds. A warm, fuzzy feeling flows through my body as my thoughts consider how much my life has changed in just a few months.

I pass a few cars on the road, each one driving carefully as though snow is a rare occurrence. It is New England, people—we get a lot of snow. That's one of the reasons I bought a Jeep. Sadly though, I am fully aware of how much damage even just a little bit of snow and ice can cause at any given moment.

All of a sudden, I am aware of a car trailing closely behind me, its headlights bright in my rearview mirror. I speed up thinking maybe that I'm driving too slowly, too cautiously, but the sedan keeps following closely. An uneasy feeling whizzes through me, the hair on the back of my neck stands up, my heart beating a little faster. Since I know these streets like the back of my hand, I turn onto a side road through the industrial park which will still take me to Adam's house. The car proceeds to turn behind me. I turn left onto another side road and the car follows. *What the hell?* My instincts tell me something isn't right. I can't see the driver of the vehicle because every time we pass the street light, the car slows down, widening the gap and then comes close again. *Think, Mia. Think.* My father's words come back to me. *"Mia, if you're ever being followed, drive to the police station or any populated area."* That would be great advice except Adam lives in the middle of nowhere on the outskirts of town and the police department is back a few miles in the opposite direction.

I press the green button on my phone to answer Adam's call immediately.

"Mia, where are you? I thought you'd be here already," he asks before I can even say hello.

I don't want to seem paranoid, but this car has me a little worried. "Adam, I'll be there soon," I respond distractedly.

"Mia, what's wrong? You sound anxious?"

"I think I have a car following me. I've turned onto a couple different streets trying to figure it out, but the car follows me on every turn."

"What does the car look like?"

"From what I can make out, it's a dark sedan with only one person," I tell him.

We find ourselves unsure about what to do. He certainly can't wake his sleeping children to come meet me and leaving them home alone would never be an option for either one of us.

"I want you to turn around and go back toward town, drive straight to the police station," Adam insists. I can hear the apprehension in his command.

Just as I make my way back into the more populated part of town, the car slows down, turns right towards the highway and disappears. Adam keeps me on the phone the entire time, constantly asking where I am now and what the car behind me is doing.

My eyes scan the road as I pull into my driveway, looking for any sign of something amiss. I park my Jeep and get out slowly, holding on to the door so I don't slip and fall in the snow. The motion-sensor light mounted on the garage quickly turns off just as I unlock the back door and step inside. *What the hell? It usually stays on for longer than that.* I'll have to check the batteries or maybe it's those damn deer always running across my yard.

I crawl into my big bed all alone, missing his body wrapped around mine. Adam and I whisper words of affection and lust to one another on the phone as we each take matters into our own hands—literally. Of all nights when we're so desperate for each other, we have to settle for this. Those feelings of unease and paranoia are quickly replaced with utter bliss and contentment knowing that my words alone could send Adam over the edge to his release. I love this man with all that I am and all that I have.

"No, stop! Don't go in there! Please!" I scream at the top of my lungs, running frantically trying to reach them. I watch in slow motion as Adam walks toward the building, holding Madison and Luke's hands, leading them away from me. My heart pounds in my chest, my voice screeching loudly, begging them to come back, but he doesn't hear me. Madison's head slowly turns to face me, an innocent smile on her face as she lifts her tiny hand, her fingers curling, waving goodbye.

Just as they cross the threshold of the open door into the building and disappear, my body is slammed back against the wall. In an instant, a monstrous plume of black smoke and orange fire light up the night sky, consuming them. "NOOOOOOOO," I scream. "Come back! Come back to Mama."

"Come back!" My screams jolt me awake, hot tears streaming down my face, uncontrollable sobs shake me. I drop my face into my palms and pant heavily, trying to calm myself down. Breathe in and out. In and out. Brady whimpers at the sight of me so I pull him close to me, reassuring him that I'm fine and that it was just a bad dream. A really bad fucking nightmare is more like it.

Walking downstairs to get a drink of water, I notice that it's really cold in my kitchen. I think about how winter is making its approach much too quickly this year. Brady barks, indicating that he wants to go out so I open the back door. I watch him run out into the backyard, barking angrily while chasing after some wild animals. No doubt it's the raccoons that like to feast on my garbage at night.

I make my way to the bathroom to wash my face. And that's when I notice the window is slightly open. No wonder it's so cold in here. The kids must've opened it earlier today. I secure the latch on the window before calling Brady several times to come back in. Stupid dog wants to stay outside and chase wildlife in the middle of the night.

Sleep doesn't come easily. I toss and turn, fluff my pillows, and even consider drinking Vicks NyQuil to get some sleep, but it's almost time to get up for work so I just lie there thinking. I think about my father. I think about my mom and my brother. I think about Adam. I think about Maddie and Luke. I think about the one whose tiny fingers and toes I have never touched, but I love still the same.

Chapter Thirty

SATURDAY AFTERNOON, WITH THE EARLY SNOW NOW melted and gone, the kids and I rake my entire front yard and make a family of scarecrows while Adam is away on his business trip. His phone calls and texts have been brief because he's either on a job site or in a meeting. His annoyance and anger were clear as day when I asked him about the female's voice calling his name in the background during one of our quick phone calls. *"You're just one of the many women he's fucking."* Gina's words stirred my insecurities that I'm not enough for Adam, but my heart fluttered like a hummingbird when he told me that his kids and I were his life.

I watch as Brady chases the kids through huge piles of colorful leaves. I feel like we've become a family. Thankfully, Adam and I still have our own weekends when the kids go visit their grandparents, although there have been a few times when Maddie asked if she could stay home instead. Sometimes, the answer has been yes, other times no. I've come to an agreement with Madison that she has to keep things quiet at school with the other kids. Adam and I don't hide our relationship anymore, nor do we flaunt it around on display for the world to see. Needless to say, the Wicked Bitch is not happy.

I even managed to piss off another DeGennaro this week when Gina's older brother, Chris, came in to pick up his niece. He was livid when I made him go to the office to get approval to take Sophie home because his name wasn't listed as an authorized person and he didn't have any identification since his wallet was in the car. I smiled the most insincere smile imaginable, quickly reminding him that I was just doing my job and following the rules. He walked away muttering something about me being stubborn just like my father. My eyes flashed up in anger when he snorted and mumbled, "Look how that turned out." That son of a bitch!

A FEW DAYS LATER, AFTER MY BROTHER CALLED TO TALK about our Thanksgiving plans, I decide to go for a run while I have some free time. The air is frigid when Brady and I reach the summit. Most of the leaves have fallen off, young and old trees stand bare. My one-sided conversation with my father is filled with apologies for not coming often enough and stories of how my mom is doing and about how happy I am with Adam and the kids. I know my father would like Adam because he's hard-working, honest and treats me like a princess. Sometimes it makes me sad that my father was taken away, never having the opportunity to walk his baby girl down the aisle or to see and hold his grandchildren. Well, that's not entirely true...I believe with all my heart that he holds one precious, tiny hand every single day in Heaven. I imagine he would be a loving and doting Grandpa—the kind that would give you an extra scoop of ice cream even though your parents already said no.

When I get home and shower, I send Adam a quick text to let him know that I'm going to stop at Shelby's, go to the grocery store to pick up steak for dinner, and then I'll be on my way over. I chat with Angie Jackson at the store and welcome her squeals of delight when I confirm that Adam and I are indeed a couple. "I just knew it, girl. I just knew it. When's the weddin'? I'll need some time to lose weight, you know." I laugh at her craziness and tell her to settle down with talk of a wedding.

It's been such a long time since I've felt this happy. I love Adam and his kids so much, they're all I've ever wanted. The Philip Phillips song on the radio reminds that the Lawson family has become my home. It's late afternoon and the sun has just begun to set when I pull into Adam's long driveway. Immediately I spot *her* Mercedes in the driveway parked alongside the Escalade. While I park my Jeep in front of the garage, I notice that my palms are sweaty and my anxiety is high on alert. I can't imagine why she's here on a Saturday. I know they are still business associates, but I don't see the need for her to be here at his house on a Saturday evening. Can't she just leave him alone? My heart warns me that something isn't right.

Like every other time, I walk into the house through the garage which leads through the mudroom into the kitchen. My pulse starts to quicken as the muffled words, "Shhh...it's okay. Don't cry," invade my ears. My eyes tighten in confusion, scanning his vast kitchen and then I see them. Maybe it's my body's way of protecting itself that causes me to falter back slightly, but I can still see them in the reflection of the sliding glass door. Adam's arms are wrapped around her body, embracing her as he does to me. I freeze. The sound of my heart cracking fills my head loudly, I can hardly think. I stand there, immobilized, speechless, watching my worst nightmare unfold before my eyes. Again. The scene before me is too much to bear—it's like an awful déjà vu from seven years ago. Adam's face slowly morphs into Dylan's and I literally cannot breathe as I watch them.

Gina lifts her head from his chest and presses her lips to his. *Don't kiss her back. DO. NOT. KISS. HER. BACK.* He tenses and immediately jumps back, pushing her away. "What are you doing?" With the back of his hand, he wipes her red lipstick from his lips as his handsome face scrunches in disgust. "Gina, why would you do that? What's wrong with you?" His words reek of contempt.

"Adam, I know you want me. You always have." She steps forward, trying to grab him. "Listen to me, baby. You think you want her, but you don't. You don't know the things she's done. I'm so much better for you. We were meant to be together."

His face contorts into revulsion. "What? No, Gina. You're wrong. We are not meant to be together. You're...you're like *family* to me. It's never been anything more than that. You already know this."

"You're right, baby. We can be a family, just the four of us." Her voice begins to whimper as she reaches out to touch his face as if he hadn't just rejected her.

The four of them? Doesn't she mean five of them? I know she didn't graduate in the top ten percent of the class or anything, but two plus three still equals five.

"Four of us? What the fuck are you talking about, Gina? Listen, I'm sorry to hear about your father and I'll do what I can to help, but you're obviously not thinking clearly. I think you need to go. Now." He backs away again.

"We belong together, Adam. Even my father agrees." Her tactic, as well as her voice, changes. Her father would do anything and everything in his power for his little girl. He'd already proven that a few years ago. Carl DeGennaro is a ruthless man who has money and the power of persuasion on his side.

I step back quietly into the garage, silently cursing my phone when it begins to vibrate. I should just ignore the call, but it's my mother calling again for the third time in a row so I quietly close the door and walk out to the driveway. I don't really hear the words she says even though I am listening. My mind and my heart are back in Adam's kitchen. I sense immediately that she's not on her medication even though we haven't talked that much in recent weeks. She's rambling about not making it to my brother's for Thanksgiving this year because she's going on some new-age spiritual retreat in the Dominican Republic.

With a deep intensity, my eyes stare straight ahead at the door where just beyond it stand two people. One is the person I love most in life and the other is the person I hate the most in the world. My thoughts are still focused on what's going on inside Adam's house. My mother's conversation is all over the place before she abruptly ends the call, saying her friends are there to pick her up. My poor mom. My dad would turn over in his grave if he ever saw how poorly she dealt with losing the love of her life that fateful night. We all lost something that night—some of us more than others.

It's the sound of the back door slamming so loudly that makes me look up. A haggard and distraught looking Gina rounds the corner of the house and freezes when she sees me leaning against my Jeep.

I stand there bewildered, wondering about what happened inside. Maybe I should have just walked in and confronted her. Maybe the time has come for me to claim what's mine and finally put that bitch in her place.

"You! You fucking bitch! This is your fault! You think you can have him. You're dead wrong, Mia. And I mean *dead* wrong. Dead like your father. Dead like Dylan. Dead like your *baby*." Her cruel words spit out with acid, spewing venom like the cold-blooded viper that she is.

I don't respond. I can't respond because I have no words. I am stunned. My heart has been ripped to shreds again by this vindictive witch. She looks deranged as if she had been pulling at her blonde hair leaving it in a wild mess. Her usually flawless makeup is smeared across her face. I watch silently as she gets into her shiny car, backing out recklessly before screeching away.

I feel faint. The sky above me starts to spin, everything moving in slow motion as I lower my weak body down to the ground and sit against the side of my Jeep, the floodgates of my soul opening.

I don't even have the strength to pick up my phone to respond to Adam's texts probably wondering where I am. It's here that he finds me a short while later. My head rests against the front tire, my eyes looking upward, but I see nothing. It's as if I'm staring into an empty oblivion. The sound of his voice coming through the back door draws my attention. With his phone cradled between his ear and his shoulder, he steps out onto the patio to light the grill, ending his conversation. I vaguely hear him say something about her losing it and having to move faster than planned. Just seeing this beautiful man who holds my heart brings on another round of emotion. My arms are wrapped around my knees, slowly rocking myself back and forth while snotty tears flow from my eyes and nose. With mascara smeared across my eyes, black streaks mar my face. Muffled sobs attract his attention.

Immediately, Adam drops to his knees, cradles my face, and comforts me, asking what's wrong. I feel betrayed. I feel dejected. I feel broken. Those beautiful dark eyes look at me, revealing a mixture of his love and apprehension, while his words repeatedly tell me how sorry he is. I'm not sure what he's apologizing for exactly, but I let him wrap his arms around me, forming a cocoon to rock me gently until exhaustion takes over and I succumb to the darkness which beckons me.

I wake up under the covers of his plush king size bed and look over to find him working quietly on his laptop, a serious, almost worried, expression on his face. I don't remember coming to bed. I don't remember anything but his arms wrapped around me. He looks up thoughtfully and goes back to typing what looks like an email.

His phone vibrates alerting him of a text. I watch him carefully as his lips purse and he shakes his head. He taps out a response before setting the phone back down on the nightstand. I memorize his face. I memorize the way his lips meet or the way his tongue darts out to moisten them. I know that this will be the last time I get to lie next to him. I know that after tonight, we will no longer be together. I know I won't survive this. I can feel the edge of darkness creeping in, closing in, shutting out the light.

He must feel the weight of my stare because he looks over at me. Our eyes meet—there is no need for words. After setting his laptop down on the bedside table, he pulls my body against his, his fingers reach out to brush my hair away from my face. Our faces are only inches apart. God, I love this man.

"Hi," I say my voice raspy and dry.

"Hello, my beautiful girl." He smiles, kissing my nose lightly.

"I'm sorry." My eyes close and my voice falters on two little words, but he leans down to silence me with his lips.

"What do you have to be sorry for?" He pulls back to search my face. "You didn't do anything," he mutters against my lips.

Oh, Adam. There's so much I need to apologize for. I should've told him everything that happened so he could truly understand the person I am. He would have known to run far away from me. Death and destruction tend to follow me.

"I'm the one who needs to apologize. I'm sorry for what you saw yesterday. I didn't realize you were here until I found you outside. When I saw you crying, I assumed that you had seen what happened."

Yesterday? I turn over to look out the window to see the early morning sun casting its morning glow. The time on the clock tells me is not yet 6:00 am. I can't believe I've slept all night. That's over twelve hours of sleep.

He continues, "Gina—" he starts but stops when my eyes flash to meet his. I can't even stand to hear her name fall from his lips. "She stopped by to drop off some property listings for me to look at and told me about her father's heart attack. She got really upset and when I tried to console her, she came onto me. She kissed me, but I pushed her away immediately, Mia. I swear I did. I have no idea what she was thinking."

I just stare in silence, tears welling up threatening to fall.

I know this; I watched the whole familiar scene unfold in front of me as if it were in slow motion.

"She's fucking crazy. She was rambling on and on about how we belong together. How we can be a family." He shakes his head, his words evident of his disbelief. "How did I not see this before?"

My eyes continue to blink to keep the tears at bay, but I speak no words.

"Talk to me. Tell me that you believe me," he begs, kissing my forehead.

I nod imperceptibly. "I believe you." I know how crazy she can be. I've been on the receiving end of her craziness for too many years.

"She hates me so much, Adam." Stupid tears well up again.

"Why?" he demands quietly. "Tell me what happened, Mia. Help me understand this animosity between the two of you."

My heavy eyelids close, tears spill from my eyes, and my fingers find their way to my necklace as I silently ask God for strength to do this. I beg him for the strength and courage to tell Adam what I've kept hidden from him all these months.

And so there on a quiet, cold November morning, I divulge my deepest secrets, I expose my guilt, reliving the painful memories of how at twenty years old I got pregnant. I tell him about the baby that I carried for almost eight months and lost in an instant. An innocent, young life ended before it really ever began.

Adam cries with me. His heart breaks for me as I recall the events of that cold, icy winter night. The explosion that killed my father was the first of three horrific events. Tremors ravage through my body as I detail the sequence of everything that happened that night, as if I were reliving each moment all over again. Some of the events I can't remember, my therapist said I've repressed those because they are too painful. But the image of entangled, naked bodies, the snow falling, the motion of my car spinning, those memories will haunt me for the rest of my life.

When I found out that my father, who was my hero and rock, was killed, I needed Dylan. Dylan Marx was my first real boyfriend and I loved him beyond words. I needed to tell him what happened to my father. I needed him to hold me and comfort me.

I was in such a despondent state when I pulled into his driveway that I didn't even notice the compact, white BMW there next to his father's old pickup truck. I didn't knock on the door; I just walked into the quiet house like I always did. And that's when I saw them.

Dylan was naked, his lean body stretched out on top of Gina, fucking her on the living room floor. I froze, thinking that I was hallucinating, but the nightmare was real. My boyfriend of two and half years, the father of my unborn child, was fucking my best friend, the girl I loved like a sister, right there in front of me. Screeching, feral screams exploded from deep within me and pierced the room, causing them to jump up and scramble for their clothes, but not before I saw it. The swell of Gina's belly told me all I needed to know—in that moment, I clutched my own swollen belly and knew that I wasn't the only one carrying Dylan's baby.

Running back towards the refuge of my car, I couldn't even see through my tears and the falling snow that whirled around me. Scrambling to get a sweatshirt on over his head, he pulled the passenger door open to stop me from driving away. He had no choice really but to jump in since I wasn't slowing down and I definitely wasn't stopping.

I remember the pain shooting through my hand as I pounded it on the steering wheel, screaming and asking the same questions over and over, "Why?" "How he could do this to me? To us?" I thought we were going to get married in the spring and start our life together, after our daughter was born. Oh God, how could you let this happen? How could I have been such a fool? Their betrayal was right in front of my face and I didn't see it.

He kept yelling at me to slow down in between his pleas for forgiveness. He kept saying, "I'm sorry. We were going to tell you." His explanation of how Gina started hanging around more often while I was away at school and how things just happened fell on my deaf ears. I didn't want to hear it. I couldn't stand to hear it. My heart was shattered beyond any chance of repair. My boyfriend and my best friend, the two people I loved and trusted the most, obliterated my heart, leaving a huge gaping hole.

The snow-covered road was slick. Even though I knew all the

twists and turns of the road like the back of my hand, hot tears coursed down my face, blurring my vision and it all happened so quickly. I was driving too fast and my car skidded across a patch of ice, sending us into a tailspin, heading straight for the steep embankment leading down to the river. Instinctively I slammed on the brake, but it was useless. My body was like a rag doll, being tossed around, crashing into the steering wheel. Dylan's arms flew up to protect himself as his face crumbled with fear of what was to come. There was nothing I could do but hold on and pray. Prayers and screams filled the small space. And then silence.

"Mia, I am so sorry." Adam's arms circle my back and he holds me close. I can feel his chest shudder with unshed emotion. He gives me the strength and conviction to go on.

I continue to tell him how eight days later on Christmas morning, I awoke. My eyes fluttered as I took in my surroundings of the sterile room and saw my mother asleep on a chair. I tried to swallow, but my mouth was dry and my throat hurt. I closed my eyes and breathed, hoping this was just a bad dream. I pushed my hair back, careful not to pull the IV out and then rested my hand on my stomach, exhaling loudly. It took a moment for the panic to set in as memories flooded my mind. My round belly was now flat.

The explosion. Dylan's house. The car accident. Quiet sobs erupted from my chest while I repeatedly mumbled the words, "No, no, no." The beeping became louder, almost frantic as if calling for help before a nurse came in to sedate me. Call it mother's intuition. Call it whatever the hell you want. I knew without a doubt what had happened. My father was dead. My baby's father was dead. My baby girl was dead.

"I'm so sorry." Adam's face was white as a ghost as he uttered those words over and over again as if he had been the one who inflicted such horrific pain. "I am so sorry. I wish I could take it all away, baby." For hours, Adam's strong arms held me and cradled me.

Adam mourned with me that morning. He cried with me. He

cried for me. He cried for the pain I suffered. He cried for the little baby who lived for a mere eight minutes. He cried for all I loved and lost. He cried as if he endured my pain, pulling me close to shield me from further unseen pain.

Something shifted in our relationship. I have never in my life been closer or more connected to another human being. Adam Lawson is my soul mate. He is my life. He is my home. He knows me like no one has ever known me. He loves me despite the fact that I carry a heavy burden and will never forgive myself for killing my child and her father. His love for me is unconditional.

We make love several times throughout the day without words, for no words are needed. Our bodies reveal the depths of our love for each other. His lips kiss my lips, my neck, and my breasts before pausing at my stretch marks. He places his forehead against my stomach, kissing up and down the dark pink lines, the physical evidence of a life that once was.

Exhaustion from the hours of crying beckons me and I fall into a deep slumber. When I awake a few hours later, I am alone. Grabbing the flat sheet, I go in search of Adam when I hear the shower running. The air is thick and hot, steam billows throughout the large bathroom. A strangled cry sends chills down my spine. It's hard to hear with the sound of the water so I step further into the space. "Why? God, why?" Adam pleads with God for answers. Immediately my thoughts race to the kids. Did something happen to them? Of course, I realize that he wouldn't be standing here, he would've rushed out to be with them. Those kids are his everything. To hear my beautiful man sob and the thumping of his forehead against the tile crushes me to the bone. I want to grab the door and ask him what I can do to ease his burden, but I can't. This moment is private, a moment to be alone with your thoughts and God. Whatever is causing this ache in his soul is something that he needs to work out on his own.

I step back, closing the bathroom door quietly and crawl back into bed to wait for him. I will give him the time he needs.

"I CAN ONLY IMAGINE HOW BEAUTIFUL YOU WERE." HIS fingers traced the lines. "Can I ask you a question?"

"Mmmm..." I hum, keeping my eyes closed.

"What was it like?" he asks and then hesitates. "...to feel her grow and move in you?"

I keep my head down, but my eyes flash open to find his. I can't imagine why he would ask me that question. It's like pouring salt on an open wound. I swallow hard and reach for my necklace.

"What do you want to know?" I whisper.

"Everything. You can give me something that I never had to chance to experience."

"I'm not sure I understand."

He looks down thoughtfully and then clears his throat before speaking. "I told you already how when Johanna was pregnant, she didn't tell anyone. I never got the chance to see my babies grow in her belly. I never felt them move within her. I never got to kiss their tiny fingers and toes or hold them as newborn babies. She denied me those opportunities. I'll *never* forgive her for that. Never." His last words catch in his throat.

I run my hand through his hair, smoothing it back to look at his handsome face. "I'm sorry she denied you all those things." I close my eyes momentarily, breathing in and out slowly. I can give him this. I can share my story with him and hope that someday he can forgive Johanna.

I massage the back of his head which rests against my belly as he continues to shower me with tender kisses. "It was scary ... and absolutely wonderful at the same time." My words are quietly spoken.

His back rises and falls, breathing sharply, as he waits for me to tell my story.

"I was terrified when I found out I was pregnant. I was a twenty year old college student. God knows I wasn't ready to become a mother. I had my whole life ahead of me. My parents were so angry. They said we were careless and irresponsible to think that we could bring a child into this world when we were just kids ourselves." I shake my head at the memory. "Dylan's father was too drunk to care. But we loved each other—at least, I thought we did. I thought we would get married after the baby was born and make things work."

Adam looks up at me and I see his face transform from interest to remorse. It makes me a little sad that we were willing to marry other people for the sake of our unborn children. At least Dylan and I were a couple. Adam asked Johanna to marry him even though he didn't love her. I don't think either marriage would have lasted.

"He left school and started working full time for my dad at the DeGennaro's plant to save money. He came to a few of the doctor's appointments with me." I shake my head in quiet disbelief. "When he saw the heartbeat on the screen, he broke down in tears." I remember wondering if he was crying because he was happy to see his baby girl's tiny heart beating or was he sad because the reality that he got me pregnant and was going to become a father was too much to handle. I realized years later that he probably couldn't believe the situation he was in—two girls and two babies. That would be a lot for anyone to handle, I guess.

"I wanted to go back to school and finish the semester, only coming home for my appointments. My mother insisted that I come home and go to the local community college, but I argued with her saying that I was on a full scholarship and was determined to finish school."

"The first time I felt her move, I was lying on my bed reading, studying for the final exam for a summer class I was taking. It was like a quick flutter. It happened so fast I almost missed it. She must've liked when I was resting because that's when she moved the most." I reach down and circle my navel.

"I wish it had been me and you." Adam whispers as rests his head on my belly again. "Our lives could've been so different."

"We weren't meant to meet then. It's our time now—with Maddie and Luke."

"I would never have done those things to you, Mia. Never. I would have loved you and married you."

I offer a small smile while my fingers play with his dark, wavy hair wishing his words were true, but the fact is that we probably wouldn't have worked out either.

"I love you." He kisses my belly.

"I know you do."

"I will *always* protect you no matter what." The conviction in his voice is strong.

I smile at his words. "Okay."

Chapter Thirty-One

LATE SUNDAY MORNING BRINGS A RENEWED SENSE OF purpose, a new beginning to us. I awake enveloped in Adam's arms, holding me close. His promised words to never let her or anyone else hurt me again were reassuring but brought on another deluge of tears.

"Come shower with me." I'm pulled out of bed and carted off to the vast marbled shower.

Hot water rains down on us while Adam's hands wash away tears and some of the guilt I felt for not being completely honest with him about my past. "Shhh, stop with the crying."

"I can't... I just love you so much." I hiccup.

"I know, baby. I love you, too. Turn around so I can wash your back."

His hands travel across my shoulders, down my back and over my backside to my legs, rubbing circles in every direction. He lowers himself to squat to wash my feet and the front of my legs. Rising slowly, he washes my stomach and my breasts before angling my head against his shoulder to kiss my neck. "You are everything I never knew I wanted."

With shampoo in his hands, he lathers and washes my hair before he applies conditioner. Over my shoulders to my breasts, Adam caresses me, pulling my back to his front. His need for me is evident as he circles his hips, pushing himself into me. The marble is cold against my breasts as hot water pours down on us. The heat of our bodies makes me forget about the hard surface. He warms my body, he warms my heart.

I DRIVE HOME THAT AFTERNOON INSTEAD OF TAKING Adam up on his offer to go with him to pick up the kids from their grandparents. I haven't met them yet. I'm not sure I'm quite ready to meet Johanna's parents.

I change the station on the radio after the weather forecast calls for an early winter with lots of snow, warning drivers to take it easy on the roadways. Two inches fell overnight and cover my driveway. I park the Jeep and walk over to get Brady back from Mrs. Longo before going into my house. I was thankful that Adam called her last night and asked if she'd keep Brady because he knew that I wouldn't want him to be alone all night.

The freshly fallen snow is beautiful, hanging onto the branches of the evergreen trees, pulling their branches low to create a Winter Wonderland. Mr. Longo shoveled a narrow path on the walkway leading up to their back door.

"Come in, darling." Mrs. Longo ushers me in from the cold where Brady yelps frantically on the other side of the door. I drop to my knees and let him shower me with kisses. "Hey, buddy. I missed you, boy. I'm sorry Mama wasn't home last night."

"Thank you for keeping him." I hug her thin body.

"Oh, honey, you're quite welcome. Any time. You know that."

I accept her offer for a cup of coffee and we sit in her tidy kitchen. Mr. Longo snores quietly in the living room with the TV still on.

"I hope you don't mind my asking, but is everything okay?" she asks as she cuts and serves me a generous slice of pumpkin bread.

"It is now." I simply smile. "Thank you."

I dunk the corner piece of my bread into the cup of coffee and smile. "This is delicious. Adam would love this. You'll have to give me the recipe, but if I eat any more of this, I'll have to put myself on a diet."

"Speaking of diet. Did you change Brady's food or anything?" What an odd question. Why would she care what food I'm feeding my dog? She must see the puzzled look on my face because she explains her inquiry.

"The reason I'm asking is Brady kept me up half the night, yelping and barking to go outside." He has been doing that a lot recently, waking up in the wee hours of the morning. Those damn wild animals are driving him insane.

"As soon as I opened the back door, he took off like a bat out of hell into your yard, barking like a lunatic."

"Yeah, he's been doing that the past few weeks. Poor guy's getting older. I need to schedule an appointment with the vet to have him checked out."

"That's a good idea, dear. You know, the older they get, the less their boy parts work properly," she says with a wink. Ewww...I think I just threw up in my mouth. The thought of Mr. Longo's boy parts is just so...so wrong. I swallow the bile that threatens to rise.

After Brady and I say a final thank you and head on home, I decide that I should probably shovel my walkway before the temperature drops overnight and the snow freezes. I send Adam a quick text as I walk over to the garage to dig out a shovel. I notice the door is ajar and some things are moved around. I'll have to remind Mr. Longo to put things back after he uses them. I climb over my paddleboard to get the shovel. *What the hell!* I can't imagine why Mr. Longo would have put the shovel so far back after using it. Maybe Mrs. Longo needs to make an appointment for him, too.

Brady trots back over to me. I grab my phone out of my jacket pocket and tap out a response to Adam's attachment. It's a car selfie of him and the kids with the words, "We love you." A cheeky grin slides across my face when I see it. I send him a picture of Brady and me, "We love you, too."

Winter in New England really is so beautiful with a blanket of white covering the ground, the tall pines tree branches hang low from the snow's weight. Something dark in the white snow catches my eye. I walk over and pick it up; it's a glove. What the hell? I haven't been here and Mr. Longo doesn't usually go past the garage. But what sends chills down my spine are the footsteps that lead away from the garage into the woods going down toward the lake. I retrace my steps only to find out that these large footsteps lead to my back door to the garage and then into the woods. I'm deep thought when the sound of my phone startles me.

"Hello, Peter!" I hate calling him by his full name, but he insists so I oblige. Every once in a while, I want to call him Peter Peter Pumpkin-eater, but I know he'd get mad. He's such a pansy sometimes.

"Hey, gorgeous. What's going on? Are you home?"

"Yeah, I'm here. I just got home. What's up?"

"There's someone I want you to meet."

"Um...Okay, sure." I'm not really in the mood for company, but it's Pete and I can't ever say no to him.

I lie in bed that night with Brady at my side, thinking about Pete and his new "friend" Tyler, who came over and watched the Patriots game with me. I tried to pay attention to the game, but between Adam's constant texts to make sure that I was really okay and Pete and Tyler's ogling over Tom Brady and Julian Edelman in their uniforms, I couldn't concentrate. Pete swears that if he had five minutes with Tom Brady, he could make him forget all about Gisele. And that is why I love Pete so much. I think we won, but I'm not really sure. I'll have to text Josh in the morning to find out the final score. He's much more animated than the commentators on Sports Center.

Chapter Thirty-Two

To say that Adam has become very protective of me would be a serious understatement. One might say he's borderline domineering, even rushing out of an important business meeting to help me when my Jeep got a flat tire during a light snowfall.

"Babe, I do know how to change a tire." I laugh into the phone when he insisted that I stay put and wait for him. Maddie and Luke sit patiently in the back seat.

"I know you do. But it's my job to be there for you, baby. Tell me exactly where you guys are."

Twenty minutes later, Adam pulls up and saves the day. The kids and I wait in the warmth of his luxury vehicle while he tends to the flat tire. The name "Nora" flashes on the dashboard screen when his phone starts to ring. I shouldn't answer his phone. I'm sure it's just a work call, but this "Nora" calls him a lot. I remember him saying that some people couldn't take "no" for an answer or the time he canceled our New York trip at the last minute, claiming something came up. Before I pick up his phone, I look around to see where he is. I feel guilty, like a snoop. *Oh right, maybe that's because I am.*

"Hello?" I answer quietly, swiping the green button on his phone.

I'm met with hesitation and then, an agitated voice asks, "Where's Adam?"

No hello, no cordial greeting of any kind. Why does she need to know where he is anyway?

"Uh, I'm sorry. He's unavailable at the moment. Can I give him a message for you?" My breathing starts to become uneven and my heart races in my chest. I'm terrified to know what kind of message she wants me to deliver.

"Yeah, you tell him that I don't appreciate him storming out in the middle of a meeting. Who's this anyway?"

"Excuse me?"

"I asked who you were. Are you the reason he's been so distracted lately?"

I don't know what to say to this woman who obviously is comfortable with him. If she's only a business associate, why are goose bumps lining my skin?

"I'm Mia. Who are you?" I glance back and see Adam walk around the back of my Jeep to get my spare tire.

"You're the school teacher. The girlfriend?" There's a definite change in her tone as she sighs audibly, but I can't seem to figure it out. How does she know about me?

"I'll tell him you called," I mutter quickly.

"You better. It's important." She disconnects the call.

Adam opens the trunk of his Escalade and tosses my flat tire in before slamming the door shut. His eyebrows are furrowed and he looks worried, distracted. I feel guilty for having him rush out here to change a flat tire. He's covered with a dusting of snow when he opens the passenger door for me. The white flakes against his dark hair and black jacket make him look delicious.

"You are all set," he enunciates each word as he leans over to kiss me chastely.

My nerves haven't calmed down yet after Nora's phone call, but I manage a small smile and kiss him back.

"Hey kids, let's go. Put the movie on pause." He clears his throat as he taps the DVD screen mounted on the upholstered ceiling. "I have to go back to work for a little bit, but I'll see you for dinner."

I want to tell him about the phone call and ask who exactly she is, but I don't. His cold fingers brush the hair away from my face,

"You okay?"

"I'm fine." I smile weakly. "I told you I could've changed the tire myself. You didn't have to rush out here." I look into those chocolate eyes and know without a doubt that he would do more, so much more, for me.

"Stop." He silences me with his lips. "I said Stop." His lips press against mine when I try to talk. "I'll see you around seven or so. I have a couple of things to take care of."

"Okay." I step out into the cold and lead Maddie and Luke back to the Jeep.

Looking pensive, Adam walks alongside us, his eyes scanning the road. My poor man! He's got so much going on at work and he thinks he needs to protect me like I'm helpless. No, my love, I've been on my own for quite some time and can handle most things without anyone's help.

Later that night after the kids are asleep in their beds, Adam and I soak in a hot bath to relieve the stress of the day. "So how was your day?" His strong hands rub deep circles into my shoulders while he places kisses on my neck.

"Mmmmm...It was fine until I got a flat tire. Those are brand new tires."

The circling of his fingers pauses momentarily and then resumes.

"Why'd you take my tire anyway? I was going to swing by Mr. Jackson's place and have him fix it."

"It's okay. I'll take care of it." He pushes my hair over the other shoulder and inhales at the nape of my neck. "I love this part. *Kiss*. Right. *Kiss*. Here."

It's my turn to ask the questions. "So, other than saving a damsel in distress, how was your day?" I smirk, offering my cheek for a kiss.

"I've had better days," he sighs. His words make me sad. I feel like I'm an added burden.

"Want to talk about it?" Water swishes around as I turn to face him.

"Not really. It's nothing for you to be concerned about." He reaches forward to grasp my arms so I can straddle him. My legs slide along his thighs while his erection pokes out from the deep water. "I do have something to tell you, though." I stiffen at his words. Is he going to tell me about Nora or what's going on with his work?

"You can tell me anything. You know that." I kiss his chest, licking up to his neck.

"What I have to say is very important so you need to listen closely."

He's so serious, not a hint of amusement detected.

"Okay, I'm listening." I swallow hard in anticipation of his words.

"You and my kids are my life. I would do anything to protect you guys." I watch as tears fill his eyes. "I love you more than life itself." Our chests collide when he crushes me against him. His heart pounds frantically in his chest making me push away to look at his face. His eyes are closed, his nostrils flare and he's trying desperately to hold back the tears.

"Baby, why are you upset?" My thumbs wipe at his cheeks as my fingers caress his scruffy face, willing him to talk to me. "What's going on?"

"I need you." He attacks my mouth ferociously, lifting me up to impale me with his stiff length. Oh, God! He feels so good even if I'm not quite ready for him. He stills the moment he enters me, savoring it.

His hands roam all over my wet body as I lift and lower continuously, needing a deeper connection with him. He's not making sweet love to me. He's fucking me hard. And I love every minute of it.

Long fingers reach in between us and rub circles on my clit while he angles my body to plunge deeper. My eyes start to close, but his demands to look at him force them open.

"I'm going to c-c-come." I toss my head back, look to the ceiling, reveling in the high of my orgasm.

"Oh my fucking God," he groans and breathes heavily into my breasts as he releases and spills into me.

I smile lazily into his neck as he pants against me. He knows I'm smiling. "What are you grinning about?" The image of the very first time I saw him on the summit comes to mind. He was panting so hard, bending over, supporting himself on his knees. I remember wondering if that's what he sounded like when he comes. Yep, it's confirmed for the umpteenth time. Once again it's me that got him this way, not the hike up the expert trail at the park or some other woman. I'm embarrassed that even from the first moment I laid eyes on him, I was attracted to him. The buzzing of his phone makes me roll my eyes as I reach over the side of the tub to retrieve his phone. Maybe I can grab his phone and "accidentally" drop it in the bath water. *Oops. Silly me.*

When Nora's name lights up the screen, it earns him narrowed eyes and a dirty look. "Oh, I forgot to tell you Nora called earlier," I say nonchalantly.

His eyes flash to mine. "Yeah, she told me." I wonder if she told him how rude she was to me. He declines the call and sets the phone down. What kinds of people conduct work at such late hours? There has to be more to the story than just work. I am determined to find out.

"Who is she?" My voice is small, lacking conviction.

"What do you mean, 'Who is she?' She's an associate. One of our agents." He says it like it is common knowledge. I wonder if she works for a rival real estate agency.

"Have you ever fucked her?" I look away afraid of what his face might reveal. Yes, the green-eyed monster appears even though his words of love are sincere. Dylan's words were sincere, so were Shane's and look what happened there. Both times.

"No."

"No?" I ask in disbelief. "You've never done *anything* with her?"

"No." It doesn't escape me that his eyes look away.

I know he's lying. I grab the side of the huge bathtub to push myself up and step out, wrapping a white towel around me.

I hand him a towel, but he doesn't take it. Instead he sits there staring at me. "You don't believe me."

"I'm sorry," I whisper and run my fingers through my hair to pull at the long strands. "You know I get insecure about the women from your past." I think of the two women I have seen Adam with. The ginger and the blonde. I know there are so many more.

"Mia, none of those women ever meant anything. You know what I did and why I did it. Those women were a means to an end. You are the means to my future."

I know this. He has said it to me enough times already.

"Remember the night at that club? Why were you so mean to me?" I shiver when remember the harsh words he spoke and the look on his face when he stepped into the light.

Adam breathes a deep sigh and subtly shakes his head like he's trying to erase the image. "You shouldn't have been there. That wasn't a place for someone like you." He takes the towel from me and drapes it over his lap. "Come here. Sit."

I lower myself onto his lap. "What do you mean, 'a place for someone like me'? It was just a club." Even as I say the words, I know that that's not entirely true.

A small chuckle escapes his lips and he shakes his head. "Baby, it's not a dance club."

My eyes beg for further explanation.

"It's a sex club. A swingers club to be exact."

My mouth gapes open. "What? You're lying! It is *not* a sex club!"

The raised eyebrows on his face tell me he's not kidding.

"Oh shit! It is?"

"I was checking out the VIP rooms when you saw me standing on the balcony." His voice is low; he sounds ashamed.

"Eww! You were going to have sex with that redhead in a sex

club?"

"No, I said I was checking it out. One of the owners is a friend of mine."

Friend of his? Devin? He's friends with Devin? Oh Lord, if he only knew what Devin wanted to do to me.

"I was just looking around the refurbished club when I looked down and saw you. I couldn't believe it. I assumed you were there to...you know, find someone for the night." He couldn't even say the words. It's like the thought repulses him that much. Good! Now he knows exactly how I felt. "I wasn't positive that it was you at first, but then I *felt* you. I had to get out of there. I was so angry that you were there to...you know and that you had seen me there. You were, after all, my daughter's teacher." *Oh, if this isn't the pot calling the kettle black! Humph!* A wry smile crosses his face.

"I was so mad at Kate, she just left me there to fend for myself."

"Who's Kate? I didn't see you with anyone."

"Krazy Kate. She's a friend from college. She brought me there that night and ended up leaving with other friends. It was pretty fucked up. I heard that she's in rehab again."

"Is she in for drugs or alcohol?"

"I'm not sure. Probably both," I answer honestly.

He shakes his head. "That's too bad. I hope she gets the help she needs. Drugs aren't anything to mess around with."

I think about all the crazy things she's done over the years.

"So, Kate left you there and then what happened?"

"I gave some asshole a bloody nose."

"*You* did that?" His eyes pop open. "I heard about that."

"The jerk had his hands all over me, telling me that he wanted to fuck me."

Adam winces and then growls at my crude words. "He what? That motherfucker!"

"It was disgusting!"

"Like I said, not a place for you."

"Yeah, well, it's not a place for you either."

"That was my first and last time. When I saw you there, I was determined to make you mine." He kisses my forehead. I remember when he found out that I was Maddie's teacher. I wonder if that's why he asked if I was married.

"What about the blonde at the bar?" I ask now that he's on a roll, talking openly.

"Blonde? Which blonde?" Oh great, there were so many he can't keep track of them.

When I describe the blonde from the happy hour at the Pour House, he nods in remembrance. "Oh, that blonde. That's Nora." Nora? He was at the bar with Nora and she still calls him all the time and at all hours. *What the fuck!* My body tenses immediately.

"Babe, work associate, remember? She's one of our agents. Relax." He rubs my back trying to soothe the tension.

"We had a business lunch meeting that ran late." He places tiny kisses along my bare shoulder.

"Whatever." I roll my eyes. I know I'm being childish, but that's what jealousy does to me.

"Why were you were so mad at me all that week?" It seems like yesterday Shelby and I were talking about Adam being a fine fucker. I let out a small chuckle.

"Oh, you were such a jerk! Always flirting with me and then walking out with your arm around the Wicked Bitch. I wanted to slap you." I laugh louder at the memory.

"I wanted you so badly, but I wasn't sure if you were interested. You were hard to read. So I had to see for myself." His shoulders rise in a nonchalant shrug.

"You...You did that shit on purpose? You were trying to make me jealous? Oh, Adam Lawson, you are in big, big, big trouble, mister!" I stand up and snatch his towel off exposing his semi-erect shaft. I twist the towel into a whip before snapping it against his thigh, leaving a red mark. "Get up! Let's go! Bedroom! You owe me!!"

The roguish grin on his face tells me that he's going to play along. "Yes, ma'am." I snap the towel once more catching it on his ass cheek. "Ouch, woman! I don't think I want to see what you can do with a real whip." He rubs the red spot and smirks.

I sprawl out on the oversized bed with my knees slightly bent and call him to me. "You. There. Now." I demand with seriousness on my face, pointing to the apex between my thighs. "You made me jealous on purpose. You owe me."

"Oh, baby, I always pay my debts." He smirks and licks his lips before lowering his head.

Adam Lawson pays his debts and then some.

Chapter Thirty-Three

ADAM TAKES EVERY OPPORTUNITY TO PROTECT ME FROM Gina and anyone else who would try to hurt me or his family. Our nights are never spent apart—every night we are together, just the four of us, splitting time between his house and mine. The kids love sleeping at my house, it's like sleep away camp.

My encounters with Gina are minimal because she doesn't come in to pick Sophie up at school anymore, she sends Chris or Samantha, a nasty bleach-blonde snotty bitch who works for her. At first when I would see Gina's car driving slowly around my neighborhood, it would piss me off. Is she stalking me now? But then the realization hits me like I'm an idiot. She's a realtor who happens to be selling a house on my street. I think maybe I should mention it to Adam but then decide against it. It's really not important. She's not important.

BY FRIDAY AFTERNOON, ADAM AND I ARE LOOKING forward to dropping the kids off to visit their grandparents since they won't see them for Thanksgiving. We've decided to fly to Texas to visit my brother for the holiday even though my mom won't be there.

I spend the entire hour long ride with my eyes closed, trying to sleep off the migraine I feel coming on. I could vaguely hear the conversation Adam is having with his mother. I wonder what she's like. I wonder if she'd like me. Deep breaths do little to quell my nerves which are on high alert as we drive to the suburban town where Johanna grew up. The children's grandparents have asked to meet me because apparently I'm all they talk about. Adam's constant circling on my thigh only serves one purpose and I don't think it's what he was going for.

"Why are you so nervous?" He smiles and questions me.

"I don't know really. I guess I just want them to like me." I tug at my pendant.

"I don't care what they think. Why is it so important to you, Mia?"

I turn in my seat and nod toward the back where the kids are watching a movie. "Because I love those two kids and I want them to *always* feel love, to *always* be surrounded by people who love them."

I continue, "And I guess I don't want them to ever think that I could or that I would ever try to replace their mother. I'm sure it's hard for them. Johanna's parents have never had to deal with another woman loving their daughter's children."

"You're incredible, you know that?" he says, leaning over to kiss me.

I wasn't sure what I was expecting, but it certainly wasn't this. The simple white Colonial was warm and welcoming—a grandchild's refuge filled with genuine love. Adam parks the Escalade and we get the kids' bags out of the trunk. Walking up the slate stairs and into the house, a sweet aroma of cinnamon and apples infiltrates my nose, reminding me of my own childhood.

A tall, statuesque woman and an equally tall man appear from what seems like a formal dining room. Luke and Madison drop their bags and run into the awaiting arms of their grandparents. Adam steps forward to shake hands with the older gentleman and then kisses the woman on the cheek. I stand there awkwardly as they share a tender moment. For some reason, I feel like I've seen them before; they look oddly familiar to me.

Adam reaches back and extends his hand to me, calling me forward to join him. Hesitation falters my steps, but I quickly gain my confidence when I see his eyes beckon me. I slip my hand into his and smile.

"Nathan, Katherine. This is Mia. Mia Delaney." He presents me as though I've just been awarded first prize. I extend my hand to them. "Hello. It's a pleasure to finally meet you both." The woman he called Katherine just stares at me, thoughtfully but doesn't speak. Nathan, the grandfather, gently places his hand in mine. "Mia. Welcome. The pleasure truly is all ours."

Katherine shakes her head slightly as if waking from a daydream and smiles. "You're very beautiful. Welcome to our home." Her arms reach around to embrace me, but she holds on a second longer when I start to pull away.

Adam encourages the kids to put their things away upstairs and come back down quickly so they can say goodbye to us before we leave. The expression on Katherine's face falls. "Oh...I thought you were staying for dinner."

"I'm sorry Katherine, but Mia and I have dinner reservations already. Thank you for the offer though."

Without thinking or looking at him for consideration, I blurt out, "I don't mind cancelling our dinner plans." Adam's eyes dart to mine curiously and he swallows hard, his jaw beginning to tick. "Mia, may I have a word with you?" He pulls me into the foyer, away from prying eyes. "What are you doing?"

"I'm sorry I blurted that out, but I think we should stay for dinner. Did you see the look on her face?" I counter.

"Did you see this?" He pulls his jacket back and points to where his pants are tenting between his legs. "You're killing me here."

"Baby, I'll make it up to you. I promise," my voice whispers in his ear as I nibble on jaw.

The six of us sit at the formal dining room table to enjoy Katherine's homemade dinner of roasted chicken and baked macaroni and cheese. This feels like a family. And I'm happy to be a part of it. Maddie and Luke keep dinner interesting with their stories of dance class and football practice. Nathan promises that he'll come to one of Luke's games.

After dinner, Adam, Nathan and the kids head outside to toss the football around while Maddie plays on the tire swing that looks like it may have belonged to her mother. I stay inside to help Katherine clean up even though she insists that she is fine. We work side by side while she washes the dishes and I dry them, placing them on the dish rack. From the kitchen window, we can see them running around, playing in the big backyard as the sun begins to set.

"I knew it was you." Katherine dries her hands on a dish towel, turning to face me. "That phony woman was almost comical, fawning over Adam, doting on the children as if she really cared about them. Anyone with eyes could see it."

"Excuse me? I'm not sure I understand," I tell her honestly.

"At the birthday party. I saw the two of you talking. I knew he was in love with you. It was the subtle touches and the stolen glances. I watched him as he watched you. Every move you made, his eyes followed you. I knew you were more than just Madison's teacher."

Holy shit! That's it! That's where I saw them. They were the older couple standing quietly off to the side. I never put it together, but now it all makes sense.

"Wow. I don't know what to say."

"I saw what you gave Maddie for her birthday. I knew right then that you loved her. And I think you know my grandson quite well, too."

I smile warmly. "Madison had shared with me that her mother was a ballerina. I thought she would like the jewelry box. I had one just like it when I was a little girl. Luke is a wonderful boy."

"You're very considerate, loving," Katherine declares, staring out the window to the yard below.

"You remind me a lot of my daughter. Bless her soul. You even look a bit like her."

"Johanna was very beautiful," I state. I never really considered that we looked similar, although Madison could be my mini-me with her long dark hair and brown eyes.

"But she was very troubled, always wanting to live in a fantasy world."

I wait for her to continue, I can sense there's more to come.

"I remember when she finally told him that he fathered those babies, boy, was he livid! He accused her of lying and demanded a paternity test." She shakes her head at the memory. "What did she expect? Those babies were almost three years old when she revealed their existence." This revelation is nothing new, but instantly, anger flares within me for the lost years that Adam could never get back.

"He tried to do the right thing. He asked her to marry him and everything."

A loud sigh escapes Katherine's thin body as she hangs the towel to dry on the front of the stainless steel stove. "She was so damn stubborn. So strong-willed. She didn't want anything from him. Except his money."

"He became a wonderful father, providing everything for those children, but it was never enough for her. What she wanted most in this world was to dance and she hated that motherhood had taken that away. She resented him for that."

Suddenly, I feel as though I'm violating Adam's privacy. Why hasn't he ever told me how she felt about him? I know he feels guilty for what happened, for not being there when she needed him.

"I think a small part of him loved her, though. He obviously liked her enough to take her to his bed." Katherine's eyes open wide and then roll. "I think he loved her for giving him two beautiful, healthy babies even though they were quite the surprise."

I watch through the window at my handsome man who loves his children more than anything.

"That man out there, he's completely in love with you. And more importantly, Mia, so are his children." Tears pool in the corner of her aged eyes.

"Be a good mother to those children."

I want to correct her and tell her that I'm not their mother, but the hand she lifts, causes me to halt my words.

"You *are* their mother now. Love them. Take care of them. Protect them. Always."

AFTER WE SAY GOODBYE TO NATHAN, KATHERINE AND the kids, my heart swells and overflows with love. Adam's expression was one of surprise when I was welcomed back anytime by his children's grandparents. The ride back home is dark and quiet; Adam and I are each lost in our own thoughts. It's amazing how content I am just to be with him, to feel him near me.

Justin Timberlake's sexy voice sings about falling in love with him. That's exactly how I feel. I know without a doubt that being in love with Adam Lawson and his children isn't such a bad thing. Our fingers are laced together, taking and giving what we need.

A loud ringing breaks our moment as Adam reaches forward and taps the screen to take the call. I send up a silent prayer, thankful that it is not Nora or the Wicked Witch. It is, however, a DeGennaro. This time it's her brother, Chris, who calls.

"Hey, Chris. What's up?" Adam asks as we turn onto the highway. An angry voice booms through the speaker, making me flinch and shift in my heated leather seat. "Where the fuck are you? What's your fucking problem, bro? I don't know what you think—"

Immediately, my hand is released so Adam can hit the button, silencing the call. A somber look crosses his face and then he stares straight ahead at the road. My carefree, loving Adam is gone, now replaced with a tense, irritated man.

"What's that about, Adam?" I ask tentatively, my head motions in the direction of the screen, my hand reaching for his, wanting to soothe away his tension.

"Nothing," he snaps, pulls his hand away, running it through his dark hair, inhaling sharply.

"Adam, don't lie to me." My words are careful and controlled, my eyes search his face for a clue.

"It's nothing for you to worry about. Just drop it." Dark eyes beg me to heed his words as he lets out a deep breath.

"Don't shut me out. Talk to me." The thought of Adam tangled up in some kind of problem with the DeGennaro family doesn't sit well with me. I know this family. They are ruthless and will stop at nothing to get what they want.

Adam reaches down to the center console to retrieve his phone when Chris' name appears again on the screen, but what he does next shocks me. Instead of answering the phone, he powers it off. Adam never, *ever* does that. It's his lifeline to those he loves most in the world.

I don't know if Adam realizes that he's just voiced murmured words about "no one being able to help," which scare the living shit out of me. I know this can't be good. Fear and anxiety race through my pounding heart as I conjure up every possible situation that he may have found himself in with this family.

FLICKERING CANDLES PLACED ALL AROUND THE DEEP, porcelain Jacuzzi tub provide the only light for us. Snow Patrol floats through the steamy air, calming us. Our bodies rise and fall as I lay my back against his chest. Warm, wet hands caress my arms, my neck, my breasts and even my belly. Down my neck and ear, his soft lips kiss, nibbling, sucking and tasting along the way.

"If I lay here, if I just lay here, would you lie with me and just forget the world," with a quiet, almost whispered voice, I sing to

Adam.

"I wish I could." Adam's stubble skims across the top of my head, then down my cheek. "I never thought I would ever feel this way. I never thought I could love this much."

I turn around and kneel between his legs so I can face him. I caress his face through his scruff and smile. His eyes fall longingly to my breasts, then back to my eyes. "I love everything about you." His wet hand caresses my face. "I love this." Pointing to my temple, he says, "And I love this." With his hands sliding down to touch my hips and then continuing lower to the neatly waxed sex, he whispers with a sly smile, "I absolutely love this."

Warm water splashes when I lean forward to kiss him. With his mouth crushed against mine, he says, "But what I love the most," he pushes me away gently, "is this." He sits forward and kisses the spot above my left breast where my heart beats. "I love your heart."

I move quickly, desperate to feel him in me, to taste him. I want all he has, all he is willing to give me. Forcing him up onto the side of the Jacuzzi, I love him completely with my mouth. His fingers weave through my hair as his hands grip my head, guiding me as I lick, suck and swallow along his thick shaft. Electricity courses through me, sending every blood vessel between my head to my toes on high alert. Before he climaxes, his thrusts become harder and deeper. I relish everything he's doing, everything he's giving me.

When he frees himself from my mouth, he pulls me close, smiles before he kisses me hard, his tongue tasting his own remnants. "Your debt has been paid." I owed him a debt? What the hell is he talking about? "You made me wait. You agreed to dinner with Nate and Katherine, remember? I ached all throughout dinner. You have no idea."

I smile. "Ah yes, I remember now. It was worth the wait, wasn't it?"

"And now you owe me again." His wet hands slip and slide all over me, over the swell of my heavy breasts to the curve of my backside, reaching up exploring me. "Nate and Katherine fell in love with you tonight. I want you all to myself." With his hands exploring my hidden parts, Adam showers me with his love. I close my eyes and enjoy the ride before I leap off the proverbial cliff into the abyss of utter satisfaction through release.

Chapter Thirty-Four

IT SEEMS THAT EVERYBODY AND THEIR MOTHER IN THE tri-state area decided to fly out on the Wednesday before Thanksgiving. The slow-moving traffic that we found ourselves stuck in from Connecticut to New York's JFK International Airport was utterly insane, earning Adam a few sideway glances from me when he shouted some choice words to errant cab drivers who cut him off.

"Dad, Maddie won't let me have it," Luke complains, tugging the iPad away from his sister, who sits next to him in the back seat of the Ford Explorer we rented once we arrived at San Antonio International Airport. Needless to say, we just need to get to my brother's house and chill out.

Josh insisted that we stay at his house for Thanksgiving, saying that it would like old times. I wasn't sure how Adam would feel about sharing a full-size bed in my brother's home with the kids on an air mattress in the kids' room. He certainly could have afforded to put us all in a luxury suite for the weekend, but he surprised me when he said it would be great to get to know my family. Could I possibly love him anymore?

Luke plays outside in the backyard with my brother's kids, Ashley and JJ, while Maddie takes a nap because she isn't feeling well. The guys bond over a game of football on the TV. I help Araceli in the kitchen, peeling potatoes, chopping and slicing away as needed.

"He's so freaking hot, chica." She winks at me, elbowing me

gently to get some juicy details, which I, unlike Shelby, will not share. "How can you stand to look at his face? Ay dios mio! He gets me all warm and fuzzy and you know my wooha is loose from giving your brother those two big-ass babies." Oh my God! Listening to my sister-in-law talk about her "parts" being loose is just...gross because I know that Josh is the reason they're like that. From what she's told me, they're almost as bad as Shelby and Mike.

"Ewww, you're disgusting, *chica*," I tease, throwing a piece of cubed celery at her, hoping to change the subject.

"C'mon, give me something..."

"Okay, okay, you perv. He's a very generous man when it comes to showing his love for me."

"Que mierda! No me digas, por un momento, que no hay mas que eso, chica!" Oh boy, when Araceli switches over to her native tongue telling me that she knows I'm withholding information, I know I'm in trouble. There might be a sandal or two that whiz past my head next. "I can't believe you won't tell me. Pero, nena, somos hermanas. You're like my sister!" Oh no, here comes the Spanglish!

A knock on the back door diverts our attention. "Hello, anyone home?"

The sliding door leading out to the patio opens and in walks my brother's best friend, Max. Yes, the best friend who I thought was heading back to Germany. Yes, the best friend I had sex with last summer in the back of a Land Rover. My eyes, wide with shock, travel down his body as I try desperately to remember if he looked this good in the summer. The muscles of his upper body are covered by a t-shirt and an unbuttoned long sleeve shirt, rolled up at the sleeves. His face, perfectly tanned, reveals that sexy smile. My cheeks redden with embarrassment as I vaguely remember lowering his pants and pulling him down on top of me. I swallow nervously.

Max's face lights up when he sees me standing next to Araceli as he walks over, kissing her cheek and placing a pecan pie on the counter.

"Happy Thanksgiving." He smiles at me. I wonder if he's thinking about that night. I was so drunk, you would have expected me not to remember it, but I did and I still do. Sort of.

I offer my cheek awkwardly when he leans in to greet me, his lips lingering a moment too long, making my eyes close briefly. It's not that I want him; I just wasn't expecting to ever see him again. And let's face it, he's freaking hot!

"My brother didn't mention that you'd be here for Thanksgiving," I state.

Araceli steps into the pantry looking for stuffing mix.

"Yeah, it was last minute thing." His voice drops to a shy whisper, "I was going to call you, but I lost your number." I don't know what to say when he looks at me with those incredible hazel eyes. "And I couldn't exactly ask Josh for your number now, could I?" Max asks, looking at me with implied meaning. His broad shoulders shrug apologetically before casting his eyes to the tiled floor.

"Oh my God, no worries! Seriously...it's fine," I promise, smiling before turning to wash my hands in the sink, not wanting anyone to notice how they're trembling.

Taking a break from the TV, Adam saunters over to me and slides his hands around my waist, pulling me into his hard chest. "Hey, beautiful, I've missed you."

I angle my head so I can lean back to kiss him. "I've been right here, babe, slaving away for you."

He growls in my ear. "I can be a slave driver, if you want me to be." I don't think he used his inside voice because my sister-in-law walks back in and erupts into a fit of giggles, drawing Adam's lips away from my ear to see what's so funny, but what he finds is Max standing there staring at us, watching our interaction.

Quickly, I jump into action, making introductions between Max and Adam.

"Max is my brother's best friend. They met in the Air Force."

I turn to Adam and smile. "Max, meet Adam. He's my...my

Adam." What am I supposed to call him? Boyfriend seems so trite. Lover is not an adequate description of what Adam is. Soul mate? That would be the correct definition of what he is to me, but that just sounds weird.

"Good to meet you, man." Max extends his hand and Adam returns the handshake. "How long have you two been together?" he asks and I can't help but wonder if he's trying to figure out if I was with Adam over the summer. I'm slightly offended by the question because I would never be unfaithful to Adam or anyone else for that matter. I'm not a cheater. Period.

"Well, that depends. Would that include all the time I pursued her and she ran fast and far away from me?" Adam smirks because I think he knew he'd eventually catch me just like he did. "We've been together a few months. She's everything to me."

"That's good to hear. She's a good girl." Max smiles at me. I wonder if he means that I'm a nice person "good girl" or I screwed her in the back seat of my Rover "good girl." Either way, it doesn't matter, it's over and done with. I can't change the past.

"Miss Delaney," a teary-eyed Madison cries, running into the kitchen in search of me.

"What's the matter, honey?" I ask, reminding her that she can call me "Mia" when we're not at school.

An eruption of tears streams from her little body when she bursts into sobs, gripping my hips tightly with her arms. I look to her father for some guidance.

"Maddie girl, what's wrong?" Adam asks, squatting to her eye level, pushing her hair away from her face, but Maddie tightens her hold on me.

"I was so scared. I was looking for you, but you weren't there."

Upon hearing her tearful words with such fear in her voice, I lift Maddie up and cradle her against my body, her legs wrap around my waist without hesitation. With her arms around my neck, she buries her face beneath my long hair.

"Shhhh, honey. It's okay. It was just a dream. I'm right here."

Adam stands there helplessly as I console his daughter, comforting her as only I can. His worried eyes meet mine, searching for some unknown answer.

"We'll be outside," I whisper and carry Maddie out to the patio to sit on the hammock. Her petite arms still hold on for dear life as her quiet sobs slowly begin to subside.

"Talk to me, Maddie." I use my fingers to smooth her hair back and kiss her forehead.

"I...I was so...scared," she hiccups. "I was walking with Luke and Daddy. We were holding hands. I turned around to see where you were, but you weren't there." She wipes her eyes with the tips of her small fingers while her hiccups continue. "When I told Daddy that we had to go back to get you, he said you had to go away. He...he said you didn't love us anymore. You didn't love me."

I bite back the unshed tears that will fall heavily onto my cheeks at any given moment. "Madison, I'm not going anywhere, sweetheart. I love you, honey. You're my sweet Maddie girl. I love you, your brother, and your daddy very much." My arms can't hold her close enough. "And you know who loves you, too?"

"No," she sighs exhausted from crying.

"C'mon, sure you do. Think about."

Her big brown eyes filled with sadness look into mine.

"Brady! That dog is crazy about you! He loves you so much!" We laugh together thinking about what a loveable and goofy boy he is.

Rocking back and forth slowly on the hammock, I close my eyes and imagine what it would be like to hold my daughter like this. To have held her at birth, to feel her suckle on my breast, all these things I would never know. I can't imagine my life without Adam and his kids, I would be devastated if I lost them, and yet Johanna couldn't imagine her life with Adam and her kids, she couldn't stand it so she ended her life, taking Madison and Luke's innocence with her. The irony is too familiar.

"Miss Delaney."

"Madison, honey. Remember you can call me Mia when we're not at school. I don't mind."

Apprehension dots her now subdued face. "But, Sophie said it's not right. She said you want to be my mommy. She said you can't be because you only get one mom and mine went to Heaven."

And I wonder where Sophie heard that. I smile down at Adam's sweet little girl.

"Well, Sophie is 100% wrong! You know my brother, Josh, inside?" I motion toward the house. "He has two mommies. When he was just a teeny tiny baby, his real mommy, the one who carried him in her belly, well, she couldn't take care of him. So she gave baby Josh to my mom and dad because she knew that my parents would love him and protect him."

"Josh has two mommies?"

"Yep and just because I'm not your mom because Johanna was your mommy, that doesn't mean that I can't love you. I'll always love and protect you. So don't listen to Sophie anymore, okay? You call me whatever you want. Deal?" I hold out my pinky to lock in her promise. Her little pinky wraps around mine. "Deal."

Back inside, we find everyone helping to set the tables. Josh and Araceli have a modest home in this quiet military town. A makeshift kids' table is set up adjacent to the adults' table. When we sit down to eat, we hold hands, bow our heads and say grace, each of us sharing what we are thankful for this year. Everyone got to say their piece, but I couldn't do it. The words wouldn't come forth, only tears uttered my silent and many thanks for Adam, Luke, and Madison. For my brother and his family. For my crazy mother. For my friends. And lastly for Brady, who has been there faithfully beside me for the past seven years.

Everyone at the table laughs nervously when I break out into a full on sob after Adam thanks me for being the love of his life and for completing his family, kissing me with such love and adoration.

He was right. All those months back as we walked along the seaside, hand in hand, he said, "It'll happen." It finally happened.

Chapter Thirty-Five

FLYING HOME LATE ON A SUNDAY AFTERNOON FROM A busy but fun holiday weekend was probably not the best choice. We are all exhausted. The kids have been arguing and whining since we said goodbye to Josh, Araceli and the kids. Thankfully Max didn't show up to say goodbye like he said he would. That wouldn't have gone over well with Adam.

The brief but noticeably friendly encounters between Max and me were a huge source of contention after we stuffed ourselves full on our Thanksgiving feast. Adam knows me too well. The tension that riddled throughout my body was palpable when Adam figured out that the subtle nuances that Max aimed at me were more than playful banter, it was outright flirting. Max didn't seem to care that my brother, or more importantly, Adam was present. Adam's face was a mix of emotions from hurt to disgust when I confessed later night about sleeping with Max.

"He fucked you? In the back of his truck?" I had to cover his mouth with my hand to quiet him because his voice could, no doubt, be heard through the thin walls.

"SHHHHH! BE QUIET! It was before I met you. I didn't even know you existed!" I answered through gritted teeth, defending myself. Surely he couldn't be mad for something that happened before him? If I remember correctly, he was the one who said, "Do we really want to delve into each other's pasts?" No! I don't want to know about all the women who've shared his bed. Lord knows he's probably slept with half of the women in New York City so he shouldn't want to know or care about whose bed I've been in. Although the back seat doesn't constitute a bed. Adam slid his hands over mine to remove them from his lips, cupping my face while forcing me to look at him. In his eyes, I expected to see anger, but instead I was met with compassion and love. "Baby, I don't care that you had sex with him. Well...that's not entirely true." His chest rose and lowered on a ragged breath. "I hate any man who's ever had the privilege of kissing you, touching you or pleasuring you," he winced, but continued on, "but, it's the *way* he treated you. How could he have been so careless with you?"

Closing his eyes, Adam lowered his head and shook it briefly as if he were shaking away an unwelcomed thought before resting his lips against my forehead. Images of all the women before me come to mind. I wonder if Adam is thinking about how he treated them.

"You have no idea how incredibly precious you are. No one should ever treat you like anything less." Once his varied emotions over the situation subsided, he showered me all night with a love more precious than the rarest gem on Earth.

"YES, I UNDERSTAND...OKAY, THAT'S FINE...I'M GETTING everything we need...Yes. Okay, I'll be there. I've gotta go." Adam's whispered conversation wakes me as he parks his Escalade in my driveway and turns off the ignition. As I open one eye slowly, I find him in a thoughtful state, his face troubled and weary. My promise to stay awake to keep him company was soon forgotten by the time we hit the Merritt Parkway when I curled up and fell asleep, midsentence.

"Who was that?" I ask quietly, my voice laced with concern, not wanting to wake the kids who have been asleep the entire time.

"Hmmm?" Adam hums, snapping out of his reverie.

"The call. Who were you talking to?" I ask again, shifting my body to face him so he can see that I mean business. Suddenly, I feel uneasy again. It was the same feeling I had when I asked him about the constant phone calls he had taken over the weekend, even excusing himself from the table to walk outside to speak privately. I mean, really, unless you're a doctor on call, who takes a business call right in the middle of Thanksgiving dinner? Although his tight smile and a kiss on the forehead attempted to appease me, my returned eye roll let him know that I was not happy with him.

"Business. Like always." His strong hands reach up to scrub his face and scratch his beard, loudly exhaling a deep breath before turning to me. "Do you know how much I love you? Do you know that I would do anything to protect you and the kids?"

I nod and grab his head, kissing him hard. "Yes, baby. I know." Brown eyes search brown eyes, looking for some clue. I hear his words, I feel his lips, but I can't help feel a sense of unease and foreboding. Adam isn't being completely honest with me, he's keeping secrets. Jealousy and insecurity have joined forces and are raising their ugly head, taunting and teasing without mercy.

Adam opens the trunk and gets my suitcase out before he leaves. We decide that it's probably a good idea that he go back to his own place tonight so the kids can sleep comfortably in their own beds and rest a little bit more before school in the morning. With one last kiss, I wave goodbye as he leaves.

I yawn and wipe the sleep out of my eyes, squinting carefully to look at the side of the SUV. I smile when I realize that Maddie is awake, looking at me. Her tiny, curled fingers press against the glass, waving at me, a sad smile mars her beautiful face. Before I can raise my hand to wave back or blow her a kiss, she's gone. Just like my dream. Or rather my nightmare.

Brady runs over to me when I unlock the back door. Mrs. Longo's kind offer to bring him home earlier was welcomed. I sit in the Adirondack chair to wait while Brady tends to his canine business for the last time for the evening. My eyes are heavy and they close, but I bolt into an upright position when barking in the woods startles me. Goosebumps cover my skin, the hair at the nape of my neck stands to attention. Darkness prevents me from seeing anything between the tall pine trees, but I have a sense that someone or something is watching me. Standing up, I scan the vast yard, looking for any sign of life. The Longo's house is dark except for the back porch light and the light above the kitchen window, casting a shadow through the thick shrubs lining the driveway. Mrs. Longo told me once that her husband has a tendency to come down in the middle of the night to get a drink and sit on the back porch. She said some nights his mind won't rest, he's always thinking about the past. I'd never sleep if I did that.

I call to Brady who is nowhere in sight, but from a far distance down by the lake, I can hear his vicious, protective bark. His growl reveals that he must be getting annoyed with all this wildlife crossing his territory, gathering what they need for a long New England winter.

I wait and I wait and I wait some more. When he finally comes trotting into the yard, he looks agitated, not like my happy-go-lucky dog. A visit to the vet is a must because I think he could use a little Prozac, too. These little critters are driving him crazy. Brady and I crawl into my neatly made, cool, lonely bed. I miss Adam. I can't remember the last time I slept without his warm, hard body entangled with mine.

"Love you more," I respond to his sweet text before drifting off to sleep. I'm starting dream number two when Brady's deep growl wakes me. The dim garage light filters into my bedroom, casting just enough light to help me find Brady's head. I pat his head, shushing him, telling him it's just the rabbits and raccoons.

Chapter Thirty-Six

THE HUSTLE AND BUSTLE OF CHRISTMAS IS UPON US, drawing shoppers into the malls for great deals and the latest ridiculously overpriced gadgets. Father Winter and Jack Frost have come out to play, each bringing their fair share of snow and ice, as usual. Red, green, silver and gold adorn every hallway and classroom display, letters to Santa are written, each child detailing their Christmas list.

Maddie and Luke have each chosen a name from the "Giving Tree" displayed in the foyer of our school. I've been delegated as Christmas shopper since Adam, who has grown even more agitated since Thanksgiving, finds himself working longer days, traveling often outside of the state for business meetings. With his frequent absences, the kids and I eat dinner without him and my bed becomes cold and lonely. I feel like a single mother to his children.

After dealing with impatient drivers on the highway, I park the Jeep in the packed parking lot of one of our state's biggest malls. Don't ask me why I thought this was a good idea. Frantic shoppers flock in multitudes. Christmas spirit and good cheer are replaced by greed and rudeness. The kids promise to stay close by, each having to hold my hand as we navigate through the sea of people. Finding the perfect gift for the children whom, without the help of the "Giving Tree" would have no gifts at all, was no easy task, but we manage to escape unscathed.

I let the kids decide where they'd like to eat lunch. Lights flash, thunder rumbles, gorillas beat their chests as we dine at the Rainforest Café. My texts to Adam have gone unanswered all morning. That's not like him. As brief as his responses of "Can't talk" or "In a meeting" are, it's better than being met with absolute silence.

With our bellies full and legs tired, we can't wait to get home and relax. Luke has been a trooper— I don't know many boys who can endure a day of shopping without a single complaint. Maddie is as happy as a clam just to be with me.

Exiting the restaurant bathroom, I pull the heavy door open, laughing at the silly antics performed by this adorable seven year old. The weight of the door is eased as I come face to face with a pair of angry blue eyes which dart quickly from my face to Maddie's. It's a standoff—one of us will have to move so the other can get by. Maddie's hand slips into mine. Maybe it's a sign of solidarity—us against them.

"Mom! Hurry up. I need to go," Sophie pipes up from behind her mother.

I feel Maddie shift her body to stand behind me, shielding herself from Gina's lethal glare.

"Excuse us." I step to the side to let them through.

With an audible huff, Gina saunters in with Sophie in tow. No "thank you." No nothing.

The soft voice of this normally quiet little girl surprises me. "That was not nice, Gina. You should say thank you."

"What did you say to me?" Gina's head whips around and snarls with narrowed eyes focused solely on Madison while Sophie dashes into an empty stall.

"Nothing," I retort quickly.

"How dare you! After everything I did for you!" Her manicured nail points down at Maddie.

"Drop it, Gina. She's seven!"

"You, little shit! Do you have any idea what I've done for you?"

I step in front of Gina when she tries to get close to Madison. With my chin lifted high, I stand tall defiantly. "Leave her alone, Gina."

She doesn't move, standing there frozen with contempt across her face.

"Back. The. Hell. Up. Now." I whisper through gritted teeth as I step in closer so our faces are only a few inches apart. I am in mother bear mode, all my defenses up and ready to attack. Do not mess with my family. I'm well aware that Maddie isn't my kid, she's Adam's daughter, but I will defend and protect her as if she were my own.

"Mommy, I need help," Sophie calls from the stall, but Gina doesn't move to help her daughter.

Gina snorts. "You hear that? '*Mommy.*' Has a nice ring to it, don't you think?"

I pull Maddie back into the restaurant with me before unshed tears fall. I will never let that bitch hurt me again.

Luke waits patiently by the men's restroom, looking at the wishing well, lost in thought. "Can I have a quarter?" Luke asks before adding, "Please."

"Uh, sure, bud." I reach into my wallet to get a coin. "Sorry, I don't have any quarters. Will a penny do?" He looks at it and asks if I have a dime or a nickel. I'm not sure what's going on in that little head of his, but I oblige and give him a dime. I give Maddie the other dime, but she asks for a penny. I love these kids, but sometimes, they're a little strange. "Sure, honey. Here." I hand it to her and watch as she closes her eyes, tossing the penny in. Her face lights with a bright smile that would rival the star on a Christmas tree.

I settle our bill; I notice the two texts that came in from Adam while we were in the bathroom.

AL: Meeting is running late. Be home later.

AL: Love you.

I toss my phone into my bag, too annoyed to answer him now. I won't be responsible for my words if I do.

The traffic is a little lighter since all the Christmas shoppers have gone for the day, possibly preparing for a night of frenzied wrapping and labeling. As I wait at the traffic light at the four way intersection, a black Escalade slowly comes to a stop and sits across from me on the opposite side of the road.

My heart drops from my chest to my stomach. A lump the size of Texas forms in my throat, my knuckles turning white as I grip the steering wheel. I swallow hard and pray that my eyes are deceiving me, that I've just eaten some bad chicken and am having a hallucination. But I know that my eyes are working perfectly fine. I know that Adam is sitting opposite me in his Escalade. I also know that Adam is not alone. Seated in the passenger seat is a woman. It's the tall, blonde woman from the bar the night Shelby met Adam for the first time. It's Nora. Even though it's been months and I've only seen her once, her sharp, platinum blonde bob and pretty face are unmistakable. In a meeting my ass! Oh, Adam Lawson...you, my friend, have just fucked up!

I will him to look at me, to make our eyes meet so he knows that I know he's fucked up. I put the Jeep in park, sprint across the intersection, avoiding being run over by several cars, and stand before the SUV. Our eyes meet—bull to matador. I walk deliberately to his window, bang a closed fist and demand that he step out. I look past him into the car and I see their hands are laced together and he's drawing reassuring circles on her hand, just like he does to mine. My eyes are transfixed as his body leans over the console to whisper something before he places a chaste kiss on her lips. He turns and opens the door to face me.

"Mia, I'm sorry. We were going to tell you." The words that Dylan had used to justify his actions are now being said by Adam.

My heart explodes in my chest. This man, whom I love and trust implicitly, is shattering me. "Why, Adam?" I step up to him, getting within an inch of his traitorous lips. "How could you do this to me? To us?" Adam's lips begin to move, but I can't understand the words, his lies and excuses for breaking my heart which will no doubt cause irreparable damage. All I can hear is the pounding and cracking of my heart and the desperate scream that emanates from deep within. I slap him hard across his face and beat against his chest. I will never recover from this. My legs crumble, unable to bear my weight and I fall to my knees. Adam doesn't offer to help me nor does he wrap those strong arms around me to embrace me. Instead, he looks at me with pity in his eyes. He steps around me to collect his children from the back seat of my Jeep. Kneeling in the middle of the intersection with cars whizzing by, I watch Adam take my life away.

"HEY! Jingle bells, jingle bells, jingle all the way…" My eyes flick up and look into the rearview mirror as Madison and Luke's singing brings me back to reality. When I look straight ahead to where Adam is, I can only see the red rear lights and the right turn signal flashing as he enters the highway. A quick "beep beep" draws my eyes up to look into the rearview mirror and then back to the traffic light which is now green. I offer a courtesy "sorry" wave and proceed. I blink away the tears and I take cleansing, calming breaths.

Why would he lie to me and say that he's in a meeting? Where was he going with her? Is he cheating on me? Why would he always tell me how much he loves me and claim that the kids and I are his life? These questions and a million more swirl around my head like snowflakes during cold New England blizzard.

Would he take these kids away from me? What am I going to do?

Chapter Thirty-Seven

AFTER MAKING A LIGHT DINNER, AND GETTING THE KIDS showered and ready for bed, we sit, snuggled together, on the soft leather couch in Adam's living room watching *Rudolph the Red Nosed-Reindeer* and wait for their father to get home.

While the original plan was to stay at my house that night, I decided that if Adam was going to admit to his infidelity and break things off, it would be best if the kids were at least already at their own home. It's not their fault their father is a douche bag.

The sound of a door opening wakes me, my eyes darting around the living room before reaching for my phone to check the time. 11:25. What the hell? I am careful not to wake the kids whose arms are draped across me. A movement draws my attention toward the doorway. Adam stands there leaning against the frame, arms crossed at his chest, his face somber, clothes wrinkled and untucked. His dark hair looks like fingers have been running through it—he looks like he's been thoroughly fucked. Our eyes meet and in that moment, I am fearful of what is going to happen. He doesn't look happy to see me. In fact, apprehension tarnishes his face. I know what he's going to say. He's going to tell me that he loves Nora and he always has. She's good for him, good for the kids. What is it with these men and blonde women?

He walks slowly into the room, stopping at the couch, looking at the three of us entangled. "Hi," is the only word he says. One word? I get one fucking word? Picking up Luke's limp body, he carries him upstairs to his Superhero-themed bedroom. "Hey, buddy. Shhh...it's okay...I've got you."

I follow suit with Maddie in my arms, her little body, covered in red and green polka dotted flannel, is so warm and comforting. I pull the covers back, lay her down gently and tuck her into her pretty pink bed. "Good night, sweetie." I kiss her forehead and smile at the dark-haired angel in front of me.

"I love you," she whispers before turning over onto her side, curling her body into fetal position.

"And I love you."

I know the end is near, I can feel it. Everything I've ever wanted is going to be taken from me. Again. It's going to be so much harder because now I know exactly what I'm losing.

Adam waits for me outside Madison's room and holds his hand out for me. I want to take it. I really do. But I think back to what I imagined. Adam's fingers laced with hers, rubbing circles, reaching over to cup her face, Adam touching her in private places.

He waits for me to take his outstretched hand, a questioning look on his face. Is he serious? He's been gone all day, it's 11 o'clock at night. Does he not think that I would be wary of him?

"Come here. I need you." He needs me? What could he possibly need me for when he's got Miss Tall, Curvy Blonde? He pushes off the wall, stepping in to close the gap between us. Long arms entrap me, circling around my back, pulling me against his chest. His face nuzzles into my neck, inhaling deeply. My arms don't move, they are defiant, choosing to remain by my side. It's my turn to inhale deeply. I relish the feel of him, of his body on mine. He smells like he always does—there's no hint of perfume from his earlier rendezvous with the blonde.

"What's wrong?" he asks immediately, concern in his voice.

I swallow hard.

"Mia, what's wrong?" he asks again when he's met with silence. "Baby, are you okay? Are the kids okay?" My face is cupped in his hand as he searches my eyes.

Finally, I speak. "Where have you been?" I ask. I need to be strong. Breaking down into tears is not an option.

"Oh my God, it was such a long fucking day. I'm exhausted." He steps back and scrubs his eyes and face.

"I asked where you were not how your day was." My words have a bite to them, making his eyes flash up to mine.

"What?" he asks confused with a hint of anger.

"It's a simple question, Adam. Where have you been all day?" I retort.

"Where do you *think* I've been all day?"

Oh no! He's not going to pull that crap of asking a question instead of answering mine.

"I don't *think*. I *know* you were driving around with that blonde in your car."

His eyes widen in surprise.

"Nora, is it? I saw you with her." I step away from him.

"Dad?" Luke calls from his room.

"Don't move," Adam commands before he walks into Luke's room. I can hear him whisper reassuring words to his son.

After he closes the door, Adam looks flustered. He looks like a guilty man. *Oh, maybe that's because he is!*

"Come downstairs."

"Are you going to answer my question?" I ask, not moving a single step.

"Downstairs. Now."

I don't want to follow him or to hear his excuses. I want to pull out my shield of armor to protect my heart from the words of lies and deceit that he's going to hurl at me.

I follow him into the kitchen where he opens the refrigerator and pulls out leftover chicken pot pie and pops it into the microwave. I stand quietly against the cold granite counter, waiting for him to speak. The only sound in the room comes from the hot plate

rotating in the microwave until the beep indicates that his food is
ready.

This isn't how things were supposed to be. Part of me wants
to immediately forgive him for reverting to his old ways when he's
stressed out or the pressures of life are too much. But fuck that
shit! That's a piss poor excuse! I will never be that person again. The
person who sees the signs, but chooses to ignore them and who is
then left shattered in the process. Nope, not me! Never again.

"This is good," he says with a mouthful of chicken.

"This is good?" Really, Adam? That's what you choose to say.

I stare at him as he eats in silence, waiting for him to say
something more.

He eats. I wait.

Finally, he stands up and puts his dish in the dishwasher before
sitting in the middle of the leather couch. I don't want to sit next to
him, but I'm left with no choice so I stand instead.

"Sit with me, Mia." He pats the vacant spot between us. "We
need to talk."

Oh, God! I am not prepared for the words he's about to say.
Why did he pursue me? Why did he make me fall in love with him?
Why would he let me fall in love with his kids only to tear them
away?

"Just say it, Adam. Just fucking say it." Say whatever you need to
so I can leave and go back to my oblivion. In this moment, I hate
him. I hate him so much. After everything we've been through, I
can't believe that he's going to rip my heart out like this.

"I fucked up. I never meant to hurt you." Adam sits forward
and leans with his elbows on his knees, his head bowed in shame. A
shiver runs through my body like an electric current.

Even if I wanted to speak, I can't.

"I've made some really, really bad choices. I don't know how I let
things get so out of control." He sounds broken, remorseful even.

"Please sit with me. I need you." He doesn't even have to

decency to sound embarrassed. He fucks another woman and has the audacity to ask me to sit with him and tell me that he needs me? Who is this man in front of me? He looks like Adam, but he's not. My Adam would never do this to me.

I stand there for what seems like forever, just watching him as his shoulders sag further and he buries his face in his hands. "Oh, God. Oh, God," he mutters repeatedly. "So fucking stupid. If only I could change the things I've done."

I love this man. I love this man with every fiber of my being. To stand here and not help him is more than I can bear. Yes, he's been unfaithful and yes, he's broken my heart, but I love him. Plain and simple.

Walking to him, I drop to my knees in front of him and pull his hands away from his face to find his dark eyes troubled. Instinctively, his hands cup my face and he leans forward to kiss me. I turn away. The hold on my face becomes firmer as he pulls me in to gently kiss me.

"Adam, stop." I feel the tears coming forth, I shake them away. I won't let him see how he's broken me.

"Baby, I can't lose you." The pads of his thumb wipe away at the tears that have spilled. "I'll die without you."

"How could you do this to me?" My chin quivers. "How could you do this to us?"

He searches my eyes pensively. "I don't know how things got so fucked up. I didn't mean for any of this to happen." How do you accidently put your dick in the wrong vagina? What did he think would happen?

"I never thought things would get this complicated. I didn't mean to drag you into the middle of this." Middle of this? Him and Nora? He's been carrying on with Nora the whole time? I'm the other woman? Are there others? Maybe Gina was telling the truth about there being others.

It doesn't escape me that he's not answering my questions. It's like he's having a conversation with himself.

"Answers. I need answers, Adam." My knees hurt, but when I shift my weight to sit on my ass, Adam pulls me up to sit on his lap. I can't look at him even though he's staring at me.

"God, I don't even know where to start."

"You can start by telling me why you lied about Nora. Tell me how long you've been sleeping with her." I'm surprised by the confidence in my voice.

Adam's back stiffens and he gasps, "What?"

The fact that he has the nerve to sound offended nearly kills me. Did he think I wouldn't ask? Is he surprised that it took me this long to figure it out?

"You heard me," I snap.

"What are you talking about?" My shoulders are pushed back, angled so he can look directly in my face.

"I know about you and Nora."

"Is that what you think? That I've been fucking around with Nora?" he asks with a humorous tone.

I don't find anything remotely funny. Not one single bit. "She calls you all the time. You run when she calls and you said you were in a meeting today, but you lied. You were out and about with her. I saw you. Please don't try to deny it. Give me some fucking credit." I struggle to get out of his arms.

He laughs. I mean, "throw your head back" laughs before pushing my hair back away from my face. "Baby, I'm not sleeping with Nora or anyone else. I *love* you." His words sound sincere, but I'm still cautious.

"You're not?" I ask incredulously, eyeing him suspiciously.

"No, baby, I'm not. But there is something that you need to know. Come have a bath with me and I'll tell you everything."

Chapter Thirty-Eight

As far away from Adam as I can possibly get, I sit on the edge of the oversized tub. I want to look at his face, to detect any hints of deceit as he tells me everything I need to hear.

"I wish you would sit closer to me." His hand reaches out and caresses my bare leg.

"I can't..." I pull my leg away, just out of his reach.

He takes a deep breath and begins. "Okay, so you already know that I met Chris in college and that we do business together. That's how I met Gina and the rest of the family." I do know this, but it doesn't explain how we are in this situation with Nora.

"They had given me some pretty lucrative jobs and I've made a lot of money with them. I guess deep down, I had my suspicions about some of the deals but turned a blind eye. It wasn't until more recently that Chris suggested I start another business where he could hide his family's money. He said no one would suspect anything because my name is clean." The thought of that family's money makes my stomach turn because I can only imagine where the money that my mother got came from. I'll never touch that money, it's blood money.

I think about all the uncles that always hung around Gina's house when we were growing up. They always seemed a little shady to me even though I was just a kid. My dad used to make me wait in the car sometimes instead of letting me go in to play with Gina.

"At first, I didn't think it was a big deal. I was young and stupid."

Adam rolls his eyes and shakes his head at the thought.

"Can you just get to the part about Nora?" I ask impatiently as I lower myself into the bathwater.

"I'm getting there...About a year and a half ago, my company was audited by the IRS. I had everything in order so I wasn't really concerned. But when they asked me to produce the invoices, bank statements, and tax returns for the second company, I couldn't. Obviously."

"So your company was just a front for Chris' money?" He's right. He was stupid to get involved with their shady business.

"Chris wanted me to close up shop and open up under a different name, but I wouldn't do it. It wasn't just me anymore—I had my kids at this point. I was approached by a federal agent who was part of a team investigating Chris for illegal activities with ties to corruption in New York. Money laundering, bribery, coercion, gambling, prostitution. You name it, he did it."

My eyes rounded like giant gumballs. I couldn't believe what I was hearing.

I pull my knees in and wrap my arms around them, listening intently, hanging onto every single word.

"The blonde woman you know as Nora is the agent who approached me."

Nora is an FBI agent? But she's sexy and gorgeous and so... feminine. I guess I picture Sandra Bullock in Miss Congeniality before the makeover when I think "female FBI agent." I realize my mistake immediately. He was honest when he told me that she was an "agent." I assumed that he meant she was a real estate agent, like Gina.

"You're not going to like this part..." he says, letting his fingers circle my knee. "You know how before you I didn't date, I just...well, you know..."

It's my turn to roll my eyes at him.

"Yes, you were a man-whore...I already know this."

"Well, to keep tabs on Chris and his business dealings, Nora acted as my lover, even escorting me to business lunches and social events. She plays the part of a pretty, dumb blonde quite well."

And another eye roll.

"When you crashed into my life, I had no idea what I was in for or how hard I'd fall for you." He smiles lovingly as he unwraps my arms from my legs to pull me close. Water splashes as I scoot forward.

"Nora told me to stay away from you until this was all over, but I couldn't resist you."

My eyes roll and I suck my teeth. I'm sure she didn't want to just "play the part" of his lover. "That's not why she wanted you to stay away from me, I'm sure."

"No, it's not like that, babe. She knows how people like Chris can be and she said it wasn't fair to get involved with you until this was over." Before I know it, I'm turned around cradled against his chest. I love it here. It's my favorite place in the world.

"So, what was with all the late night calls?" I make small circles on his soapy thigh. "You always said it was business."

"It was. There are a lot of agents on this investigation who are always following leads. The name 'Nora' is programmed into my phone for about seven or eight different people—all agents."

"Remember the day we were supposed to go to New York and I had to cancel?"

I nod, remembering how hurt I was that he canceled. I also remember giving him the cold shoulder and not wanting to hear his explanation.

"Nora needed me to be in New York with her that morning. We had to make it seem like we were there for the weekend. We just 'happened' to be nearby when Chris met with his associates that morning and since she was my 'lover,' Chris never questioned anything about her being there. A lot of crazy shit went down that day."

326 - L.M CARR

"So are you in trouble with the Feds for fronting that business?" The thought that Adam is involved in anything illegal makes me sick to my stomach. It was that kind of activity that ultimately killed my father and pushed my mother over the edge.

"No. I could've been, but since I've agreed to work with them, they've offered some immunity. It'll be swept under the rug, so to speak." His fingers lace with mine and squeeze softly. "It's been months of secret meetings and looking at prospective 'job sites' while they gathered information about Chris and his ties to New York."

"Are you really a real estate developer or is there something else you need to tell me?" I laugh quietly.

"Mia, I have worked so hard to build my business. It took a long time to get my shit together after partying so hard for years with Chris. You can't even imagine the situations we used to get ourselves into. Besides, I'm good at what I do. C'mon, you've seen me in action." Ah, there's the arrogant man I love so much. "I wasn't about to let Chris DeGennaro or anyone else ruin what I've built."

"I have one last question. Gina. How involved is she in all of this?"

Adam's lips have moved from my shoulders to the nape of my neck, kissing and inhaling simultaneously.

"She's not involved in the illegal part of it. She's a good realtor with a legitimate business. I'm not sure she even knows about her brother's activities."

"Is that why you were always with her?" I know the answer to this question, we've been over this before, but I'm feeling insecure after my run in with her and the whole Nora situation.

"I thought you said you had only one more question." I can't see him, but I know he's smiling against my neck.

"I lied."

"Yes, mostly. She was really helpful when the kids were little, but then when the investigation started Nora suggested that I get closer to her to find out what she knew. I never would've agreed if I thought for one second that my kids were ever in any kind of danger."

"So what happens now?" I ask, but Adam must misunderstand my question because he tenses behind me.

"With what? Us?" His words are filled with sadness.

"No, I meant the investigation." I can tell my words reassure him because he lets out a deep breath.

"It's almost over, but we have to wait a little longer." A chuckle of disbelief seeps out. "Chris has no idea that they're onto him or that I'm involved in any way."

"You sure about that?" I ask shyly.

With absolute confidence in his voice he answers, "I'm sure." His hands trail across my breasts before moving lower down my belly. I know where he's headed and I'm happy to widen the space between my legs to allow him better access.

"Good because I know all too well how vindictive that family can be."

"Come to bed with me." Tiny circles go round and round on my swollen bud while fingers delve into me. If he wants me to go to bed, he should probably stop what he's doing, because Lord knows I don't want to move an inch. How is it possible that one man can be so talented?

"I can't move..." I murmur. The spark of heated energy courses from my head to my toes while he tugs on my nipple and increases the speed below. "I can't m-m-move...Oh, God..." My back arches, my eyes close, my head is thrown back and my body shudders in pleasure as all the pent up anger, frustration and my need for him release.

"You love that." It's a declaration not a question. Adam knows exactly what I need when I need it.

I crane my neck to offer my lips. "I love you."

Chapter Thirty-Nine

I AWAKE EARLY THE NEXT MORNING, EVEN BEFORE THE sun comes out to play, with a blanket of hot, hard sculpted muscle draping over my naked body and his large hand cupping my breast. I could wake up like this every day for the rest of my life.

Adam's breathing is quiet but labored as he nestles in the crook of my neck. Part of me feels guilty for not trusting him lately, but with a past track record like mine, who can blame me. There's no question that Adam loves me, but I wish that he had trusted me enough to tell me what's been going on with Chris and this investigation sooner. I'll admit that hurt a little. After what Johanna did to him all those years ago, I guess I understand why he's a bit distrustful.

I pluck gently at his dark hair and run my fingers through the short strands, smoothing it down from its waywardness. I feel him stir in my arms.

"Mmmmm." He inhales my scent. "Mornin' beautiful," he mumbles hoarsely.

"Hi, baby." I kiss the top of his head as he pulls me closer.

He's breathing so quietly, I think he's fallen back to sleep. He's been working so much, I'm sure he's exhausted. I wonder how he can function on so little sleep. I continue to lie there with him draped across me.

"Owww," I wince. His fingers pinch my nipple hard, pulling it taut. I feel him smile against my neck. "What was that for?" I yank back on his hair to see his amused eyes.

"That was for not trusting me." Adam shifts his weight so he's completely on top of me, trapping me beneath him. I can feel his morning erection coming to life as he swivels his narrow hips. "You owe me." He smirks.

"I have to pee. Get up," I plead.

"Nope. You'll have to wait."

Oh, crap! I know what's coming and I'm pretty sure it's going to be all over me.

Effortlessly he moves to straddle me, his knees meeting my ears while he sits on my chest. Thank God his weight is supported by his legs or else I think he'd kill me. His morning wood is delectable, encouraging me to lick my lips in anticipation. He guides the tip to my lips, sliding it back and forth like he's applying lip gloss with his moisture. I must look needy because I am desperate for him to part my lips so I can taste him. With hooded eyes, he watches me carefully, teasing me with his beautiful manhood.

"Open."

I obey his command. I open my mouth and lick him before closing my lips around him. I hear him hiss in pleasure, sliding further into my mouth. It always amazes me how much I love to do this to him. To know that I can give him what he wants and needs is enthralling and it gives me the confidence to take *all* of him in. One hand grips firmly at the base while the other hand reaches around to cup his ass. I am feeling confident and I want to show him how much I love him. The wall of distrust needs to be knocked down, freeing us from any barriers. He needs to know how much I trust him and that he can trust me in return.

I slide my hand down over my belly into myself to gather moisture that's pooled between my legs and cup his ass again. With a mouthful, I smirk, my eyes dancing with lust. I part him and slip my finger around his puckered hole. He twitches in my mouth, approving of what I'm doing to him. "Ffffuck! Do that again."

My mouth continues to pleasure him as my finger slips in further, circling around his tight, forbidden place. "Oh my fucking God. That feels so good." I watch his face transform to one of pure lust and he takes over and strokes himself fast and hard. I follow his lead and plunge my finger in deeper until he releases his seed all over me before settling back into my mouth. That has got to be by far the hottest, sexiest thing I have ever seen or done with him.

"Holy shit. That was incredible." He rolls over and takes me with him, squeezing my ass hard. "So that's how you want to play?" He kisses me hard, moaning as he tastes himself in my mouth.

With a swift motion, he lifts himself and rolls onto his back, pulling me onto his chest.

"You know what? I think I might be over the moon in love with you." My sudden epiphany earns me a slap on the ass.

"Good because I *know* I'm over the moon in love with you."

"We have a big day ahead of us."

"We do?" I kiss his scruffy jaw, nipping along his neck.

"We do. We have to go cut down our tree."

"You, Mr. City Slicker, are going to *cut down* a Christmas tree?" I eye him skeptically.

"Hey, are you doubting my skills? I'm actually pretty good with a saw. Did you forget that I know how to use a hammer, too?" We both laugh remembering the time he fixed my shower and Luke complained about the hammer making too much noise.

The smell of bacon and eggs wafts throughout the kitchen as Adam walks around in black pajama bottoms and a white Yankees t-shirt making Belgian waffles for us. My offer to help was declined, he said it was the least he could do for all I'd done for him in the past few weeks. He was right. It felt as if Madison and Luke were *our* children, not just his. I felt awful earlier that week when I had to discipline Luke by making him sit in time out for pushing his sister down. When I called Adam, he told me to do what I thought was right. It's easier said than done when you're disciplining someone else's kid.

With the four of us sitting at the oversized kitchen island, we feasted on this gourmet breakfast of waffles with fresh whipped cream, strawberries, bacon and eggs.

"This is delicious. How'd you learn to cook so well?" I ask as I spoon another dollop of whipped cream onto my waffle. "Are you holding out on me, Mr. Lawson?" I realize that I should be saving this whipped cream for later. We could have a lot of fun with this upstairs in his bedroom.

"I have many talents." His eyebrows waggle like the pervert he is. He continues, "Speaking of talents, I do believe that you showed me one of yours this morning." He leans over and kisses the spot just below my earlobe.

"Mmmmmmm." My eyes close and let a moan escape. Sometimes it's so easy to get lost in him.

"Ewwww...gross," Luke pipes in, his nose scrunching in disgust.

My eyes pop open, my face turning all shades of red. Adam's face dances with amusement.

"You know, Luke, someday soon you're going to like girls," Adam teases, mussing his son's hair. "And some girls like Mia, smell really good." He moves to stand behind me, pushing my hair over my shoulder to inhale at the nape of my neck. I feel his warm breath move closer to my ear.

"And taste even better," he whispers, nipping at my earlobe.

His simple words and delicate touches set my heart and my body racing. The tingling sends shivers down my spine, into my belly and in between my legs. He makes me desperate for him. How did I ever think I could resist him?

Madison's sweet giggle interrupts my erotic thoughts. "Daddy, are you going to marry Mia?"

I feel Adam's body tense immediately. It's not something that we've ever really talked about. I mean, I know he loves me and we are together, but I don't know if he is in it for the long haul as in marriage. When I told him about my pregnancy, he said he would have married me, but I think it was just because it would've been "the right thing" to do. I know I would marry him in a second.

A chaste kiss is placed on my cheek before he answers his daughter's question. "Do you want me to marry her?" He moves from behind me to turn Maddie around to face him, lowering himself to her eye level.

"Yes!" She grins.

"And why would that be, Maddie girl?" Adam looks into her brown eyes, asking playfully.

"So I can have a mommy again!" Her face beams with giddiness while Luke looks on.

I'm not sure what answer he was expecting, but the look on Adam's face tells me this wasn't it.

I drop the fork and knife, startling myself at the sound of them hitting the dish. I love this little girl and her brother, but the thought of me being someone's mom scares me. I couldn't protect my own baby. "Sorry." I smile weakly.

Her little face is cradled in Adam's big hands as he pulls her forward to kiss her forehead. "Sweetheart..." He's at a loss for words. Disappointment fills me when I see the sympathetic look on his face.

Tears threaten to spill as they silently pool in the corners of my eyes. I gather my dish and walk to the sink, rinse it and put it in the dishwasher. Light snow falls outside the window, reminding me that Christmas will be here soon. Adam and Madison's conversation becomes muted as I watch the snow fall, getting lost in my own thoughts.

"Mia, I think you'd be a good mom for us," Luke whispers and smiles up at me as he stands next to me at the sink, offering his sticky plate. I look down at this beautiful little boy, so full of life and adventure, who captures my heart every single day. The words I want to speak are lodged in my throat, so I smile and nod then lean down to kiss the top of his head.

"Alright you two, go brush your teeth, and get dressed. We're going to get our tree!" Adam chases his children out of the kitchen and up the stairs. I quickly clean up the kitchen since he cooked. Just as I start the dishwasher, I feel his arms wrap around me, pulling me close. He knows that my mind is reeling from the earlier conversation, my body is riddled with tension.

"You okay?" He skims his nose along the nape of my neck.

"Yeah, I'm good."

"Don't lie to me," he teases.

"I'm not lying. I'm good. Now let's go get your tree." I turn around in his embrace and kiss him chastely. I really want to ask him what he said to Madison. Does he want to marry me? Why can't I just believe that his words are completely sincere? I know he's not Dylan or Shane, but my experiences with them have left me with doubts. I will never love anyone as much as I love him. I'd rather spend one day loving Adam than spend a lifetime looking for love with someone else.

"It's *our* tree, baby. You hear me?" His lips meet mine, his tongue sweeping across my bottom lip, begging for entry. "All of this is *ours.*"

My mouth opens and I accept his words and all of him. I love this man so incredibly much. The fact that he knows my past and loves me in spite of it, mends my heart every day. What happened with Johanna, what happened with Dylan—those things are in the past and can never hurt us. What's done is done. I will never want more than this. He is my everything.

Chapter Forty

BEFORE WE GO TO PICK BRADY UP FROM THE LONGO'S, I help Adam bundle the kids up as we venture out on this cold, blustery day to find the perfect Christmas tree. I earn a slap on the backside when I mistakenly call it their tree not our tree. His words from earlier this morning still fresh on my mind, "All of this is ours."

Broken Arrow Tree Farm is breathtaking with acres and acres of tree lined paths each home to a different kind of tree. The light, fluffy morning snow has begun to fall heavier, coating each branch, weighing it down close to the ground. Green wreaths with red bows adorn the old barn door where the smell of hot cocoa drifts through the air as favorite Christmas carols are heard.

Adam, looking sexy as ever with his two days' worth of scruff, is dressed in a dark, North Face winter jacket and knit cap. He walks up ahead of us to get a saw and a tree cart while the kids and I scold Brady when he lifts his hind leg to mark his territory on the trunk of a small Charlie Brown tree, leaving the snow around it bright yellow. He's such an Alpha dog, staking his claim. Typical male.

I love watching Maddie and Luke play with Brady, spoiling him with affection. Wanting to capture the moment, I reach into the deep pocket of my long, goose-down jacket to get my phone so I can snap a picture. All three of them look when I call their names, snow falling lightly around them. It's picture perfect! I take picture after picture of their smiling faces when I notice two figures in the background of the screen. An uneasy feeling surges through me.

My phone slips out of my gloved hands and drops into the snow.

The erratic beating of my heart pounds in my ears, causing them to ring loudly. Adam's body becomes stiff, tense, and defensive as he stands there listening while Chris berates him. Although I can't hear what is being said, I know that Adam is not happy, in fact, he's pretty pissed. His eyes narrow, causing his eyebrows to furrow up and a harsh scowl transforms his handsome face. Chris is only a few inches taller than Adam, but he is bigger, with bulky muscles wrapped in a gray jacket. They stand toe to toe, neither one of them backing down. Whatever is being said, Adam seems to be listening while standing his ground.

I watch in slow motion as Chris stabs his index finger into Adam's chest, making a point to their conversation. That's when Adam loses his temper. Before I know it, Adam reaches out and wraps his hand around Chris' thick neck, catching him by surprise. Since they're a short distance away, I can't hear what Adam is saying, but it can't be good. The look on his face is fierce—his jaw ticks and the veins in his neck bulge. I've never seen it before and I don't ever want to again. I am reminded of the angry man at the club months ago. The thought that my loving, handsome, sexy man can flip a switch and become this person scares the living shit out of me. I've seen people get angry, but this is way past angry. It's murderous.

Chris' eyes enlarge to the size of saucers, he's caught off guard. Silent words fall from his lips and he angles his face to look in my direction. Adam immediately releases Chris as if his hands were on fire. His eyes find mine and lock immediately. Across Adam's face is the look of a man in pain, the kind of pain that reaches down into your soul and rips your heart out. I can't look away from him. I want to run to him, wrap my arms around him and take away that pain, but I don't. It's merely a few minutes, but it feels like a lifetime. The world around us slips away while the snow continues to fall and his children laugh with Brady, but I can't see or hear any of it, all I see is Adam.

I wait and watch patiently to see what he's going to do. Finally, he pulls his eyes from mine to glare at Chris who is standing there with a smug look smeared across his face, defiantly watching our wordless interaction. It's no secret that Adam and I are together, but I have the feeling that seeing us together, seeing our connection just upped the ante. Whatever Chris' problem is, it now involves me. I feel as if I'm a pawn in a dangerous game.

Chris nods slowly and then proceeds to back up, disappearing into the thick row of blue spruce trees. I feel a chill run down my spine.

"Adam?" I ask warily when he reaches me and slips his hand into mine, pulling our bodies flush against one another before inhaling and exhaling to slow his breathing and rein in his emotions.

He nestles into the red scarf wrapped around my neck and simply shakes his head. Whatever is going on, I know he's not going to tell me now. My hands reach up to smooth his face and cradle his head and my gloves massage the nape of his neck. It's the only thing I can offer to comfort him right now.

My mind races a million miles a minute with questions about their conversation. Why was Chris so angry? Why would he push Adam to the point where, no doubt if we weren't standing here, in the middle of a Christmas tree farm, Adam would've have landed a punch to Chris' face and probably wouldn't have stopped there. The look on Adam's face...it broke my heart. You would think that someone just told him the most devastating news that a loved one died tragically or something along those lines. But he was looking directly at me? Why would he look at me like that?

I pull away so I can look at his face. "Baby, I love you. Whatever is going on, we'll get through it. Together."

Troubled, dark eyes search my face before he cradles my cheeks and kisses me chastely on the lips. I want to shake him and demand that he tell me what's going on. I hate the thought of him being involved with any of the DeGennaros. I want to run after Chris and tell him to leave Adam alone and that he, like his father and sister, are horrible people who deserve to rot in the deepest pits of hell.

"Look, Daddy. We made Olaf," Maddie calls his attention to the mini snowman that she and her brother built.

"C'mon, Dad. Let's go." Luke interrupts our moment. I'm thankful for the interruption because I can feel the tears creeping their way up into my eyes. The last thing I need to do is cry here in front of Luke and Maddie.

"Let's go get our tree," Adam says on a deep exhale before giving me another peck.

Maddie squeals with delight as she is lifted high into the air onto Adam's shoulders. A grimace shoots across Luke's face. He looks disappointed so I squat down, allowing him to climb piggyback style onto my back. "Hop on, bud. And hold on tight." I fall in love with this little boy even more when he leans forward to kiss my cheek.

Adam blinks a few times as he scans over us with a look of complete adoration, fierce love pours out of his eyes. I love this man. I love this man's children. This is what I want. This is the life I want.

Chapter Forty-One

THE YOUNG COLLEGE KID HELPED ADAM SECURE THE tree onto the roof while the kids and I climbed into the Escalade, cranking the heat on full blast. Brady wasn't too happy when we dropped him off at home, but he needed to get in from the cold. He's been behaving so oddly lately. I watched as he plopped himself on the couch after doing his business outside, letting out a huge sigh indicating his displeasure.

For an early Sunday afternoon, it's pretty busy at Maple's Restaurant with all the families hustling and bustling in from the frigid day. The temperature has dropped and the winds have picked up, swirling the snow around the tree farm like a snow globe.

A hostess escorts us to the only empty booth that overlooks the lake. Maddie and Luke bicker about who gets to sit on my side to which Adam whispers and says that he's invisible when I'm around. Luke finally relents and sits with his dad after Maddie argues that he got to ride piggy back. Adam grins as his eyes dart back and forth between his children like he's watching a tennis match.

After removing our jackets, scarves and hats, Maddie snuggles closely to me to read the menu. I decide on a grilled cheese sandwich and a cup of tomato soup to warm up. Maddie decides to have the same while Luke and Adam select cheeseburgers and fries. Within minutes, a pretty waitress comes over to greet us and take our order. It doesn't escape me that she notices Adam before she sees me. I mean really, how can you not notice him? He's freaking gorgeous with his dark eyes, scruffy jaw, rosy cheeks and dark, sexy hair that you just want to run your fingers through and those lips that you just want to kiss and bite. I recognize her as one of the college students who worked at our school last spring. She was working on her degree in education. I think she may have even worked in my room then, but the months of March through June are pretty much a blur.

"Hi there, I'm Nicole. I'll be taking care of you today." *Yeah, I'm sure you'd like to take care of him alright. Back up, bitch. He's mine.* Her eyes light up when he places his phone on the table and looks at her. She smiles and tucks her shoulder length strawberry blonde hair behind her ear.

"Hi. How are you? It's busy in here today, huh?" Adam says and smiles as he looks past her at all the patrons before bringing his gaze back to her. He's bringing out the charm. Perhaps he thinks we'll get better service.

"Yeah, it is, but I can handle it. I'm quite experienced." Nicole winks. What a flirt! And right in front of me. What is wrong with some women today?

"That's good to hear because we're starving." He turns to look at me. "Baby, what would you like to eat?" I watch our waitress struggle to pull her eyes away from Adam and address me. "What can I get for you, ma'am?" *Oh no, she didn't!*

I wait for some sort of recognition from her, but it doesn't come so I place my order and watch as she takes everyone else's.

Adam and Luke both order a vanilla milkshake. A devious grin appears on our waitress' face. "Vanilla? Hmmm...I wouldn't take you for a vanilla guy. Forbidden chocolate, maybe." *Oh my God!* I can't believe how this brazen woman is outright flirting with Adam like I'm not even sitting across from him. *Am I fucking invisible?* Maybe she thinks I'm his sister or something like a nanny, but he did just call me "baby." I've got to give it to her, this chick has some pretty big balls.

Adam nods and returns the grin. "Actually, I'll stick to vanilla, but you can give her Forbidden Chocolate." Again, I watch her struggle to address me. Give me a break. I know Adam is an Adonis, but it's not like I'm snaggletooth. "Whatever you want, sir." Nicole smirks and turns to leave when another customer calls her attention.

"Wow! Can you believe her?" The shock on my face melts away when Adam reaches across the table and takes my hands in his. "I see no one else but you. You know that, don't you?" Warmth flows through me, moisture pools between my legs. "I do." A smile dances on my lips. "Vanilla, huh?"

"Any flavor is good with you." He kisses my knuckles before releasing my hands to answer his phone. I surprised myself earlier when "Nora" flashed across the screen on the Escalade. While the tiny green-eyed monster wanted to make a grand appearance, Adam's reassuring words and warm lips against mine, quelled the feeling.

Luke and Maddie distract me as Adam taps out a text message. I watch as his eyes widen momentarily as his jaw tightens. He looks around the restaurant and I follow his gaze. Our eyes land on a piercing blue glare. A look of scorn and hate stain Gina's face as she stares back at us. I notice the large body sitting across from her is Chris. Sophie sits quietly playing on an iPad. How did I not notice them when we walked in? They've been there for a while as their half-eaten plates are still on the table, waiting to be cleared away. Her lips move silently but quickly. I know she's just told her brother that we are here because he immediately turns in our direction.

Chris DeGennaro is a big man, but it's the ferocity of his face that is menacing. He scares me. He intimidates me. I know what he is capable of. I shiver when I think of the business transactions that Adam has been involved with or the kinds of people that he's met through his association with Chris.

Adam turns back, grimaces and taps out another message. What the hell? I would love to know what is so important that he needs to be interrupted on a Sunday afternoon when he's out with his family. *Family?* Where the hell did that come from? I'm not his family. Not technically anyway. His children are his family.

Nicole returns with our drinks, placing the vanilla shake in front of me and the chocolate in front of Adam. The grin on her face disappears in an instant when he looks at her with disdain. "Are you serious?" Gone is the incorrigible flirt, now replaced with a stern, serious, and very annoyed man.

"Oh, sorry." She smiles sheepishly before she switches our drinks. It amazes me that he didn't even have to tell her what the problem was. She knew.

"Adam..." I lace my fingers with his hoping that my simple gesture will calm him. I'm not sure if he's agitated because of Nora, Chris, or Nicole. Whatever it is, I refuse to let it ruin our day with the kids.

"It's okay, babe. I'll be fine." He offers a small smile, but it doesn't reach his eyes. "I'll be right back." He stands up and heads in the direction of the restroom which happens to be near the kitchen.

My heart nearly flies out of my mouth when I see Chris rise and walk in the same direction. I want to follow them to see what's going to happen especially after what I witnessed at the tree farm. My gaze drifts to Gina who is staring at me even though her daughter is tugging on her arm to get her attention. I can't waste any more time, she's not worth it. Instead I pick up a blue crayon and challenge Luke to a game of tic-tac-toe on the paper placemat while we wait for our food.

What seems like a long time later, Nicole comes to the table carrying a large tray with our lunch. I thank her by name when she places it all down.

"How's school going?" I ask casually as I pass Maddie her tomato soup.

Her eyes dart to mine immediately, now with recognition. "Oh, Miss Delaney. Hi! I...I...um didn't recognize you." *Yeah, right. I'm sure you didn't.*

"Yep," the "p" making a popping sound, "it's me." I feel my phone vibrate in my jacket pocket.

"You look different."

"Do I?" She probably didn't recognize me with my hair now layered and highlighted. Or maybe it's the fact that I'm actually smiling, not walking around like someone just ran my dog over. When she came to work in my classroom, all that shit had just happened with Shane. I was catapulted back into my dark place, even Shelby and Pete couldn't pull me out. The day of Mike and Shelby's wedding was the only exception. My friend, Xanax, helped me through the day. I smiled for pictures and mumbled the right words through the toast as maid of honor.

"Yeah, you look good. Happy."

Adam excuses himself and sits down, mussing Luke's hair and winking at Maddie.

"I am. Thanks." I smile at Adam.

"Well, let me know if I can get you anything else." I'm happy that her attention is now directed at me.

"Everything okay?" I ask as I dunk the corner of my grilled cheese into my soup.

Adam nods a curt, "Yes" and proceeds to dip his french fries in ketchup.

Christmas songs from the jukebox help to get us back into the holiday spirit. I don't want anything or anyone to ruin it for the kids. My phone buzzes once again, reminding me that I never checked the earlier message. I pull my phone out and see that it's from Adam, but he's sitting across from me. I know I look confused as I open the message.

AL: I'm a starving man. I want to eat you. All. Night. Long.

My head drops to my chin and I try desperately to hide my grin. If my cheeks weren't already red from the cold, they're definitely red now from lust. I look at him just as he sinks his teeth into his burger. His tongue darts out to lick the ketchup on the corner of his mouth. But he doesn't stop there. He continues his tongue tease as he brings his thumb to his mouth and licks it before turning his thumb again to suck on the pad, his index finger resting on his cheek, forming a V. Oh, Adam! Why must you torture me here and now?

A slow throb begins and my heart beats faster. If we didn't have the kids, I'd drag him to the nearest bathroom and take him into my mouth before letting him drive into me.

Me: I think I'm in the mood for Italian tonight.

AL: Sausage or meatballs?

Me: Both. You can't have one without the other and my appetite is insatiable. You know I'm a greedy girl.

AL: And I'll have your sweet cream for dessert.

Oh my God! Leave it to him to get me hot and bothered on food sex talk!

Chris, Gina, and Sophie walk past us as they leave the restaurant. Gina shows her obvious and desperate need for attention when she says hello to Adam and no one else. Not even the kids. If she was hoping for more, she was sorely disappointed when he simply nodded and said, "Gina."

On the way back at Adam's house, we pick up Brady and bring him with us. We decorate the perfectly shaped, beautiful evergreen which stands almost 8 feet tall in the corner of Adam's expansive great room. I've earned a few smacks in the rear when I kept "mistakenly" calling it "his" tree instead of "our" tree. But in reality, it is his tree. The little artificial tree sitting in my garage is *my* tree. It's all I need. I used to love Christmas, it was my favorite holiday. Well, it was up until seven years ago. I guess it's easier to go through the motions than to explain all the events that led up to my melancholy over the holiday.

The four of us change into warm, comfortable clothes. Maddie and I are nestled in Adam's arms on the leather sofa while Luke sprawls on the plush rug with his head on Brady's belly. "Our" tree is really beautiful with its white lights and handmade ornaments. A warm smile spreads across my face when I see the small green wreaths, covered in silver glitter that has the kids' school pictures in the center. They're the ornaments that Maddie and Luke made in school last week. Maddie tugged on my heartstrings when she asked me privately if she could make two ornaments, she wanted to hang one on the tree at her grandparents' house, too.

My body is weary and my eyes are heavy and I would love to stay awake and watch the Patriots game. As Adam runs his fingers through my hair, pulling gently at the long strands, I feel Madison's little body slip into a deep sleep in my arms. Before my eyelashes meet and close for the last time as I begin my nap, something on the mantle catches my attention. The addition of two new stockings hanging beside their three makes me smile, and I get a warm and fuzzy feeling in my belly. My sleepy eyes drift downward to the small fire that dances and crackles in the fireplace, providing light and heat. If I could freeze time, I would because in this moment, I know that I am exactly where I'm supposed to be.

Sheer joy fills me as I walk through the woods on a narrow trail that leads to a vacant lot. My father's voice beside me encourages me and tells me that I look stunning in white and how happy he is that he can be here to celebrate this day with me. Adam stands tall, smiling at me. His face is full of love and he looks so incredibly handsome in his black tuxedo and crisp white shirt, his dark hair coiffed elegantly. Maddie looks precious in a simple pink dress with tiny, white flowers on the trim. Luke's dark dress pants and a white collared shirt make him look older than his seven years. They all look so dressed up like they're going out to a Christmas party or even a ball.

A soft melodious hymn fills the air while my loved ones and other faceless people watch as I step slowly, keeping in tune to the music while my father guides me toward Adam who waits patiently for me. I have never been happier in my life. Everything I've ever wanted is mere feet away, just within my reach. My father's large, rugged hand reaches down to grasp my slender hand. He places my hand in Adam's.

I pull my gaze from our clasped hands and all I want to see is the man of my dreams, the love of my life. Instead, an angry Chris DeGennaro looks down at me with the face of Lucifer himself.

"Hello, Mia. I've been waiting for you." The devil smiles at me.

ABOUT THE AUTHOR

L.M. Carr is the author of realistic and relatable Contemporary Romance novels. Each story is crafted to draw upon your heartstrings while taking you on an emotional journey. Infused with an element of suspense, pages are turned until the characters reach their destination of a HEA. Since 2015, seven novels have been published by L. M. Carr.

Email: authorlmcarr@gmail.com
Facebook: Author LM Carr
Twitter: @LM_Carr
Website: www.authorlmcarr.com

Made in the USA
Middletown, DE
23 June 2023

33335293R00210